THE RENEGADE

SINDIEL SIGHTED ON a masked helm and fired, jerking the shot so badly in his eagerness and panic that he missed it altogether. He saw two of the soul thieves drop so suddenly it seemed as if the earth had swallowed them up; probably Linthis and Belth getting the kill shots they were always so quietly competitive about.

The Dark Kin's reaction was instantaneous. Half of them turned their weapons on the treeline and rip-sawed at the foliage with streams of poison-laced hypervelocity splinters. The others grabbed their fallen comrades and dragged them unceremoniously back through the portal.

A WARHAMMER 40,000 NOVEL

PATH
OF THE
RENEGADE

ANDY CHAMBERS

BLACK LIBRARY

Dedicated to Jes Goodwin and Phil Kelly for bringing the dark city to life, to my mum and dad for being awesome and to my wife, Jessica, for being even more awesome.

A BLACK LIBRARY PUBLICATION

First published in Great Britain in 2012 by
The Black Library,
Games Workshop Ltd.,
Willow Road, Nottingham,
NG7 2WS, UK.

10 9 8 7 6 5 4 3 2 1

Cover illustration by Neil Roberts.

A CIP record for this book is available from the British Library.

UK ISBN: 978 1 84970 136 5
US ISBN: 978 1 84970 137 2

See the Black Library on the internet at
www.blacklibrary.com

Find out more about Games Workshop
and the world of Warhammer 40,000 at
www.games-workshop.com

Printed and bound in the UK by the CPI Group (UK) Ltd, Croydon, CR0 4YY

Torturers and sadists, nightmare made real, the dark eldar are evil incarnate. Cold and beautiful, slender of bone, their lithe appearance belies their deadly talent for slaughter and cruelty.

From the hidden city of Commorragh, the dark eldar launch their lightning raids into the depths of realspace, sowing terror and leaving devastation in their wake. They hunt for slaves, fodder for the hell-pits and the petty amusements of their lords who draw sustenance from the blood shed in ritual battle. For in this hellish realm, living flesh is currency and Overlord Asdrubael Vect rules above all with the greatest share.

Beneath their supreme master, the archons of the darkling city murder and cheat to keep one step ahead of She Who Thirsts. For the dark eldar harbour a terrible curse, a wasting of their flesh that can only be slowed by the infliction of pain. Life eternal is the reward for this soul harvest, and the favour of the ancient haemonculi can extend an eldar's mortal coil yet further... for a price. The alternative is damnation and endless suffering, a withering of body and mind until all that remains is dust.

But such hunger cannot ever be sated. It is a bottomless pit of hate and depravity that lurks within the dark eldar, a vessel that can never truly be filled, even with oceans of blood. And when the last drop has bled away, the soul thieves will know true terror as the daemons come to claim them...

'Consider the moment of godhood. The desires of an entire race meeting and merging, caught and reflected endlessly in the Sea of Souls. Think of the billions upon billions of psyches merging in impossible depths, drawn together by the deadly undertow of their own lusts to meet and intertwine, finally awakening to become something Other.

'Imagine the moment of merged consciousness awakening, tearing free from the last bonds of sanity. Picture the glory of release, the unbridled forces of the id ripping open the walls of reality and feasting upon the shattered ruins of the super-ego.

'Ultimate ascension awaits the ravening meta-entity, a place in a pantheon of ruling powers as old as the stars themselves. In the fever realms of otherspace it becomes as a god fuelled by the death-screams of its progenitors. Reality is breached, godhood achieved and the cosmic balance tilts yet further against the fragile substance of reality and order.

'Mourn, if you will, for an entire civilisation so cruelly snuffed out at the height of their power, and then begin to consider what manner of survivors such a cataclysm might breed.'

— *The Dark Mirror*,
by Veslyin the Anchorite

PROLOGUE

Rain.

Rain encompassed the world, it thundered down in a ceaseless torrent, cascading from the treetops in twisting waterfalls. All that could be seen was greenery distorted by a wall of water. Sindiel had never experienced anything like it. He huddled miserably in the bole of a titanic hardwood tree wrapped in his camouflage cape as he had done for three days now, suffering through periodic downpours and the steaming tropical humidity that followed them. Three days also spent enduring the biting insects and inquisitive predators that seemed drawn magnetically to him, to the point where Sindiel had simply given up on trying to remove his flexmetal gloves or hood for relief. Now he endured the cloying sweat-slicked touch of his armour and tried to be patient.

He squinted through his scopesight at the gate in

a futile effort to see it through the torrential rain. He didn't need to see the gate to picture it accurately, the two primitive-looking upright stones and capping lintel etched firmly into his mind. Night, day, rain, shine he had watched the gate with the others for three days and seen absolutely nothing out of the ordinary.

Sindiel wasn't overly fond of patience, and his limited supply of it was rapidly becoming exhausted. He was seriously considering petitioning Linthis again that they should move on. The Dark Kin weren't coming here, despite what her complex lunar calculations said about the inactive gate they'd found. Corallyon and Belth couldn't be any happier than he was, although in the end they were bound to align themselves with whatever Linthis wanted just like they always did.

Sindiel had found himself starting to question all the half-hushed whispers he had heard about stopping the wicked soul thieves. All the talk of secret lore and hidden paths had come to this: sitting in a sodden jungle watching an inactive gate and hoping they would show – or rather hoping that they didn't but hanging around *just in case* they did. It was pathetic, and Sindiel felt more pathetic for allowing himself to be trapped by his ego into staying. Leaving now meant proving himself to be less tough than the other Rangers, the old hands, and that simply stuck in his throat too much to be borne.

The rain eventually stopped as suddenly as if it had been turned off at a tap, leaving the jungle fresh and dripping. Within minutes steam was rising from the forest floor where a hundred tiny pools and rills glittered in shafts of light that pierced the high canopy. Sindiel looked at the gate again. It was still there, still exactly as he had seen it a hundred times before; a silvery rivulet of water was running through it, quite picturesque.

A brightly coloured tree snake slithered into Sindiel's hiding place, seemingly intent on making its way into his lap in a friendly yet determined fashion. Sindiel evicted the venomous reptile as gently as he could, earning a few dry bites to his gauntleted hands in the process.

He looked at the gate again. It had changed. Silver now filled the entire space between the uprights and the lintel, a shimmering wall of mercury. Spiral markings on the stones were glowing with a faint inner light as the webway portal aligned and reopened for the first time in three hundred years.

+–l's active,+ Linthis's voice whispered in his mind. He was so intent on the active gateway the interruption made him flinch.

+Say again?+ Sindiel thought back. +Yes, the portal's active, I can see it. What do I do?+

It wasn't clear if Linthis's response was just to Sindiel or to the whole group. It was flat and emotionless. +Shoot anything that comes out of it.+

Sindiel fumbled to focus his scope and disable the safety locks on his long rifle, his hands and mind disjointed and disobedient in his sudden panic.

Shapes were emerging from the silver wall. Lithe humanoids clad in darkly burnished armour stepped forth, their weapons jagged with blades and barbs. The nightmarish figures swept their avaricious, red-eyed gaze over the virgin forest in anticipation of new conquest.

+Shoot!+ came the hard, clipped thought of his leader.

Sindiel sighted on a masked helm and fired, jerking the shot so badly in his eagerness and panic that he missed it altogether. He saw two of the soul thieves drop so suddenly it seemed as if the earth had swallowed them up; probably Linthis and Belth getting the kill shots they were always so quietly competitive about.

The Dark Kin's reaction was instantaneous. Half of them turned their weapons on the tree-line and rip-sawed at the foliage with streams of poison-laced hypervelocity splinters. The others grabbed their fallen comrades and dragged them unceremoniously back through the portal. The shooters put up a creditable enough suppressing fire that Sindiel only got off a few snapshots at them before they also ducked and weaved their way into the portal a few seconds later. A sudden silence descended on the scene as the whip-crack echoes of the brief firefight faded away.

'Close in,' Linthis whispered. Sindiel reluctantly slithered closer, barely hearing any sound as the other Rangers moved in behind him. He kept expecting the nightmarish figures to erupt from the portal at any moment, a feeling that got stronger the closer he got to it. He noticed blood sprays where two of the Dark Kin had fallen. They were bright, arterial and definitively fatal. He found he wondered at why the cruel, sadistic soul thieves would risk themselves to recover their dead.

He noticed something else, a small polished sphere half-buried in the mud that looked as if it had been dropped by the fleeing soul thieves. His heart froze when he realised he could be looking at a grenade. No, it was too big for that, and what kind of grenade looked like stone banded in different colours? He realised it was something else entirely just in time to hide it beneath his foot when Corallyon wandered over to find out what was so interesting. Linthis and Belth were busy doing something to the gate to shut it down.

'They took their dead with them,' Sindiel offered by way of explanation. 'I wasn't sure if they were really dead but see,' he pointed to the bloodstains and drag marks, 'dead. We would just take the spirit stones, why bother with empty vessels?'

He'd given Corallyon exactly what she wanted, an opportunity to illustrate her superior knowledge. Sindiel had joined Linthis's band years ago, only a short time after Corallyon, but as an even fractionally senior member Corallyon took pains to belittle Sindiel as a newblood as often as she could. It was the great cycle of life. Eventually a new recruit would come along and it would become Sindiel's privilege to make them miserable in their turn.

'They don't have spirit stones, lackwit,' Corallyon said with relish. 'They go off to the daemon city to get brought back to life in a test tube.' Sindiel felt his own waystone give a cold pulse of warning. The empathic gem had been with him his whole life, it was his soul-anchor, his moral compass. To live without one was so unthinkably dangerous that it was just... well, unthinkable. A private part of him found the thought thrilling.

'Don't talk like that, Corallyon,' Linthis said as she walked up, her silvery hair floating free after its confinement beneath mask and hood. Behind her the portal was closed, and the ancient arch had returned to looking as it had done for centuries. 'It's no daemon city that they come from, it's a real place and they certainly do not suffer daemons to rule there.

'They eke out eternal lives by preying on the souls of others, taking back what they lose with pain and torture. That's why we work against them. But they aren't daemons, not yet. In some ways I think they're worse.'

The rounded shape beneath Sindiel's foot felt as if it were going to explode after all. He was experiencing the wildest vicarious thrill of his life just by hiding it from Linthis and her pompous little band. It was all he could do to keep from laughing out loud at them. He shifted his weight, pushing the sphere completely out of sight beneath the mud.

'Why didn't you just destroy the gate,' Sindiel asked innocently, 'if you knew they were going to use it to come here and steal people?'

When Linthis replied she spoke as if to a child. 'Because that would damage the webway just that little bit more, Sindiel, and another piece of it would be forever lost.'

'It seems like they get more use out of it than we do,' Sindiel persisted truculently.

'Of course they do, they live in it!' Corallyon blurted.

'That's enough, Corallyon,' Linthis admonished.

'We do not speak of such things. All you need know is that our work here is done. We repelled the Dark Kin and now we move on.'

'Where next?' Corallyon asked, suitably chastened.

'To another maiden world named Lileathanir, a place very much like this one. Our cousins there have also grown lax and all but forgotten the peril of the gates.'

Sindiel reflected that they hadn't so much repelled the soul thieves here as given them a slight pause. Four snipers would not have held them back for long if they had only realised how few stood against them. They were simply lucky that Linthis had the craft to shut the gate from this side before they returned in greater numbers. Most likely once they had gone the Dark Kin would come creeping back anyway; as Corallyon had said, they knew more about the labyrinth dimension because they lived in it.

He decided he would return to the spot later, alone, and see if the object he'd hidden was really what he hoped it was. He felt sure he'd seen that kind of striped banding before on spheres held by old statues on his craftworld. He remembered it was reckoned a symbolic object, like a crown for rulership or a spear for hunting. The sphere represented speech with distant stars.

CHAPTER 1
THE ACCURSED HALLS OF SHAA-DOM

'Do you know what it is when you must question your every action in light of what punishment it may bring? Do you understand what it is to feel the eyes of your owner upon you even when he is not present? That is what it is to live in fear, to live the life of a slave. You tell me to beware of raising up that which I cannot then put down. I tell you that I will make any pact or bargain to gain the strength to free myself from the clutches of the tyrant. I will have my freedom, no matter the cost.'

– Archon Ysclyth of Talon Cyriix, as quoted
in *The Articles of Hubris*

WALKING IS CONTROLLED falling. Every step means abandoning oneself to gravity and then trusting that an outstretched leg will prevent disaster. Nyos Yllithian felt as if he were falling towards his destiny, being drawn inexorably onwards as if in a dream. He was in the dark places under the world, walking cautiously through worming corridors of scratched and mouldering stonework. Shadows gave back reluctantly before him and came clustering in behind him as he passed. He walked cautiously because ur-ghuls and carrion slaves still lurked in these tunnels, although even alone as he was he had little to fear from them. The dark, secret places of the eternal city always had their perils and he was well armed against such mundane foes.

In truth his caution was born of an uncharacteristic tinge of fear at what lay ahead of him. Everything he'd done up until now was deniable, excusable, explain-able, and perhaps even laudable once garnished with a little bluster and bribery. Even if he were caught right now, sneaking through the catacombs of Talon Cyriix, there was no crime in that in the tyrant's laws. Not yet. Talon Cyriix was certainly an ill-starred locale to be found in, the scene of an invasion and dreadful mas-sacre in times past, but the eternal city of Commorragh had many, many places that could fit that description.

However, what lay ahead was a blatant act of betrayal if the great tyrant should ever come to know of it. Yllithian consoled himself that caution, and even some fear, was an appropriate response to that state of affairs. Betraying the great tyrant of the eternal city bore all the consequences that might be imagined to extend from that distinguished title. Death was the least uncomfortable prospect, and inevitably one that would be long deferred in favour of far more visceral punishments.

The great tyrant had disposed of a vast number of would-be rivals down the ages, including several of Nyos's own ancestors in the coup when Vect first seized power. The scrofulous slums Nyos was now entering had once belonged to Archon Ysclyth of Talon Cyriix, a great house almost as old as his own, until only a few centuries ago. Ysclyth had broken Vect's laws and made pacts with unspeakable, otherworldly entities to overthrow the tyrant. When he made his own coup attempt Archon Ysclyth was aided by an unstoppable legion of daemons from beyond the veil.

Unfortunately for the ambitious archon he had reckoned without the tyrant's command of ancient failsafes within the city. Before the horde could debouch into other districts the whole of Talon Cyriix spur was sealed off from the rest of Commorragh by impenetrable shields of energy. Trapped, denied the blood and souls they had been promised, Ysclyth's untrustworthy daemonic allies turned on him and sated themselves on his holdfast before disappearing whence they came. Now the ravaged halls of Talon Cyriix stood abandoned and silent, fit only for skulking wretches and slaves that would dare the unclean spirits said to lurk there. The tyrant's sycophants still celebrated the ironic downfall of the faithless Archon Ysclyth in poem and song, praising the just punishment meted out by their master.

Nyos emerged into an open courtyard between broken towers. High above him he could glimpse a patch of dark sky, an oily shimmer that was barely lighter than the deep gloom all around him. He sought and found the rambling outline of a mansion that occupied one edge of the court. Whatever grandeur the building had once possessed had been ripped away, daemon-fouled and defiled to leave it a mouldering corpse reminiscent of some long-dead sea-monster. A dull miasma of old horror hung over the place, an indelible psychic taint left by the abhorrent feasts that had been enacted there. Yllithian steeled himself and pressed on inside.

He found himself in a hallway lined with plinths. Once they had supported lifelike busts of the proud antecedents of Archon Ysclyth, carved with cunning artistry in stone so pure and white that it seemed luminous. Now most of the heads lay smashed and broken, while the survivors still on their plinths had been obscenely mutilated by daemonic claws sharper than steel knives. Thousands of years of pure-blooded lineage had been wiped out by the misplaced hubris of one descendant. Ysclyth's line had ended here and although Yllithian cared not one whit about that, save perhaps for rejoicing in the removal of a poten-tial rival, the loss of Talon Cyriix grieved him on some level. Such a loss could never be recovered, and through it the majesty of the eternal city was lessened just a little more, driven further down the paths of entropy and ultimate dissolution.

In some ways Ysclyth had got off lightly. Neither Ysclyth, Nyos nor the tyrant himself were members of the crude and lumpen race called men. They were eldar, members of a race of beings incomparably superior to those insane barbarians currently most prevalent in the Great Wheel. As such the tyrant's pun-ishments were imaginative, protracted and ultimately fatal. The tortures the tyrant reserved for traitors had been honed to arts of screaming perfection down the thousands of years he had reigned. As eldar perfection was their birthright in all things, so Nyos could expect nothing less at the hands of the great tyrant, Asdrubael Vect. The shrieking agony that Ysclyth had endured at the end of his life had been mercifully brief by comparison.

As Nyos himself would be quick to inform those ignorant of such manifest facts, eldar are beautiful, lithe and quick, keen-eyed, sharply-sensed, long-lived and highly intelligent beings. In every conceivable realm the eldar stand as proud adults above the idiot children of the younger races, whether it be the arts, culture, aesthetics, wisdom, intellect, technology, subtlety, majesty, morality or, naturally, cruelty. The games that the trueborn eldar played with one another were deadly, the stakes total. A single missed step meant the long fall into oblivion had begun.

He moved deeper into the manse, wary of traps as his routes of advance narrowed inexorably the closer he got to his objective. He sought steps that would take him downwards, moving from one wrecked chamber to another, searching carefully. As he found none his anxiety grew. Nyos had a great many enemies that would relish the opportunity to catch him alone like this. He was confident in his abilities, a trained warrior from birth and a master of the blade, but he was cunning enough to understand his own mortality and that his own skills must be measured against a city filled with peerless killers. Secrecy had been paramount and so he had come alone, but the longer his fruitless search went on the more the fear grew in him… a false lead… enemies closing in. He'd dispatched some of his own enemies in the same way.

He spotted steps leading downwards in the kitchens and his paranoid fantasies evaporated like mist. He still went warily, but the debris partially blocking the stairway seemed undisturbed and masked assassins in singularly short supply. He found an archway opening into a low cellar, where a gleam of silver at the far end made his heart race.

He stopped himself from rushing forwards to investigate. This was the danger point: in sight of the objective, when the quarry was distracted and focusing on the wrong thing. He looked around the cellar, trying to pierce the gloom. Crumbling columns supported the sagging roof and broken, unidentifiable detritus lay scattered all over the floor. He stepped out, ready to spring back into cover in an instant. Nothing moved. He worked his way carefully around the angles of the pillars, ensuring he was completely alone before reaching what he'd come to find, a simple silver loop that hung from the cellar's far wall.

A point that Nyos would be more loath to concede about the eldar was that despite all their glittering prowess there was one realm in which they fell short of their promise of greatness: that of power. Once upon a time the whole Great Wheel of the galaxy had been the plaything of the eldar and a portal like this could have led anywhere, connecting to others like it on a million different worlds. Those times were long past. Now the scattered survivors of the eldar race were in bitter, squabbling factions clinging to their sanctuaries while the universe passed them by. The once-great splendour of the eldar was forced to skulk miserably in the shadows and scheme for a return to past glories.

Nyos spoke the words to activate the portal. This portal only led to one place now, an accursed place forbidden to the citizens of Commorragh on pain of death. That was the tyrant's law.

A fact Nyos also less habitually shared with others was that he had grown determined to lead his soon-to-be grateful and obedient kin into another golden age. That golden age could only begin with the removal of the great tyrant, and on that Yllithian had sworn his near-immortal life.

Although unassuming in his current appearance, Nyos Yllithian was possessed of considerable resources to bring about a resurgence of his kind. He was of a proud, pure bloodline that could be traced unbroken to before the Fall of the eldar race. He held the title of Archon of the White Flames, making him the feared and beloved head of one of the oldest and most noble kabals in all of the eternal city of Commorragh, the last bastion of true eldar culture in a benighted universe. The White Flames for their part controlled an entire tier of the mighty port-city with their own docks and shipyards, armouries and training grounds.

Despite all this, Nyos Yllithian's personal power, like the power of every other archon across the sprawling city, was but a grain of sand beside the mountain that was the great tyrant, Asdrubael Vect.

For generations Vect had kept his place by ensuring

the intrigues of the archons were directed against each other, picking off rivals before they grew powerful enough to challenge him. From the outset the tyrant's reign had been founded on bloodshed and betrayal of the basest kind. It was easy to see that as long as Commorragh remained in Vect's grasp the eldar race would continue to slide ever deeper into obscurity as they expended their energies in internecine bickering.

Yllithian had spent many, many years quietly intriguing to align the forces he required. There had been the most delicate business of seeking allies, of which there were potentially many but only a few that could be trusted in their turn. Then had come endless sifting through the web of lies surrounding Asdrubael Vect to seek some clue as to how he could be defeated. Now Nyos's determination to unseat the tyrant had led him to a forgotten slum in Talon Cyriix in the decaying underbelly of Commorragh. Here, it was whispered, a way to topple Vect might be found.

Nyos gazed at the mirror-like surface of the active portal before him as if it might betray what lay beyond. There had been rumours that Ysclyth had delved deep to find the forbidden sorceries that became his undoing. Even now there was a chance that Nyos had been tricked into walking blithely to his own doom. As Ysclyth and others had illustrated, Vect was particularly fond of dispatching opponents by using their own hubris against them. But Nyos Yllithian had been very careful, only using the most obtuse and roundabout sources to find the information he was now trusting his life to. In all the subtle checking and crosschecking there had been no inconsistencies or telltale signs of a trap.

This portal led to accursed Shaa-dom, that was certain, and he bore a psychically-charged opal the size of his fist that should serve to take him to the individual he needed to find there. Entry to Shaa-dom broke the tyrant's laws; indeed even the mention of that place was a crime. Yet this formed the next step in the conspiracy he had planned so long for. Once he passed through the portal there would be no turning back.

All that remained was to see if he had the strength to survive the horrors that lay within the accursed halls of Shaa-dom. Yllithian had dressed for the occasion in a suit of angular black armour that was possessed of its own fierce little war spirit. It was clever enough to extrude monomolecular blades on command or playfully nip off a crippled limb to save its wearer's life. He kept it unadorned for now, and vanity forbade wearing a helmet. He armed himself with a long, thin blade keen enough to cut stone, summoned up his courage and stepped through the portal.

NYOS'S FIRST IMPRESSION was of a breathless moment of cold and then a sultry heat. He was standing at the edge of a thoroughfare after emerging from an arch. The elegant flagstones were blackened and cracked, the decorative trees and statues lining it were twisted, skeletal remnants that seemed to claw at the roiling skies in agony. Away beyond the blasted facades Nyos could sense the epicentre of the destruction of Shaa-dom. There, he knew, there was a rift where unnatural fires still burned in the aftermath of the cataclysm that had occurred here. Warp-taint hung heavy in the air and reality itself had a sickly, greasy feel to it. The subtle thrill of She Who Thirsts sucking away at his life, always present but carefully controlled within Commorragh, gusted through him and he realised with a chill that just to remain here for too long could be deadly. He had thought Talon Cyriix terrible but it was a child's playground, a slave's copy, when compared to Shaa-dom.

This was the horror the great tyrant had unleashed when he was challenged in the past. All his immeasurable power was used not to glorify the eldar but instead to destroy them, dragging them ever further down the path to oblivion. Generations ago the prosperous satellite realm of Shaa-dom had grown too proud for Asdrubael Vect to overawe and too powerful for him to humble. When El'Uriaq, the archon of all Shaa-dom, gathered his forces and declared himself emperor, Vect had publicly vowed that all of Shaa-dom would feel the edge of his blade and this was the result. Genocide unleashed on an already dying race.

Nyos regarded the smooth gem he was holding carefully. Bright motes wavered and darted within it as if battered by spectral winds. With agonising slowness they coalesced into a single brighter spark that floated at one edge of the gem in a determined fashion. Nyos set out in the direction indicated, finding himself drawn along the thoroughfare and crunching through occasional drifts of fragile bone, pitiful remnants of the widows and orphans that had suffered in the aftermath of Vect's retribution.

The legends told that El'Uriaq had laughed at Vect's posturing when he heard of it. His forces were well-armed and outnumbered Vect's. Few of the other kabals would commit themselves to fight on behalf of the tyrant while many had sent secret emissaries to El'Uriaq. The emperor of Shaa-dom had returned to the completion of his plans to conquer Commorragh confident in the knowledge that any attack made by Vect would only play into his hands. A few days later the blade of Vect arrived in the form of a burning, crashing starship lurching suddenly into reality above Shaa-dom.

The glowing spark was leading him at a tangent to the impact site near the centre of Shaa-dom. He quickly came to what had been a covered avenue with a ribwork of high arches that once held panes of coloured crystal. Glittering shards scattered over the pavement added an incongruous splash of vibrancy to the hollow-eyed dwellings on either hand. Nyos advanced warily along the avenue, his superb senses taking in every facet of his environment. He reassured himself that here at the periphery of Shaa-dom the risks of encountering a denizen from beyond the veil should be slight, although an unwelcome part of his mind whispered that they would be certain to voraciously seek him out if they should sense his presence.

The vessel that struck Shaa-dom was one of those built by the upstart younger races – huge and crudely made, armoured in thick slabs of ignorance and wishful thinking. It tore through the supposedly unbreakable wardings between El'Uriaq's realm and the Sea of Souls like a bull charging through cobwebs.

El'Uriaq and the core of his warrior elite were immolated instantly when the ship crashed into his palace, but what came after proved to be the worse fate. The open breach left behind in the warding attracted a swarm of horrors from beyond. Shaa-dom was ravaged even more thoroughly than the unfortunate Talon Cyriix, the gusting energies of the breach sustaining a plague of daemons that harried the pitiful survivors without respite. The tyrant ordered the whole realm of Shaa-dom sealed off to protect the rest of the city. The wretches left inside who had somehow survived the catastrophe and the daemons that came afterwards were damned to a lingering demise as their trapped souls were relentlessly drained away by She Who Thirsts.

So had ended Shaa-dom.

The scuff of a footfall whipped Nyos's attention to one side of the avenue. He caught a pale flicker of movement at a window and flourished his blade aggressively at the hidden watcher. This could be no daemon hiding and skulking with a tasty soul so close at hand. It could only be some twisted remnant of an eldar devoured by She Who Thirsts, a soulless and mindless wretch, ever hungry and driven only by instinct. One alone could pose no threat and it wisely stayed hidden from sight. Nyos pointedly turned away and moved on down the avenue, listening carefully for stealthy sounds of pursuit.

At the end of the avenue steps led upwards to a tall building that must once have impressively overlooked the covered avenue below. Now it appeared crumpled and sagged in upon itself as if its internal structure had been warped. The spark in the gem Nyos was holding strained strongly in that direction. As he set out again he could feel the fatigue in his limbs as She Who Thirsts sapped his life away. He set himself to hurry despite his fears, even though at every step it felt like an insidious marsh lay beneath his feet waiting to suck him under.

Nyos's mighty ancient kin had long ago mastered the other realm – the Sea of Souls, the realm of Chaos, the immaterium, the warp or whatever else anyone cared to call it. The great city of Commorragh and its satellite realms were testimonies to a time when the eldar created their own enclaves in the warp and connected them with a fantastic skein of interdimensional pathways encompassing the whole galaxy. The predatory denizens of that other realm were kept safely sealed away, bound and constrained by eldar power and wisdom.

The Fall had brought an end to all that and thereafter the theme of daemons feasting upon souls had become a distressingly recurrent one in eldar histories. She Who Thirsts was the greatest daemon-goddess of them all, and She was ever-hungry for the souls of the race that some believed had created Her.

Whatever doors had closed off the building at the top of the steps had been torn away, and inside an atrium lay half-choked with rubble. Entering it Nyos stiffened as he heard a faint voice sound above him, an echoing whisper.

'He comes!'

Nyos stepped into the shadows by the shattered

doorway with a speed that belied the fluid elegance of the motion. He waited tensely for the first crash of weapons-fire or a rush of enemies. The seconds dragged out longer but nothing came. He caught the same voice again, scratchy whispers that groped their way into the atrium, definitely coming from above.

'Only the first, the visionary.'

The bright spark in the gem he held strained towards the sound of the voice. Nyos made an instant decision and regally stalked out into full view in the atrium before looking upwards. A handful of tiered balconies rose toward another shattered crystal roof, brutally opened now to show the roiling clouds above. Withered vegetation overhung the balconies and trailed artistically down pillars; on the lowest balcony, a darker shape lurked among the shadows.

Seeing no other way upwards Nyos sheathed his sword and secured the gem before climbing nimbly up the cracked stonework. He studiously avoided the treacherous streamers of dead vegetation and their spurious promise of a secure handhold. Swinging himself suddenly over the cracked balustrade he confronted the whisperer.

At first glance it looked like a pile of black rags, but a lustrous river of long, black hair spilled from beneath a cowl where the head would be. Skeletal spider-like hands emerged from the rags to wander between a scattering of small bone-white objects on the floor. It lifted one and showed it to him with a titter: a tiny rendition of the rune of vision.

Nyos's guts churned with instinctive disgust. The manifold gifts of the eldar extended to very

considerable psychic prowess and their ancient civilisation had been built as much with thoughts as
with hands. But after the Fall the use of psychic powers became a sure way to attract daemons, effectively
signing the sorcerer's death warrant along with any
other unfortunates in the vicinity.

It was a hard vice to resist, akin to losing a limb,
but the eldar kindred of Commorragh and its satellites soon learned to shun their psychic gifts, and to
destroy those that pursued them despite the consequences. Now every scrap of their mental training
focused on internalising their powers and hiding
their presence from She Who Thirsts. The few that still
pursued such knowledge, like Archon Ysclyth, usually came to a sticky end however clever they thought
they were. Some still dabbled in the meaner warp-
arts, using cards and grimoires and other fetishes to
protect themselves. Rune-casting to see the future was
another crime replete with its own set of horrid pun-
ishments for anyone involved in it.

+He's afraid now that he's found what he's looking
for,+ the warp-dabbler said and tittered again.

'Be careful, Angevere, your soul is still precious to
you or you would have been devoured long ago,' Nyos
replied coolly. 'If you wish to retain it you'll obey me
or I'll send you to your richly deserved appointment
with She Who Thirsts without further delay.' He was
gratified that the witch drew back a little at that. She
still knew fear.

'That is your name, isn't it? Angevere, who was once
handmaid to Dyreddya, concubine of El'Uriaq?' Nyos
spoke with mocking politeness, mercilessly pressing

his advantage. 'You're looking surprisingly sprightly, all things considered.'

+I apologise, my lord, I meant no disrespect,+ the wretched thing whispered in his mind.

'Better. Now prove yourself by telling me the reason I chose to visit this charming locale.'

The spider-like hands crawled obediently among the scattered runes, gathering them up before casting them again. The bone-white sigils clicked and clattered unnaturally together as they fell, twitching slightly as they struck the ground as if imbued with a life of their own. Once the runes had stilled the wretched crone reached out and touched the closest to her.

+Salvation inverted, for one who passes from light into darkness,+ she whispered before touching another and then another. +In the skein of desire: freedom, meaning transcendence and victory. In the place of the enemy stands the rune of mastery. You seek to overthrow your master.+

Nyos bridled at the description of the great tyrant as his master, but could not deny it.

'Simple guesswork any street entertainer could mimic. If you wish to continue your miserable existence you must do better, crone,' he said, and drew his fine, keen sword. The crone appeared to ignore him as she continued fondling the scattered runes.

+Here in the line of kinship are pleasure inverted to denote suffering or pain, and generosity inverted to indicate the miser. Both are touching the rune of brotherhood. You have two allies that share your goals sufficiently to trust, at least until the objective is achieved.+

That was interesting, Nyos thought to himself. The crone had accurately divined traits of his two strongest supporters, confirming Nyos's premonition that this little interchange could only end one way once he had all the information he needed.

'Very good, or very lucky,' Nyos sneered. 'Now tell me what I came here to find out. How can I fulfil my heart's desire and rid my people of Asdrubael Vect?'

The crone hissed at that name, although whether in pain or anger Nyos could not tell. She turned her face to him for the first time, silken hair falling back to reveal a visage out of a fevered nightmare. The face was gaunt and deeply lined. Its eyes and lips were crudely stitched shut, but he still felt the weight of her blind eyes gazing upon him. Nyos had witnessed many greater horrors, and inflicted not a few of them himself, but his spine still conveyed an icy stab of fear as she mind-spoke to him again.

+And what horrors would you unleash to rid yourself of him?+ The crone's mind-voice seemed stronger now, an unwelcome pressure against his thoughts. 'How far will your lust for power carry you in your endeavour? Vect has slain all that opposed him. You stand amid the ruin he makes of his enemies!'

Nyos replied with fervour. 'Vect is a parasite, bloated on the blood of the true people. I would gladly break the Great Wheel itself if I could bury him in its downfall!' He had seldom dared to utter such words while in Commorragh, even while dealing with the most solicitous of his allies, and it felt deliciously liberating to speak them now. The crone remained silent but seemed to approve, the spider hands stretched out again to gather up the little runes into her gnarled fist.

Click, clack. The runes fell to the ground once more. The crone moved to touch them but drew back suddenly as if they burned her hand. A tiny wail of distress keened through Nyos's consciousness.

'What is it? What do you see?' Nyos demanded, placing the flat of his keen blade upon her shoulder for emphasis. A simple flick of his wrist and she would be a head shorter.

With shaking hands she reached out to the runes again. Reluctantly they moved from one rune to another as her scratchy mind-voice intoned the symbolic meanings before her.

+The end of your heart's desire is beyond sight, unachievable with your current means, but the pathway towards it is littered with many portents. Here is the Solitaire, the rune of the soulless, sign of the living dead but also the symbol of hope or rescue when inverted. Connected with it are the runes of the world spirit and history, symbols of the forgotten and of escape, these in turn point to the runes of phoenix for renewal or rebirth, salvation and then freedom again–+

'Then my heart's desire will be achieved somehow,' Nyos said bluntly, 'Why do you hesitate? Advise me of the course I must take succinctly and immediately, I grow weary of your endless prevarication.'

Even with death at her throat the crone hesitated before replying. +The line you follow eventually leads to the rune of Dysjunction – unthinkable entropy and change will come about should you follow this path. Commorragh will be torn asunder and remade.+

The crone's hands hovered above the rune as if fearing to touch it. Nyos pondered finding such a calamitous portent. Beyond the metaphysical implications the concept of Dysjunction had a very real meaning for the denizens of Commorragh. Their city rested in a delicate balance between the material and immaterial worlds. Dysjunctions had occurred in the past when reality rippled and the unthinking energies of the warp crowded in close to bend themselves to the unmaking of the eternal city. Chaos and disaster attended such events, and only through the most strenuous efforts had Commorragh and its sub-realms avoided sharing the fate of Shaa-dom. Nyos concluded that the crone was trying to frighten him and brushed aside such thoughts as more psyker mummery.

'I should expect so,' Nyos replied impatiently. 'Interpret the rest of this mess or I'll have your head.' Some of Nyos's fellow archons held that threats were a crude and inelegant form of inducement to employ, but in Nyos's experience they were highly effective providing that the promised retribution materialised in a timely fashion. He twitched his blade back in anticipation.

+You must look to the past,+ the crone whispered. +Return the one that challenged Vect so closely that the most desperate measures were used to destroy him. To destroy Vect you must rebirth the shade of Archon El'Uriaq, the emperor of Shaa-dom–+

'Impossible, El'Uriaq was consumed when his fortress was destroyed,' Nyos snapped, but he found there was doubt in his words. The eldar of

Commorragh had discovered many ways to conquer death. Over the centuries the cult of haemonculi, the artist-surgeons and torture-scientists of the dark city, had perfected unnatural methods to preserve themselves against the tide of years and to be remade from even the smallest morsel of their flesh. True death was a rarity among the highborn, and all the more feared because of it. Who knew what the practitioners of the arts of flesh might be able to achieve?

+No. A part of him still dwells in his ruined domain. A pure heart could still call him back from the abyss.+

Nyos lowered his blade as his mind weighed the possibilities. El'Uriaq had failed to topple Vect, but he had come so very close that the tyrant had been forced to destroy an entire satellite realm to thwart him. The secret pacts and alliances El'Uriaq had made among the kabals were ancient history now, but the legend of Vect's retribution upon Shaa-dom formed a substantial part of the invisible web of intrigue that protected the tyrant to this day. The re-emergence of Vect's old rival would be a crippling blow to Vect's prestige. The intellect and experience of such a co-conspirator would be worth legions of troops in its own right.

'It sounds far-fetched, Angevere. Where might I find this part of El'Uriaq and the pure heart? Your seeings are useless without that knowledge.'

+El'Uriaq lies at the breach where he fell. A pure heart you will not find here nor anywhere else in Commorragh. Beyond that I cannot say, the way is hidden.+

'I see. Presumably you've divined how our little consultation is going to end, Angevere?'

Her reply was reluctant. +Yes.+

'And you're saying you can tell me no more?'

+You will bring about a Dysjunction. Turn aside from your path before it is too late.+

'I think not. Farewell, Angevere.' Nyos flicked his wrist and the crone's head smoothly parted company from her body as the monomolecular blade swished through her neck. Nyos felt only the very slightest shiver of her passing soul and looked down in bemusement at the severed head where it lay among the scattering of runes in a spreading pool of blood.

The stitched mouth still writhed and the eyes rolled sluggishly beneath their sutured lids, eliciting an admiring grunt from Nyos. He reached down and carefully retrieved the head by its now blood-slicked black locks. The crone might have further uses after all.

The sickly sweet caress of She Who Thirsts was still sucking at his soul, piling up subjective years of ageing. It was time to leave.

Outside the crone's dwelling ancient, unseen eyes watched Nyos Yllithian flee from Shaa-dom. They followed his progress with unnatural intensity and an unspeakable humour. The first piece was in place, the first motion had begun. Threads of fate were tightening towards an act of vengeance three millennia in the making, their mesh becoming inescapable. All that remained was to save what could be saved and destroy the rest. Beyond the veil hungry predators began to gather in anticipation of the feast to come.

CHAPTER 2
THE ARTS OF FLESH

'So many believe that pain is inflicted only by the physical application of torment. Blades, hooks, chains, racks – these are all crude physical tools that serve their part in mortifying the flesh. Anticipation, repetition, conciliation and hope – these are the finer instruments to be wielded when it comes to the mortification of the soul.'

– Master haemonculus Bellathonis

NYOS YLLITHIAN RETURNED by secret ways to his fortress-palace on the corespur, deep among the soaring central spires of High Commorragh. Yllithian's domain was an ancient one, an heirloom of his noble house that had been doggedly carved out and protected against usurpers since before the Fall. Nyos's ancestor, Dralydh Yllithian, had first expanded and fortified his family's spire-top manse by seizing the adjacent levels and incorporating them into his holdfast. After six centuries' worth of skirmishing, intriguing and intimidating, Nyos's great-grandfather, Zovas Yllithian, completed the conquest of the whole spire by driving out the last of the Archon Uziiak's poisonous kabal from the lower levels. The fortress had been the White Flames' exclusive territory ever since. Petty archons might have to rub shoulders with one another by sharing territory within a single tier but not Archon Yllithian of the White Flames.

The sloping, armoured eaves of the fortress's precipitous rooftops overhung a three-kilometre drop on two sides to where its gnarled foundations abutted onto Ashkeri Talon and the docking ring. Two of the three closest spires were controlled by kabals Yllithian rated as vassals or allies to his own. The remaining spire, a skeletal affair of dark metal, was home to Archon Uziiak's surviving offspring and a number of other petty archons hostile to Yllithian.

He was little troubled by their proximity. Decorative barbs, columns, rosettes and statues scattered artfully across the surface of the White Flames' palace concealed a profusion of detection arrays and extremely potent weaponry. The palace was continuously patrolled by kabalite warriors and a hundred invisible eyes followed every occurrence inside its precincts, whispering constantly to Yllithian about what they saw.

Secure again on the White Flames' tier of the city amidst his warriors and slaves Nyos Yllithian rapidly recouped the strength he'd lost in Shaa-dom through the suffering of his minions. No doubt the spies of the great tyrant that Nyos suspected to be in his household reported on his brief absence but he had few concerns about that. He kept his activities secretive as a matter of course just as all archons did. Assassination by ambitious underlings or jealous rivals was a risk so commonplace that it was seen as a form of natural selection in the eternal city.

Some days after his return Nyos summoned the chief of the haemonculi in service to the White Flames Kabal, a twisted individual known as Syiin. Nyos ordinarily had little to do with haemonculi save to secure the pacts required to ensure rebirth in the unfortunate event of his death. He found the delicate artistry of the practitioners of the arts of flesh too dispassionate and academic to truly admire and too time-consuming to usefully employ. Nonetheless it was a foolish archon that did not keep haemonculi in their employ.

Syiin was deep in the bowels of the White Flames' fortress when he received the archon's summons. He and his underlings dwelled in a saw-edged spiral labyrinth of cells and torture-surgeries where they pursued their art. Here dozens of strangely altered captives howled, screamed, tittered and mewled within their razor-lined oubliettes, a bizarre cross-section of practice subjects and ongoing experiments. At the time Syiin was in the process of completing a new face he had sculpted for himself by extending his bones to stretch the pallid skin into a taut, flat circle. Like all haemonculi Syiin had made many alterations to himself in the lifelong pursuit of his art. His abnormally lengthened limbs would have made him tall were it not for a curving spine that bent him almost double. Instead he tended to the appearance of some four-limbed creature walking on its hind legs with elbows to knees and a leering, moon-like face twisted to look up from beneath an impressively hunched back.

He hurriedly garbed himself in the traditional stitched hides of his victims to present himself properly before Archon Yllithian. The garment comprised hundreds of soft vellum-like patches sewn together to make a mosaic of past suffering, all keepsakes from victims driven to a perfect pitch of agony. Donning it helped to settle his concerns a little, for it was rare for the archon to consult him directly and not a little worrisome to receive such a summons. He went as quickly as his bent body would allow by narrow, twisting walkways lit by corpse-eyes, worming up from the depths like an obscene insect wriggling its way out of a rotting log.

Syiin blinked when he emerged into the unaccustomed light and space of the upper palace. There seemed to be more warriors than he had recalled seeing before. Everywhere he looked he saw black-armoured figures poised on guard or patrolling the corridors. The final ascent to the archon's audience chamber was up a long flight of steps carved of an alabaster-like stone so pure it seemed to glow with an inner light. Every third step was occupied by pairs of guards armed with ceremonial lances hung with icons of the White Flames. Syiin found himself wondering whether this show of power was being made for his benefit but dismissed the thought. Archon Yllithian was scarcely likely to be trying to impress his chief haemonculus with a show of force. Syiin decided that the rumours he'd heard of the archon's absence of late must have some substance to them and that he was none-too-subtly reasserting his authority over the palace. The bent-backed haemonculus laboured up the steps as swiftly as he could, filled with foreboding at what such signs might portend for him personally.

One of the *Ilmaea*, Commorragh's captive suns, was casting a wan, poisonous light through the wide embrasures of the archon's audience chamber as it slowly died in its distant sub-realm high above. Elegantly twisted pillars of polished porphyry marched in a double rank along both sides of the processional, casting purple-black shadows across the exquisite mosaic floor. At the head of the processional Nyos Yllithian lounged upon a bladed throne forged by Zovas Yllithian from the broken weapons of his enemies. The archon appeared distracted and was viewing the scene outside with apparent disinterest as Syiin entered the chamber.

Blank-helmed incubi regarded the haemonculus from both sides, their great curved klaives held upright before them ready to end his life at the merest twitch of Yllithian's finger. Brightly garbed courtiers drew a menagerie of exotic beasts on gilded leashes into the shadows: snuffling, whip-thin ur-ghuls whined piteously, sinuous haemovores writhed as their lamprey-like mouths quested for blood and golden-eyed androgynes watched with inhuman interest. A coterie of sensuously painted Lhamaean concubines, each ritually bathed in aconite and perfumed with extract of hellebore, giggled languidly at Syiin as he approached to a respectful distance from his archon and abased himself before the throne.

Nyos ignored the kneeling haemonculus and continued to gaze outside. Syiin stole a glance towards what seemingly occupied his archon's attention. Beyond the black sun multi-coloured veils could be seen betraying the presence of the outer wardings that protected the city. They formed a shifting canvas of faerie fire criss-crossed by the drive flares of distant star craft. Nothing unusual was to be seen there, so Syiin settled himself to wait.

In the case of any other minion Yllithian would have heightened their discomfort by keeping them waiting longer before deigning to acknowledge their presence. He knew that such subtleties were wasted on haemonculi, however, as they valued patience to a degree that most true eldar found perverse. Instead he addressed his assembled court.

'Leave us,' Nyos said. 'The words I speak are for Syiin's ears only.' His command started a small, but richly appointed avalanche of warriors, concubines, pets and slaves hurriedly leaving the audience chamber. The incubi were the last to leave, only removing themselves after they had assured that the archon's orders had been obeyed. Once they were alone and the gilded doors had silently closed Nyos turned his attention to the haemonculus cowering before him.

'I have questions pertaining to the arts of flesh for you to answer,' Nyos said without preamble. 'If you cannot answer them I will require you to find me someone that can, do I make myself clear?'

'Absolutely, my archon, how may I assist you?'

Syiin's tone was respectful, even obsequious; but his words implied Nyos would owe him a debt for answering, a concept the archon did not relish.

'You will not "assist" me, you will obey me by answering my questions or seek service elsewhere,' he snapped.

'Apologies, my archon, how may I serve you?' Syiin fawned.

'Better. Now tell me: how would you remake a highborn who had been lost for a very long time – centuries, perhaps even millennia?'

Syiin's taut face creased in a slight frown as he weighed up how far he could lie. 'A complex process, my archon. The fresher the remnant the more quickly and safely regeneration of the whole can be achieved.'

'I see. Without a "fresh remnant", as you put it, what conditions would be most conducive to success?'

Syiin's thin lips puckered with distress. Discussing such secrets even with an archon made him uncomfortable.

The haemonculus's distress was an unexpected pleasure for Nyos. He rose from his bladed throne and stalked toward Syiin to savour the sensation more closely.

'The more potent the – ah – catalyst the better the chances, my archon, but to bring back one who was lost thousands of years ago…'

Nyos sensed Syiin's weakness and pounced. 'You mean victim when you say catalyst, don't you? A powerful enough sacrifice would be needed.'

Syiin squirmed slightly within his hide robe as Nyos began to circle him. He made a feeble attempt to change the direction the discussion was taking.

'There are risks, my archon, with returning the long dead, risks which do not exist with the remaking of those newly passed.' Syiin wet his thin lips with an obscenely pink tongue. 'Terrible risks.' The archon paused for a moment at that and Syiin somewhat daringly sought to press the point further.

'Some among my brotherhood hold that the efforts to return Vlokarion directly contributed to the fifth Dysjunction, my archon,' Syiin whispered, fearful. A dreadful secret to share but Syiin was desperate. Now it was Nyos's turn to frown as he recalled the crone's warnings about Dysjunction. Even so something about Syiin's evasive answers still troubled him.

'Such things can only be known,' Nyos said slowly, 'because some of your kin have attempted it before. Tell me of them, tell me who can fill the gaping void that evidently exists in your knowledge.'

That barb struck true. Syiin's discomfort stemmed from not wishing to admit that others knew more than he did. Nyos chuckled to himself; ever-reliable hubris was a weakness even among haemonculi it seemed. Perhaps especially among haemonculi. He waited to see if Syiin would try to lie outright and deny such a manifest fact.

Syiin squirmed under his relentless gaze before finally giving up a piece of information he would soon come to regret.

'There is one among our brotherhood who has delved deep into such matters,' Syiin admitted reluctantly, 'a master by the name of Bellathonis. I understand he dwells in the Aviaries of Archon Malixian beyond Metzuh tier–'

Nyos silenced the haemonculus with an upraised hand, denying Syiin even the opportunity to save face by telling him more. 'Go now, Syiin, your "assistance" is no longer required here,' he said carelessly. He waited until Syiin had almost reached the threshold before calling out to him again.

'One more thing, Syiin,' said Nyos pleasantly. The haemonculus tensed at the archon's words, but Nyos only smiled his most charming smile and said, 'It goes without saying that you will not share this precious little moment of ours with others. I would hate to have to find a new chief haemonculus for my kabal.'

Syiin's round face nodded silently in understanding of the implicit threat. Nyos consoled himself that it would have to suffice. Haemonculi were a notoriously clannish lot and having one of their number killed out of hand would sit poorly with the rest of that strange brotherhood. Instead Syiin would be left to scuttle back to his sunken maze of pain and contemplate his failure to adequately satisfy his archon.

After Syiin had left, Nyos took a stroll through the palace, his incubi bodyguard closing protectively around him and heralds scurrying ahead to ensure that everything possible was being done to avoid the archon's displeasure. Nyos meandered through blazing weapons forges where sweating slaves laboured beneath the lash, he sniffed narcotic blooms in his pleasure gardens, toured exercise yards where his warriors practised their deadly skills and promenaded beneath erotic fractal sculptures that merged and coupled with a life of their own. At every turn a gratifying thrill of fear shot through his minions at his presence, enervating Nyos delightfully with their negative emotional energy. He distributed punishments and favours according to his whims, leaving a trail of pain, disruption and jealousy through his household.

Once he had satisfied himself that his earlier consultation with Syiin would be buried beneath a dozen other inconsequential reports from the tyrant's spies he made his way to a docking port in the highest reaches of his domain. Here, the titanic vista of Commorragh beneath its circling crown of captive suns could be viewed in some small part. Impossibly high structures of metal, crystal, flesh, bone and polished stone rose at every side; thousand-metre images of kabalite archons seemed to battle against spiralling starscrapers that clawed their way upwards from the depths.

Barbed spires and blade-like spines were crowded together as if straining toward the light of the *Ilmaea*, each interconnected by a profusion of slender arches and jagged bridges that sprang impossibly across the dizzying void. Everywhere the air was filled by speeding grav vehicles, the winged figures of scourges high above and hellions recklessly careening on their skyboards far below.

'I think I shall tour the city for a while,' Nyos mused to no one in particular, his silent incubi bodyguard knowing better than to reply. 'Ready my personal barque and rouse some of those worthless scourges to escort us.'

Nyos's personal grav craft was a creation of quite stunning beauty. The curving armoured plates of its fiercely jutting prow were inlaid with ruby and alabaster depicting the White Flames. The graceful lines of its long, narrow-waisted hull swept majestically backwards before flaring to accommodate the pods containing gravitic engines at the rear. Nyos mounted the open platform at the centre of the barque and settled himself in a richly appointed throne that was twin to the one in his audience chamber. His incubi moved to take their positions at long-throated splinter cannon and disintegrators ranged on mountings around the hull. At a nod to his steersman Nyos's craft smoothly ascended and slid away from the docking port.

A flock of winged figures descended towards them, prompting the incubi to swing their cannon to menace the potential threat. They cared not that these scourges were a part of the Kabal of the White Flames, many an archon had fallen prey to his own supposedly loyal troops. Only the watchful incubi could ever be truly trusted, thanks to their monkish warrior codes of duty and honour; the loyalty of others had to be bought or imposed.

The scourges arrogantly dived past the craft before spiralling outwards to form a wheeling defensive sphere surrounding it. The hiss and snap of their altered wings was clearly audible through the layered shields protecting the barque. Many scourges had gone further than merely altering themselves to have wings of sculpted flesh, some had bird-like feet or heads of raptors, and the hands that gripped their weapons were often clawed. Each one had pursued their personal vision of taking flight – most with leathery pinions, but some with insectoid wings and many in hawk or eagle feathers.

'Take us to Metzuh tier, let's see what pleasures

are to be found along the Grand Canal,' Nyos said to the steersman and the craft dipped obediently. Jagged spires and barbed steeples whipped past in ever-greater profusion as the barque descended into the depths. The titanic spires now formed glittering canyon walls connected by bridges and arches that flashed towards them like giant blades. The steersman weaved expertly through the chaotic tangle, always descending into shadow. The scourges kept pace, their powerful wings beating lazily.

'Faster,' Nyos ordered.

The canyon walls became a blur, the giant blades leaping out of the gathering gloom without warning, and the steersman had to haul mightily to control the speeding craft. The scourges were working harder now, their great wings beating the air as they hurled themselves forwards to follow the barque's descent. The faintest breeze blew through the barque's protective fields from the rushing winds outside. Nyos gestured to the steersman, *Faster*.

Even the peerless dampening fields of the barque could not entirely shield its occupants at such speeds. The incubi braced themselves and swayed with the craft's motion as they careened past obstacles close enough to touch. The scourges were truly racing now, with only the strongest keeping pace. Nyos chuckled at the sight of one slamming headlong into a razor-edged archway. The impact reduced it to nothing but a cloud of blood and a scattering of severed limbs.

The lower reaches of Commorragh were spreading out before them now, the spire canyons giving way to the old trade districts and docking spurs that clustered around the feet of High Commorragh. In the spires this was known as the *Ynnealidh*, the necropolis below, where the uncounted billions of the dark city laboured, sweated and died. Tiny stars of light picked out endless tangled streets and plazas. The fungus-like mat of a thousand different architectural styles marked the flesh markets and barter shops where the miserable underlife of Commorragh strove to eke out their existence.

It could be dangerous for one of Nyos's status to enter Low Commorragh. It was easier for enemies to muster strong forces there where the streets were always so rife with agents and desperate mercenaries. The sudden, apparently unplanned arrival of Nyos's retinue would help preclude such unpleasant surprises materialising, but he would still need to conclude his business quickly and be gone before assassins started crawling out of every hole and underpass.

Nyos's craft was curving around the mountain-like flank of one particular spire now, rapidly dropping past Hy'kan tier to reach Metzuh tier at its very bottom. A thin black line running around Metzuh tier thickened into an oily-looking canal with a handful of brightly lit pleasure craft winking on its smooth, dark expanse. The steersman braked to glide just above the pitch-black surface with evident relief.

'Grand Canal, Metzuh tier, my archon,' he intoned solemnly.

Nyos eyed the scourges circling above him with distaste.

'I feel dissatisfied with the performance of our scourges, they seem lacklustre, do they not?' Nyos opined aloud. The steersman was quick enough to pick up on the proffered opportunity to agree with him.

'They do indeed, my archon, distinctly lacklustre,' the steersman echoed obediently.

'If only I could consult a worthy individual with expertise in the field,' Nyos sighed and gazed out over the velvet expanse surrounding them, 'I'm sure they would be invaluable in rectifying such matters.' It was a gamble but the steersman was eager to please. Nyos waited to see if he would take the bait. He was not disappointed.

'If I may offer a suggestion for the archon's consideration?' the steersman asked meekly. Nyos favoured him with a curt nod.

'By great good fortune we are very close to the Aviaries of Malixian, my archon. It's said that Archon Malixian has an unsurpassed passion for all creatures of the air and many scourges in his kabal. Malixian the Mad some call him,' the steersman added in a conspiratorial whisper. 'Without doubt he would be a worthwhile consultant in such matters.'

'Fascinating. Dispatch some of our worthless escort to the Aviaries immediately. Instruct them to convey my compliments to the noble Malixian and most humbly seek an audience with him.' The steersman's carefully composed face twitched a little with surprise at that but he complied without question. Almost immediately a smaller group of scourges broke away from the wheeling flock above and disappeared along the canal. The steersman hauled his ornate tiller bar and brought the barque around to follow them a few seconds later.

The Grand Canal twisted around the base of Metzuh tier, bounded by the outer wardings on one bank and the notorious pleasure palaces of Metzuh on the other. There were stories that the canal had once been filled with a pure, sweet-smelling narcotic oil acquired in limitless quantities from some enslaved alien world. Now it was a black morass of nameless excreta, wastes and compounds that some swore had gained a strange, sluggish sentience of its own. Even the mists emitted by the weirdly altered substance were hallucinogenic, and its touch brought madness or oblivion. Commorragh's jaded denizens still came by their thousands in pursuit of hedonism in the flesh shops and drug dens along its serpentine course. Metzuh's main claim to fame was that it formed a natural crossroads of sorts thanks to its possession of several of the larger dimensional gates leading to the satellite realms of Commorragh.

Nyos always contemplated the satellite realms with some ambivalence. Commorragh had originally been just one of the extradimensional enclaves made by the eldar. There had been numerous other port-cities, fortresses and private estates created. Over the centuries Commorragh had reached out across the webway and subsumed one after another of them like a slowly spreading parasitic growth. The conquered satellite realms were slaved to Commorragh, their gates locked permanently open to allow the eternal city to plunder their contents at will. Shaa-dom was one of the few that had raised a creditable attempt at secession, but the tyrant was too strong and too ruthless to let anything go once it was in his grasp.

The satellite realms seemed to breed a special kind of madness notable even in the dark city. Those at the fringes of Commorragh appeared most readily afflicted by the medium surrounding it, the limitless energies of the warp breeding strange obsessions and weirdly altered states of being down the centuries. In Aelindrach the very shadows flowed and writhed with a life of their own, in Maelyr'Dum the spirits of the dead could return to confront their killers, and in Xae'Trenneayi time itself jumped back and forth with scant regard for subjective continuity. The archons of the periphery were contemptuously regarded as idiot yokels by those of High Commorragh, fools saddled with unproductive domains, but they were also unpredictable and surprisingly powerful.

After he seized control Vect's laws demanded only the mightiest should rule the kabals, his cynical attempt to wipe away the nobility and replace it with some grubby meritocracy. Beaten and bloodied by Vect's betrayal the noble houses had dutifully transformed themselves into kabals but even under that guise the purest blood came to the fore.

The house of Yllithian lived on through the White Flames, just as their ancient allies of Xelian and Kraillach lived on through the Blades of Desire and the Realm Eternal. Among the satellite realms no such genteel rules of privilege and status existed; raw ambition and deadly ability drove their archons to the fore and struck them down just as readily. 'Mad' Malixian had outlasted most of his contemporaries and fed plenty of his rivals to his famed collection of airborne predators.

The most public entrance to Malixian's realm lay over a slender silver bridge across the canal that terminated at the Beryl Gate. The hedonists and epicureans that thronged the Grand Canal often frequented the Aviaries of Malixian to marvel at his exotic collection of avians brought together at unthinkable cost from every part of the Great Wheel. Some visitors had the great fortune to see the majestic white rukhs or darting shaderavens in their famed hunts, some of the less fortunate visitors in their turn became the hunted instead. Malixian had a well-deserved reputation for having a capricious nature even by the warped standards of Commorragh. The tyrant often indulged the mad archon in his insane vendettas for his own amusement, the volatile nature of Malixian making him an ideal tool of retribution when one was needed.

Beneath the steersman's sure hand the Beryl Gate soon slid into view as the barque rose silently to the level of the bridge to meet it.

BELLATHONIS WAS A haemonculus who had emerged from the benighted torture pits beneath the corespur of Commorragh centuries ago to make his own way in the city above. Thus far his skills had sufficed to find him patronage with a variety of archons including, most recently, the Archon Malixian of the Ninth Raptrex. The haemonculi covens below continually dogged him to align with one or another of them on a permanent basis, muttering darkly about the disrespect shown by his dilettante pursuit of the arts of flesh. Bellathonis professed to care nothing for their criticisms, although he had found it necessary to take increasing steps to ensure his privacy and safety of late.

Archon Malixian's generous offer of a tower within his satellite realm for Bellathonis's personal use had done a great deal to ease both issues, sparking something akin to gratitude in the master haemonculus's withered black heart. So when Bellathonis received a summons to attend to Archon Malixian he came forth willingly enough even though he anticipated another interminable discussion on the virtues of differing flight musculature.

Bellathonis instructed his assistants to shut down the apparatus he was testing and made his way up from the torture laboratories in the base of his tower. Outside a grav skiff manned by Malixian's kabalite warriors awaited him. He mounted and gripped on tightly as the warriors shot skywards with a bone-cracking jolt of acceleration. Bellathonis's modest tower lay on the outskirts of the Aviaries of Malixian and even at such speeds it would take several minutes to reach Malixian's eyrie at the centre. Titanic cages and enclosures reared up higher and higher as they flew up towards the heart of Malixian's realm, the lean grav skiff straining for height with every ounce of its considerable power.

The cages of the Aviaries swam past in a baroque panoply. Simple pagoda-like cages of gilded bars shouldered against immense wire spheres, leaded glass cubes and cones of interwoven bone. Their numbers belied their scale, each one a skyscraper-sized habitat for a unique winged life form plucked from some far-off world. Breaching through the mass was Malixian's eyrie, a single spike of silver rearing up to scrape the heavens. As the grav craft strained higher the tip of the spike resolved itself into a silver sphere, a pierced bead a hundred paces across, more empty space than metal but with landing points and railless walkways for the convenience of those that strode upon two legs.

As they swept in to land Bellathonis noted an unfamiliar and rich-looking grav vessel already docked at the eyrie. He regarded it more closely as he disembarked, and saw the symbol displayed on its bow. Malixian had company it seemed, and Bellathonis recognised the kabalite icon at once. The White Flames were a High Commorragh kabal that had remained rich and powerful thanks to their noble origins, and the noble kabals were forever scheming against the Supreme Overlord Asdrubael Vect. Intrigued, Bellathonis made his way along the curving pathways of the eyrie to its heart.

The master haemonculus was momentarily confused when he beheld Malixian talking with another eldar dressed in simple black. Beside Malixian in his spun-gold raptor mask and his feathered cloak of semi-sentient eyes – one of Bellathonis's finer creations, he noted proudly – the interloper looked like a mere warrior. The eldar in black turned to gaze at Bellathonis and in that moment he understood. The stranger's eyes declared him to be the archon he evidently was – proud, cynical, utterly ruthless and accustomed to absolute obedience. More than that, the newcomer's glance was lit with a kind of visionary fervour and radiant sense of command as if he were already wearing an invisible crown. This one had great ambition for certain, Bellathonis thought to himself as he lowered his eyes deferentially.

'Ah, here is my master flesh-sculptor now,' Malixian trilled on catching sight of him. 'Come forward, Bellathonis, and meet the noble Archon Yllithian!'

Aside from his chalk-white skin the master haemonculus Bellathonis appeared physically different to Syiin in almost every way. Where Syiin was permanently stooped Bellathonis stood rigidly upright. In place of Syiin's moon-like face Bellathonis's features were angular and sharp. Syiin's loose hide robes were replaced with Bellathonis's glossy black ribbed skinsuit. It was their eyes that marked their brotherhood: Bellathonis's eyes were black and glittering orbs that had drunk in torments of unimaginable cruelty and malice.

Bellathonis approached and abased himself with a formality that seemed to please Archon Yllithian. Malixian appeared to be in what Bellathonis thought of as one of his gregarious moods. Energetic and excitable, he was constantly bobbing up and down on the anti-gravitic spikes he wore to keep him permanently raised a few inches above the floor.

'Old Yllithian here felt his scourges were getting soft so he brought them to me to test against my own winged warriors!' Malixian's eyes glittered with amusement behind the raptor mask. 'A useless flock they were too! Couldn't win a single race!'

If Yllithian felt embarrassment at the performance of his minions he didn't show it, he merely nodded in rueful agreement.

'I fear the noble Malixian is correct, but he was generous enough to suggest that I might be able to engage your renowned services to rectify the matter, Master Bellathonis.' Yllithian said smoothly. 'He was extremely effusive about your skills when it comes to the reconfiguration of beings to enable flight.'

Bellathonis smiled ingratiatingly and bowed again. 'Archon Malixian is too kind. In truth, what mean skills I have were only honed to usefulness by access to the incomparable resources here in the Aviaries.'

'Indeed?' Yllithian seemed intrigued by the thought. 'So in the past you have honed other areas of your art with equal skill?'

Bellathonis looked to Malixian for approval before replying, acutely aware that he didn't wish to appear as trying to be a more interesting or accomplished companion than the mad archon. Malixian twitched his head marginally to signal him to proceed.

'I have had the great good fortune to study the arts of flesh beneath a variety of patrons,' Bellathonis replied carefully. 'Each had their own interests and I consider it simple courtesy to learn all I can to please them in the subject of their heart's desire.'

'Fascinating. My own haemonculi would do well to share your attitudes rather than frittering away their energies to inconsequentialities,' Yllithian said with feeling. Bellathonis found it hard to believe that this hard-eyed archon of the White Flames could be so indulgent of any inconsequential activity.

'Archon Malixian suggested that I might tour your workshops and discuss with you the alteration of the scourges under my control,' Yllithian continued.

'I would be most greatly honoured, Archon Yllithian,' Bellathonis responded obediently, all the while wondering what it was that Nyos Yllithian really wanted to discuss.

NYOS ALLOWED THE haemonculus to lead him through his untidy little tower full of torture implements. The tall, thin creature apologised continuously for his lack of preparedness for the visit of his august personage, lashing its own servants, his wracks as they were properly termed, into a positive frenzy for their tardiness. Bellathonis demonstrated the alterations he was making to turn imprisoned slaves into the twisted monsters known as grotesques, the haemonculus's long-fingered hands deftly wielding scalpel and flesh welder to sculpt their shuddering bodies. Nyos was shown whip-thin, skinless predators suitable for hunting and ursine-looking brutes being broken for the arena.

Members of the Ninth Raptrex who were undergoing the transformation into scourges were demonstrated to him in great detail. Their bodies were stretched on suspended frames as they painstakingly grew the bone, muscle and cartilage necessary for their new forms. Bellathonis launched into what sounded an erudite dissertation on the finer points of flight musculature but quickly subsided when Nyos showed little interest in the topic. Nyos was pleased to note that the haemonculus's attitude shifted slightly at that, as if he had confirmed a suspicion.

Finally Bellathonis led Nyos into a central area filled with a variety of pain racks and examination tables and directed his attention upwards. Dozens of crystal-fronted sarcophagi were arrayed in concentric circles disappearing up into the gloom above their heads. A handful of the sarcophagi were occupied by the semi-cocooned figures of eldar, the yellow-white bones showing on some contrasting with the raw red meat evident on others. The latter, Bellathonis explained, were fallen warriors that were close to reaching the conclusion of their regenerative process while the former unfortunates were only beginning theirs. The haemonculus then lapsed into silence as if waiting, his piercing gaze directed squarely, and somewhat impertinently, at Nyos.

'And so, most honoured guest, how is it that I may truly assist you?' Bellathonis asked eventually.

Nyos smiled thinly. Now they came to the meat of it.

'I was advised to seek you out in a matter my own haemonculi were unable resolve satisfactorily,' he said. 'Your reputation as a reanimator precedes you, it seems.'

'How very flattering, might I enquire which of my brothers brought my unworthy self to the archon's attention?' Bellathonis replied, and there was steel in the words. It seemed that Bellathonis had little love for his brother haemonculi, or possibly archons.

'We can discuss that later in concordance with my level of satisfaction in your highly lauded knowledge,' Nyos countered to regain control of the discussion. 'Now – tell me how the process is performed. I have been told it is complex and has many pitfalls; you cannot return one lost for more than a day, for example.'

There was a long pause before the master haemonculus replied.

'At its most elemental level the process is simple,' Bellathonis said emphatically, eyes shining with black intensity. 'My brother haemonculi insist on mystifying the procedure but only two steps are required.' Nyos could sense he was hearing an old argument being played out to a new audience. The master haemonculus raised a corpse-white hand with two fingers extended.

'Firstly the body must be regrown. For this, the smallest fragment of the subject can be used – even ashes will suffice,' Bellathonis said as one obscenely long, thin finger was lowered.

'Secondly – the animating spirit must be recalled into the body and then nourished with sufficient pain and suffering of another.' The second horrid digit lowered to join its twin.

'If these two requirements are fulfilled it is my belief that any regeneration may be performed. Death cannot hold us with either weight of years or violence if we have but the will to survive!' Bellathonis's fist was gripped tightly by now. Nyos found himself nodding, old Syiin had put him on the right track after all – probably by accident in all honesty, but the right track nonetheless.

'I was led to understand there were terrible risks involved, that overly ambitious attempts had triggered Dysjunctions in the past,' Nyos said. Bellathonis's sharp features curled in disgust.

'Fear leads my brethren to create connections where none exist,' the tall haemonculus replied dismissively.

'The key to restoring the long-dead is a secret they all seek – after all, what greater power could a coven wield than life or death itself? Their future would be assured for all eternity. So each coven pursues its own ends and tries to foil the attempts of the others, not least through stories of dreadful failures and dire consequences. Pure hypocrisy.'

'Fascinating. So if you were provided with the requisite means – a viable fragment and a sufficient source of suffering – you believe you could return one lost for hundreds or even thousands of years?'

Bellathonis paused before replying, weighing Nyos's words carefully.

'The resonance of dark energies required to return one so far behind the veil would be immense. The empathic connection to the source could be nothing less than perfect…' the master haemonculus mused.

'An individual of "pure heart" could make the connection,' Nyos prompted. 'Someone not to be found in Commorragh.'

Bellathonis looked at him sharply again, calculating.

'You are surprisingly well informed, archon. You are correct in surmising that, to put it in crude terms, quality and not quantity is required for the undertaking. A single subject of the right characteristics would bring better chances of success than a pen full of slaves… Yes, a pure heart…'

'You do not know where such an individual might be found?' Nyos asked. 'If not in the eternal city, then where?'

Bellathonis's face was growing taut with excitement, his dark eyes glittering with the thrill of the hunt for new knowledge. Nyos was beginning to see why the other haemonculi shunned this individual. It appeared Bellathonis took entirely too much pleasure in the exchange of thoughts and ideas for their tastes.

'Such questions have plagued the covens of the haemonculi for years without number, noble archon. Some have sought increasingly esoteric subjects, particularly among the human chattel, but thus far without success. Others have attempted to substitute quantity with notably disastrous outcomes. I have theorised for some time and to any that would listen that the lesser races lack a powerful enough connection to the Sea of Souls to serve such a purpose.'

'It would appear that despite your obvious eminence your colleagues failed to see the wisdom of your words.'

Bellathonis's eyes glittered darkly. 'They had no taste for the conclusions I had drawn, no, merely carping criticisms of the impossibility of obtaining appropriate subjects.'

'Oh? And what manner of subjects would these be?'

Bellathonis abruptly turned on his heel without a word and entered a doorway leading off the main chamber, leaving an astonished Archon Yllithian behind. The tall haemonculus returned a few seconds later bearing a huge, hide-bound tome that was fully half his height. Thumping it down on the notched surface of an examination table Bellathonis began to rapidly leaf through its man-skin pages. Obscene anatomical sketches, runic inscriptions and esoteric diagrams flicked past, the thin pages rustling

unnaturally as if angry at their disturbance. Bellathonis paused at a certain page, reading intently with
one long finger tracing the silvery runes.

'Vlokarion believed...' Bellathonis checked himself
and began again, 'Vlokarion was one of the greatest
haemonculi ever to grace the dark city. His achieve-
ments have only been equalled by the great Urien
Rakarth in recent centuries and they have never
been surpassed. Vlokarion was fascinated by the
muddy branches of our race that turned aside from
the true way to mire themselves in primitivism and
monasticism.'

Bellathonis swivelled the tome towards Nyos to
point to elements of a complex diagram picked out
in silvery ink on the pale skin of the pages as he
continued.

'See here the unbroken line of the ancients leading
to their inheritors in Commorragh. See here the twin
branching paths of the sterile eldar of the craftworlds
and the simpleton followers of Isha, the Exodites.' In
truth Nyos could only vaguely follow the branches
Bellathonis was pointing to: the lines intersected,
parted, curved around one another and reconnected
in a dizzying profusion.

'Vlokarion believed that during the Fall the racial
soul of the eldar was divided like colourless light
striking a prism. The division led to each branch of
our race embracing, or rather expressing, different
parts of our nature to the exclusion of others.'

The broad, straight path leading from the ancients
to Commorragh bore a version of the mark of Khaela
Mensha Khaine, the dragon-rune denoting Fury.

Bellathonis pointed out a prominent rune on the craftworld path, a variant of the sign of Asuryan – Discipline. Finally he pointed to a different rune on the Exodite path, this one showing the sign of Isha – Purity.

'Vlokarion proved on many occasions that the quantity of dark energy that could be harvested from eldar subjects exceeded that of the slave races many times over,' Bellathonis explained, 'and the Exodites most of all. He speculated that with a pure enough specimen to work with he could resurrect the greatest legends of eldar history.'

Bellathonis heaved the tome shut before resting his hands meditatively on the embossed cover.

'A pure heart could be found on a maiden world, among the Exodite clans. The Exodites bind their souls to what they call the world spirit of their home planet in order to escape She Who Thirsts, just as our deluded kin on the craftworlds hide their dead from Her by binding them into the very fabric of their vessel.'

Nyos's lip curled in disgust at the concept. The eldar of the craftworlds chose to hide forever, clinging to their psychic gifts in sterile little facsimiles of the home worlds and never venturing forth. The regressive Exodites were no better than those of the craftworlds, living in the mud of a single world and calling that their whole universe. True eldar, the ones the milksop eldar of the craftworlds called the Dark Kin, chose to live forever and took what they needed from the slave races to survive.

'You said that this individual could be found among

the Exodite clans, not that any one of them would do. On a planet full of savages how could this singular pure heart be found?'

Bellathonis grinned in triumph, a dreadful and menacing shark-like smile. 'You are most incisive. In the course of my studies I have discovered a caste that would be ideally suited for our purposes, ascetic warp-shapers that form a life-long spiritual bond with their home world. Once removed from that… embryonic environment I believe a member of this caste could be employed as a living conduit of dark energy.'

Nyos arched his brows thoughtfully. He'd spent a long lifetime keeping his position by being able to read what others sought to conceal. His finely tuned senses could detect the distinct taint of omission in the haemonculus's words now.

'If such individuals exist and you know of them why has none been secured before? It's not as if the Exodites could prevent us from taking whatever we want from them. I fear you're not being entirely forthright with me, Bellathonis.'

The master haemonculus paused and bowed his head. 'Forgive me, noble archon, my enthusiasm perhaps runs ahead of me. The caste in question is seldom mentioned even in the oldest records, and to the best of my knowledge no member of it has been brought to the eternal city alive.'

The master haemonculus reached out to caress the embossed surface of the great tome on the table before him. 'Some claim that their existence is entirely mythical,' Bellathonis continued, 'possibly even a concoction by Vlokarion to misguide his rivals. However, Vlokarion himself mentions that they seldom leave their shrines buried deep in the heart of their worlds, and that these places are normally completely inaccessible to outsiders.'

The haemonculus raised his head and locked his disquieting gaze on Nyos. 'But if you could find such a *worldsinger* and bring them to me I feel confident that I could resurrect Eldanesh himself.'

'I admire your hyperbole, Bellathonis, but the first-born of our kind is not quite who I had in mind,' Nyos said. 'Make such preparations as are necessary and I will find a way to supply you with the means to make a dark miracle the like of which this city has never seen.'

Bellathonis bowed deeply 'I am greatly honoured, archon, but beginning the preparations would be a great undertaking to make on faith alone. I sense that such activities would be best pursued outside the Aviaries of Malixian and beyond the sight of the tyrant's agents or you would have been more forth-right already. Are such costs and risks to be accepted entirely without compensation?'

Nyos was taken aback by the sudden twist of acquisitiveness, thinking that he had already snared Bellathonis through his own thirst for knowledge. 'I would imagine the promise of participating in such great endeavours would be spur enough for one such as yourself, haemonculus,' Nyos replied danger-ously, before checking himself. Bellathonis would be key to the scheme ahead so placating him was best. Full accounts could be made for impudence later. Nyos smiled disarmingly 'However, I am a generous patron and I do have a plaything in my possession that would handsomely recompense any marginal inconvenience that such activities might incur on your part.'

Bellathonis's brows arched with obvious interest and Nyos knew that he had him.

WHEN YLLITHIAN'S BARQUE returned to the fortress of the White Flames the hunch-backed haemonculus Syiin had emerged from his pits and was lurking at the docking port to dutifully give voice to his joy at his archon's safe passage. He was left behind as Yllithian and his retinue swept into the palace, lingering to talk with the steersman and his crew, plying them with elixirs distilled in the pits below.

Syiin was particularly attentive to the steersman's stories of their journey to the Grand Canal and the Aviaries of Malixian the Mad, congratulating him on his perspicacity in suggesting such a rewarding diversion to Yllithian. Syiin commiserated with the flightmaster at the losses to his scourges, and listened patiently to his distraught excuses as to why his winged charges had performed so poorly when put to the test. His broad, moon-like face smiled disarmingly as he pieced together his archon's activities one by one and saw them for what they were.

Syiin's mind clicked through the calculations like a wicked old abacus. Yllithian had gone virtually straight to Bellathonis. Despite all the archon's smoke clouds and misdirection Syiin could see through them to what lay at their heart. He had gone to meet with Bellathonis and… what? That precise piece of data was missing and known only to Bellathonis and Yllithian, forcing Syiin to speculate in a most unsatisfactory fashion.

The archon had asked Syiin about a dangerous brand of necromancy. Returning an individual thousands of years dead wasn't just dangerous, it was impossible as best as the moon-faced haemonculus knew. He wasn't about to go asking opinions from others of his calling. Covens and individual haemonculi guarded their secrets carefully, exchanging their knowledge only with a chosen few when there was profit to be made.

When Syiin had suggested Bellathonis he had hoped that the master haemonculus might find himself landed with an impossible request, and at the very least be discomfited by having to disabuse Yllithian of his half-crazed notions. Now Syiin found himself wondering if Bellathonis had, in fact, accepted the seemingly impossible task and what would become of his own tenure with Yllithian if his rival should somehow succeed at it.

Syiin returned slowly to the pits, ruminating on how best to be alert for signs of further contact between Bellathonis and Yllithian. Whatever mad schemes the archon might come up with they could do little harm as long as no haemonculi indulged him. But Bellathonis could be dangerous, he was a renegade after his own fashion that belonged to no coven and had no permanent ties to a single kabal. While it was not unprecedented for a master haemonculus to pursue their arts that way such behaviour spoke volumes of his overweening ego. It might fall to Syiin to rouse his coven-mates into finally doing something about the upstart Bellathonis.

CHAPTER 3
A THOUSAND SOULS TO QUENCH

*'What could be finer than the soughing kiss of blade
on flesh? Come to me and I will love you with such
strokes as will make you swoon. We will dance and
caress with edges so fine the very stars themselves
are sundered by their divine movements.'*

– Qa'leh, Mistress of Blades, to Duke Vileth,
in Ursyllas's *Dispossessions*

AMONG THE SPIRES of High Commorragh the great
citadel of the Blades of Desire Kabal held a special
place in the dark hearts of many Commorrites. Its
gigantic arenas played host to elaborate displays
of fighting prowess unmatched anywhere in the
universe, carnivals of blood and suffering honed to
artistic perfection. The arenas fulfilled a vital role in
Commorragh society. The miasma of pain and fear
they generated, the excitement of murder and wanton

slaughter witnessed at close hand invigorated and rejuvenated the spectators. This is no mere pastime or simple diversion for the jaded hosts of the dark city. Without the crimson displays of the arena Commorragh would soon collapse in upon itself to slake its eternal thirst for suffering. The archons had a term for it: *Llith'antu Klavu*, the knife that stays the blade.

Many spires featured arenas of their own – toroidal raceways, multi-layered platforms or specialised environments – but few rivalled those of the Blades of Desire for sheer scale and complexity. Archon Xelian, mistress of the Blades of Desire, conducted endless realspace raids to fill the slaughter pits with fresh victims and offered patronage to any wych cult or hellion gang of sufficient stature to meet her famously high standards. Every day thousands of slaves and beasts flowed into her arenas to be gorily sliced apart for the pleasure of the crowd, but today was different.

Today's events marked the culmination of a six-day orgy of carnage fuelled by Archon Xelian's most recent raid. The foray had netted unexpected jewels in the form of Imperial Guard troopers. Commorraghan experience of the human warriors of the Imperium's shield could be divided into two flavours: terrified conscripts unable to quite believe the nightmare they had fallen into, and seen-it-all veterans that didn't realise the nightmare they had fallen into until it was too late. The latter variety were much more entertaining.

Xelian herself was already fully recovered from her taxing sojourn in realspace, her body firm and supple beneath hooked breastplate and razor-edged greaves, her lips full and red beneath her half-masked helm. She strode through the training complex beneath the arena primus with an ornate agoniser whip gripped in her hand. Anyone crossing her path was lashed aside with a wordless snarl, the agoniser's neuronic circuitry leaving a trail of writhing, screaming victims in her wake. She forged her way to the confinement cells in a fury, barely sparing a glance for the wyches at practice in blade-filled chambers and gut-wrenching gravity anomalies all around her. Her beastmaster, Varidh, quailed at her coming, as well he might.

'You said they were ready!' Xelian thrust the agoniser whip at him accusingly.

'They will be, my archon! I swear it!' Varidh yelped.

'That's not what I was told. Explain!' The whip lowered to her side but still lashed like the tail of an angry cat.

'The scenario will still be played out, it is only that the turncoat became unreliable and had to be replaced. Please, my archon, observe if you will.' Varidh turned and touched the wall before gesturing towards it in an expansive fashion as he quietly backed out of lashing range. The wall shimmered and vanished to reveal the interior of a large confinement cell where they could observe the inhabitants unseen from outside.

A group of hairy, lumpen-looking humans were in the act of rising from equally lumpen-looking beds as a door opened to admit a human female bearing a tray. An eldar warrior in armour stood in the doorway as the sow distributed some sort of disgusting food to the others. Xelian smiled to see the simple plot playing out. The guard was lax and disinterested – in point of fact he was a drugged-addled criminal recruited specifically for the task. The sow exchanged little knowing looks and whispered words of encouragement to the brutes as she moved among them.

The men were suspicious and wary but they couldn't seem to quite quell the tiny spark of hope that she kindled in them. Eventually the sow withdrew and the guard shut the door, leaving the brutes huddled together croaking and grunting in their crude tongue as they doubtless planned their imminent escape. Xelian's full red lips smiled cruelly.

At the appointed time the turncoat would return and open the cell. From that point the drama could be orchestrated in many ways: the heroic escape might begin there and degenerate into a nightmarish pursuit through the training complexes, the slaves might seem to fight their way through impossible odds to reach a portal or a ship. The turncoat might be taken away and tortured to induce guilt, or given a weapon and instructed to slay the leader of the escapers to induce horror and a sense of betrayal. In every one of the well-worn scenarios the escapers eventually found themselves emerging into the arena proper to meet their final fate.

So simple yet so glorious. It always worked the best with veterans as they were the ones with the arrogance to truly believe that they could escape in the first place. The enormity of the jest being made at their expense always hit them the hardest of all.

Xelian felt satisfied enough to leave the quailing

Varidh to complete his preparations in peace and moved on to terrorise her other beastmasters. In truth the trip to the confinement cells had only been a diversion to take her mind from the imminent meeting with her allies. The thought of dealing with Kraillach always drove her into a vindictive frenzy that could only be quenched with suffering.

As the hour of the games approached deep-throated horns and sirens began to sound high above to summon the highborn citizenry to the feast. Xelian cursed and abandoned the gibbering slave she was scourging, stalking off to a bank of gravitic risers that would bring her to the observation tiers. While the invisible energies of the riser pushed her upwards Xelian tried to centre herself and bring her irritation under control. Kraillach was a disgusting worm, but he was a necessity. Without the backing of Yllithian's White Flames and Kraillach's kabal, the Realm Eternal, Xelian's most recent raid could never have succeeded. Much as it galled her to admit it the wonderful events she was staging today were as much to honour the Realm Eternal and the White Flames as the Blades of Desire.

The observation tier felt cool and clinical after the heat and sweat of the training complex below. Curving terraces of pale stone reared up, like frozen waves caught breaking over a floating central platform with thirteen surrounding satellites. At present the platforms were empty save for a few slaves scattering shovelfuls of glittering white sand over their surface. The sand was a traditionalist touch that Xelian insisted on despite the inconvenience; nothing else quite showed the loops and whorls of spurting arterial blood so artfully. Xelian took a pipe of *vreld* and settled herself into an unadorned throne of black metal to watch the spectators assemble.

Elegantly sculpted grav craft and darting individual skimmers were already arriving in some numbers. They settled on to the terraces like a rapacious flock of predators descending on a kill. The approaching culmination of the past six days of carnage was a highly anticipated event and a febrile thread of excitement ran through the growing throng. Kabals from all across High Commorragh were in evidence: preening catamites of the Baleful Gaze reclined beside ornately armoured mechanicians of the Obsidian Rose, masked terror-scions of the Broken Sigil claimed their places alongside steely-eyed warriors of the Last Hatred.

The icon of Vect's lackeys, the Kabal of the Black Heart, could be seen everywhere, outnumbering all the other kabals present. Xelian's delicately pointed teeth ground in impotent fury at the sight of the swaggering warriors so proudly bearing the supreme overlord's mark. She would have slaughtered them all if she could.

Rank upon rank, row upon row of fantastically armed and armoured warriors from a hundred different kabals flowed into the arena. Nowhere else in Commorragh would so many kabalite warriors lay aside blood feuds and honour debts to gather for a single purpose. Nonetheless quick, bloody duels, stealthy murders and acts of perfidy still occurred, thrilling the growing crowds as their tiny tableaux played out against the backdrop of the greater event. It was to be expected that the crowd would entertain themselves while they were waiting; nowhere in Commorragh was ever truly safe.

The horns and sirens sounded again with a higher, sweeter pitch that was redolent of howling madmen and screaming infants. The second summons was for the archons and their cliques to enable them to arrive at the last possible moment with fashionable tardiness. The rapidly filling terraces quieted in anticipation of their coming. The notes still hung in their air as the first arrived.

Archon Khromys of the Obsidian Rose, the self-styled Queen of Splinters, rode in upon a heavily beweaponed and razorthorn-encrusted Ravager craft to be greeted by a thunderous cacophony from her warriors clashing their weapons together. Archon Xerathis of the Broken Sigil swept over the arena on a spoked wheel festooned with the mnemonic projectors and psychic amplifiers he used to convey his messages of terror and discord to the trembling populations that fell beneath his hand. A succession of other fantastic, threatening and sometimes gaudy craft slid into view across the open top of the arena, each archon greeted by a bestial roar of approbation from their followers.

Some of the craft hung motionless in the air while others descended to debouch their passengers onto terraces. The dimension-warping properties of the observation tiers would ensure that every viewer in the arena could witness the action from scant metres away. Some preferred to do so from the isolation of their personal craft, while others trusted their bodyguards sufficiently to rub shoulders with their kabalite warriors on the terraces. After the archons had settled into their places two final craft nosed their way over the rim of the arena. From one hand came the sleek barque of Yllithian of the White Flames, from the other the mollusc-like golden chariot of Kraillach.

Xelian stood up from her throne as Yllithian stepped nimbly from his craft surrounded by a small cadre of incubi. She stood up straight as a rod to force him up on to his tiptoes in order to kiss her cheek in ritual greeting.

'Xelian, you are as magnificent as ever,' Yllithian murmured appreciatively.

'Yllithian, you remain… unchanged,' Xelian replied coldly.

Fans of golden metal slid back on Kraillach's craft to reveal a sumptuous interior of silks and exotic fur before the view was obscured by disembarking incubi. Kraillach's chief executioner, a giant incubus warrior known as Morr, led his brethren as they spread out and suspiciously eyed Xelian and Yllithian. Only when Morr was satisfied did the emaciated figure of Kraillach himself emerge from the opulent depths of his craft.

Kraillach was so wizened that he looked like a dried-out mummy. Deep lines and creases marked skin stretched so thin it seemed a miracle it didn't tear open and spill his yellowed bones onto the ground. The impressive vermillion robes he wore only served emphasise the tremulous decrepitude of their occupant. His eyes seemed to be the only part of him that were truly alive, glittering chips of onyx trapped in a crumbling face of shale.

Kraillach was old, one of the few members of his noble house that survived when Vect took control of the city. Eternal, unblemished youth was the aim of every Commorrite but even for one so wealthy and powerful as Kraillach the growing weight of years could not be easily turned aside. Over the centuries more and more suffering was needed to fill the unceasing hunger inside, and the restorative properties of the process became increasingly short-lived. Kraillach lived his life in an unceasing cycle of orgies and debasement, feeding almost continuously on wretched slaves and unsatisfactory underlings. His current state had no doubt been induced by the lack of sufficient stimulation during his journey from his palace.

Unsurprisingly Kraillach was keen for events to begin and eyed the still-empty display platforms hungrily.

'Xelian, Yllithian,' he acknowledged each of them with the barest nod.

'Kraillach.'

'Kraillach.'

Two identical black thrones were brought forwards and Xelian's guests seated themselves to each side without further ceremony. Xelian strode to the front of the dais to address the restless crowd, her presence carried before every viewer with perfect clarity. She had posed the scene carefully, herself standing tall and magnificent between trailing banners with Yllithian and Kraillach lounging in their thrones behind her.

'Welcome, friends!' She kept her voice low and thrilling. 'Be most welcome and partake in the fruits of the labour of our three kabals: the Blades of Desire, the White Flames and the Realm Eternal.'

Xelian allowed that to sink in for a moment. By presenting a solid front the kabals that had grown out of the old noble houses were reaping rich rewards. It was a fact that was pulling not only wych cults but whole kabals into their orbit. Xelian raised her voice as she continued. An atavistic sense of hunger and anticipation was filling the giant arena, an almost palpable tension that crackled in the air.

'We come to the sixth and final day of our events. As befits any great occasion we have saved the best until last for your entertainment and delight. Today we shall finally see the so-called deathworlders find the true meaning of betrayal. Today they will see the pilgrims they sought to protect die screaming, and today they will join them!'

A low murmur of appreciation and avid desire rippled through the crowds.

'We dedicate these gifts to the greater glory and everlasting majesty of our ancient city of Commorragh, may it ever stand eternal.

'Let the games begin!'

The horns and sirens sounded out in a shriek that rose into ultrasonics before crashing out in a explosion of bass. White light flared on the thirteen rotating outer platforms before dying away to reveal thirteen slaves. Some wailed and gibbered, others dashed around helplessly, some prayed and others stood defiantly screaming. Young, old, fat, thin, male, female, they all swung smoothly around the central stage in their individual bubbles of captivity.

The platforms began to float higher or sink lower in response to the audience's interest in them. Those the audience found most intriguing would be matched against combatants by the beastmasters. The least interesting would be fed to warp beasts if their platforms sank low enough, something that often increased their number of viewers markedly.

After a few seconds the occupant of the highest platform – a hook-armed, red-furred specimen – vanished and reappeared on the central stage to be met by a single wych a moment later. The nearly naked wych looked slender when measured against the brutish human but she moved with a fluid grace that made the human look positively comical. The wych picked up on the possibilities and led the lumpy human around like a shambling ogre chasing a nymph. She improvised a series of slick engagements that sliced the man up so slowly that he wound down like a clockwork toy, quick trysts that left him only kissed by the edge of the blade each time.

Before she could finish him a white flash erupted and another slave appeared. This one was a shaven-headed, tattooed fanatic that rushed straight at her with a hooked knife held low. The wych pirouetted lazily out of reach before lunging just the tip of her blade into the fanatic's eye socket. He screamed and staggered, dropping the knife. *Flash*. A third slave appeared and was hamstrung a heartbeat later. *Flash*. The wych seemed to barely avoid the sweep of a cleaver; her counter left her opponent dragging his entrails in the sand. *Flash*. A second wych joined the first, the two of them leaping and cavorting together like lost lovers reunited as they ripped through the injured slaves. *Flash*. More slaves. *Flash*. More blood.

The voice of the crowd rose and fell like surf against a shore, enraptured as they drank in wave after wave of pain and suffering. The first batch of slaves had vanished from the outer platforms, one way or another, and were rapidly replaced. Five wyches were working the central stage by now and they left an ever-speeding influx of slaves leaking their lifeblood out on the sand. Xelian felt satisfied that the opening warm-up was well under way and turned her attention to her two allies.

Kraillach looked somewhat recovered, his lined face showing patrician features instead of the death mask of a mummy. Yllithian was hunched forwards, careless of the entertainment but obviously eager to talk. The dimension-warping technologies artfully concealed within the arena structure permitted a spectator to cast their presence into the midst of the action, feeling the blood drops on their face and hearing the death-screams ringing in their ears. They also permitted Xelian, Kraillach and Yllithian to converse together inside a co-sensual reality safe from outside observation.

'I have found the key to ridding ourselves of Vect,' Yllithian began without preamble. 'The answer lies in Shaa-dom as I suspected.'

'How can you know this? Are you telling me you went there yourself?' Kraillach sniffed derisively.

'I did go there, as you well know from your own spies.'

'Well, I don't believe it. You're still alive after all.'

'Enough,' grated Xelian. She promised herself that one day there would be a reckoning for moments like these. 'Speak. Tell us what you found out on your... expedition, Nyos.'

'With the right preparations it may be possible to recall El'Uriaq from beyond the veil.'

'El'Uriaq!' Kraillach spat, his face blanching at the name. 'What madness is this? The old emperor of Shaa-dom has been dead for three millennia!'

'It can be done,' Yllithian insisted with surprising vehemence, 'and it is our path to victory. With one of Vect's most deadly enemies at our side the kabals would abandon the tyrant in droves. The value of someone who has defied the tyrant previously cannot be overestimated.' The sudden tirade seemed to wear Kraillach out and he fell back in his throne waving one hand feebly as if to brush Yllithian away.

Yllithian lapsed into silence. On the central stage the wyches' dance of death was almost over. Now they skirmished with each other over the crimson dunes of sliced meat they had made, skipping grotesquely over the still screaming, quivering piles of maimed slaves.

Her favourite, a highly ranked succubus named Aez'ashya, was taking on two other wyches at once. Her knives blurred in gleaming arcs as she pressed them back with a lightning fast flurry of blows. One of her foes was a *yraqnae* with an electrified shardnet and impaler but Aez'ashya gave him no space to make a cast. Her other enemy tried to slide around behind her and come at her unprotected back while she was occupied.

'He failed, Nyos,' Xelian said. 'Vect crushed him and his entire realm in a single night. I'm not much given to recruiting failures be they living or dead.'

The crowd gasped as Aez'ashya suddenly dropped, but the shardnet flew through the space she had occupied and wrapped itself inexorably around the wych behind her. Aez'ashya flipped back onto her feet and resumed her assault with a lusty peal of laughter. The netless *yraqnae* had only sharp-tined impalers left to defend himself with and quickly succumbed to the dancing knives of the lithe succubus.

'El'Uriaq's only failure was underestimating Vect's desperation and lack of imagination!' Yllithian snapped. 'Our own illustrious forebears fell to the same ruse, only in El'Uriaq's case the tyrant dispensed with the artifice of using a foreign vessel as a distraction and crashed it on his damned head instead.'

Yllithian's barb about their illustrious forebears was well-placed. The noble houses that once ruled Commorragh were virtually annihilated by invaders deliberately provoked into attacking the city by Vect. While the lords of High Commorragh fought to protect their holdings Asdrubael Vect and his allies had picked them off one by one on the battlefield. By the time the invaders were driven out Vect was well placed to fill the power vacuum left by the recently deceased high archons. In the centuries of anarchy that followed the old order was swept away and Vect instituted his new system of kabalite law.

Kraillach grimaced. He had been only a child when Imperial Space Marines smashed through his family's quarter of High Commorragh but he recalled the night all too well. The leaping, hissing flames and the distinctive staccato roar of boltguns in the shattered streets had never left him. He remembered the running and the hiding, the shock of hearing that the high archon was dead, killed by the blast of a dark lance from his own ranks, though by accident or design no one knew...

'Vect must pay,' Kraillach said bitterly. 'The tyrant has to suffer for his crimes against the city and my house.'

On the central stage haemonculi were moving through the drifts of injured. They bore gravitic wands that they used to pull glistening loops of viscera from the fallen and send them skywards in dancing arches and whorls. Some of the haemonculi raised up red and screaming almost-whole victims to be artfully vivisected for the entertainment and edification of the crowd. Others stabilised the dying and roused the insensible with elixirs and pain goads. From the terraces thousands of eyes watched every move hungrily, savouring the dregs of the first course and whetting their appetites for the next.

'The tyrant became so and remains so because he's willing to use the biggest weapon he can find,' Yllithian said. 'If he's threatened he'll use it to strike without hesitation or warning. We need our own weapon, we cannot defeat him otherwise. We need an unthinkable weapon and the will to wield it, if the tyrant has taught us nothing else he has taught us that. Both of you may carp and complain about my plans but where are your own? We all desire this thing, we are all bound together by blood and vengeance.'

The outer platforms of the arena were reconfiguring themselves, flowing like mercury to touch one another until they formed a continuous strip hanging scant metres from the fluted stonework of the terraces. The Reaver race was about to begin.

'What do you say, Kraillach?' said Xelian. 'I want to at least hear Yllithian's idea in full. None of us is getting any younger.'

'Subtle as ever, Xelian. Very well Yllithian, make your case.'

'We can effect the return of El'Uriaq with two simple steps. First we raid a maiden world with its own crop of Exodites and seize one of their worldsingers to act as a catalyst. Second we retrieve a fragment of El'Uriaq's body from Shaa-dom. I have secured the services of a master haemonculus to undertake the task and he assures me that it is perfectly viable.'

Yllithian timed his deposition nicely with the beginning of the race. A cluster of lean, predatory-looking jetbikes and their half-wild riders had snarled into place both above and below the race strip, preparing to race in opposite directions. An expectant hush fell over the crowd as every eye strained to Xelian awaiting the signal to begin. Xelian raised a gloved hand imperiously and paused for a moment before letting it drop. The bikes instantly leapt away with a multi-throated howl and shot off along the course at an eye-watering rate of acceleration.

The Reavers expertly threw themselves around the curved track at breakneck speeds, only their extraordinary reflexes preventing them from smashing into the arena walls or each other. After the first lap obstacles began to appear: saw-edged teeth protruding from the track, moving blades sweeping out from the arena walls, drifting gravitic anomalies and monofilament nets.

The appearance of the death traps was also the sign for a general melee to break out among the Reavers. They began to side-swipe one another with their bladevanes and loose off blasts at the leading bikes with their built-in weaponry. The dance was a deadly one. Every Reaver had a mass of hooked, razor-sharp knives mounted on their craft in their own customised array. All too often a quick twist and roll brought an incautious attacker onto an impaling dagger before they could make their own blades connect.

'If this thing can be achieved, how do you propose to control El'Uriaq?' Kraillach said, 'He was renowned for being proud and wilful. We would simply exchange one tyrant for another.'

'Aside from El'Uriaq's obvious common cause with us the haemonculus has assured me that certain… checks and balances can be introduced into his regenerating body that will afford us complete control if we deem it necessary. We would hold his life in our hands and we could dispose of him at any time. Such a puppet tyrant might even help to ease the transition of the city back under the rule of the noble houses.'

Below them the race was entering its final stages. The contra-rotating packs of Reavers had thinned to include only the luckiest and most skilful riders. The gleaming strip of the raceway began to ripple and twist to test their nerve and coordination even more, sending the speeding jetbikes even closer to the cliff-like walls. One Reaver was struck by splinter fire from behind and careened straight into the crowd, plunging into the screaming mass like a fiery comet before exploding in a shower of white-hot fragments. Xelian yawned.

'Interesting,' she said with a smile, 'and just what steps do we take to avoid Vect divining our plans?'

'One among the tyrant's own pets will be the one to suggest the maiden world raid and our forces will simply offer to join it. During the raid itself an elite clique of our agents will slip away to abduct the worldsinger in the confusion. Only when the worldsinger is secure do we move to reclaim a physical link to El'Uriaq from Shaa-dom.'

The vicious g-forces exerted by the twisting track were now flinging out both packs of riders so far that they passed through each other before plunging on their separate courses. Explosions of blood and viscera marked each pass. Some machines plunged straight into each other and fell locked together as a single flaming mass of tangled wreckage.

Soon only two Reavers were left, a jade-green carapaced jetbike with a bare-headed rider that threw itself against a glittering black one in a rolling dive. Bladevanes flashed as the two came together head-on, the jade-green vehicle jinking at the last second to sweep a sharpened wing above the other's curving prow. The black-clad Reaver had anticipated the move and jerked below the onrushing jetbike, laying open the guts of his enemy with an upthrust dorsal blade. The jade-green cycle spiralled away spitting smoke and flames, disappearing out of sight. The victor roared around the track in triumph accepting the acclaim of the bloodthirsty crowd.

'Truly you have all the answers, Yllithian,' Kraillach sneered. 'All we need do is trust that honeyed tongue of yours and we'll be wafted to happy golden uplands in no time at all.'

Xelian had an impulse to attack the wizened archon there and then, sating her growing ire with a gush of blood. Kraillach's chief executioner, Morr, shifted subtly behind his master's throne in a tacit admission that the silent incubus had picked up on Xelian's impulse even if his archon had not. Xelian forced herself to relax and focus. She had her own doubts about Yllithian's scheme but Kraillach's opposition was relentlessly driving her towards embracing it. Was Kraillach manipulating her? No it was more likely Yllithian's doing. He was always a clever one.

Xelian gave her attention to the next performance now starting in the arena while turning over Yllithian's insane plan in her mind.

The central stage was empty again, its white sands perfect and unblemished. A rapidly flickering holo-radiant hung above them now. It retold the story of the raid in a breakneck kaleidoscope of jump-cut imagery: black, hook-winged craft plummeting through atmosphere, a night-time scene of a primitive settlement, missiles flashing upwards, disintegrators flaring in reply, terrified families fleeing into a night that suddenly blossomed into fire and steel.

The content was of little interest to the restless crowd and some jeered at it with a crass lack of finesse. Xelian had insisted that they retain a context for the exhibition of the deathworlders that even now the turncoat would be releasing from their cell.

The last scenes of the holo-radiant montage showed the last stand of the settlement's defenders. They fought a brave but futile battle against eldar superiority in both numbers and technology that supplied a few images worth showing: a howling, bearded human thrusting a bayonet into the guts of a kabalite warrior, a barrage of laser bolts knocking another eldar off his feet. Haywire grenades crackled and a rush of wyches stormed a shot-scarred building that formed the last node of resistance.

The holo-radiant shifted to a direct sensory implant woven into the turncoat's nervous system, just the first of several such carefully prepared viewing points. A hundred thousand hungry souls rode behind the human sow's eyes as she hurried to open the locks to the deathworlders' cell. They felt her fear and avarice for the reward she had been promised burning inside her as she pulled the door open. The hairy, ugly deathworlders were ready and waiting. Two of them slipped out into the corridor while their evident leader took his betrayer protectively under his arm. The two scouts found the coast was clear and the rest filed out silently to follow them.

'What really makes you think this plan of yours will work, Yllithian?' Xelian said. 'I'd like to offer my whole-hearted support but I can't shake the sense that you aren't being entirely open with me.'

Although they were primitives the humans clearly thought they were both skilled and stealthy. Despite their wariness they were surprised by their guard blundering into them – as scheduled – from an unseen entryway. They reacted with deadly speed to the threat, one grabbing for the guard's splinter rifle while the other dived at his back.

The first lost fingers on the rifle's monomolecular blades but got a grip somehow and held fast even after the guard reversed his grip and punched a curved blade into his attacker's guts. The second assailant dragged the guard to the decking and after a brief, vicious struggle broke his neck.

A vicarious thrill shivered through the watching audience. Xelian relished the rush of excitement, and the undercurrent of loathing for the dangerous brutes that swept in after it. As she'd hoped, sacrificing one of their own had made the drama a hundred times more visceral.

'Securing a worldsinger is apparently a delicate matter, although I have assets in place that will smooth the way,' Yllithian said carefully, but Xelian simply stared at him waiting for the rest. Sensing the impending battle of wills the archon of the White Flames gave a small shrug and surrendered gracefully. 'It's also possible that returning El'Uriaq will bring about a Dysjunction in the city, although it's my belief that with our forewarning of the occurrence we can use this to our advantage.'

'Aha, you mean you'd hoped to use it to your own advantage while telling us nothing!' Kraillach said. Xelian found to her distaste that she was actually inclined to agree with the withered old fossil about something.

The deathworlders were fleeing now. Alarms sounded shrilly all around them and lights were strobing at an oscillation chosen to induce panic in humans. The turncoat ran with them, always being held protectively in their midst – the deathworlders desperately wanted to believe that they had found a friend. The one that had been injured fighting the guard was left behind with a captured splinter pistol to hold off pursuit as long as he could.

The injured deathworlder's end came ignominiously at the jaws of hunting beasts set on their trail. He managed to shoot the first but the others patiently crept up on him as he struggled to stay conscious through shock and blood loss. The howling beasts were soon back on the trail of the dead man's friends. Yllithian and Kraillach continued their bickering without regard to the unfolding drama.

'A Dysjunction could wreck the city!'

'The city has survived worse. The tyrant would be the one to suffer the most harm.'

'Madness to take such risks.'

'Madness to expect change will occur by sitting idly by.'

'Hush now,' Xelian said dangerously. 'Our guests are about to arrive and I want to enjoy the moment.'

The deathworlders had reached a deserted-looking oval bay dominated by a bronze metal arch at the far end. The turncoat had been instructed to tell them that the portal visible as a shimmering curtain inside the arch led back to realspace and safety. She had not been forewarned about the ambush.

Kabalite warriors emerged from hiding and shot their splinter rifles at the deathworlders with a startlingly poor show of accuracy. Shots flew everywhere, smacking into walls, ceiling and floor. Xelian grimaced unhappily; the warriors were supposed to drive the deathworlders through the portal but they were overdoing it with their obvious ineptitude. She needn't have worried. After a moment of confusion the deathworlders stampeded headlong for the arch while diving, darting and rolling for all they were worth.

Xelian withdrew her attention from the sensory link and focused on the central stage. The deathworlders flared into existence still running. They stumbled to a halt on the white sands as they took in their surroundings. As the hapless primitives finally apprehended the joke being played on them gales of cruel laughter echoed around the arena from the watching crowd. Some of the deathworlders stood dumbfounded, others fell to their knees or cursed their tormentors in their primitive, grunting language.

The psychic malaise of their despair was utterly delightful – so pure and natural that it had a kind of lost innocence to it. The primitives had been convinced the universe worked a certain way, that they were the heroes in their own tale of derring-do. The last shreds of their ego had finally been stripped away, revealing them to be the playthings of older, darker powers utterly inimical to humankind.

Xelian rose to make a final address to the crowd before the last act was played out. She had a hand-picked coterie of wyches standing by to fight the deathworlders in one-on-one combat. The primitives would be armed and permitted to fight their hardest for the pleasure of the crowd. More layers of self-belief would be destroyed as they discovered just how laughable their much-vaunted fighting skills were when compared to the grace and speed of a knife-wielding wych. Talos torture-engines were standing by to take what quivering remnants were left and commit them to an eternity of suffering inside their adamantium ribs. Xelian stood proudly and pointed to the filthy primitives on the central stage.

'Here are the beasts that have declared themselves rulers of the Great Wheel! See them grovel before you, my brothers and sisters! They thought to deny our greatness, to defy our glory–'

The whole arena trembled slightly and Xelian paused. An involuntary chill ran through her. Dysjunction already? Surely not, there would have been some warning from the crones and card-fondlers of Low Commorragh at least.

A vast, jagged ziggurat of black metal was rising over the rim of the arena and blotting out the light of the captured suns above. Hovering grav craft overhead scattered before it like a cloud of insects. Long shadows raced across the white sands towards Xelian's dais and swallowed the forgotten deathworlders completely. The assembled crowd fell to their knees like wheat falling before a scythe, abasing themselves as if they were themselves primitives intent on worshipping some strange new moon. Xelian grimaced and reluctantly went down on one knee. Behind her she could hear a silent Yllithian and a protesting Kraillach doing the same.

They had no choice. The tyrant was at hand.

Thorn-like probes and antennae on the underside of the ziggurat flared into life. Shafts of greenish light swept through the crowds like searching fingers before closing together into a luminous inverted pyramid. A face the size of a mountainside flickered into being, the visage of the creature that had held the dark city in thrall for six millennia. Asdrubael Vect, Supreme Overlord of Commorragh.

The arena echoed with the cheers of the kabalite warriors present, a bestial roaring that rose and fell around the terraces with a life of its own. When the face finally spoke it was with a voice of falling glaciers and grinding ice floes that stilled every throat.

'My apologies for interrupting your little soirée, children, the necessity for tiresome public rudeness is one of the burdens I was forced to shoulder when I became custodian of this peerless city. I can assure you that scheduled events will proceed momentarily.'

A deathly silence hung over the arena. Vect hadn't come to spectate, he had come for someone there. A traitor had been named and Vect had come to punish them. Every archon present felt a momentary gust of fear that some disloyal scheme of theirs, real or imagined, had come to the attention of the great tyrant. By long habit each of them strove to cultivate an attitude of nonchalant disinterest. Such tests of nerve were frequent steps on the path of the archon. The coward and the fool did not prosper in Commorrite society for long.

Vect evidently decided to be true to his word and did not keep the crowd in suspense for long. The stablights flicked out again, this time focused on a single point on the terraces.

'NARTHELLYON! You stand accused!' the god-voice roared.

Ninety-nine per cent of the arena's occupants allowed themselves to breathe a collective sigh of relief. Narthellyon's retinue closed around him protectively but it was looking to be a futile display. Hundreds of Vect's followers, warriors of the Kabal of the Black Heart, had already surrounded them in response to some hidden signal from their overlord. The renegade archon made some unheard reply to Vect, prompting a terrifying rumble of laughter from the great tyrant.

'I'm not sure that's anatomically possible, Narthellyon, but my haemonculi will be perfectly willing to test the theory on you. Seize him – alive, if you please.'

Xelian watched in helpless fury as fighting erupted in the baleful glare of the stab-lights. Wickedly curved blades flashed and poison-laced splinters whickered across the pale stonework. Vect's black-armoured warriors struggled to bring their superior numbers to bear against the tight knot of Narthellyon's followers immediately, forming a dense thorny ring as they fought to close in. Shots flew wild, bystanders were hit and soon several more battles broke out elsewhere on the terraces as the retinues of different archons took the opportunity to even old scores amidst the resulting chaos.

It appeared that Narthellyon had been expecting some kind of trouble during the day's events and had come prepared – so he thought – for it. Energy weapons suddenly flared through the struggling mass of warriors, the vivid emerald stars of disintegrators firing on full automatic. Screaming, kicking bodies could be seen as glowing after-images as they burned like candles in the hellish glare. Gaps were torn in the ring of Vect's kabalite warriors and the struggle hung momentarily in the balance.

A Raider craft bravely swept in to try and pick up Narthellyon. Lances of dark energy stabbed out from the ziggurat and crucified the sleek craft before it even got close. It was unclear whether they hoped to drive it off or to exact some measure of revenge for the fallen Raider, but Narthellyon's disintegrators targeted the ziggurat next.

Livid green sparks of high-energy plasma ricocheted off the imperturbable dark metal without so much as scorching the surface. Despite the lack of visible effect the feeble attack was apparently enough to exhaust Vect's patience. Disintegrators and dark lances studding the ziggurat abruptly swept the terrace with the fury of an angry god. Entropic darklight beams and plasma bolts rained down and obliterated the scene. All that was left of Narthellyon, his retinue and the Black Heart kabalite warriors fighting them, was a patina of blackened holes punched into the stonework. The awesome display of firepower did much to quiet the fighting in other parts of the arena. The tyrant's visage appeared again, leering at the carnage with a cruel smile on his lips.

'Such a shame,' the glacial tones said without any hint of regret. 'Now we shall have to wait to rebirth Narthellyon before we can have any fun together. Enjoy the rest of your event, Xelian, I do hope I didn't disrupt things too much.'

The black metal ziggurat rose silently and drifted away. As the shadow slid back across the sands the torn bodies of the deathworlders came into view. Xelian bowed again and attempted to keep her face impassive as she boiled internally with impotent rage. It was possible, just possible, that the deathworlders had been accidental victims of the crossfire, but Xelian felt sure that there was nothing accidental about their demise. Vect had timed his arrival and triggered the fighting specifically to upstage the culmination of Xelian's entertainment in the worst possible way.

She turned back slowly to her two allies. Yllithian met her gaze unflinchingly, a supercilious smile playing about his lips as he tried his best not to bait her when she was in a killing mood. Kraillach quailed backwards in his throne at what he saw in her eyes.

'No more games. No more bickering and manipulation. We move forwards with Yllithian's plan immediately.'

'I... I–' Kraillach stammered.

'If you are not with us on this you are against us. Kraillach, are you against us?' Xelian spoke with cold precision. If Kraillach objected he would not be leaving the dais alive, bodyguards or no, and he knew it. The wizened old archon wisely kept his silence.

Xelian turned around to survey the smoking ruins of the terraces.

'Vect must die. Everyone that supports him must die. I don't care if we have to burn the whole city to do it. The tyrant must be destroyed.'

CHAPTER 4
THE HUNTERS

'In the time before the fall of Shaa-dom, it is said that El'Uriaq's favoured concubine Dyreddya had seven handmaidens all of unsurpassed youth and purity. Each complemented El'Uriaq's mistress in one of the arts, and assisted by their tender ministrations Dyreddya was always able to quicken her lord's heart to flame. Some say that when disaster befell Shaa-dom the handmaids' souls were carried off directly to She Who Thirsts, such choice and delectable sweetmeats were they. Others say that She was so delighted with their delicate promise that She clasped them to Her bosom and remade them into something as dark as they were once light. Some even believe that the handmaids were carried away not by daemons but by the Dark Muse Lhilitu and escaped the wreck of Shaa-dom to become part of her strange pantheon. All the legends agree that *the cleverest handmaid hid herself by stitching shut her eyes and mouth to thwart the searching daemons. The hellish minions returned to their mistress and shamefacedly admitted they could find no breath nor sight of the one they called Angevere.'*

– Veslyin the Anchorite, *The Sudden Fall of Shaa-dom*

SOME DAYS AFTER the events at the arena of the Blades of Desire, Bellathonis summoned one of his wrack servants to him: an individual named Xagor, a promising and earnest pupil in the arts of pain. Xagor duly appeared, breathless and pleasantly apprehensive at why his master might call for him personally. Unmasked the wrack showed a pale, haggard face to the world, with red, staring eyes, a heavy jaw and a determined scowl that looked to be a permanent fixture. The thick brows beneath Xagor's glistening, naked skull were knotted with worry. A long, ribbed coat of dark hide flapped from the wrack's shoulders as he rushed into Bellathonis's cluttered quarters with unseemly haste to grovel before him.

Bellathonis was busy feeding a selection of his carnivorous plants, the last survivors of hybridisation experiments on behalf of Archon Pyrllivyn a number of years ago. Although the experiments had generally been another of many disappointments Bellathonis had grown attached to the fleshy little monsters it produced. He continued to drop fragments of raw meat into their snapping mouth-parts as he talked to Xagor, his long fingers too quick and sure to be caught by their thorn-edged jaws.

'Ah, Xagor, there you are. Is everything all right? You

seem a little… rushed,' Bellathonis smiled. He did so enjoy the earnestness of the young, and tormenting them for it. In truth his wracks had good cause to fear him. Each of them had sworn themselves to him utterly in exchange for their apprenticeship in the arts of flesh. Part of that apprenticeship was to experience Bellathonis's cruel skills at work on their own bodies. As he always told them, a would-be haemonculus had to first know pain before they could bestow pain.

'M-master, your faithful servant Xagor came as quickly as he could!' the wrack gibbered with his face pressed into the rich carpets.

'Oh don't worry, Xagor, I haven't called you to punish you, do get up. In fact I have a reward for you, isn't that nice?'

'Yes-yes, very nice!' squeaked Xagor in confusion as he struggled to his feet.

'Yes, you have been so diligent of late that I have a special task for you. Complete it to my satisfaction and I will look upon you with favour, do you understand?'

Xagor understood all too well what that really meant – pain and death would attend any failure to fulfil the task to Bellathonis's complete satisfaction. The wrack nodded frantically.

'Excellent. My first instruction is that you are to tell no one else of this task either now or later. You will proceed to the flesh markets of Metzuh in Low Commorragh and go to one of the most reputed exchanges there, a place known as the Red House, close by the Street of Knives. Do you know the place?'

'Yes-yes, master!' Xagor stammered. 'Xagor has

visited the Red House many times. Matsilier, who is a gourmand there, is my batch-brother.'

'Excellent, I'm pleased you did not try and lie to me by denying it,' Bellathonis murmured as he dropped another morsel of meat into the straining jaws beneath his fingertips.

'I have a very important package at the Red House that must be delivered to me in person. You will collect this package – a jar – and return it to me here at the tower intact and unopened. That part of the task is simple enough but absolutely critical – intact and unopened – do you understand?'

Xagor nodded obediently. Bellathonis could almost see the words 'intact and unopened' etching themselves into the wrack's brain in fiery letters. The haemonculus nodded back in satisfaction. He'd thought of a way to implant a suitable cover story that might also serve a useful dual purpose.

'The other important part of your task is to keep your ears open while you're in the flesh markets. I need information of the kind you can only get from Low Commorragh – find out what the dabblers and charlatans are saying when they try to foretell the future, see what ridiculous rumours the slaves have been cooking up lately – there's a grain of truth at the bottom of each one. Something's in the wind, Xagor, I just know it!'

Xagor nodded with barely repressed excitement at Bellathonis's somewhat fanciful oratory. He had been elevated from courier and potential victim to co-conspirator in a single stroke, an exciting development in his young life.

'All clear? Very good, then run along. Bring me the jar and any juicy rumours you hear, I'm hungry for news.'

Once Xagor had left the master haemonculus sent some discreet messages to his agents in Low Commorragh alerting them to follow the wrack's progress and, most importantly of all, to ensure the jar containing Yllithian's gift arrived in his hands intact and unopened. A single wrack should not overly excite the interest of his rivals in the haemonculi covens and Bellathonis was gambling on the fact to ensure the prize would not be intercepted before it was in his grasp. Nonetheless the decrepit warren of streets and alleys around the flesh markets had plentiful predators of their own to contend with. Ordinarily the servant of a haemonculus would enjoy a certain measure of protection, but the omnipresent pulse of violence and desperation in the city had been growing stronger of late. Something bad was coming and the masses could feel it.

Bellathonis had barely completed his arrangements and turned back to the clients on his tables when a summons arrived from Malixian. He had heard little from the mad archon since his meeting with Yllithian and wondered if this missive heralded some new burst of manic activity on Malixian's part. After a moment's thought Bellathonis dispatched one more message before he left, this time to agents in Aelindrach that he was normally loath to call upon. Although the cost would be high Bellathonis wanted absolute certainty that he could collect on Yllithian's payment.

* * *

ONE OF BELLATHONIS'S sometime agents and occasional informers was crouching on a half-eroded roof beam in an abandoned slave mill when the call came. He had spent days staking out the crumbling structure deep in the sprawling inner districts of Low Commorragh waiting for his mark to show up. Now just as the overseer was finally meeting with his cronies the agent's tell-tale pulsed with the whisper of a new and potentially lucrative mission.

The agent, a slender young eldar named Kharbyr, cursed inwardly at his misfortune. The overseer and his little gang of cohorts were mere slaves, ordinarily dirt beneath Kharbyr's recognition. Nonetheless someone had posted a small murder-fee for this overseer, and despite his pride Kharbyr was also very, very hungry. It was probably other slaves that found themselves under the overseer's too-ready lash that had pooled their miserable resources to rid themselves of their oppressor once and for all. The reward for this kill was paltry, but Kharbyr had not quenched his murderlust in several days and was loath to let his mark escape him now. A victim in hand was worth two on the loose, as the saying went.

Gazing down on the small circle of slaves below Kharbyr fancied he could take them all at once. Two with the pistol, three with the knife; it would all be over before they could wipe the stupefied expressions from their faces. A seldom-used, cautious part of his mind held him back. The slaves were wary, burly and crudely but effectively armed with metal cudgels and scrap-knives. He couldn't be sure that one of them wouldn't get in a lucky blow that would leave him open to getting overwhelmed by the rest. He fondled his favourite blade disappointedly. The half-metre curve of razor-sharp metal would not taste warm blood after all, just as Kharbyr would not get to quench his own unending thirst.

As Kharbyr fretted, the meeting broke up. The overseer and his friends split, each making their own way out of the decrepit structure. Kharbyr's heart sang with joy and he ran light-footed along the corrosion-furred roof beams to get ahead of his mark. Through a shattered window he watched the overseer leave the abandoned mill and cross a filthy, refuse-strewn alley to enter a crumbling row of storage barns on the opposite side. Kharbyr slid after him soft and silent as a shadow.

Only rats and peeling walls confronted him inside. At some point the interior of the barn had been partitioned off with sheets of a cheap, resinous compound. The walls had split in some places and fallen in others turning the place into a crumbling, unstable maze. Kharbyr crept along listening intently for a sound of his quarry. He felt sure the overseer was still somewhere in the building, but he couldn't hear anything but his own quiet breaths. Rounding a corner he found a set of rickety-looking steps that led upwards. He crept up them cursing internally at the slight creaks and groans made by his progress.

As his head came level with the floor above he stopped and cautiously scrutinised the part of the landing he could see. Nothing was in sight and the floor was in a ruinous state. If the overseer had come this way, Kharbyr decided, he would have heard him on the stairs anyway. The lean assassin turned and descended to the floor below as gracefully as he could.

A slight creak made him spin around in surprise. The overseer was right behind him! The big slave had crawled silently down the steps and was stretched out preparing to plunge a rusty scrap-knife into Kharbyr's exposed back. The overseer thrust desperately when he saw he had been spotted but the blow was weak and awkward from his semi-prone position. Startled by the sudden turnaround in fortunes the assassin leapt back and fled out of sight around a corner in a momentary panic. The overseer jumped to his feet with a roar and charged in pursuit.

At the third twist in the maze the overseer was brought to an abrupt halt by Kharbyr's outstretched blade sheathing itself in his guts. Choking on his own blood, the slave tried to bring his knife to bear but found his wrist gripped by steely fingers.

'Not so easy, is it?' Kharbyr whispered to his struggling victim as he dragged the half-metre of sharpened metal up to the slave's sternum. Blood and viscera sprayed over his pointed boots and he cursed again; he always forgot to step back at the correct moment. He ignored the momentary distraction and drank hungrily from the departing soul as it suffered on his blade, quenching but not satiating his eternal thirst.

He used his tell-tale to burn his kill mark on the twitching corpse. He couldn't take the time to drag it somewhere where it was more likely to be found, he'd just have to rely on someone reporting it for the finder's bounty. The idea of collecting payment was already fuzzy and half-forgotten in his mind anyway, he'd got what he wanted when he made the kill. This job for the haemonculus though, if he could find the courier first, promised almost unbelievable riches. He wondered whether he should take the 'important package' and deliver it himself or see if he could sell it to someone else.

Find the courier first, Kharbyr decided, then worry about the package once he's dead. He licked his lips with anticipation.

A SLEEK GRAV craft was waiting outside Bellathonis's tower to sweep him skywards to Malixian's eyrie. The pierced sphere atop its impossibly tall silver spike was the centre of a veritable hive of activity. A small armada of aerial craft jockeyed for position among a halo of swooping hellions and wheeling scourges. It looked to Bellathonis like the whole Kabal of the Ninth Raptrex was airborne.

Bellathonis's craft didn't enter the eyrie itself, instead it angled higher still to slide in beside a large, sleek Raider craft presumably bearing the archon himself. Malixian's war craft was slender and skeletal like the polished chromium bones of some aerial giant, and featured more open space than solid platform in its design. Malixian's warriors ran along its palm-wide spars and curving blades to take their positions with startling agility.

Bellathonis had long since evicted all traces of emotions akin to fear from his strictly ordered persona, but even so he felt an unpleasant instant of vertigo as he stepped across the kilometres-deep gulf between the two craft. The vessel he stepped from bobbed alarmingly as he pushed off from it, but Malixian's Raider was as solid and immovable as a rock. Malixian himself was dangling precariously from the Raider's spritsail as he hungrily drank in the sight of his assembled forces, and he was not alone. Bellathonis eyed the newcomer with professional discourtesy. Syiin's round moon-face blinked back at him innocently, the crook-backed haemonculus seeming to be fully engaged in clutching at one of the Raider's slender guard rails and not looking down.

'Ah, Bellathonis, my master shaper! I'm so glad you could come!' Malixian trilled happily, apparently forgetting that Bellathonis valued his life too much to ignore a summons from his archon. 'You know of Syiin, Yllithian's flesh carver? He came by to offer compliments on your fine work with the scourges so I thought he should come along too!'

'My heartfelt gratitude for that kind indulgence, my archon,' Bellathonis replied, somewhat pointedly looking at Syiin. 'May I enquire as to the occasion?'

'A hunt, my dear Bellathonis, a hunt!' Malixian crowed. 'After that business in the arena I picked up a job lot of Xelian's slaves. It seems the pain lady has some rebuilding to do and had to liquidate some of her assets – or rather that's what I'm about to do for her.'

A maggot of concern wriggled to the surface of Bellathonis's mind. Syiin's presence was unwelcome but not unexpected. Yllithian's chief haemonculus was inevitably going to start sniffing around at some point. His appearance just as Bellathonis was looking to take delivery of a reward from Yllithian was suspiciously timely, but what truly dropped the clawed fiend into the slave pit was Malixian's sudden impulse to hold a hunt.

Malixian liked to keep his winged pets well fed and exercised. On occasion a few score of slaves would be released into the Aviaries' grounds and allowed to scatter. Some time later the cages would be opened to release their flocks of aerial terrors – skinwings, bloodtalons, Iridian pteraclaws, vespids, rare white ruhks, shaderavens, poisonous Ymgarl shrikes and many more. The Ninth Raptrex would ride aloft with their archon to enjoy the pain and terror of the dying slaves as the hunt proceeded. They would also deal with any of their prey that were impolite enough to hide too successfully or desperate enough to fight back.

Anything on foot in the Aviaries during the hunt was fair game. If a warrior fell from their craft or a hellion became dismounted they became more prey alongside the hapless slaves. The barely restrained anarchy of Malixian's legendary hunts brought great numbers of scourges and hellions into his kabal, the wild warriors finding a common kinship in their contempt for their earthbound kin. Ordinarily Bellathonis would have been delighted to see Malixian's menagerie at play, but now Xagor's innocuous-seeming mission was apt to meet its end at the razor-sharp talons of the mad archon's pets when the wrack returned.

'I am deeply honoured, Archon Malixian,' said Bellathonis, while covering his dismay with a bow. 'We are particularly fortunate to have one of my colleagues here to enjoy the festivities too.'

'Hoo, it's nothing, you'll find it informative to see what you've been working on so diligently finally get into action. I'd been meaning to do something for a time, but Syiin's arrival clinched it – it's been too long since we shook out our wings and took to the skies!'

'Isn't it wonderful? Your kind archon indulging us in this way, Bellathonis? simpered Syiin. 'Lowly haemonculi like ourselves so seldom get a chance to know our place in the grand schemes of our betters. When such opportunities come along we really should seize on them so we can learn how to serve their best interests all the better. Don't you agree?'

'Why yes, Syiin, keeping our place is ever at the forefront of our minds, is it not?' Bellathonis replied tartly.

Bellathonis had to admit his curiosity was genuinely piqued by the idea of a hunt despite his more pressing concerns. The fate of the earnest young Xagor was out of his hands anyway. He was effectively trapped on board Malixian's hunting-chariot with Syiin and the archon for the duration of the hunt. Bellathonis consoled himself that if the jar survived and was delivered to him the loss of Xagor was regrettable but scarcely germane to the greater objective.

The master haemonculus rejected the passing notion of letting Malixian in on the secret of Xagor's mission. With Syiin present it was out of the question, and beside that the mad archon would be in no mood for objective discussions while his blood sang with the joy of the hunt. No, Xagor would have to take his chances and Bellathonis must be ready to pick up the pieces later – literally as well as figuratively – if matters were to go awry. Bellathonis silently blessed the streak of paranoia that had prompted him to seek help from his seldom-called allies.

With an imperious gesture Malixian sent his Raider plummeting earthwards, apparently the signal for a mass descent as the air around them was filled with pinioned scourges, hellions, jetbikes, Raiders and Venoms as if they were in the midst of a glittering waterfall. They levelled off above the highest peaks of the cages and the kabal slowly dispersed over the area in some pre-arranged scheme. Below them Bellathonis could see streamers of winged shapes emerging from their places of confinement like traceries of wind-blown smoke. The flicker of rainbow scales among the closest marked them as Iridian pteraclaws but further away he could discern the slow-beating wings of white ruhk and whirring clouds of shaderavens.

Malixian raised a long silver tube to his lips and blew through it to produce a low, shrilling whistle that carried through the armada and was taken up in many places. In response the deadly flocks descended into the canyons between the aviary cages to begin hunting for the slaves that were no doubt fleeing for their lives somewhere below.

Malixian's Raider flashed downwards in pursuit of some pteraclaws. Their frantically beating wings indicated they had spotted prey and they hissed at one another excitedly as they chased it down. Though the Raider could have easily overtaken the reptilian predators it hung back once they had caught up to them. Hellions dropped into place like outriders around their archon and a pack of jetbikes closed in to circle

protectively high above their stern. As the Raider settled on its course Syiin just managed to nerve himself
to creep, hand over hand, along the railing to come
closer to Bellathonis.

'Why do they trouble to guard against attacks from
above?' Syiin hissed urgently as he gazed up the circling Reavers. 'Surely we're not also at risk from the
archon's marvellous pets?'

'The Ninth Raptrex use their hunts not just for
pleasure but to practise the arts of war,' Bellathonis
replied, relishing the opportunity to lecture the other
haemonculus, 'a noble tradition that dates back to the
earliest days of our species. In the course of the hunt
the kabal learns to choreograph the diverse elements
of Raiders, Reavers, hellions and scourges in all three
dimensions with all the natural fluidity that serves
them so well on the battlefield. Hence the Reavers
position themselves as if an enemy may come upon
the archon unexpectedly because it is natural for them
to do so even when no danger threatens.'

He was distracted by the excited cry of Malixian.
The pteraclaws were folding their wings and diving
on their prey. The areas between the aviary cages were
parklands of manicured lawns and decorative arbours.
Three or four dark smudges on the ground were hurrying away from the winged doom descending upon
them. They moved pitifully slowly in comparison to
the pteraclaws, like insects trying to crawl away across
a tabletop. The predators dived on them in packs, striking down first one slave and then another with their
razor-edged claws. More of the pteraclaws dropped on
the fallen figures, ripping and tearing at them hungrily.

They were lower now and Bellathonis's cat-like eyesight picked out one of the fleeing slaves quite distinctly. It turned and flung itself at one of the squabbling packs, swinging a crude weapon it had fashioned in a futile effort to save one of its fallen comrades. The pteraclaws flapped backwards with a burst of outraged hissing, the slave yelling wordlessly as it belaboured them with its club.

A second later the brave but foolhardy slave was crushed beneath the plummeting delta shape of a white ruhk swooping on it from above. The ruhk was huge, fully three times the height of the mangled slave it was now pinning beneath one claw as it tore off its bloody limbs to feed. The pteraclaws continued hissing at the new arrival but stayed safely out of striking range while the white ruhk imperiously ignored them and continued consuming its freshly killed meal.

The Raider coasted slowly above the noisily feasting creature. Malixian grinned back at Bellathonis and Syiin appreciatively.

'My beautiful white ruhks always love to take down the ones that try to fight. I think they take any kind of challenge as something of a personal affront,' Malixian chuckled.

'Quite magnificent,' muttered Syiin weakly. Bellathonis was pleased to note that Malixian's aerial antics seemed to have a distinctly detrimental effect on Syiin's physiology. His stretched, circular face looked distinctly green around the edges.

'I was surprised to see one slave going back to try to save another like that, they must have been a bonded pair of some sort,' Bellathonis remarked.

'Perhaps,' Malixian said dismissively. 'The first kills in every hunt are the stupid ones – ones that have no better plan than to try to run. The clever ones are in hiding right now and the true hunt will begin when we start flushing them out of their holes.'

'Do any ever escape?' Bellathonis's question formed in his mind and popped out of his lips before he even considered the potential tantrum it might trigger in Malixian. He cursed himself inwardly for his distracted mind. Fortunately Malixian appeared to be in too good a mood to be upset by impertinent questions.

'My Aviatrix swears up and down that none of them escape, but I've got my doubts about that. I mean, the shaderavens will leave nothing but a wet smear when they've finished feeding – how can we be sure that the slaves are all accounted for without bodies? Sieve through their droppings?'

Malixian cackled appreciatively at the thought. It was quite within his power to order such a thing, but it simply hadn't occurred to him before now. 'No, I'm sure some of them do survive,' he continued 'but I say good luck to them if they can get out of the Aviaries alive under their own power. I don't begrudge them thinking they have a chance, it makes them run all the harder before they get caught.'

'Very true, noble archon!' Syiin said. 'Why, in my personal experience keeping a subject alive long enough to extract the maximum dark energy from them is impossible unless you somehow make them cling to a shred of hope – release, rescue, death, whatever it may be.'

Bellathonis nodded politely at Syiin's doggerel. It was true enough, without hope slaves plucked from realspace sickened and died far too quickly to be useful. He made a mental note to mention the phenomena to Yllithian, it would be an important factor for his schemes. Bellathonis was shocked out of his reverie at Malixian's next words.

'I have some news I've been meaning to share with you, Bellathonis, and you too, Syiin, since you're here,' Malixian said. 'I've persuaded Archon Yllithian to plan a joint raid on a place held by our grass-chewing simpleton cousins, the Exodites.'

'Indeed?' was the best Bellathonis could manage by way of reply at first. He darted a glance at Syiin but his flat face was unreadable. Bellathonis's mind raced wondering what kind of inducements and blandishments Yllithian had used to make Malixian think he was the one persuading Yllithian instead of vice-versa. Of course it was most likely that he'd simply played on Malixian's most obvious weakness.

'I imagine that there are some fantastic specimens to be found for your collection upon maiden worlds, my archon,' Bellathonis said.

'Just so! Did you know Exodites ride giant pterasaurs on some worlds? They make my white ruhks look like midgets. It's a long time since I've seen that.'

The smaller pteraclaws had finished their meal and now rose into the air with a thunderous whirl of iridescent wings. The white ruhk was left still feasting alone. As the Raider moved to follow the disappearing pteraclaw flock one of its escorting hellions caught sight of something on the ground. The lightly armoured warrior's knees bent and then braced as he pitched his skyboard over into a vertical dive. As he dropped the hellion brought up his hellglaive and triggered the splinter pods on his skyboard, spraying a stream of near-invisible hyper-velocity splinters from its built-in weaponry.

Below they saw a slave roll desperately out of the brush where it had been hiding to avoid the burst. It immediately broke into a run straight towards where the white ruhk was still perching on the remnants of its victim. As the slave no doubt intended the hellion was forced to shear off his attack for fear of hitting one of the archon's prized specimens.

As it ran forwards the slave levelled a lance of its own, some piece of piping or tree branch it had torn free, a pitifully tiny weapon to match against something as huge as a white ruhk. The tall, angular-looking creature twisted its head around to watch the little thing rushing towards it inscrutably. The three-metre-long bone-white beak of the ruhk suddenly clacked shut on the slave's head and torso before it got into striking range with its puny spear.

The creature lifted its helpless victim into the air with arms and legs kicking feebly before tipping its head back to swallow its catch whole. The white ruhk looked obscenely pleased with itself for getting second helpings without even having to move.

'Hoo, that one's going to be useless now – it'll be moping around digesting for the rest of the hunt now it ate a whole one, the greedy monster!' Malixian fretted. 'Speaking of greedy monsters an interesting thought struck me when Yllithian said yes to the idea of a raid – no one normally wants to go after the annoying tree huggers because they're so hard to pin down. No profit in it.'

Bellathonis wrenched his attention away from his own feeding on the pain and suffering being inflicted by Malixian's pets. The spear-wielding slave was still alive down there, being digested in the white ruhk's gullet. Syiin wore a frightened look; Bellathonis strove to make sure his own face didn't mirror it.

'You suspect that Yllithian has ulterior motives for the raid, my archon?' Bellathonis asked delicately. He disliked the direction Malixian's line of thinking was taking him.

'You can't normally interest a soul in the maiden worlds and now Yllithian's keen to throw in with his own kabal and his friends too? Smells strange to me. He didn't mention anything to either of you by any chance?' Malixian's voice was silky smooth and dangerous.

Bellathonis suddenly felt very alone on the archon's craft surrounded by Malixian's warriors. He glanced at Syiin and found him looking panicked. Evidently this was no scheme of Syiin's to win Malixian's favour, he had just found himself suddenly caught in one of Malixian's random bouts of paranoia. Bellathonis badly needed something to distract the mad archon with and something Yllithian had mentioned did come to mind, just a possibility but too perfect a foil to neglect.

'It has come to my attention that there are rumours of a coming Dysjunction, my archon,' Bellathonis offered. 'Yllithian's interest may be related to that.' He glared at Syiin to prompt him into some sort of affirmation. The haemonculus's moon-face lifted to look at him intently when he mentioned Dysjunction, like a sensor dish locking onto a signal.

'My – ah – my archon is ever cautious in safeguarding his assets,' Syiin eventually bleated.

'Dysjunction, you say?' Malixian echoed. Bellathonis felt as if the silent, immobile warriors on the archon's craft were hanging on his every word.

'I'd not thought to raise the matter with you before as there are little more than rumours at present, although I'm seeking to have them confirmed,' Bellathonis lied glibly.

'Hoo, a Dysjunction could have serious consequences here in the Aviaries, Bellathonis, very serious consequences.' Malixian gazed sadly out over the artificial mountain range of cages as if already seeing them broken and tumbled into ruins.

Bellathonis desperately wanted to take this chance to reveal that his faithful wrack, Xagor, could soon be returning with definitive news. A deep well of suspicion and paranoia stopped him. If Xagor were to arrive after Bellathonis had made such a revelation Malixian would want to meet with him and question him, and the jar would be mentioned. Malixian would want to know what was in it and then he might find out who it came from. Perhaps that was precisely what Syiin had come to find out, some clue as to the private plans of his own archon.

If that happened the whole scheme could unravel by linking Bellathonis back to the suspicious-seeming Yllithian at a most inopportune moment. Ultimately

Malixian was one of the tyrant's favourites, albeit in a distant and half-joking fashion, and if his suspicions were aroused then Vect's could soon follow suit with deadly result. Once again the mental equation of cold logic clicked out the same result. Xagor would have to take his chances alone and Syiin would have to keep fishing for answers without any help from Bellathonis.

'Please do not allow such matters to interfere with your enjoyment of your sport, my archon,' Bellathonis said soothingly. 'I should know more soon and then I can perhaps advise you on the validity of these claims of imminent disaster. They will doubtless prove to be without foundation.' To Bellathonis's relief Malixian nodded.

'Yes, first things first hey? I promised you a demonstration and you shall have one.' Malixian gestured to his steersman and the Raider shot away, quickly leaving the satiated white ruhk and still-hunting pteraclaws far behind.

They approached an open space where the omnipresent cages only formed a jumbled horizon in the distance. Around a great park, howling jetbikes and hellions were driving a herd of running slaves to a point beneath a circle of flying scourges.

'Here now, watch this, Bellathonis, Syiin,' Malixian trilled, hopping to the bowsprit again.

As the slaves came close the winged figures swooped down on them like avenging angels. Many of the scourges had their feet grown into powerful avian claws and simply latched onto their victims' shoulders before carrying them aloft. Others used shardnet

ANDY CHAMBERS

launchers or agoniser rounds to disable their victims before seizing them and bearing them away. Within a few seconds from when the whirling circle had begun to dip into the herd the scourges had carried every single slave screaming into the sky.

With their victims gathered the scourges began to play, dropping them and racing to catch them, taking a limb each and tearing them apart. More blood and viscera showered down when the hellions and jetbikes darted in trying to hook away victims for themselves. They were seldom able to win such bouts, the scourges were simply too strong and too agile for the machines to beat however skilfully they were piloted. Bellathonis had to admit it was a crude but impressive display. All the more impressive given that the number of scourges present represented only a fraction of those the master haemonculus had enhanced on behalf of Malixian over the preceding months.

'Magnificent work, Bellathonis!' applauded Syiin, his thin hands rattling together like bundles of twigs. 'I find myself in awe of the skills you show in this field. You seem to have found yourself a perfect niche.'

'I have to say they make a fine sight, my archon,' Bellathonis said dryly. 'Truly none can hope to escape your mighty winged warriors.'

'Cursed mud-dwelling Exodites might if they're dug in deep enough,' Malixian remarked sourly.

'I understood that our rustic inferiors were more given to running away and hiding than confrontation, so that stealth and speed were the only viable techniques for capture?'

124

'No, they're unpredictable, wild. They'll fight some-times if their settlements and shrines are threatened.'

The Raider was drawing away from the scourges' massacre, drifting higher again. Malixian gazed out over the jagged landscape as if he was seeing another one from his past, the primordial realm of a maiden world.

'Woods full of beasts, traps and snipers, everyone else barricaded in their holes waiting for the clans to gather. Once they do everything on the planet that walks, crawls or flies will be looking to take a chunk out of you. That's why a stealthy snatch is the most viable technique, because they know our kind can't stay for too long once they make a fight of it.' Malixian shook himself, his feathered cloak rustling mournfully, before lapsing into a brooding silence.

Bellathonis nodded. Regressive as they were Exo-dites were not stupid and they had their legends about the Dark Kin who came by night to steal the souls of the unwary. The eldar of the craftworlds also had some proprietary sense of duty to the maiden worlds. They would often come creeping through the labyrinth dimension to appear in their defence at the most inopportune moments. Yllithian's real objective for the raid of seizing a worldsinger, surely a mem-ber of one of the Exodites' most prized and protected castes, was beginning to sound like an extremely thorny prospect.

Malixian cocked his head to one side as if listening to invisible voices. He gestured sharply to the steers-man and the Raider immediately slid away towards the outer edge of the Aviaries, picking up speed as it angled towards where Bellathonis's tower lay.

'Well, Bellathonis, it seems that not one but two of your servants have opted to enter the Beryl Gate on foot while the hunt is in progress,' Malixian said as he perked up with a nasty grin. 'I thought we could go and see if they make it home or not.'

The maggot of concern that been boring patiently away at Bellathonis's mind metamorphosed into a buzzing fly of panic that he strove unsuccessfully to crush. Syiin was watching him with interest; it was obvious now that he knew or guessed that Bellathonis's servants were returning from some task related to Yllithian's visit. Silence seemed the best and only option under the circumstances and Bellathonis strove to maintain a slightly shaky expression of polite disinterest.

The skies were noticeably quieter on the outskirts of the Aviaries. A few scouting hellions zipped back and forth and the occasional spiral of flying creatures emerged from the cage canyons to seek for new prey. Malixian pointed silently downward into the deep shadows lining the avenue below. Bellathonis saw movement and picked out Xagor, easily recognisable by the flapping of his hide coat as he dashed comically from one hedge to another. The wrack loped along awkwardly, desperately clutching something to his chest. Bellathonis hoped for his sake that it was the jar he had been sent to collect.

'Taking delivery of something, Bellathonis?' Syiin whispered conspiratorially. 'It must be important to risk–' Malixian angrily shushed the haemonculus into silence before again drawing their attention below.

Malixian's eyesight must have verged on the preternatural. His semi-sentient cloak of eyes combined with the image enhancement augmetics in his bird mask certainly gave him the kind of visual acuity his beloved pets could only dream of. The mad archon pointed out another individual a dozen paces behind Xagor that was moving with a feline grace that Bellathonis's own enhanced eyes could barely pick out in the gloom. One of the agents he had engaged? He looked like he was stalking Xagor rather than protecting him. Perhaps it was a catspaw of Syiin's sent to waylay Xagor and only claiming to be Bellathonis's servant in order to access the Aviaries?

Syiin seemed to lack the gloating air Bellathonis would have expected if that were the case. On balance, Bellathonis recalled, his instructions had only extended to ensuring safe delivery of the prize rather than protection of the courier. It seemed more likely the agent had interpreted that to include murdering the unfortunate Xagor and delivering what he carried in person. Bellathonis stifled a cruel laugh.

'Look,' Malixian whispered as he pointed again, 'our two star-crossed lovers have additional suitors.'

The hunter was himself being hunted. Invisible to the agent but clear from above once Malixian pointed them out, the shapes of several slaves could be seen. They were creeping towards the agent while his attention was fixed on Xagor. The three factions formed a perfect little tableau: Xagor hesitating at a corner as the agent raised a pistol to gun him down as the slaves rushed at his unguarded back. It was like seeing an allegorical triptych on one of the thirteen foundations of vengeance. Bellathonis, Syiin and Malixian drifted god-like above the scene, dispassionately awaiting its outcome.

The pistol spat and the tiny flash broke the moment. Xagor panicked and fled, the cloaked agent's aim being spoiled as he momentarily disappeared beneath a rush of club-wielding slaves. His swift fall elicited a disappointed hoot from Malixian, but the archon's dismay proved premature. A moment later the struggling figures broke apart with both slaves down and writhing in their own blood. However incautious the agent might be when it came to watching his back his reflexes were apparently beyond reproach. Sadly his indiscipline showed again as he paused to satiate himself on the slaves' death agonies before sprinting around the corner in pursuit of Xagor.

'He's a lively one. Must be a stripling,' Malixian whispered as the Raider silently drifted down the avenue to follow him. There was no chance of being heard down below but the mad archon seemed to be enjoying the artifice of being hidden observers watching animals at a watering hole.

'Yes, it would appear he has much potential but also much to learn,' Bellathonis murmured darkly. 'Although naturally I'm glad that he's offering my archon and my esteemed colleague such impromptu entertainment.'

'It's all quite fascinating, Bellathonis, I can assure you,' whispered Syiin. 'A real insight.'

As Bellathonis fought with the momentary urge to push the hunchbacked figure off the Raider a pistol cracked several more times from around the corner.

The sharp sound attracted the attention of a pair of passing hellions, who rapidly arced their skyboards around to go and investigate.

Malixian gestured sharply for the Raider to follow them, the steersman sending the long craft shooting forwards with a sudden burst of power. They breasted the flank of an enormous, pagoda-like enclosure and swung around its edge in time to see the pair of hellions sweeping down upon the lone agent in an attack run. Once again his reflexes saved him, sending him rolling out of the path of the first hellion's bladed skyboard and punching the second from his mount with an accurate burst of splinter fire. Malixian seemed so delighted he neglected to whisper.

'Hoo! That's a lively one all right! After him!'

As if striving for an encore the agent now sprang onto the fallen skyboard and fled with the first hellion in hot pursuit. There was no sign of Xagor but Bellathonis thought he'd caught the telltale flicker of shadows oozing away beneath an underpass when the hellions made their attack. Nothing that Syiin or Malixian would have noticed with any luck because they were too busy watching the agent fight the hellions, but something Bellathonis had been half-expecting and half-hoping to see.

His allies had responded to his call. Shadow-skinned mandrakes were gliding silently through the Aviaries at his behest to ensure the prize would still come to him despite all the caprices of the mad archon and the interferences of Syiin. Inwardly the haemonculus heaved a gigantic sigh of relief. Now all that remained was to see if this worthless agent of his would have the wherewithal to escape Malixian or at least the good grace to die in the attempt.

The racing agent quickly outpaced Malixian's Raider by plunging into narrow places it couldn't follow. The hellion pursued him avidly, bobbing and weaving expertly through the gruelling course the agent set. The hellion only became unstuck when he attempted to trigger his skyboard's splinter pods to shoot his quarry in the back.

The tiniest miscalculation and one of the skyboard's forward-thrust blades kissed a cage bar as the hellion slalomed past it. The hellion was instantly hurled off, his body pinwheeling helplessly away into the darkness as the skyboard careened into the bars with a vivid red flash. Malixian roared with laughter at that. Now there would be another new client to be placed in one of Bellathonis's crystal-fronted sarcophagi, trapped there until they could painfully re-knit their shattered bones. The thought sparked an idea.

'Perhaps I should go and attend to the preparations necessary to reviving your hellions, my archon?' Bellathonis ventured, attempting to sound contrite.

'Hoo, I suppose so, I want everyone fit for when we go to the planet of the mud people. Mind you give that servant of yours my regards if he makes it back to you, Bellathonis. He bested two of my hellions and I won't grudge him due praise.'

'My thanks, my archon. Should he survive both your hunters and my displeasure I will be sure to pass that along to him.'

'By all means. You can also add that if I catch him

in my Aviaries again I'll feed him to my white ruhk personally.'

Syiin chortled in appreciation. 'May I offer my assistance, Bellathonis? It would be a pleasure to visit your tower and discuss matters of the art at your leisure.'

'Perhaps another time would be more appropriate for visitations. With the unexpected news of the coming raid I have many matters to attend to – as do you, I would imagine. Also I would not wish to deprive my archon of your scintillating company for the remainder of the hunt, I believe there will be some considerable hours for it still to run. Until we meet again. Archon. Syiin.'

Bellathonis bowed to them both. Although no signal had been given a leaner, simpler Raider craft was already silently drawing alongside. The master haemonculus crossed to the smaller craft and it bore him swiftly away towards his humble tower. He felt a moment of misgiving at leaving Malixian and Syiin together. Yllithian's haemonculus could become tiresome if he kept sniffing around, potentially dangerous if he latched onto something incriminating. The removal of a fellow haemonculus was never to be undertaken lightly, but extraordinary times could sometimes require extraordinary measures.

As the Raider cut swiftly through the air the thought of the prize awaiting him soon erased Bellathonis's immediate concerns about Syiin. He passed inside his tower barely able to suppress his anticipation. He was very much looking forward to getting his hands on the prize that Yllithian had dangled so artfully before him, a reward so secret and forbidden that it had to be transported across the city concealed inside an innocuous-looking jar. Yes, he was very much looking forward to meeting the severed and yet apparently undying head of the crone, Angevere.

CHAPTER 5
THE UNEXPECTED GIFT

'The moment can never equal the anticipation of the moment. The perfection envisaged by the mind is never matched by the body, the high hopes that consciousness has raised are dashed beneath the inevitable weight of mortal clay. Yet our city embraces that moment of anticipation drawn out through eternity. We accept the flawed nature of our materials and yet raise towering edifices with them if only for the space of a single breath. Knowing that our tools will ever break beneath our hands we pursue the ideal moment and refuse to turn away from the dark splendour of godhood – however fleeting it may be.'

– The philosopher-poet Pso'kobor,
The Forbidden Ambitions

KRAILLACH HAD DREAMED of Commorragh many times in his life. He felt the great port-city could only be fully appreciated in a dream. Certainly, it was possible to view the corespur from near-space, where one could see the thrusting spires of High Commorragh, the sprawling mills and tenements of Low Commorragh, the outstretched docking talons, the endless succession of tiers. These things could be seen by the eye well enough to confound the mind with the sheer enormity of their expanse, but in truth they formed only the tip of the iceberg of what was the eternal city.

Only in a dream was it possible to perceive the subrealms of Commorragh that lay strung about it like a jewelled necklace. A thousand realities that were scattered throughout the infinitude of the labyrinth dimension were at the same time shackled to the eternal city through open gates and impervious wards.

In his dreams Kraillach saw each sub-realm with its own hue: deep amber, smoky russet, jade green, opalescent white, they swung by in stately procession. The tyrant had pulled them all into the inescapable orbit of Commorragh during his reign, thrall states to be slowly sucked dry by the eternal, parasitic city. He coveted those precious baubles and the power they represented with an obscene yearning. Sometimes he even dreamt of stealing them for himself.

ARCHON LUQUIX BORR Kraillach, eight hundred and eighty-ninth pure-blooded and trueborn ascendant of the Kraillach dynasty and absolute ruler of the Kabal of the Realm Eternal, stirred and stretched luxuriantly in his nest of golden silks. Bulbous censers floating nearby responded by switching from narcotic smoke to a stimulant mist with a faint chime. Kraillach enjoyed a rare moment of serenity. He was safe at last within his inner sanctum after being exposed to the energising but frankly frightening death and destruction at Xelian's arena the day before. He was safe in his sanctum and able to finally relax behind walls of unbreakable stone lined with unbreachable metal. A faint, subsonic buzz gave him a comforting reassurance that the hermetic shields surrounding the chamber were still in place and still fully functional.

He glanced around. The blood-daubed sigils covering the walls, floor and ceiling were unbroken and unchanged from the night before, evidence that nothing from beyond the veil had attempted to breach the arcane wardings. The only entrance to the sanctum, a metre-thick iris valve of baroquely inscribed metal, was sealed shut and guarded by the room's only other occupant – Kraillach's chief executioner, Morr. The armoured incubus stood resting both hands lightly on his immense klaive, a deadly double-handed power weapon that had dispatched thousands at Kraillach's command. Morr's stance was unchanged from when Kraillach had closed his eyes hours before and he had no doubt that the fearsome warrior had stood statue-like watching over him for the entire time.

Kraillach fully intended to live forever. Commorragh might be a deadly snake pit of enemies and She Who Thirsts might be waiting to consume any soul that fell into Her daemonic clutches but Kraillach was clever and Kraillach was very, very careful. Should the whole of Commorragh have the mischance to fall to some unthinkable, reality-mangling catastrophe

Kraillach could most likely survive the cataclysm in his sanctum and be left floating through the ruins.

'Greetings, Morr,' Kraillach said as he stifled a yawn. 'What news?'

The burning slits of Morr's ornate tormentor helm turned to regard him balefully once Kraillach acknowledged his presence and gave him permission to speak. Like all incubi in Kraillach's experience Morr had little passion for dialogue other than commands or acknowledgements. Incubi preferred sepulchral silence while they meditated on the ways of war and bloodshed.

'No news, my archon,' Morr intoned solemnly. 'All is well.'

'Excellent, have a slave brought to me so that I may break my fast.'

'As you command, my archon.'

Morr turned to the sealed portal and his gauntleted hands moved across its surface pressing various points on the inscriptions that covered it in a complex sequence known only to himself and Kraillach. The leaves of the iris valve slid back to reveal the shimmering surface of the open portal behind. Morr stepped through and vanished without another word, the leaves scissoring back together silently behind him.

At the exact centre of the sanctum floor there lay a sunken bath set into a sunburst of polished onyx. Kraillach disrobed and settled his withered body into the warm, scented waters and contemplated the day ahead. At the top of his agenda was determining whether to betray his two noble allies to the tyrant or not. Kraillach feared and hated Asdrubael Vect as much as any of them but he had also lived longer than all of them. Yllithian and Xelian were pure-blooded descendants of the noble houses eliminated by Vect during his rise to power, but only Kraillach had actually lived through those dreadful times.

A loose opposition to Vect and a desire to regain past glories united the noble families and made them natural allies but Kraillach had doubts about the sanity of the others. Xelian was little better than a wild beast ever hungry for blood and Yllithian's schemes always had the sharp scent of danger about them – resurrections, Dysjunctions, returning the old emperor of Shaa-dom... It was all too much, too fantastical to place any faith in.

Unfortunately, as Kraillach sourly reflected, the sad truth was that he was bound to his allies just as Yllithian had said. His noble house, his *kabal* in the contemptible modern parlance adopted by Vect, was slowly but surely outstripping his resources. Decade by decade, century by century the once fabulous wealth of House Kraillach was being leached away just as his own vitality was being drained away by the eternal hunger of She Who Thirsts.

The orgies and debauches he needed to partake in to slake his own thirst grew ever more extreme and frequent as the centuries rolled by despite his best efforts to control the process. He could perceive a chilling point in his future where his existence could no longer maintained and Kraillach would be drained away to a pathetic, soulless thing, driven out to lurk in the deepest recesses of Low Commorragh with the rest of the Parched.

Whatever reward Vect might deign to bestow for his betrayal would inevitably fall far short of the resources he gained through his alliance with Yllithian and Xelian. It was more likely that Vect would take the opportunity to rid himself of all three kabals at once if they showed any signs of disunity. The Realm Eternal still enjoyed the reputation of vast wealth – even if its coffers were almost empty – and its sybaritic ways attracted many hedonistic devotees, but without Xelian's lethal wyches and Yllithian's cunning warriors it would be too weak to stand in battle against the tyrant.

Kraillach found himself wondering if Yllithian had engineered Vect's intercession at the arena in some fashion. It seemed unlikely but Yllithian had a well-deserved reputation as a master manipulator. Predictably enough events at the arena had driven Xelian into one of her tiresome murderous rages and gained her easy acquiescence to Yllithian's plans. Now Kraillach was left with little choice other than to join the others or else forfeit the protection of their alliance. It rankled Kraillach to be manoeuvred so adroitly. Ultimately, though, he needed to win more power and influence to stay alive and staying alive was all that mattered. Certainly Vect might catch them plotting against him and punish them in the worst ways imaginable for their trouble, but better that than the slow, dwindling death the future held in store right now.

The portal slid open and Morr reappeared bearing a flat-faced little slave effortlessly in one hand. He brought the slave to edge of the bath and secured him there with silver jaws that rose from slots in the stone.

'Shall I fetch your instruments, my archon?' Morr asked when he was finished, gazing across to a side table where a scattering of hooked and straight blades, vials, syringes and elegant little saws lay.

'No, you do it, Morr. I always enjoy seeing you use that great blade of yours like a paring knife.'

'Thank you, my archon.'

Morr unlimbered his two-metre-long blade and left it unpowered as he set about his work, using just its razor-sharp edges to efficiently flense the howling slave. Blood swirled pleasingly in the waters of the bath, forming submerged cloudscapes of pink and red as it had done a thousand times before. Kraillach sighed as he settled back and drank in the quick repast. The slave's lusty screaming was quite musical in its aspect and Kraillach found himself humming along with it, eventually fitting it into a few bars of Velqyul's eighth sonata.

KRAILLACH STRODE INTO his palace proper much revitalised, moving through colonnaded halls and arched chambers scattered with the detritus of the previous night's excesses. Supine bodies, both living and dead, lay in secluded boudoirs and public pleasure pits while slaves scurried back and forth frantically trying to clean up the palace and, in some cases, its occupants. As he walked a crowd of sycophants and hangers-on gravitated into his wake, each fluttering over fresh quips and newly minted gossip to ingratiate themselves. Morr followed him like a shadow, his threatening presence serving to keep the swarming courtiers at a respectful distance.

Once he was satisfied with the size of his gathered entourage Kraillach swept into his great hall to take his place on the multi-faceted throne of splendours, a relic from the earliest days of Commorragh and the golden age of the eldar race. Each facet of the throne shifted constantly between different heroic images of the past deeds of House Kraillach and the Realm Eternal, some animated and others still, some of them artistic representations and others that were actual recordings of events. The images were chosen by some not-entirely-random internal artifice and were held by many to be prophetic in nature, showing hints at potential futures with images torn from the past.

As he approached he could see that the throne was displaying stark images of battling figures high up in a war-torn sky. One facet displayed flights of scourges diving like renegade angels between tiny, embattled islands of archaic grav craft that had locked together in combat. Another facet showed one of the black suns so close that it was just a blazing arc on one side of the image. Periodically a blinding flare of plasma punched out from the sun to incinerate a flotilla of jet cycles racing past in an endless loop.

These and other images shown on the throne were from the War of the Sun and Moon, an era over eight thousand years ago and centuries before even Kraillach's birth. Solar cults that controlled the dark city's stolen suns had tried to topple the noble houses. For centuries aerial warfare raged through the upper gulfs of Commorragh before the solar cults were crushed. It had been a great triumph for the high archons. The eternal night that enfolded the city thereafter was admittedly in part due to the destruction wrought, but also an abiding symbol of their mastery over heaven and earth.

Kraillach seated himself amid the tumbling images and pondered the portents. The noble houses had triumphed in the War of the Sun and Moon, certainly; they had endured for another two millennia before Vect felled them in turn. A mixed sign at best, a veiled warning at worst. Yllithian and Xelian might succeed in their schemes only to be overthrown later. It was all most distressing, so he ordered his entourage to perform for him and distract him for a time. They set to with a will, giving and receiving pain, straining, dancing and teasing for his pleasure. He envied their youth and energy but felt little moved by what was on display.

Kraillach was about to send for a troupe of more entertaining professionals when Morr signalled minutely for his attention.

'What is it, Morr? Can't you see I'm busy?' Uninteresting as it was the crude orgy developing undoubtedly held more interest than whatever Morr wanted to bring up.

'Forgive me, my archon, a matter has arisen that requires your direct attendance.' Morr was apparently not above reminding his archon that however disinteresting his news might be it was important. Kraillach sighed.

'Go on.'

'A deputation has arrived from the Blades of Desire, my archon. They claim to bear a gift from Archon Xelian for your personal delectation.'

'Really? That is more intriguing than I had hoped for, but where is the issue that requires my personal attention?'

'They insist the gift may only be given into your hands, on express orders from their mistress.'

The images on the throne of splendours were changing. They tumbled in a monochromatic snow-storm all about him, seeming unable to hold a single form for more than a second. Kraillach decided that was certainly not a good sign.

'What kind of fool accepts a gift with terms attached? Did not Archon Kelithresh perish to a singularity inside a casket presented to him as a tithe?'

'Indeed, my archon, he and his whole sub-realm with him. They say it was Vect's work.'

'Everything is, my dear Morr, everything is.'

To return the gift unopened might be seen as a potential deadly insult by the mistress of the Blades of Desire, especially if it were some sort of conciliatory gesture for her shambles at the arena. Even so, caution was more than a watchword for Kraillach, it was a religion. A nasty concern creased Kraillach's brow.

'Where is this "gift" now?'

'Held in the vestibule with the party that brought it. Suppressors are in place and the package has been examined remotely. No overtly dangerous elements have been revealed, though that in itself means noth-ing, my archon.'

Another not-so subtle reminder from Morr that Kraillach did not require. Brilliant minds in Com-morragh had spent thousands of years devising peerless tools for stealthy sabotage and assassination.

Compounds of poison and explosive that were to all intents and purposes undetectable had been perfected long since. Nonetheless the vestibule itself was a richly appointed but heavily armoured blast chamber cunningly designed to baffle and deflect unwelcome energies away from the body of the palace. The damage that could be caused in the vestibule was severely limited without resorting to a dimensional warp or singularity, and those could be detected with ease.

'Very well. Relay my gracious thanks and my regrets that I cannot receive their gift in person at this time. They can leave it behind in the vestibule and return to their mistress.'

Morr's helm tilted in acquiescence as he conveyed Kraillach's orders to the unseen guards in the vestibule.

An instant later the stonework of the great hall shook slightly with the impact of a distant explosion. Alarms warbled hysterically. Kraillach enjoyed a moment of smug vindication.

'Ah ha, so they thought to bring me some crude bomb after all! Xelian must be mad to–'

'Forgive me, my archon, but that was only a small breaching charge. The assailants have broken out of the vestibule and entered the palace.'

'What! How many? How armed?'

'A dozen attackers, lightly armed. If you will proceed to your sanctum I will take charge of hunting them down once you are in a place of safety.'

Kraillach desperately wanted to follow Morr's advice but could not countenance the loss of face that would be involved. To bolt for his sanctum when his palace was being invaded by such a tiny force was too craven an act to contemplate. Archons had to be bold and fearless, or at least appear so, if they wanted to avoid assassination by their own kabal. Fear was a weakness and showing weakness was invariably a fatal mistake in Commorrite society. Kraillach scowled theatrically.

'I won't flee from these whelps that dare to assault the Realm Eternal! Bring me my armour and weapons so that I can drive them from my house!'

A slightly ragged cheer rose from the assembled entourage of hedonists and sycophants. Some brandished hooks and whips in what they imagined to be a warlike fashion. Morr's shoulders may have slumped by the tiniest amount but he remained taciturn.

MINUTES LATER KRAILLACH led fifty or more of his kabalite warriors towards the ruined vestibule. He now wore a form-fitting augmetic suit of jewel-like armour plates that shimmered richly behind iridescent force fields. As Kraillach walked he was surrounded by perfect Kraillach doppelgangers created by the protective fields, a host of illusory projections of himself that made it impossible to tell his true location. He bore *Quasili*, a metre-long blade of living metal that was old when Commorragh was first founded; a relic of the Golden Age, it could split the very vault of heaven.

The attacking group had not penetrated far past the vestibule. A vicious firefight had developed in the atrium just beyond it as Kraillach's guards sought to keep the incursion in check. Choking black smoke was drifting through the cavernous chamber and bodies lay sprawled across the decorative tilework floor where they had been mercilessly cut down in the opening seconds of the attack. Xelian's small force had almost overwhelmed the last of the atrium guards by the time Kraillach and his reinforcements arrived.

A wicked barrage of splinter fire drove the attackers back into cover as Kraillach's followers spilled into the room. He got his first look at his would-be murderers as he strode in after the initial rush with more outward confidence than he truly felt. Lithe, half-naked wyches somersaulted away from the deadly streams of hyper-velocity splinter rounds sweeping across the scene. In retrospect the atrium had been built with too much of an eye for aesthetics and not enough consideration for defence. Its wide-based pillars, low walls and trellis-work bowers provided entirely too many hiding spots for the wyches to vanish into. Hunting them down was going to demand the kind of close quarters fighting wyches excelled at.

Kraillach's warriors slowed and went more cautiously, spreading out into cover to try and pinch the attackers in a crossfire. They were quickly driven back into hiding as shots whipped back at them across the chamber from a dozen angles. Three kabalite warriors broke cover and sprinted forwards to take station behind a pillar. They retreated just as quickly when several small, oval plasma grenades came looping out of the smoke to land at their feet.

Morr and a pair of incubi broke the deadlock by ploughing forwards, whirling their immense klaives in bright arcs of coruscating energy. Desultory splinter fire from the trapped wyches ricocheted from the flickering weapons as the incubi advanced. Kraillach took the opportunity to leap heroically forwards into some better cover, his spectral cohort of images drawing fire from all quarters. The wyches didn't wait to get picked off individually in their hiding places and came bounding forward en masse towards Kraillach.

A warrior beside him collapsed with splinter rounds in his throat, the virulent toxins coating the crystalline splinters killing him before he hit the ground. A dense spray of monofilament wire from a shredder sliced through another nearby warrior, reducing him to a cloud of fine red mist. Suddenly Kraillach found himself alone and darted back behind a statue made more obscene by its half-shattered form. A wych leapt out of the smoke and ran at him swinging a wickedly curved falchion at his neck. The blurring blade swept through a ghost image harmlessly and Kraillach countered. The wych spun her blade expertly to deflect the dozen striking blades of Kraillach and his images but his sword easily shore the falchion in two before plunging on into pale, vulnerable flesh.

Two more wyches darted forwards flailing wildly at the many Kraillachs before them. The images languidly shot one of the wyches with a dozen long-muzzled blast pistols before a resurgent charge by a group of his warriors impaled the other on their combat blades. Kraillach beheaded the dying wych with a backhand blow just to be sure. As the headless corpse flopped to the ground the sounds of combat faded away save for the moans of the fallen. Kraillach's fawning entourage chanted his name with gratifying enthusiasm.

Kraillach caught sight of Morr through the confusion and smiled patronisingly.

'These fools barely raised my pulse, Morr,' Kraillach gloated. 'This has to be the poorest assassination attempt in the long history of our fair city.'

'That is what worries me, my archon,' Morr replied with tedious pedantry, 'I fear that–'

The chief executioner paused, his slit-eyed helm swivelling to regard a bare-headed warrior standing nearby. The warrior was in obvious distress. He clutched at the neck joint of his armour with eyes staring wildly. There was a crash as another warrior dropped his rifle and fell to his knees with a look of horror on his face. Morr's masked visage swung sharply back to Kraillach.

'Contaminants! Get to safety, my archon! Quickly!'

Kraillach could see the spreading circle of evidence for himself. Every warrior that had entered the atrium helmetless or only partially armoured was showing signs of contamination. The veins beneath the victim's skin were turning black even as he watched, spreading to form inky cobwebs over rapidly darkening flesh. Kraillach backed away with a sick feeling of horror.

He was not wearing a helmet himself.

He turned and ran as quickly as the augmented leg musculature of his armour would carry him.

As he fled Kraillach passed dozens more of his subjects writhing in the grip of the unseen killer. It was spreading as fast as he could move, if not faster, striking down anyone not in full armour. He wondered why he had not already fallen prey and felt every twinge in his body as another harbinger of doom. When he reached the great hall the throne of splendours was showing a new kaleidoscopic array of images. An array of tortured eldar faces predominated, each exquisitely sculpted from some black, glass-like crystal.

Kraillach slowed to a halt as recognition dawned on him. He croaked out a harsh laugh and sat down wearily on the multi-faceted throne.

SOME TIME LATER Morr came to him with the final tally of casualties. Several hundred assorted warriors, slaves, houris, pets and courtiers had fallen victim to the attack, including the entire group that had carried it into the palace in the first place. This frustrating twist left him with no prisoners to interrogate and precious little material evidence to examine. The contaminant had been identified, confirming what Kraillach had already seen in the throne of splendours – it was the glass plague.

Close to a thousand years before the fall of Shaadom a celebrated sculptor named Jalaxlar had enjoyed fantastic acclaim when he revealed his latest works in Commorragh. His amazingly life-like renditions displayed eldar caught in various poses of shock and horror rendered in a black, glass-like crystal. Jalaxlar earned immediate patronage from some of the most powerful kabals but incurred fierce rivalry from others. The very same evening his studio-laboratories were raided and smashed apart. Among the ruins Jalaxlar's secret was revealed.

The insane sculptor-scientist had isolated a viral

helix that was capable of rapidly vitrifying living tissue, transforming warm flesh into cold, crystalline glass within a few heartbeats. His stunning display of artfully posed statues were in point of fact made with the unwilling assistance of his first victims – friends, callers and assistants. The virus was accidentally released in the destruction of Jalaxlar's workshops and spread through the city with frightening speed. Thousands of Commorrites fell victim to the resulting 'plague of glass' before a haemonculi coven known as the Hex succeeded in releasing an anti-virus to quell it.

Naturally the glass plague had gone on to be weaponised and used in many guises, occasionally re-emerging naturally as a rogue mutation that temporarily defied the common anti-viral agents before they could be adjusted. The strain that had been released inside the palace was an obscure one. Several quarts of it had been concealed in liquid form inside the 'gift': a stone urn designed to release it as an aerosol when triggered. The black smoke they had seen came not from the explosion as Kraillach had supposed, but from the virus battling anti-viral agents in the air of the palace. In this case the anti-viral agents had failed and those without their own inoculations of defensive nano-phages had fallen prey to the vitrifying plague.

The glass plague meant True Death. There was no rebirth from it as no cell of living tissue survived for the body to be remade from. The precious soul was denied the slightest grip on life and slipped easily out of the altered vessel into the waiting maw of She Who

Thirsts. True Death had stalked into his palace and Kraillach had only survived thanks to his secret regimen of protective elixirs and anti-agathics. In spite of the apparent clumsiness of the attack Xelian had almost succeeded in killing him. Kraillach suppressed a shudder.

'What are your thoughts, Morr?'

'The attack seems… indirect given its alleged origins.'

'Explain.'

'Archon Xelian is direct in her approach. She establishes dominance and exerts her will through strength.'

'You're saying this is beneath her? I think you're sadly mistaken, Morr.'

'Her first attack would be one she was sure would succeed.'

'Ahh, you're saying she wouldn't betray her intentions so easily'

'Indeed, my archon.'

Morr might be correct, of course. Xelian would certainly prefer to simply come in with all guns blazing and make it a fight to the death. She lacked the kind of subtlety and experience to pursue the sort of double-bluff strategy shown by the assassination attempt. But if not her then who? From Xelian the circle of suspects widened to include the bland, scheming Yllithian and the great tyrant himself, Asdrubael Vect.

Yllithian was capable of any kind of underhanded skulduggery to get his way but it was hard to see what he could gain through Kraillach's death. Perhaps he hoped to manoeuvre a more tractable archon into control over the Realm Eternal. Dragging Xelian into the fight by setting him against her would make sense then; either Kraillach dies or he retaliates against Xelian, making it win-win. Again, though, why? The alliance between their houses propped up all three of them to some extent. Infighting among them would only serve the best interests of Vect.

Indeed Asdrubael Vect was the one with the reputation for bestowing surprise gifts on those he wished to be rid of. He would surely like to see the noble houses at each other's throats and any attempt to drive a wedge between them could have his hand behind it. Ultimately it didn't matter. Regardless of just who had sent the assassins Kraillach was still trapped by their public declaration of themselves as Xelian's followers. By now the word would have spread throughout Commorragh that Xelian had made an attack on Kraillach. Now Kraillach must confront Xelian in some fashion or lose face with the other archons.

'Gather up the household troops, Morr, I believe we need to pay Xelian a visit.'

'I will go at once, m–,' Morr began.

'Oh no, I shall be going myself, I must be seen out there alive and well cursing Xelian or the other kabals will smell blood in the water.'

'My archon, forgive me but I must object. It's far too dangerous.'

'Agreed and forgiven, it *is* far too dangerous, but you know as well as I that excess caution now will put a hundred daggers at my back instead of just one to my front.'

'One of the thirteen foundations of vengeance,' Morr said almost humbly. 'You are correct of course, my archon.'

Morr moved away as he relayed Kraillach's orders. Xelian's forces could easily overwhelm those of the Realm Eternal in close-quarter fighting, but not if Kraillach dictated how and where the confrontation took place. Wealth had its privileges.

'...and send for my spymasters. I want to know what ships are docked on the Blades of Desire's spur.'

'At once, my archon.'

ABOVE THE PALACE of the Realm Eternal a golden armada of pleasure craft began to assemble. Raiders and sinuously twisting Venoms ferried Kraillach's warriors from the rooftops to man their weapons, scalloped gun ports slid open and ornate cannon were run out. Soon dozens of thorn-armoured kaba-lites lined the baroque-fashioned rails of the waiting barges, horned helms, flamboyant crests and bare heads jostling in a bright panoply of red and bur-nished gold. Finally Kraillach rode aloft in his own sky chariot to take his place at the heart of the armada. Rippling shields of energy around the archon's craft made it appear like a strange egg in the midst of brightly jewelled ornaments.

Flying scourges and lurking grav craft from a dozen other kabals took note of the movement and sent hurried word to their masters that Kraillach was mov-ing against Xelian.

CHAPTER 6
THE BLADES OF DESIRE

'Friends and allies you call them? Black-hearted traitors one and all, I say! My reputation and my honour take precedence over their carping concerns. I will pursue my vendettas as I will for I am Vileth and I will not be constrained in my vengeance.'

– Duke Vileth to the fool Mecuto,
in Ursyllas's *Dispossessions*

NYOS YLLITHIAN SPED towards Xelian's fortress-arena at the head of a flying wedge of Raiders and Ravagers filled with White Flames warriors. He paced the narrow deck of his racing barque impatiently and his crew took pains to avoid his gaze. They knew that news of the attack on Kraillach had been unforgivably, indeed suspiciously slow in reaching their archon's ordinarily acute ears and he was apt to be looking for scapegoats.

The jagged cityscape slid past looking cold and merciless in the light of the stolen suns. The skies were ominously empty. All that could be seen were a handful of Reavers and scourges steadily pacing Yllithian's force. They always stayed some distance below and behind them, slipping through the inky shadows between the spires of High Commorragh like a pack of scavengers following a predator. They were undoubtedly spies from other kabals sent to watch the White Flames' part in the unfolding drama.

The initial reports Yllithian had received alleged that Kraillach was dead but hard on their heels had come word that Kraillach was, in fact, alive and leading his forces against Xelian. So far there had been no response to his efforts to communicate with either faction – more evidence if any were needed that a subtle hand was working against them.

The reaction of the noble houses in the next hours would be studied and dissected in the minutest detail by the watching kabals. A poised and effective recovery from the challenge would enhance all of their reputations immensely; a descent into bloody chaos would signal to the scavengers that it was time to sharpen their knives and join the feast.

Yllithian felt fury at his allies for falling for such an obvious ploy. A moment's thought should tell them that this could only be the tyrant's work, an effort to pull apart their alliance before it became threatening to his position. Yllithian had been left with no recourse but to set out with the White Flames forces he had available to seek Kraillach and Xelian in person. He had to bring them to their senses before all three houses were doomed by their mutual display of hubris and stupidity.

Nyos's steersman shouted a warning and pointed ahead. A shoal of hellions were curving into sight around the sheer flank of a nearby spire with obvious hostile intent, the razor edges of their skyboards flashing as they angled to attack. Three sleek, dark shapes shot out from concealing shadows at another angle and swung onto an interception course. Muzzle flashes twinkled along their hulls as darklight beams and streams of venomous splinters leapt across the rapidly closing gap.

XELIAN'S FORTRESS WAS built as a volcano-like mass with the arena itself nestling inside the central cone. Heroically proportioned images graven in the appearance of wych gladiators hundreds of metres tall studded the outer slopes. There had once been open spaces around each of them given over to parks and public plazas but the mistress of the Blades of Desire had little patience for such pretensions. Under her rule they had become dusty training grounds and slave pens for the lowliest of her chattels.

Kraillach's armada swept in low over the training fields, their hulls blotting out the light as they slid overhead. Slaves and slavemasters alike gaped upwards in fear at what their coming portended. The voice of the archon of the Realm Eternal cracked across the pregnant silence.

'Xelian! Your followers broke into my house! They slew my servants! What treachery is this? Come forth and explain yourself!'

Total confusion reigned below. Slaves ran for cover, slavemasters alternated between beating slaves and running themselves. Some slaves raised their shackles and greeted the skyborne host as liberators.

At least they did until the shooting started.

It was unclear who shot first. A small pack of Reaver jetbikes had just risen from the arena cone as the Realm Eternal arrived. When the Reavers dived on the pleasure craft some of Kraillach's followers decided it was an attack and filled the sky with looping streamers of fire to greet them. At about the same time one of the many armoured barbettes sunk into the flanks of the fortress came to life and spat a flurry of incandescent bolts into the floating armada. Within seconds every vessel in Kraillach's force was cutting loose with their considerable firepower at anything that moved.

The temporary nature of the slave pens made them vulnerable to attack and they bore the brunt of the Realm Eternal's retaliatory blow. Energy beams and disintegrator bolts cut through thin metal and ceramic sheeting, immolating those huddling inside. Spurting streams of splinters chased running slaves and dropped them in their tracks, writhing horribly as the venom took hold.

Soon a mass of sullenly smoking shelters and charred bodies lay where they had been cut down from above. The scene was interspersed with the brighter blazes of wrecked jetbikes and a handful of pleasure craft brought down in the fighting. Intensifying fire from the fortress defences gradually pushed the armada back out of range, where they began regrouping and bragging about their exploits. A pregnant silence fell over the scene as both sides licked their wounds and planned their next moves.

Aboard his heavily-shielded sky chariot Kraillach grimaced sourly and wondered how to extricate himself from the situation with both hide and honour intact.

The confusion that had broken out when Kraillach's aerial armada swept in over the training grounds strongly implied that Xelian had not been a party to the assassination attempt made in her name. The realisation had come too late and what Kraillach had intended as a display of power had predictably devolved into a chaotic murder spree. The bloodlust of his warriors had temporarily outrun his ability to control them. Several of the burning craft they'd left behind were the result of the disciplinary measures that were necessary to bring them back into the fold.

Now the skies above Xelian's palace were a hornet's nest of twisting Reavers and hellions aligned with the Blades of Desire. The golden cloud of Kraillach's craft hung close by, lit by the occasional false lightning of weapons-fire when Xelian's agitated sky warriors strayed within range.

Kraillach consoled himself that at least the situation had devolved into a stalemate for the present. Even aside from the Reavers and hellions too many of the weapon positions studding the towering flanks of the fortress had survived the initial assault. Now that the fortress was fully alerted the Realm Eternal would have to suffer heavy losses to press an attack.

That suited Kraillach fine. No one could call him

a coward for staying just out of range and awaiting developments. Xelian was blockaded, effectively besieged as long as the Realm Eternal kept up their vigil outside her fortress.

The problem was that Kraillach couldn't keep his followers in place indefinitely – sooner or later they would start to drift off looking for more stimulating pursuits. Equally Xelian could not afford to stay cooped up inside her demesne for too long. All that remained was to see who would blink first.

XELIAN HERSELF WAS stalking through the austere porcelain corridors of her fortress like a caged tiger. Kraillach's attack had come as a complete surprise. She had to admit, privately at least, that she rather admired the audacity of the old archon's sudden assault. It was weak but completely unexpected and had caught her with many warriors and wyches out on the docking spur loading onto ships for a new slave raid. Communications were down, jammed or sabotaged by enemy agents, so the forces at the docking spur could not be recalled. A rigorous and painful interrogation of her technicians was already under way, their thin wails of pain one of the few highlights in an otherwise grim day.

More Ravagers and Reavers were on the way. Xelian intended to lead a breakout when they arrived. She would take them into the centre of Kraillach's force and rip out his heart with her own hands. There would be a bloodbath, certainly, but Xelian was quite willing to gamble that her highly trained followers would have far more stomach for that than Kraillach's assembly of decadents. The prospect of the coming battle was enthralling for Xelian, it was something she had found herself wanting for long time and there was a kind of glorious relief in casting away the pretence of treating Kraillach as an ally.

There was only one annoying detail that still niggled at the back of her mind. Xelian couldn't fathom what had set Kraillach on the warpath. Reportedly he had made some pronouncements, hurling insults at the walls of fortress as he screeched about attacks and treachery. He seemed intent on portraying himself as the victim, justifying his unprovoked attack with lies. Not a surprising ploy but Xelian still found herself wondering if there were some grain of truth in his words. For the old fossil to stir himself into action like this was uncharacteristic. Also, Kraillach simply wasn't the type to launch a serious attack without dragging his allies in with him, so where was Yllithian?

DARKLIGHT BEAMS SCORED the shields of Yllithian's barque leaving retina-burning entropic blooms as they were barely shunted aside by the straining projectors. Yllithian's incubi loosed rippling volleys of splinter cannon fire in return, sending shapes tumbling from the attacking Raiders.

'On! Past them!' Yllithian shouted to his steersman before realising that the steersman was shorter by a head, decapitated in the crossfire. Yllithian leapt to take the tiller bar himself, swinging the elegant craft to point head-on into the diving hellions. He twisted at the power coupling ring savagely to set maximum speed and the barque leapt forwards in response.

The White Flames craft swung with him, each hosing fire into the three attacking Raiders as they sped past in echelon. A Ravager impaled the lead attacker with bolts of dark lance fire, its silhouette momentarily transfixed by twin beams of ravening destruction before it burst into flames and broke into pieces.

'Fire forward! All weapons!' Yllithian yelled, with a sick feeling that he had given the command too late.

The pack of hellions came hurtling in like a swarm of bats. Questing fingers of splinter fire chased them, disintegrator pulses flashed out and turned speeding bodies into plummeting corpses. The barque shuddered as an injured hellion ploughed headlong into the larger craft, her skyboard exploding into fragments as the barque's armoured prow sheared straight through it. Other hellions jinked and twisted aside desperately to avoid a similar fate.

Yllithian ducked beneath blurring wing-blades as more hellions shot past less than a metre above the deck. Some of his incubi were less quick and lost heads or limbs to the hurtling shoal of blades in sudden bursts of crimson. An instant later they were through the pack and in to the suddenly empty air beyond. Ahead of them the glittering flank of a spire-mountain was rushing closer by the second. Without a course change they would smash straight into it. Yllithian was turning to heave the tiller bar when a flicker of movement at the prow warned him of a new peril.

'Repel boarders!'

Out of either desperation or mad courage several

hellions had managed to hurl themselves aboard Yllithian's craft as they passed. Now they leapt lithely forwards swinging powered halberds and knives to be met by Yllithian's surviving incubi bodyguards. Swift and deadly blade work soon showed the armoured incubi to be the masters, their mighty klaives beating aside the hellions' wild strikes and carving into their lightly armoured bodies. In moments the hellions were driven howling over the sides and the deck was clear.

Ahead of them a titanic effigy of the long-dead Archon Xelicedes reared out of the spire wall as if trying to swat the barque out of the air with an outthrust sword the width of a highway. Yllithian grasped the tiller and hauled desperately to bring the speeding grav craft back onto a safe course, the colossal blade of Archon Xelicedes sweeping past just metres away.

Glancing behind he saw that the bulk of his followers were still with him, albeit with a few ragged holes in their previously pristine formation. The hellions swirled impotently in their wake, only a handful turning in time to pursue Yllithian's craft. They were soon chased away or killed by long range fire as they strained to overhaul the flying wedge of Raiders and Ravagers. Ahead thin plumes of smoke could be seen rising from among the jagged tangle of spires – Xelian's fortress was near.

KRAILLACH WATCHED THE growing swarm of light craft above Xelian's fortress with a matching sense of alarm. Their strength had tripled within the last hour and more kept arriving. Kraillach had swung from a sense of complacency about his armada being able to easily fight off such lowly trash to a fear that his beautiful pleasure craft would be wrecked by gangs of flying hooligans.

An even more disturbing development was the Venom heavy bikes now rising from the fortress, each with a cluster of wych gladiators crouched on their rear decks. Xelian was intending to make a fight of it. Kraillach was astonished. He'd expected some kind of communication from Xelian at least decrying his claims by now, but she seemed to care not a whit for talk. Just as Morr had said, she would seize her chance at victory with both hands and with no hesitation.

Kraillach wanted very much to blink now, to turn his armada for home and flee for his sanctum while he still could, but he was trapped. Quite apart from the loss of face involved in backing down, the skies were full of hostile Reaver gangs. If they were harried every step of the way back to the Realm Eternal's fortress, the losses would be catastrophic. Retreating would be a disaster, attacking would be a worse disaster and waiting to be attacked could be a disaster. Kraillach opted for the only course that held just the seeds of disaster instead of its ripe and bitter fruit. He waited.

XELIAN CLUTCHED THE curved rail on the open rear platform of a Venom jetbike as its rider, hunched beneath his crystal canopy, accelerated out of the pits beneath the arena floor at blistering speed. As they rose above the fortress she gazed out at the distant cloud of Kraillach's armada shining like motes in a sunbeam.

It was an impressive-looking array, hundreds of individual craft stacked high and deep to maximise their interlocking fields of fire. There would be little manoeuvring on Kraillach's part once battle was joined; the Blades of Desire would have to drive the action by tearing into their formation like a pack of predators plunging into a herd of prey. The Reavers and hellions would swirl around the lumbering barges to distract their fire while Venoms ran in close and dropped their deadly cargoes of wyches onto their open decks. That was the plan.

Xelian had instructed her wyches to attack and move on quickly, or to at least to turn captured guns on their former owners if they could not reach another craft. The wyches on a single Venom could easily overwhelm a single pleasure craft, but there were far too few Venoms to go around. Xelian didn't really care; her craft was flanked by two more sleek-bodied Venoms armed with dark lances to knock down the shields on Kraillach's chariot. As long as she got within arm's reach of Kraillach the rest of the battle was irrelevant to her.

Off to one side a tight wedge of speeding grav craft breached the jagged horizon and raced towards the fortress. Xelian paused from giving her final orders to study the newcomers. The leading craft bore the icon of the White Flames. So here was Yllithian at last, come to join Kraillach for the final battle.

Interestingly he wasn't heading toward Kraillach's armada but for a point halfway between them and the fortress. Requests began to flood in from the fortress guns for permission to open fire as Yllithian came with range. Xelian angrily denied them all; it seemed that Yllithian was uncommitted for now. No sense in driving him into Kraillach's arms just yet.

KRAILLACH WATCHED THE arrival of Yllithian with unmitigated relief. He was slightly nonplussed when Yllithian's flight of Raiders steered a course keeping well clear of his armada and slowing to a stop midway to Xelian's fortress. A single sleek-hulled vessel detached itself from the formation and glided down to land amid the ruined training grounds. Image enhancement showed Yllithian dismounting from the craft and wandering alone for a distance before settling himself to wait at the foot of a shot-scarred statue.

The implication was obvious enough. Yllithian wanted to parley. It could be a ploy to draw him out, but right now Kraillach was desperate enough to take that chance. Besides, he had considerable confidence in the defences of his own craft. Neither Xelian's fortress guns nor Yllithian's vessels would be able to stop him reaching safety, and if the whelp Yllithian intended treachery the trap would rebound back on him badly.

Kraillach brought his golden sky chariot gliding down to join Yllithian with the fiercest of imprecations to his minions not to follow.

YLLITHIAN WAITED PATIENTLY beneath the colossal shadow of the statue. The titanic carving had been blurred by age even before Kraillach's followers had hosed it with weapons-fire. Now it was impossible to tell if the wych it had portrayed were even male or female. It had been posed heroically with one arm thrust upwards and legs akimbo. The arm was broken off at the elbow lending an unspoken mystery to what the monumental wych had originally held aloft. A weapon? A severed head? An enemy's heart? There was a kind of irony to the dramatically posed form being robbed of its focal point. Yllithian felt as if he were witnessing some form of allegorical warning.

A single craft, rendered egg-shaped by its layers of protective energy fields, was descending from the golden cloud of Kraillach's forces. Before it had reached Yllithian a single hornet-like Venom peeled off from the swarm buzzing protectively around Xelian's fortress. The Venom plummeted down towards him in marked contrast to the sedate descent of Kraillach's craft. It pulled up sharply and flared to a stop a second later, the shapely form of Xelian vaulting from it to land lightly in the dust a short distance away.

'Xelian,' Yllithian said equitably.

'Yllithian,' Xelian replied tensely.

Kraillach's craft glided to a halt and layers of shields and armour slowly peeled back. When she caught sight of the wizened archon Xelian took a half-step forwards before checking herself. A wild notion of killing both Yllithian and Kraillach kept skittering through her mind – it was seductive and unworkable but now that her blood was up the pleasing idea simply wouldn't go away.

'Kraillach,' said Yllithian as if greeting an old friend. Kraillach's gaze darted between the dapper little black-clad figure of Yllithian and the intimidating warrior-woman Xelian. She looked ready to kill him right now.

'Someone,' Yllithian began, 'is trying to make fools out of all of us–'

'A small achievement in Kraillach's case,' Xelian snapped.

Kraillach started to object but Yllithian confidently overrode his words with silky platitudes that broached entirely new heights of patronising intent.

'Please, Xelian, poor Kraillach here has been the victim of an assassination attempt in his own house by attackers that entered under your name. Then I was assailed on my way here to play the role of negotiator in the resulting little spat. Someone has been playing us, and I don't need to tell you who.'

'You were also attacked?' Xelian's feline gaze was suddenly locked onto Yllithian.

'They were waiting for me to come riding to your rescue, dear heart. I suspect the attack on Kraillach was only intended to set the pieces in motion,'

'You think you were the intended target? They released the glass plague in my palace!' Kraillach shouted the words, unable to contain his repugnance and outrage any longer.

'And your best response was to attack me? You're a fool, Kraillach!' Xelian spat.

'And you're naïve, Xelian!' Kraillach replied. 'They came under your name! If you had even the vaguest sense of etiquette you'd know I had no choice but to act as I did!'

'Just so you see,' Yllithian purred, 'by Vect's laws

someone has to pay the price for an attack, and they have to do so publicly. That's how the strong must rule.'

Yllithian looked significantly out over the training grounds. Rows of slave pens were still burning nearby and pathetically huddled mounds in the dust marked the bodies of their occupants.

'Harm has been duly inflicted on both sides. I think we can all go home now,' he said. 'Honour has been satisfied. Perhaps we can turn our energies to raiding a certain maiden world before any other misfortunes befall us.'

Kraillach was maintaining a pose of slightly shaky hauteur but there was a look in his eye that signalled desperate agreement with Yllithian. Yllithian enjoyed a warm glow of success at manoeuvring Kraillach into a tacit compact to join the raid.

'No,' said Xelian distinctly.

'No?'

'No, I am not satisfied. I made no attack on Kraillach and I won't be a scapegoat for his own bungling incompetence.'

'I suppose you want compensation,' Kraillach blustered. 'Well, I–'

'I demand blood! Here and now! If you will not fight my kabal then you must fight me. Kraillach, if you want to quote laws and traditions I invoke my right to challenge you to a duel – for my *honour*!'

Kraillach took a step back, appalled. Yllithian was afraid he was going to bolt straight for his chariot and flee. Fortunately Kraillach had more sense than that and quickly mastered his fear. Once challenged to a duel before a witness of equal standing there was no backing down for an archon. They might cheat in any number of ways, have their opponent assassinated or exploit the event in the most perfidious fashion to emerge victorious but they couldn't back down once challenged, not without losing every shred of status. This was Vect's law, survival of the fittest, the law of the jungle. There was a long pause before the old archon spoke again.

'Very well…' Kraillach began. 'At a time and place of–'

'No. Here and now. Yllithian can bear witness, and we have–' Xelian gestured to the swarming skies above them '–plenty of seconds on hand.'

Kraillach's lips compressed into a thin line. He was trapped.

Yllithian coolly appraised the unexpected turn of events, wondering what Xelian intended. She was a deadly swordmistress in her own right, magnificent and pantherish, but she wore only the scantiest mockery of armour, with the porcelain flesh of her thighs, arms and midriff bare. Kraillach was fully armoured in a gleaming panoply that Yllithian knew from his own spy reports was full of its own tricks and traps in addition to its augmented musculature. A single strike from the ancient weapon that Kraillach bore and the mistress of the Blades of Desire would be no more.

'Take your places and we'll begin,' Yllithian said.

THE DUELLISTS STOOD ten paces apart in the drifting dust. Overhead the skies were filled by the whirling insect swarm of Xelian's followers on one hand and the drifting pleasure craft of Kraillach's on the other.

'Begin,' Yllithian said.

The two began to circle warily, first one way and then another as they sought a weakness in poise or balance that would provide an opening. Kraillach attacked first, suddenly triggering his doppelganger images and driving forwards with his crackling blade swinging in a deadly arc.

Xelian darted back out of range, momentarily confused by Kraillach's defences. Then she laughed and bounded back into the fray, whirling her knives into steely fans. The deadly brand of Kraillach darted at her in a dozen hands but she evaded them all, spinning beneath their reaching blades to deliver eviscerating blows that flashed through the incorporeal images like lightning.

Kraillach recoiled and cut at her wildly. Xelian made the instinctive mistake of parrying the myriad of slashing blades. There was a peal of thunder and one of her knives shivered into fragments, hurling Xelian backwards into the dust. Kraillach croaked in triumph and pressed his attack.

Xelian rolled in the dirt and back to her feet so smoothly it looked like part of a dance. Kraillach's thrusts seemed slow and clumsy as they quested after her, as if she occupied a skein of reality a beat out of phase with his own. Wherever his blade was, she was not. Her single knife kept slicing, darting out to touch one image after another as if she were counting them.

At least until she struck sparks from an image and found the real Kraillach.

The darting Kraillach phantoms swirled desperately

around her trying to obscure their master, but it was all to no avail. Xelian ignored them as she concentrated on the true Kraillach, clinging to him doggedly as he retreated. He fought harder and more skilfully now, his blade weaving a shimmering web about him. Xelian stayed close, ducking and diving with her knife held ready as she waited for him to tire.

Kraillach's offensive slowed down inexorably like a clockwork toy. The augmentations of his jewel-bright armour could grant him speed and strength but not true stamina. With a sudden twist Xelian lashed out. Armour split beneath her flashing blade and Kraillach's hand fell away with a welter of blood as she severed it at the wrist. His ancient, deadly blade fell to the dust still gripped in his spasming fingers. Kraillach cried out in horror and staggered back, almost falling. Xelian pounced and drove her knife into his torso up to its ornate hilt.

Kraillach swayed, held up only by the eviscerating blade. Xelian laughed cruelly and twisted the knife, carving through heart and lungs in a crimson spray. She jerked the blade free and stepped back with a satisfied air. Kraillach coughed blood and collapsed, writhing, into the dirt. Xelian knelt on his chest and pressed the bloody knife to his face.

'I want you to know you're going to need help coming back from this, Kraillach,' she whispered venomously as she started cutting. 'You're going to need more help from Yllithian's "pure heart" to come back than El'Uriaq himself!'

By the time Xelian stood back Kraillach was left as red ruin, a raw, squamous meat thing that still somehow writhed with hideous life. Kraillach's haemonculi hurried forwards from his sky chariot. The hunched, hide-clad figures squatted over their master like vampire bats as they pinched off veins and arteries, collecting the pieces left scattered around by Xelian as she slaked her bloodlust. Overhead the satiated cloud of pleasure craft was breaking up, drifting away between the spires to seek other diversions.

'Very nice, Xelian,' Yllithian said, applauding gently. 'Did you mean what you said?'

She tossed her head back provocatively, the blood still slicking her pale limbs and full mouth. If he was aroused by her he did not show it. The murderlust was strong on her, seductive and dangerous as a razor's edge. She smiled, white teeth on red.

'Kraillach was never going to agree to our plan on his own. Now he has an incentive. His own haemonculi can bring him back but it'll take too long. They'll come crawling to us and asking for our help as soon as he grows his tongue back.'

Kinship is not an emotion common to citizens of the dark city, even less so an archon of High Commorragh, but Yllithian felt something akin to it when Xelian spoke of 'our' plan. A heartbeat later, well-schooled centuries of paranoia crowded in at the heels of the unfamiliar sensation.

'All very tidy,' he said. 'So were you the one that sent assassins after Kraillach… and me?'

'That would be telling,' she mocked, smiling capriciously with sharp white teeth. 'Would you think badly of me if I did? And if I denied it would you ever really believe me?'

'I don't believe that you did send them. I think that Vect did.'

'You flatter me with your nobility, Lord Yllithian.'

'It is my honour to do so, Lady Xelian.'

'I feel a day of celebration of my victory is in order. Stay and… entertain me for a while.'

'I regret, my lady, that if we have only a day before the raid occurs many arrangements need to be made so I must forbear the undoubted pleasure.'

Xelian laughed and lifted her arms to the circling Reavers and hellions. Venom jetbikes broke from the pack and dived towards her.

'Then you should be about it, Nyos. It doesn't pay to wait around – just ask Kraillach.'

She ran lithely and made an astounding leap, catching onto a passing Venom and swinging herself aboard it in a single fluid motion. Yllithian gazed after her as she vanished towards the fortress, looked around at the bloodied circle where the duel had been fought, and sniffed meditatively. Xelian had never thought to ask him if he had been the one that sent the assassins.

CHAPTER 7
RED IN TOOTH AND CLAW

'You are all the children of destiny, red in tooth and claw. Do not think that their mayfly lives are less precious than your old wickedness in the eyes of the universe. Who can say who will prevail this day? Not I, and not you. Go forth and reap your souls, but beware the darts of the enemy for you are not yet immortal…'

– The red crone Hekatii to Duke Vileth,
in Ursyllas's *Dispossessions*

THE WHITE FLAMES kabal controlled docking rights along the Ashkeri Talon, reserving fully eighteen of the kilometres-long anchorage-spines for the exclusive use of themselves and their allies. Life among the crowded spires of Commorragh made it easy to forget that the city was originally built as a transit point, a nexus in the webway with hundreds of thousands of connections to skeins of that curious sub-realm.

The rise of the White Flames' fortunes had been in direct correlation to their expansion through the Ashkeri Talon and the docking facilities therein. When Nyos Yllithian assassinated his predecessor and rose to archon the White Flames had controlled just three anchorages along the talon. One of Yllithian's first acts had been to destroy or subvert the lesser kabals controlling the docking spines adjacent to his own. His reasoning was simple. The sprawling city consumed resources at a ravenous rate, and every day thousands of ships had to disgorge stolen cargoes to slake its hunger. By controlling even a fraction of the docking facilities around the city as he did, immeasurable wealth flowed into the White Flames' coffers.

Ashkeri Talon was normally bustling with slavers and traders, even occasional xenos ships paying their way into the dark city through Yllithian's domain. Today the anchorage-spines were occupied solely by warships. Gigantic, shark-like Torture-class cruisers took up entire spines all to themselves, greedily swallowing lines of warriors into their open maws. Smaller Corsair-class frigates were jostling together among other anchorages, loading their own payloads of torpedoes and strike craft.

The ships of many different kabals were present and tensions were running high, but with a sense of excitement and energy underlying it all. Slights and misunderstandings that would have brought violence on the streets of Commorragh were temporarily put aside. The kabalites were on their best behaviour, as if they were attending a party and didn't want to embarrass themselves in front of the host.

Xagor and Kharbyr eyed one another dubiously as they slipped through the crowds together. They were hunting for the ship of the archon of the White Flames on the express instructions of Master Bella-thonis, the haemonculus's perverse sense of humour having dubbed them ideal candidates to work as a team. Kharbyr suspected he was being punished after the events at the Aviaries. He was itching to stick a knife in Xagor the moment the wrack's back was turned, but the master haemonculus had been par-ticularly vivid in his descriptions of the torments awaiting either one of them should they return with-out the other. Xagor had accepted the situation with the same dull resignation he appeared to apply to most of his life.

'Many ships, more than Xagor has ever seen,' the wrack complained.

'Just look for biggest ones, stupid. The archons will be on those. When we find a big one with a white flame on the side that's our stop.'

'Yes, yes. Very obvious.'

YLLITHIAN WATCHED THE war host prepare from the bridge of his command ship, an ancient vessel with a revered name that would translate roughly as *Intem-perate Angel* in lesser tongues. The Ninth Raptrex had come in force, easily visible by the distinctive feather patterns that marked their Razorwing fighters and Voidraven bombers as they flew into the open bays of the ships. The nominal raid leader, Malix-ian the Mad was aboard his own vessel, the *Death*

Strike, impatiently waiting for departure. One of the cruisers was from the Realm Eternal, resplendent in the faded grandeur of lost ages. Morr was lurking aboard it, commanding in absentia for his injured master, Kraillach. As Xelian had predicted, Kraillach's regrowth was proving slow and painful. He had sent word from his regeneration crypt virtually begging to participate in seizing a worldsinger – on the condition that he would also benefit. Xelian's own hard-edged, hook-winged destroyers shared berths alongside Yllithian's black-carapaced Corsairs. Ships from a host of lesser kabals squeezed in where they could.

Despite the smoothness of preparations for the raid Yllithian felt dissatisfied. The warriors were loading, the weapons were arming, the military component of the raid was coming together with all the efficiency Commorrites typically exhibited around the business of taking slaves. But the raid ultimately was a sham, an irrelevance in comparison to the true mission to capture a worldsinger, and that part of the mission was not going at all according to plan.

Yllithian turned to reappraise the motley assortment of individuals that had presented themselves before him for inclusion in his supposedly secret mission.

Xelian had sent her own agent, a lithe succubus named Aez'ashya, to 'make sure everything went smoothly'. She stood brazenly on Yllithian's command deck eyeing him with frank insolence. She knew he could not deny her a role in the mission. Xelian's part in the conspiracy was simply too critical to risk alienating her mistress. Like all of her brother and sister wyches, Aez'ashya was quick and deadly so she was at least something of an asset. The two others that had lately arrived before him could claim no such distinction.

Bellathonis had insisted that two of his agents needed to go on the mission to capture the worldsinger 'to ensure the subject came to him intact.' It was a piece of staggering impudence that the master haemonculus had justified by 'the special requirements of the operation.' The two of them, a shivering little masked wrack and a shifty-looking sell-steel, did not engender much confidence. They stank of cheap drugs and excreta underscored with a sharp tang of chemicals and fear. He was currently weighing whether to accede to the haemonculus's request or simply have the pair of them flung out of the nearest airlock.

Perhaps most worryingly Kraillach's executioner, Morr, had been making rumbling noises about going on the mission himself 'for the sake of my archon,' apparently driven by some incomprehensible sense of duty to see his archon restored.

Incubi were supposed to possess considerable stealth skills, but a huge, heavily armoured warrior with a two-metre-long blade still did not strike Yllithian as an ideal candidate for an infiltration mission deep into the heart of enemy territory, Once again, however, he would be hard put to deny Kraillach's chief executioner his wishes if he were pressed. It was to be expected that Yllithian's allies would be alert for signs of him entirely taking over control and eager to push their own people into the heart of things, but it was getting tiresome to say the least.

Sadly the succession of troublesome unknown quantities attaching themselves to his carefully planned mission were not the greatest of Yllithian's grievances.

Yllithian's own primary agent, the individual that the entire effort hinged upon, was nowhere to be found. The elusive agent had been out of contact for several days after promising to scout the target. It was safe to assume that he was dead by now but the preparations for the raid had ground relentlessly forwards once the wheels started turning.

With Yllithian's agent gone the entire mission became a shot in the dark. It was a shot still worth taking in Yllithian's opinion on the off-chance that it succeeded, but one to perhaps limit his losses on. He addressed his visitors with ill-disguised distaste.

'Aez'ashya, be most welcome. Felicitations to your mistress, dear friend that she is to us,' Yllithian said silkily. 'Pray take charge of these two... individuals and remove them from my presence.'

'And then?' Aez'ashya arched her brows coquettishly.

'Keep them by your side, they will accompany you on the mission later.'

Bellathonis's agents looked scared. Aez'ashya looked by turns annoyed and disappointed. Yllithian felt a little better.

As PREPARATIONS FOR the raid proceeded above, Yllithian's chief haemonculus, Syiin, was busy below, burrowing his way deeper beneath the corespur. By crooked paths he went down into the most ancient pits beneath the city where the haemonculi covens had dwelt for countless centuries. Through a maze of cells and oubliettes he followed chalk marks and fetishes made in the spiralling circle that marked the seal of The Black Descent, passing along razor-edged walkways and across iron bridges as he went down, always down into the depths where his coven masters dwelt. He passed into regions where light was a defeated foe and age-long pain and misery accreted on the walls like dark clay. At last he came to the slowly-turning, trap-filled labyrinth that was the coven's lair. Here he went more slowly, stopping often to rub his hands and lick his lips as he negotiated the twists and turns. It was a long time since he had come below to seek his hidden masters and he struggled to recall the precise route.

Monofilament lines as thin as spider silk bisected the air, gravity traps lurked beneath innocuous-looking flagstones; agoniser wings, semi-sentient venom clouds and a myriad of other deadly devices were concealed behind the walls. It was clearly not a time to be imprecise. He congratulated himself that he had brought an elixir with him for just such an eventuality, a substance distilled from the synapses of a slave-scholar. He fumbled through his hide robes before triumphantly bringing forth a tiny crystal vial. Unscrewing the stopper he allowed a single drop of the viscous liquid to fall on his quivering pink tongue.

Syiin was still savouring the zesty taste when the correct route through the labyrinth came to him as if it had been sketched in lambent neon in his mind's eye. He moved along the complex, weaving path as if it were dance steps – forwards three, left one, forwards five, turn right... So by spiralling, circuitous routes Syiin made his way slowly but surely into the Chamber of Craft, where coven members of The Black Descent impatiently awaited him.

Four were present, two of them Secret Masters hooded and masked in bone, a third in the viridian and black robes of an Intimate Secretary. The fourth coven member remained hidden in the shadows, an ominous presence concealed by interference fields that easily defeated Syiin's augmented eyes.

'You're late!' the Secretary snarled. 'The coven is not yours to command, how dare you keep us waiting?'

'Humble apologies, Secretary, Masters,' Syiin puffed, bobbing bows to everyone present.

'We are only present because you promised word of Bellathonis,' one of the Secret Masters said peevishly in a thin, high voice.

'Quite,' said the Secretary brusquely. 'So out with it, what have you found?'

Syiin waited for them to be quiet. They might outrank him, noticeably so in the case of the Intimate Secretary, but Syiin held the cards in this meeting with his fresh news. As such he took his time before replying.

'Your honours, I'm certain that the renegade Bellathonis is undertaking forbidden work on behalf of Archon Yllithian.'

'Oh really?' drawled the Secretary with avid interest. 'And what do you have as proof of this?'

Syiin licked his lips uncomfortably. Proof had been

in extremely short supply. He brazenly presented his suppositions as facts instead.

'Yllithian has met with Bellathonis, and subsequent to that he sent a gift to him by roundabout means. Furthermore I have reason to believe that the renegade is creating a hidden workshop somewhere in the city.'

'I hear conjecture but not evidence,' the Secretary sneered. 'What was this gift? By your coy references it seems safe to presume you did not intercept it and learn of its contents, no more than you can precisely locate this phantom workshop. You bring us nothing.'

'Ah, but everything is in the context of these seemingly small happenings,' Syiin said smoothly before playing his trump card. 'This very hour Yllithian sets out in concert with his allies to raid a maiden world. Archon Malixian acts as patron but I have no doubt that Yllithian put him up to it, and by extension the raid was originally Bellathonis's idea.'

Syiin let that settle in for a moment, turning his round, stretched face back and forth to peer at the assembled coven members. He was enjoying himself considerably making them feel uncomfortable.

'It's my belief that Yllithian is seeking a pure heart.'

The distortion-cloaked fourth member of the coven, silent and motionless until now, reacted sharply at his words. A distorted whisper echoed about the chamber, the sound of a blade being honed on a whetstone.

'Leave us,' it said.

The masked Hidden Masters and the green-robed Intimate Secretary turned on their heels and left immediately, vanishing into shadowy openings so quickly they seemed to have been swallowed up in a single gulp. Syiin looked on interestedly as the blurred shape resolved into a darker solid, a tall and hatchet-faced haemonculus wearing the slate grey of a Master Elect of Nine. Syiin was quietly impressed with himself. He had just jumped up a full three degrees in dealing with the labyrinthine hierarchy of The Black Descent.

'An unfortunate business,' the stone-on-steel voice said, 'but one inside your own demesne. The renegade makes his new lair beneath the White Flames' fortress at the invitation of your master, Archon Yllithian.'

Syiin spluttered with outrage, feeling his stretched face become flush. That Yllithian would take up with the vagrant Bellathonis was bad enough, that he had invited the dog into his house was worse. Haemonculi were slow to anger, ridiculously slow by Commorrite standards, but once their cold, bright fury was sparked it was almost impossible to quench. Syiin felt the first stirrings of that anger kindling inside him now.

'This cannot be borne!' Syiin hissed. 'Bellathonis insults this coven, all of us! He tramples our teachings and mocks our scriptures. He endangers the city! He must be struck down!'

The Master Elect was nodding thoughtfully. Flat plates of black crystal had been used to replace his eyes and they winked at Syiin fitfully in the dim light.

'You are filled with the spirit of righteous retribution. This is good,' the Master Elect grated. 'But is your hate enough to carry you to the next degree of the descent?'

Syiin blinked in surprise. Another degree of descent would make him a master, equivalent in rank to Bellathonis before he abandoned the Coven. There were few things that Syiin wouldn't do to achieve that.

'I hate Bellathonis,' he said and found that saying the words thrilled him. 'I hate him and I wish to destroy him.' The Master Elect nodded and extended a small object to him, a key with an ornate barrel that was fluted with many sharp tines.

'Take this to the forty-ninth interstices and open the chamber there. Your enemy has a weakness for gifts, and you may find something fitting for him inside. Do not tarry overlong. I sense you have little time left. Take it and go.'

Syiin accepted the key with shaking hands and set out through the labyrinth. He began laboriously pacing out the memorised pattern to reach the forty-ninth interstices, sparing another drop of the precious elixir to keep himself on the correct course. In these depths most of the labyrinth was entirely lightless; only strict adherence to the mnemonically implanted routes known by a coven member could prevent fatal disorientation in the inky blackness. Syiin kept his head down and his eyes closed as he took the forty-nine necessary steps.

He opened his eyes to find himself in a stretch of passage that was octagonal in cross-section, and lit by a coldly glowing amethyst crystal overhead. His path was blocked by a heavy-looking circular silver door. Spiralling inscriptions across its surface emanated from a large, central keyhole. Syiin inserted the key the Master Elect had given him and then stopped.

What if this were a test? Or a trap? Perhaps some coven members were using his distraction with Bellathonis as a way to dispose of him... Syiin's fingers caressed the key uncertainly where it stood proud of the lock. Then he thought again of the insults Yllithian had heaped upon him. Syiin could never hope to strike at his archon and live, but with the coven's blessing he could still strike at his rival haemonculus.

He seized the key and twisted. It moved reluctantly at first and then more smoothly before vanishing entirely into the hole. For a few heartbeats nothing happened, and then Syiin saw that grooves were forming in the solid-seeming surface of the door, splitting it into concentric rings. The rings began to rotate and align themselves, twisting independently before folding up neatly inside one another to open a path within. A breath of stale air wafted outwards, making Syiin sneeze. The chamber must have been sealed for hundreds of years. Despite his fears no void-born entity rushed out to attack him, or to damn him by fulfilling his every wish. A half-seen glimmer from inside drew him onwards into a small octagonal chamber mostly filled by shelves made of thin sheets of crystal. Syiin emitted a little gasp when he saw what was arrayed upon them.

All manner of arcane paraphernalia was on display: bejewelled boxes, ornately bladed caskets, runic tetrahedrons, tightly-coiled spheres of shining metal, pots, amphorae, censers and crucibles. Precious treasures they seemed, certainly. They were richly made with fine if sinister artistry, but only a haemonculus could appreciate their true value. The contents of the chamber would have beggared a kabal to collect, the wealth it represented could have purchased a fleet or bribed a fortress. These rare and deadly treasures were examples of the very finest devices of excruciation.

The spheres were *Animus Vitae*, sentient ribbons of razor-edged metal tightly wound together. At a command, they would explode outwards to ensnare a victim before contracting again just as quickly to slice apart their helpless prey with delightful precision. Sadly Bellathonis would recognise one of those distinctive devices long before it could be brought close enough to him to do its lethal work…

Syiin's eyes strayed to a small, black box with ornamental blades projecting from each corner. He recognised it as a Casket of Flensing. Opening it with the correct command words would unleash a host of invisible assassins upon the target, gnawing through armour and flesh alike in a whirlwind of unseen teeth. Syiin had even heard tales that the ethereal creatures in the casket would bring the skull of their victim back to their master when the work was complete, the brain inside still delectably intact.

The moon-faced haemonculus pondered. Most of the tales featuring a Casket of Flensing portrayed it as a device of punishment and terror rather than execution, ghoulishly emphasising the agonised struggles of the helpless victim. Syiin needed a device that would reliably destroy Bellathonis completely in a single strike with no chance of survival. He regretfully discarded the idea of using the casket and moved on.

A shard of thick, angular crystal lay on a shelf close by. Syiin hissed when he saw it, moving carefully to ensure his reflection wasn't caught in the shard's mirrored surface. It was a Shattershard, legendary creation of the demented genius Vorsch. Each Shattershard had been made from a remnant of a complex dimensional gateway called the Mirror of Planes. After the portal's destruction Vorsch had painstakingly tracked down every fragment and weaponised it. By some strange dimensional sympathy understood only by Vorsch, catching a victim's reflection in the shard and then shattering it would cause the victim to shatter into pieces too. Syiin had believed there to be few, if any, Shattershards left in the city but here one lay. Perhaps this one was fated to be the doom of Bellathonis?

Syiin frowned. A Shattershard needed a courageous, deft minion to employ it successfully. He could rely on none of his wracks for that, and he could scarcely expose himself to make the attempt in person. Besides which he wasn't sure he entirely trusted an esoteric dimensional shattering as a way of permanently removing his rival. On a visceral level he really would like to see a body – irretrievably destroyed, of course, but preferably in a red and messy fashion. The thirteen foundations of vengeance had very specific instructions about that – an enemy can never be presumed dead unless their body is found. He licked his thin lips at the thought. It was a rare pleasure to strike down another haemonculus – the covens spent most of their time working to suppress such internal conflicts, rather than enable them. As such, whatever attack Syiin chose had to be totally unexpected and instantly lethal.

He ignored more caskets, orbs and crucibles, all of

them devices of psychic torment that would only titil-
late a master haemonculus like Bellathonis. He was
about to turn back to the Casket of Flensing again
when his gaze fell on the dullest and most unimpres-
sive item he had seen so far. It was a little three-sided
pyramid no taller than his thumb, made of a dull,
coarse material akin to charred bone. Silvery runes
etched into its surface warned of the dire consequences of activation.

It was a runic gate, a portable key for entering the
webway, but this particular gate led to a fragment of
the labyrinth dimension that had fallen into madness
and dissolution. Syiin had seen one like it used in his
days of apprenticeship. His old master Rhakkar had
unleashed a dark gate during the sack of a slave world.
Syiin could see it in his mind's eye even now. The
slaves' leaders had taken refuge in one of their larger
hutches with many of their armed followers guarding
them. Desperation was making the slaves fractious,
even to the point of driving back the archon's warriors with their wild firing. Careless of their shots
Rhakkar had stalked forwards and cast a small, dark
tetrahedron into the slaves' midst.

Syiin had witnessed only a black-purple flash that
disappeared in the blink of an eye – the gate opening for a fraction of a second – before the tetrahedron
dropped to the ground inert and lifeless. In that brief
instant every slave within a dozen paces of the spot
was smashed into bloody pulp, crushed into walls
and floor that were rent and scored as if they had been
raked by monstrous claws. The slaves' will to resist
was broken immediately and the survivors took their

place in the proper order of things by running and screaming until they were rounded up.

Rhakkar, in a rare moment of lucidity and expansiveness, had explained the dark gate's operation to Syiin afterwards. Impossible entities thrived in the forbidden places, he had said, things that would use an open gate to reach out and lash at anything within grasp of their pseudopods. By setting the gate to open just a chink for a fraction of a second an unwelcome lengthier incursion was avoided and the gate became an effective weapon. Rhakkar had been jealous of his dark gate and never trusted it to his minions, in fact Syiin had never seen him use it again.

Syiin licked his lips and smiled a thin smile. There was poetic justice in destroying Bellathonis with a small taste of the kind of destruction he risked unleashing on the city. A simple device to trigger, with a wide area of effect and enough lethality to ensure the job was done. Perfect.

He reached out to take the little tetrahedron with trembling hands. It felt heavier than it should and was chill to the touch as he lifted it. He left the chamber and the door silently unfurled itself to seal away its contents for another hundred years. Syiin set himself to recalling the steps necessary to get back to the Chamber of Craft and from there out of the labyrinth of The Black Descent.

Only later, once he was safely ensconced in his own lair, would he give thought to how exactly to present Bellathonis with a very special gift.

* * *

THE COMBINED WAR fleet made a brave sight as it pulled away from Ashkeri Talon. Corsairs trailed after the sedately moving cruisers in darting shoals. Their shadowfields flickered through fantastical falsehoods as they flew, turning them into mythical beasts, clouds of fire and lightning, fey castles or alien vessels at their master's whims.

The true enormity of Commorragh could only be appreciated from the void surrounding it. Only in the relatively narrow envelope between the city itself and the wardings that separated it from the roiling energies of the warp was it possible to look back and see the face of the dark city.

Perspective shrank the kilometres-long anchorages to thin fingers and then fine bristles and still the city expanded around them. The ships of the fleet flew out between the docking talons to where streams of ships moved constantly inbound and outbound, feeding the hungry city. An endless vista of lights gleamed in the darkness behind them, the city glowing like a faery fortress in the darkness. Toward its heart the spires, minarets and steeples of High Commorragh seemed to thrust upwards in mad profusion as they strained towards the crown of captured suns. The barbed spires seemed slender and fanciful from this distance, their mountainous girth rendered needle-like in the greater panorama.

Below the profusion of towers that marked High Commorragh lay the wide-flung disk of docking talons, their craggy knuckles thrusting out into the void. The tiers and districts of Low Commorragh grew in the gaps between them like plates of fungus sprouting between the gnarled roots of a tree. Below the level of the docking talons the troglodytic cousins of the upper spires hung like stalactites into the eternal cave of night. Slave mills, haemonculi pits, flesh farms and inverted tenements dangled in a dark fog of their own excrescences, lit only by the greenly glowing corpse-light of flaring gases. This was the port-city of Commorragh seen from the outside, an effect not unlike seeing an impossibly vast, spiny sea-creature feeding in the depths.

A circle of green flame appeared before the leading vessels of the fleet like an eye opening onto an infernal realm. One by one the ships of the war fleet slipped through the waiting portal and into the labyrinth dimension. In moments the entire fleet had been swallowed up and the circle vanished, leaving the eternal night around the city unchallenged once more.

Inside the webway the kabalite ships slipped rapidly along a curving tunnel of iridescent energy, its walls rippling with solid colours. Flashes of starlit sky appeared and disappeared through the shifting veil. The webway was an extradimensional marvel engineered by entities that pre-dated even the eldar. Its lattice was formed out of the very stuff of the warp and it burrowed between the material and immaterial worlds, part of both and yet separated from either. The eldar had discovered the webway early in their history, their quick minds soon learning its labyrinthine paths and mastering its ways. At its height eldar civilisation had built great port-cities, palaces and secret realms at interstices of the network, and in so doing it had unwittingly created the final strongholds it would occupy after the Fall.

At certain points the tunnel branched, splitting through immense hanging gateways of wraithbone and golden metal inscribed with eldritch runes of channelling and protection. They passed many smaller passageways leading off the major route, entrances only large enough for foot troops and light vehicles to reach some planet-based web portal. Much of the labyrinth dimension was only accessible thus; the greater ship-bearing arteries were rarer and infinitely more precious.

The webway of modern times had altered drastically since those golden days of empire. It had been torn open by war and disaster in a thousand places. Whole regions had been rendered inaccessible by the splintering of the pathways, while in other areas the wardings had collapsed, admitting strange beings from different realities. Travelling the labyrinth dimension was inherently dangerous in modern times. It took skill, intellect and experience learned through countless millennia to chart a safe course through the multi-dimensional maze of arteries and capillaries formed by the interdimensional network.

The raiding kabalite ships flew with an air of arrogant confidence through the labyrinth dimension. The eldar of Commorragh had become the masters of the webway, it was their hunting ground and their limitless domain. They slew any that they found within its fabric, although its infinite dimensions meant that it was rare to encounter such impudence. The eldar of the craftworlds still dared to use the labyrinth dimension on occasion, but they hurried quickly from one sanctuary to another only at times of need. The young races lacked the wit and sophistication to enter the webway; indeed many of its portals in the realspace carried deadly safeguards against their interference.

The greatest threat in the labyrinth dimension was from warp entities, daemons from beyond the veil that swarmed and hammered incessantly at the psychic wardings that held its arteries frustratingly just out of reach. In several places vast spirals of psychically active wraithbone surrounded the ethereal tunnels, repairing and reinforcing it against the insubstantial claws forever scrabbling at the outer walls.

Passage to the maiden world of Lileathanir could not be completed entirely within the webway. The ships would halt to disgorge their cargo of weapons and warriors into the lesser passages before moving onward to seek a transient portal into realspace believed to lie near enough to the planet to be used at this juncture. The arcane calculations required to determine *that* piece of information had been one of the more challenging aspects of planning so far. The difficulty of reaching Lileathanir was one of the reasons Yllithian had subtly prodded Malixian to select it as a target. His spy had found just one webway portal on the surface and had reported that to be long disused and virtually unguarded. No true eldar had set foot on this particular maiden world in centuries, so there was a very good chance that the short-lived Exodites had forgotten what kind of peril that portal represented.

The fleet reached the junction without incident, slowing to permit streams of grav craft to leave their bays and disappear into the narrower opening. Morr contacted the *Intemperate Angel* as it unloaded, his blank-masked helm suddenly filling every one of the curved viewing screens around the bridge.

'Archon Yllithian, with Archon Malixian's consent I have decided to accompany the expedition to Lileath-anir's surface.'

Yllithian stifled a sigh and attempted to appeal to reason.

'Are you sure your presence will be essential, Morr? It would seem that coordinating strategy from the ships should demand your full attention.'

'My place is wherever I can serve my archon's best interests. Under these circumstances that will be at the forefront of actions occurring on the surface.'

At least Morr was making an effort to not just blurt out his real reasons. Ultimately Yllithian could not prevent him going; even being informed of his decision was a simple matter of courtesy.

'Well good hunting then, Morr, I'm sure your renowned good sense and discretion will serve you admirably.'

If Morr understood the sarcasm and the veiled warning behind Yllithian's words he did not deign to respond to it.

'Thank you, Archon Yllithian. Morr out.'

Yllithian turned back to consideration of his own hand-picked group. Originally he had intended to send six of his most skilled operatives to meet his agent at a pre-arranged spot on the surface of Lileath-anir. With four others now joining the mission and his own agent unaccounted for Yllithian had reduced his own contribution accordingly. Two of his kabal members would accompany the others to seek out the missing agent, no more than that. The mission would succeed with six operatives or not at all.

The stiletto shapes of Raiders and Ravagers could still be seen streaming from the open bays of the ships and into the nearby sub-conduit. Their progress would be slow in comparison to the ships but the fleet had considerably further to go before it reached its own exit point from the webway.

According to Yllithian's calculations the ships would be on hand at just the right moment, no more than a few hours after the raid began on the planet's surface. It was slightly risky but Malixian had been unwilling to wait for the fleet to be in position before launching his attack on the surface. So the ships would arrive later, ready to fill their holds with whatever meagre selection of slaves Malixian might net from the raid while he wasn't being distracted by oversized avians.

It mattered little as long as Malixian created a big enough diversion. From what the mad archon had excitedly told Yllithian about his plans there would be no issues on that front at all.

DESPITE THE CLAIMS of Yllithian's spy, the Exodite clans of Lileathanir had not entirely forgotten the tales of their Dark Kin. Their ancestors had sensibly buried the only functional webway portal on the planet beneath a titanic mound of earth and stones to prevent its easy use. A select brotherhood of wardens kept a strict vigil at the site year after year, century after century, in case the dark ones ever returned.

Latterly the wardens' role had devolved increasingly into forbidding curious younglings from investigating the great annulus and telling horrifying stories about fiends that came in the night.

Few truly took the warnings seriously any more and the wardens themselves had become something of a joke. Within the anarchistic, agrarian culture they lived in there was always more work to be done and always too few hands to do it. A caste of custodians that performed no visible function were viewed as an indulgence by some of their fellows. In what passed for Exodite society any form of indulgence was viewed with scepticism and more than a little disgust.

Nevertheless the wardens took note when the great earthwork mound covering the gate shivered during the night as if struck by a curiously localised tremor. Runners were dispatched immediately to the nearest settlements to give warnings – that were generally ignored – and the next day tripwires were strung and crumbling stone-faced pits uncovered for the first time in centuries. The wardens' Exodite kin clicked their tongues and sighed to see such wasted effort. Lileathanir was still a young world and earth tremors were common, they said. The wardens' actions reeked of a kind of desperation to prove their worth.

The wardens were denied whatever vindication they might have felt when the Commorrites really did come a few nights later. Molecular de-bonders planted in advance of the raid instantaneously vaporised the great shielding mound and a kilometre of surrounding jungle. The ancient order of wardens that had faithfully guarded the portal for centuries vanished in the blink of an eye. A vast torus of glowing plasma was still rising into the air above the spot as the first Raider craft emerged from the newly reopened portal and sped away into the night. More and more of the waspish vessels appeared through the glowing portal, forming a continuous wyrm-like stream of bladed darkness as they glided aloft into the night sky.

The wyrm swept westwards spreading ripples of terrified alarm through the natives of Lileathanir. Flames split the darkness as the first wave of attackers ripped into the closest settlements and brushed aside what scattered opposition the stunned Exodites could muster. Clusters of slender towers toppled and fell beneath the destructive double kiss of shatterfield missiles, the Voidraven bombers that launched them invisible as they swooped away into the night sky. Beastmasters descended from the Raiders and unleashed nightmarish khymerae packs upon the stunned survivors, the twisted warp beasts bounding across the forest floor howling with bloodlust.

The Exodites fought back bravely but their cause was hopeless from the outset. Wherever knots of warriors tried to make a stand deadly accurate splinter fire slashed through their ranks from above. The proud feral warriors were quickly reduced to heaps of twitching, helpless victims by the sharp bite of paralytic toxins. Wyches darted into the tumbled ruins shrieking like children as they raced with the khymerae to root out the pitiful survivors still in hiding. Within minutes all resistance had ceased.

The Commorrites started to spread out as they hunted the handful of Exodites that had fled into the jungle at the first sign of attack. Flights of Reavers and hellions sped on ahead to seek more prey while Raider craft slid beneath the forest canopy with capture nets at the ready. Red flames leapt up in the distance where another settlement had been found. A lone Raider, unremarkable save for its passengers, split away from the main body and took a heading northwards, quickly leaving the chaos behind.

ARCHON MALIXIAN RODE at the head of the kabalite horde aboard his glittering skeletal Raider. Throughout the night his forces harried the Exodites without mercy, smashing one settlement after another with their lightning-fast advance. Resistance was light and wherever it flared up it was quickly snuffed out by the Commorrites' superior firepower. Nonetheless Malixian listened to the reports and slave tallies coming in and grew increasingly disconsolate as the night wore on with no indication of what he was waiting for. It was only as the first fingers of dawn began to thrust over the rim of the world that he caught sight of something that made his heart sing.

Mighty wings beat in the distance, catching flickers of sunlight on sail-wide pinions. He smiled happily at the thought of the mud dwellers rising to the occasion after all. A moment later keening whistles sounded and the Ninth Raptrex surged forwards to accept the challenge and begin their aerial hunt, all thoughts of the mundane, earthbound business of slave-taking temporarily forgotten.

* * *

LIFE. THE VERY air of the maiden world was thick with it. Life sprang from the earth and flew through air. Life swam in tinkling streams and deep pools. Faint starlight picked out enormous trees rising from the forest floor, their wide trunks and high canopy rendering it into a vast, cathedral-like space crowded with living, growing things in every direction. Brightly flowered, fleshy-looking creepers entwined trees and writhed across the ground to form dense, springy mats underfoot. Crawling things writhed through the rich loam at their feet, munched the leaves on the trees and were in their turn consumed by small winged creatures that whirred through the canopy overhead and darted expertly between the densely twined limbs. Bright-eyed, long-tailed marsupials took fright and fled crashing through the undergrowth at the approach of interlopers. Life was everywhere.

'It's disgusting,' said one of Bellathonis's agents, the sell-steel named Kharbyr.

'Yes, yes. Agreed. Extremely unhygienic,' sniffed Bellathonis's other agent, the wrack called Xagor.

'Silence,' said Morr. 'Communicating your unworthy thoughts is of no value.'

Morr was not in charge of the operation, in theory none of them were, but Morr's natural gravitas made him hard to ignore. Xagor cringed but Aez'ashya seemed to care little for the towering incubus's warning.

'Can't you feel it? This place is so different, the city never felt like this.'

'Life in our home is ordered, nurtured and properly utilised. This is nothing but anarchy,' replied one of

Yllithian's people, a shaven-headed, hawk-featured warrior called Vyril. He wore a chameleonic body suit that made it appear as if he were made of glass.

Yllithian's other agent, a noble-looking female called Xyriadh, was off ahead somewhere scouting out their route. To the disgust of Aez'ashya and Kharbyr the pair had insisted the group abandon their Raider shortly after they separated from the main body of the kabalite force.

Morr had quelled any argument by pointing out that despite their avowed primitivism Exodites were quite capable of detecting a lone Raider's energy signature at a considerable distance. Their favoured guerrilla tactics meant that a vehicle travelling alone was almost certain to be ambushed. Since then the group had tramped on foot for hours through a seemingly endless jungle devoid of any trace of landmarks or civilisation. The soul-sapping effects of being in realspace could be felt by all of them and tempers were growing short.

Xyriadh eventually reappeared, her chameleonic armour making her appear as a disembodied head when she removed her helm. Her features bore a close resemblance to Vyril's, an effect intensified by her shaven head. Xagor believed them cousins, Aez'ashya brother and sister, Kharbyr reckoned them a mother and daughter-disguised-as-son but he had a taste for melodramatic theatre like Ursyllas's *Dispossessions*. Morr had kept his own counsel and neither of Yllithian's agents had been forthcoming on the subject. Xyriadh certainly took the role of senior partner when she spoke, as she did now.

'The meeting stone is up ahead, no sign of our contact but I didn't get close enough to be sure before coming back.'

'Why?' demanded Morr.

'Because it seemed more important to let you know we were close than to walk into a potential trap alone,' Xyriadh replied levelly.

'If we must proceed without this "contact" to what degree will our chance of success be compromised?' Morr asked.

'Completely. I doubt we can even find the World Shrine without his help. I su–'

Morr hefted his huge blade onto his shoulder and tramped off in the direction Xyriadh had come from without another word. The rest of them hurried to catch up.

The meeting stone Xyriadh had spoken of was a titanic boulder of quartz that jutted out of the forest floor like a broken tooth. Timeworn carvings crawled across its faces, alien sigils that resembled those of the eldar but were far more eldritch in origin. A small clearing surrounded the stone, as though the trees feared to crowd in too closely around the alien thing in their midst. A stillness hung about the place that contrasted strongly with the riot of fecundity around it.

Morr strode forward with no pretence of subtlety, his blank-faced helm turning back and forth as if he scanned the undergrowth. Aez'ashya stepped lightly up to the stone and studied the sigils without comprehension.

'Who made these marks?' she demanded.

One of the glassy shadows slithering nearby replied – whether it was Xyriadh or Vyril speaking was hard to tell. 'They look like Old One sigils to me. They must have made this place long ago.'

'It is a key stone,' rumbled Morr without looking around from where he stood surveying the jungle. 'The mystic energies of this world pass through this point and others around its circumference.'

Aez'ashya seemed encouraged by her success in getting anything out of the normally taciturn incubus and favoured him with a mischievous smile.

'Morr, you surprise me. How could you know of such things?' she asked with disarming innocence.

'I am older than you know,' Morr said quietly, as if speaking to himself.

'So we just wait now?' Kharbyr whined and pulled his cloak more tightly about him. 'We sit here and hope your mystery contact shows up before She Who Thirsts gnaws us down to our bones?'

'Yes. Yes, agreed. Back before dawn the master said!' Xagor nodded frantically.

'Irrelevant. I can find the World Shrine alone,' Morr said.

There was a sharp cracking sound and Morr's eyepiece exploded into tiny shards of broken crystal. The towering incubus swayed for a moment and then he toppled like a felled tree. The others were too surprised to move for a heartbeat. Another sharp crack sounded and Xyriadh's – or perhaps Vyril's – head dissolved in a spray of crimson.

'Ambush!' Aez'ashya shouted as she raced for the treeline.

She caught sight of a glimmer of movement up in the canopy, a telltale glassy shifting in the foliage. Another crack sounded as the sniper took a shot at her but she was moving too fast to be hit. Answering splinter fire from behind her chopped into the branches and sent the chameleon shape scurrying deeper into cover. A shot struck the ground ahead of her, kicking up a spurt of grass and leaves. That one came from across the clearing from somewhere behind her, confirming at least two snipers had her in their sights.

Aez'ashya plunged into the undergrowth beneath the sniper she had seen and trusted to the others to handle the rest. Life in the dark city honed its citizens' fighting instincts virtually from birth. A daily diet of violence and bloodshed imbued them with a preternatural ability to take the best course of action in a crisis like getting caught in an ambush with an unknown number of assailants. Where an elite military unit would have been pinned down and chopped to pieces Commorrites turned on their attackers like rats in a trap. Her part was to run down the one she had seen, and she would think about helping her erstwhile allies later, perhaps...

She ran up the closest trunk and sprang nimbly onto its lower branches. She scanned the dark canopy intensely, looking for a patch of distorted starlight that would betray her prey's hiding place. There – a fork in a tree barely twenty metres away. Aez'ashya could see the outline of a cloaked figure lifting a long, slender rifle, aiming not at her but away into the clearing. She moved silently closer, padding along slender limbs with barely a sound.

The cloaked figure fired and turned to shift to a new position. Aez'ashya was waiting behind the sniper with the bright glitter of knives bared in her hands

'Greetings, cousin,' she purred as she took the sniper in her razor-edged embrace.

Xagor and Kharbyr had dived for cover before the first bodies hit the ground. Xagor cowered beneath a log with a snub-nosed splinter pistol clutched in his hand. Kharbyr drew an elegant, long-barrelled pistol and rolled onto his belly to loose off a quick volley of shots before leaping up and sprinting for the forest.

Kharbyr dodged across the open ground counting himself lucky that their enemies were using needle rifles. The single-shot weapons made superlative sniper rifles but under the circumstances automatic fire would have served their attackers better. The distinctive cracking sound made by the toxin-coated slivers breaking the sound barrier told him he was dealing with amateurs. Experienced assassins always dialled down the muzzle velocity of their weapons to ensure there would be no such telltale giveaways.

He ducked behind a tree trunk as more shots whined at him. The soft, fibrous trunk shivered as needles thunked into it. He rolled out and came up firing, pelting the canopy with streams of splinter fire to momentarily distract his attackers. He darted back into cover again without waiting to see the result. At least two snipers were tracking him, their deadly rounds coming closer each time he showed his face.

Crashing footsteps whipped his attention back to the clearing and his jaw sagged open in surprise at what he saw. Morr was on his feet and heading past

Kharbyr at a lumbering run. The incubus swung his huge klaive aloft and whirled it through the trunk of a nearby tree, carving out a giant wedge of it in two quick cuts. The tree fell with a groan of protest, moving slowly at first but rapidly gathering pace until it struck the ground with a resounding crash. The air was filled with tumbling leaves in the aftermath, and through them Kharbyr saw two vagrant flickers of motion struggling to get clear.

Morr and Kharbyr sprang forward to confront their assailants at close quarters. Their cameleoline robes had become disordered in the fall and revealed flashes of lightly armoured hands and masked faces. Kharbyr's knife was in his hand as he sprinted forwards, a curved half metre of razor-edged steel poised for an eviscerating thrust. Morr bore down on the pair like a vengeful one-eyed god as he cleaved a path towards them through the shattered limbs.

Seeing they were trapped one of the snipers turned and raised their rifle to shoot. To Kharbyr's surprise the other plunged a dagger into their comrade's exposed back before stepping back and raising open hands in surrender. Their victim gave a disbelieving cry and fell face-forwards, clawing helplessly at the dagger's protruding hilt. Kharbyr could sense their agonised soul slipping into the spiritstone they wore at their neck, a passing ripe with a sickly sweet scent of betrayal. The body twitched once more and lay still.

The other was babbling something, eyes fixed on the corpse. Kharbyr had to tear his attention away from the ripe, delicious soul waiting to be plucked to understand what they were saying.

'–serve Yllithian! I'm Sindiel! I'm his agent!'

A deceptive calm had fallen across the clearing. Kharbyr looked to Morr for guidance. The towering incubus had stopped a decapitating strike in mid-swing. He studied the stranger from beneath his poised blade for a long moment before lowering it.

'Speak. Your life hangs in the balance,' Morr said distinctly.

The stranger's accent was strange and formal-sounding as he replied. He pulled back his hood and tore off his mask, throwing it from him in apparent disgust. The face revealed looked soft and pinkish to Kharbyr's eyes, like that of a newborn. Something familiar lurked behind the dark eyes, though, a gleam of murderlust and lasciviousness that could be seen openly on every face in the dark city.

'I am Sindiel, an agent of Archon Yllithian of the White Flames Kabal,' the stranger said. 'Forgive me. I was to meet with you alone but my… former companions followed me here. I think they believed they were saving me.'

He gave a shaky laugh. He was speaking quickly and excitedly, constantly glancing back at his slain companion. Complex emotions chased across his face.

'You can guide us to the World Shrine?'

'Yes! Oh yes! That's why I'm here,' the turncoat almost babbled in relief.

'Then be welcome, Sindiel,' Morr intoned with a formality that surprised Kharbyr. 'How many followed you exactly? We must ensure that no survivors escape.'

'Three, just three others. I think your friends got

Corallyon and Belth already.' He tapped one ear nervously. 'I heard them die.'

Aez'ashya reappeared, drenched in blood and looking pleased with herself. She seemed fascinated by Sindiel and flirted with him shamelessly, much to his alternating delight and embarrassment. When Xyriadh emerged she was less amenable to their newfound companion, her proud face filled with barely repressed fury at the death of Vyril. Xagor merely sniffed at the newcomer and asked him for a skin sample. Once all of them were together again Morr turned his one-eyed gaze on Sindiel.

'We must move on,' Morr said, 'our time here is finite. How long will the journey to the World Shrine take?'

Sindiel gestured grandly to the sigil-marked quartz boulder at the centre of the clearing.

'No time at all. In fact we stand before the doorway right now.'

A THOUSAND KILOMETRES to the north, Malixian gave forth a scream of pleasure as his murderous flock dived into the attack. The giant pterasaurs beneath them swirled and scattered across the fantastic cloudscape croaking hoarse cries of alarm. Their Exodite riders were barely visible, flea-like as they scurried around on the broad backs of their mounts. They aimed slender lances upwards and the air was suddenly criss-crossed with streaks of ruby laser light. Caught in the net, a Raider belched flame and rolled over, its cargo of warriors tipped out screaming into the void. The other Raiders pulled up sharply out of range, momentarily frustrated.

A rush of hellions plummeted past the web of

fire spitting splinters in return, one expertly tearing through the wing membrane of a pterasaur with his hooked hellglaive. A second hellion attempted the same feat but was swept from his skyboard by a gigantic, gnarled claw. Other hellions fell as flaming cinders as the lancers on the pterasaurs' backs ruthlessly burned them down. Malixian was careless of their casualties; the hellions had served their purpose by drawing the enemy fire.

Scourges swept down on the distracted Exodite riders in a thunder of wings. Swarms of Malixian's alien pets were flying at their clawed heels. He'd brought razorwings and bloodtalons on this occasion – they were easily replaceable and more than deadly enough to kill mud dwellers.

The Exodites were armoured, after a fashion, in hide and scale but it availed them little against the whirlwind of claws and talons that engulfed them. Their firing faltered and Malixian led the charge of heavier grav craft down on the demoralised survivors. He leapt onto the pitching back of a pterasaur where a knot of the skin-clad primitives were attempting to make a last stand.

The riders were fighting well, warriors every one of them. They had been raised in a harsh environment, trained in the arts of war with all the phenomenal focus of their eldar minds and bodies and blooded in inter-clan feuds. Malixian still ripped through them as if they were cattle, beating aside their swords and lances in a fury of razor-edged talons. In moments the blood-drenched pterasaur was swept clear of Exodites and the prize was in his grasp.

Scourges with nerve goads ruthlessly took control of the riderless pterasaur and drove it north. The scene was repeated on other pterasaurs and soon half a dozen of the great beasts were flapping ponderously eastwards, a good haul. They would be stunned and taken aboard the ships in due course when Yllithian brought them in for the rendezvous.

Malixian privately wondered if the giant pterasaurs could ever be persuaded to hunt something as small and insignificant as a slave. He felt some confidence that in conjunction with his beastmasters Bellathonis would find a way to spur the great beasts into appropriately murderous action, although the master haemonculus had seemed rather distracted of late.

Shrill cries drew his attention to the sight of more pterasaurs labouring up through the clouds. More and more of the cruciform shapes emerged into view. At first a dozen could be seen, then two dozen, then the skies below were filling up with the inexorable ripple and snap of enormous wings beating. Malixian watched them with frank admiration for a few seconds before ordering his Ravagers to open fire. Destroying beams lanced down and caressed the magnificent, impractical beasts. First one, then another and another were sent plummeting in flames.

Their companions bore stoically onwards through the barrage, and looking below them Malixian saw the reason for their doggedness. They were only the first wave. More and more beating wings broached the cloud tops as far as the eye could see and Malixian began to feel a first insidious thrill of fear.

* * *

THE MAIDEN WORLD, Sindiel had explained, was functionally its own universe on certain metaphysical levels. The flow of elemental forces through focal nodes in its crust effectively gave the planet its own webway. With the correct triggers a portal could be opened from one place on the surface to another; even from, for example, the nearby meeting stone to the World Shrine itself. The triggers themselves were a jealously guarded secret kept by a select few. The band of 'Rangers' Sindiel claimed to have joined were among the few to hold forbidden knowledge about this and many other subtle paths in the greater webway.

'How long were you with these Ranger friends of yours?' Aez'ashya had asked.

'Years, half a lifetime it seemed. I started out believing they were free-thinkers, dangerous radicals treading the path of the outcast,' Sindiel replied, 'I was wrong.'

Sindiel's bitterness seemed to surprise even him. He had tried to explain what life on a claustrophobic craftworld was like with its myriad restrictions and unwritten laws. Resolving conflicts through confrontation, for example, was anathema in a society where everyone was guided through every step of their lives. Each life, every experience they had, was pigeonholed and mapped out almost from birth. Failure to conform to the constant subtle pressures to fit in with the other castaways led to censure in the form of a kind of living social death.

'No one understands that the seers have made us prisoners of the future. The only "path" they offer is rooted in fear of the past.'

'And you're going to show them they're wrong?' Kharbyr had mocked.

'I can't change the society of my craftworld and I don't want to either,' Sindiel replied seriously. 'I just know that it isn't how I want to live. The paths they follow are hardly like living at all.'

The newcomer was certainly clever. He hid himself on the far side of the meeting stone so that they could not observe him activating the gate. When he reappeared, the broken tooth of quartz was broken no longer, its upper part made whole again by the appearance of a grey, misty-looking portal. They clambered up to it and Sindiel was about to cross its wavering boundary when Morr clamped a gauntleted hand onto his shoulder.

'Unwise. You have led enemies to us once already. Do not imagine you will be permitted to do so again,' Morr said.

'Kill him now, Morr!' Xyriadh spat venomously. 'We don't need him any more.'

'Have you been inside the World Shrine before?' Sindiel squawked. 'I didn't think so. Well, I have! I can take you right to where you need to go.'

Morr did not relax his grip, but he did not raise his killing blade either.

'Also… before you decide to kill me later you might want to consider the value of the hidden webway paths I know about. Lord Yllithian would be displeased to lose access to those secrets, I should think.'

'No secret exists that the haemonculi can't tear from you,' said Xyriadh.

'Another telling argument in favour of not killing me

then. I must be alive for them to do so, presumably?'

'Not necessarily,' responded Xagor quietly. He was ignored. Morr suddenly released Sindiel, who rubbed his shoulder gratefully.

'Lead us there,' Morr said, 'and know that I am watching.'

Entering the portal was like and yet unlike entering the webway. The shifting walls were shadowy and indistinct. Out in the darkness beyond the twisting pathway there was a sense of vast presences lurking, as if huge beasts slept all around them just out of sight.

They followed the pallid silver of the path as it crooked and curved, Sindiel leading them silently past innumerable forks and branches. He had not lied, they would have never found their own way through the gleaming paths. The pale light they followed gradually grew stronger as they approached the core.

CHAPTER 8
THE HEART OF THE WORLD

THE WORLD SHRINE of Lileathanir was called Lil'esh Eldan Ay'Morai; 'Holy mountain of dawn's light first gleaming'. It lay thousands of kilometres away from the webway portal, marking the termination of a mystic spiral that girdled the entire planet. For the past several hours Laryin Sil Cadaiyth had been there trying to soothe the raging world spirit as it shuddered and rebelled in response to the incursion of outsiders. Laryin was young as eldar count such things, and she had never before experienced the level of discord that now flowed through the psychic conduits of her world. In concord with the disturbed spirits she herself felt angry and frightened.

The holy mountain was safe, the World Shrine buried at its roots beneath hundreds of metres of solid rock. A small honour guard had remained there but most of the clan warriors had gone to help fight against the invaders. Those that had been left behind were surly and nervous as they stood fingering their double-handed clanths of star-metal and their laser lances. They whispered among themselves with mind speech when they thought Laryin wasn't paying attention. Dark Kin! The soulthieves had come to Lileathanir!

Many of the guards had secretly laughed at the wardens' dire warnings of the Dark Kin, and questioned the necessity for their endless vigil. Keeping watch for a threat unseen in living memory seemed foolish to the clan warriors. Life was hard enough on a maiden world and the Exodites chose to live there for precisely that reason. It bred a people shorn of temptation by the day-to-day necessities of survival, the kind of society which set little value on ancient lore.

The World Shrine itself was, of course, naturalistic in its aspect. Living rock formed its sweeping buttresses and towering pillars, water rushed from cracks in the stone to form glittering waterfalls and deep, clear pools. The ancients had seen fit to seed tiny crystal suns in the upper reaches of the shrine so living things grew there too, from simple ferns and mosses to miniature Eloh trees and gloryvine. The rich veins of minerals and fantastic crystal growths that glittered along the walls added a fey sheen to the pools and grottoes.

Here and there polished sections of stone were carved with runes that pulsed with their own phosphorescent witch-light. Laryin moved from one to another of these attempting to calm the spirits of the wild flowing through the holy mountain, singing to them quietly of love and harmony and the hope of better days to come. She welcomed the souls of her own kind that had been violently loosed into the world serpent by the coming of the Dark Kin, mourning their passing and weaving songs of their rebirth. She had felt death many times before, the cycle of life inevitably passed through death like the turning of a great wheel, but she found that this was different. Lives were being cut short, souls being snuffed out as the flame of war was carried into their land.

A discordant noise suddenly diverted her attention from her work. Something unusual had sounded over the gentle tinkling of water and the whispering susurration of mind-voices. Laryin looked about her and realised she was alone. The honour guards that had been nearby a moment ago had vanished. She wiped her hands on homespun robes as she looked around in momentary annoyance, expecting some adolescent prank. As she did so a wave of sickness began to spread through her, a creeping sensation of violation and horror.

Strange shadows were moving in the lower grotto, the imprint of their alien psyches invading her mind with the stench of their murderlust. An impossibility: the Children of Khaine had entered the sanctuary of Isha! She wanted to run, to cry out a warning to her unseen guards, but horror clogged her throat and bound her limbs in icy manacles. A nightmarish feeling pervaded the scene, as if the slightest sound from her would bring the sinister shadows to her hiding place.

The world serpent was roaring in her ears.

Unbridled now and roused further by the Children of Khaine it was manifesting into its Dragon aspect. The shrine trembled in sympathy and shook loose a shower of dust and stones from the ceiling that rattled down in a hard rain. The creeping shadows had reached the foot of the ramp that would lead them up to her. They paused for a moment during the tremor and then began to move up the ramp. Laryin's stifled voice finally loosed itself in an endless scream.

At that instant violence blossomed within the shrine like a physical punch to Laryin's guts. Hissing lines of ruby light raked the shadows as her hidden guards fired their lances. A whirling, half-naked she-devil charged into sight, leaping over the sweeping beams and running along the tips of stalagmites. A towering, one-eyed, automaton-like figure reared up suddenly beside one of the distracted lancers and killed him with a single sweep of its enormous blade. Laryin gasped as she felt the guard's soul flee his body and plunge headlong into the world serpent as if being cast into a rushing river. The flow of spirits was changed in that moment, uncounted souls becoming angrier, wilder as they understood that their sanctuary was under attack.

The shrine shook again with greater violence. Larger rocks clattered to the floor and caromed into pools. Two guardians ran forwards to fight the murderous cyclops with their energised clanths trailing lightning. They were cut down in turn by the figure's inexorable blade as though they were nothing more than children. The she-devil flung herself on a surviving lancer as he struggled to bring his unwieldy weapon to bear.

She took the luckless guardian in a lover's embrace, satiating her wild lust in ways Laryin witnessed with horrifying vividness through the psychic mirror of the world spirit.

Laryin's heart began to beat again and her limbs stirred. Her rational mind knew there was no escape, but her soul just wanted to flee. Part of her wanted to leap into the river of souls that flowed through the shrine and by destroying herself merge completely with it. She could not escape physically but she could rejoin her ancestors within the world spirit and escape the horrors of the material realm that way. She would dissolve into the greater gestalt until the wheel turned and she was born anew. It would take just one step from the ledge where she stood to fall to the sharp rocks below…

'No, no. Unacceptable,' a dry, frog-like voice said behind her. A sharp sting in her back flashed tendrils of fire through Laryin's body. Her treacherous limbs folded beneath her again but strong hands caught her before she could fall.

The Dragon's roar was in her ears, rising to a triumphant scream as it broke free.

SKIMMING HIGH ABOVE the cloud tops, Malixian was having to face up to some unpleasant facts – namely that they were the ones being chased. The Ninth Raptrex was being pushed inexorably in front of a solid wall of pterasaurs like a sailing ship running before a storm. His surviving hellions and Reavers skirmished and fenced with the leading edge of the mud dwellers when they got too close but Malixian simply couldn't afford to get entangled with the whole horde. His warriors had burned at least a hundred pterasaurs but the Exodites' numbers seemed to keep increasing.

Reports coming from the green hell below told a similar story; the tree huggers had brought their biggest animal friends out to play. Huge packs of carnosaurs had appeared and savagely attacked any-one they found on the ground. After the raid's initial successes further slave taking had become virtually impossible. By unspoken consent all elements of the raiding force were now either heading north to ren-dezvous with the ships or fighting their way back to the webway portal where they had first arrived.

Malixian told himself that there was no shame in declaring the raid over and its objectives complete. According to the plan he would have been moving to rendezvous with the ships by now anyway. Being pushed there still galled him on a deeply irrational level – the very level of himself that Malixian liked best. He crouched at the keel of his skeletal Raider, watching the trailing pterasaurs and muttering impre-cations. As such, he was well-placed to observe a change suddenly come over the Exodite horde.

A ripple passed through the pursuing ranks and they came to a halt, milling in confusion. Even Malixian felt a ghost of *something* changing despite his utterly atrophied sense of empathy. A few seconds later the wall of beating wings was suddenly slumping away as the pterasaurs folded their great pinions and dived for the forest below. A scalp-tingling sense of imminence hung across the world, as if it had paused and sucked in its breath for a primal scream.

Beneath Malixian's craft the leafy canopy was tossing like the sea in a storm. A great crack suddenly split the ground from east to west, leaping from horizon to horizon like a jagged black lightning bolt. Fire and stone shot skywards from the crack, followed by an expanding bubble of volcanic ash that came roiling out to engulf both land and sky. Static lightning flickered around the cloud as it raced forwards, swallowing the few grav craft near it even as they turned to try and flee.

Hissing rocks and lava scoured the skies with the deadly effectiveness of anti-air batteries. A house-sized boulder rose directly in front of Malixian's Raider. As it reached the top of its parabolic arc it hung there for a moment before slowly rolling over like a beaching whale and plummeting earthwards trailing sparks and fumes. Malixian sent his vessel scooting after it, falling like a leaf in its slipstream. At the last instant his craft pulled out of the dive and shot away to the north like an arrow.

THE HOLY MOUNTAIN groaned and shook beneath the fury of the unleashed world spirit. Morr had his klaive raised and was attempting to advance on Sindiel. The floor was pitching so violently that the towering incubus had to alternately brace himself and stagger forwards as if he were on the deck of a ship in a storm. The delay probably saved Sindiel's life.

'Wait! It's not too late! I can still get us out of here!' he yelled desperately.

'Explain!' the giant incubus roared above the thunder of shuddering rock all around them.

'I can use a temporary burrowing to enter the webway! There's a hidden path!'

'Don't be stupid! The world spirit will destroy us!' screamed Xyriadh.

'No,' Sindiel said with a guilty glance at the slender form slung over Xagor's shoulder. 'Not while we've got her.'

Phantasmal tendrils were beginning to manifest in the air, the opalescent strands questing blindly for the invaders. Instinctively they drew closer together around the unconscious worldsinger, either to protect her or be protected by her proximity. Cracks started spreading across the floor, slowly yawning open to reveal bottomless pits at their feet.

'What choice do we have?' shouted Sindiel. Without waiting for an answer he drew a small object from his cameleoline robes and cast it into the air. It hung there, turning slowly at head height, a multi-faceted spindle of caged wraithbone. Sindiel sang desperately to the thing as it spun, now slower, now faster, in time with his tune. A silver teardrop wavered into focus beneath it and expanded, seeming as fragile and insubstantial as a soap bubble.

'As good as it gets! Go!' shouted Sindiel and leapt into the temporary portal. One after another the others scrambled after him. Finally only Morr remained, his single eye glaring balefully around the desecrated shrine.

'Only the naïve try to forgive and forget!' he snarled to the raging spirits. He spat two more words before contemptuously turning his back and stepping through the portal. The portal vanished, leaving only the incubus's final words to resonate around the shrine like the tolling of a great bell.

'Arhra remembers.'

THE SHIPS OF the raiding force rode in low orbit over Lileathanir's terminator, their long, jagged hulls precisely bisecting the border of night and day as the maiden world turned. Yllithian had been observing the course of the raid from aboard the *Intemperate Angel* ever since his ships had slipped into the outer reaches of the system through a little-used gateway. Naturally he had heard nothing from his agents as yet, he would only know if they had succeeded if and when they returned to the ship.

The fleet's approach to the planet had been stealthy and silent. There were no signs of planetary defences or, worse yet, interfering craftworld eldar forces. Yllithian suspected that the alarm had gone out; a faint ripple detected in realspace shortly after they had emerged from the labyrinth dimension probably indicated a scout vessel fleeing back to its home craftworld with the news. That mattered little, the raid would be long over before the fools had finished debating and runecasting to determine if they should get involved.

Yllithian had heard that the craftworld eldar relied completely on seers to steer their destiny, forever trying to tighten the weave of fate toward some indeterminate future. If that were true they seldom chose to put themselves in the path of the true eldar. Perhaps they recognised a stronger destiny than their own.

The first ships had begun to dip into the atmosphere, rendezvousing with Raider-borne parties of kabalite warriors in the thin upper air. Freshly taken slaves were transferred aboard, comparatively few for a raid of this size but that was only to be expected when hunting Exodites. Yllithian received reports that several large avians were being taken aboard the Ninth Raptrex ships so presumably Malixian was happy, or at least he would be if he weren't mired in some huge aerial battle kilometres away from the rendezvous coordinates...

Yllithian focused more closely on the sensory feeds emanating from Malixian's personal forces. He saw the seemingly endless waves of fliers pursuing them with crystal clarity. He saw, also, the flapping pterasaurs suddenly retreat moments before the world seemingly went insane. A dozen sullen glows kindled on the nightside of the planet within as many minutes, while on the dayside huge plumes of volcanic ash could be seen climbing into the stratosphere. Fantastic cloud formations coiled around the eruptions forming concentric rings where storm-force winds were kindling. Calls for retrieval from the surface doubled and redoubled, sending more ships hurrying down into the ash-choked upper gulfs.

Riding high above it all, Nyos Yllithian watched the spreading chaos with clinical detachment. He wondered only whether it indicated success or failure on the part of his agents.

A FLICKER OF otherworldly chill and suddenly Morr was standing beside the others. Something immediately seemed very wrong. Mist swirled knee-deep around them and the familiar tube-like passages of the webway were nowhere to be seen. Instead a deep pall of gloom clustered closely in all directions as if they stood in the midst of a dark forest. Straining eyes vaguely hinted at paler shapes like trees or pillars that seemed to lie just beyond their immediate circle of vision.

Xyriadh was screaming at Sindiel, Kharbyr was squabbling with Xagor and Aez'ashya was egging on both pairs even-handedly.

'Silence,' ordered Morr, cutting through the arguments. The incubus turned his implacable one-eyed gaze on Sindiel.

'Explain.'

'We – ah, we may be a little off course.'

'Lost!' shouted Xyriadh. 'The whelp has only lost us beyond the veil!'

'We're in the webway,' Sindiel insisted, 'but we've become caught in deformed strata of it.'

'In other words we're lost!'

'No–'

'Can you point which way to go?

'No–'

'Then we're lost!'

A savage, hopeless howl, more felt than heard, keened distantly in the darkness. It was taken up by other strange voices, some closer, some farther off.

'Fun as this is, we had better get moving,' Aez'ashya observed. 'No point in making it easy to find us.'

'Which way?'

'I doubt it matters. Anywhere but here.'

A great weariness quickly stole upon them as they

slogged through the clinging mist. The unholy thrill of She Who Thirsts was strong in this twilight realm and it inexorably sucked the strength from their limbs. The desolate howls seemed to grow more distant but the pale tree-pillars never seemed to get any closer. After a few minutes it became apparent that the mysterious shapes were too irregular to be pillars or trees. Kharbyr swore that they moved whenever he looked away – twisting, changing position, creeping closer by the time he looked back.

Eventually Kharbyr glimpsed something that stopped him looking out into the gloom altogether. He grew quiet for a time and concentrated on putting one fog-shrouded foot in front of another. Xagor walked beside him carrying the worldsinger. Kharbyr's previous attempts to murder the wrack in the Aviaries seemed all but forgotten in their current peril.

'Observed something, yes?

'I thought it was lightning out there at first, echoes of it or something, and that's why it moved. It isn't lightning.'

'Sharp eyes. Good, good. Sharp eyes see what?'

'More like whirlwinds made out of little motes of light.'

Xagor pondered this for a moment. He shifted the recumbent worldsinger over his shoulder into a more comfortable position, though he seemed to barely notice her slight weight.

'Souls being taken,' he concluded flatly.

Kharbyr nodded unhappily. 'They all seemed to connect at one point off in the distance. I was afraid to look at what was there.'

'Wise, I think.'

After a timeless period, obstacles began to rise in the gloom before them. Jutting translucent shards were scattered chaotically about the mist cape, initially no more than waist high but rearing up to tower overhead as they travelled further. The shards looked solid, but there was something glistening and gelatinous about their consistency that made them suggestive of mucus.

The howling keened behind them, still distant but getting closer. Something was following their trail. By common consent they silently pushed onwards through the shard-ruins looking for a means of escape or, failing that, somewhere to make a stand.

'What is this place?' Aez'ashya asked.

Sindiel, eager to re-establish his credentials with his new allies, rushed to answer. 'I think we're in the region of a destroyed gate. We're looking at fragments of the wreckage.'

'Wreckage? The gate must have been huge.'

'No, there are still traces of the psychic wardings in place on most of the pieces. Trapped warp energy accretes around them and forms something like cysts in the contextual reality of the–'

'Vyril?' Xyriadh said in disbelief, stepping closer to the nearest glistening obelisk.

Beneath its surface a humanoid shape moved sluggishly. Vyril's shaven head turned to face them with his mouth open in a silent scream. His limbs thrashed slowly as if he were drowning in clear gel, one hand stretched imploringly towards Xyriadh. The female warrior reached forwards to grasp his hand without hesitation.

'Unwise,' said Morr as he knocked her hand aside. She spun with an oath to strike at the incubus but found her wrist caught in a vice-like grip. 'Observe,' Morr intoned calmly and turned her back to face Vyril.

Looking now she saw the hand extended to her was in reality a grasping claw, and the face behind it was not that of Vyril but some saucer-eyed, fang-mouthed daemon. Xyriadh recoiled in horror. An agonised howl from close by broke into insane, tittering laughter.

'Bravo, that was a close-run thing,' said a new voice. Morr released Xyriadh and spun to face the newcomer with blade at the ready. A slight figure dressed in motley garments stepped into sight.

'Oh, put away your over-sized cutlery, incubus, no one is dining just yet,' the stranger responded airily.

The individual had the appearance of an eldar dressed in an archaic-looking doublet and hose made with so many variegated colours that from a distance they appeared to be grey. A black and white domino mask hid the upper part of his face, but the mouth and chin beneath it looked full and mobile. Right now the full mouth was grinning impudently with its red lips and white teeth.

'Do not toy with me, apparition,' Morr rumbled dangerously.

'You are a fierce one, aren't you?' The newcomer's accent was strange, neither a High Commorrite cant nor Low Commorrite vulgarity, but somewhere between the two. 'Well, fear not, I bear no weapons and I bear you no ill intent either, I was merely surprised to see fellow travellers abroad... and why, hello, Sindiel! I didn't see you lurking back there!'

Morr wheeled to glare at Sindiel. The grey figure took advantage of the momentary distraction to slip over to where Xagor and Kharbyr stood. The motley-clad individual smoothly disappeared and reappeared as if he had moved in one extraordinarily long step. The domino mask peered at the worldsinger slung over Xagor's shoulder appraisingly.

'You've been busy, I see. Recent events make a lot more sense with that little piece of information. Thank you.'

Morr snarled and whirled his deadly blade through the grey figure in a decapitating arc. His target seemed only to bow courteously and razor-edged destruction flew through the space where it had been.

'I'd love to dance, Morr, really I would, but we simply don't have the time,'

'Identify this... individual, Sindiel,' Morr said.

'Pish posh, I can speak for myself. I'm the one that gave Sindiel the little bauble that brought you here.'

'It's true,' admitted Sindiel. 'Linthis introduced us.'

'And how is Linthis, hmm?' asked the grey one brightly. 'In fact how are all your little woodland friends, Sindiel? Did they help you find what you were looking for? I'm thinking that your new friends indicate that they did not.'

'No. Linthis was just as hollow and full of lies as all the rest,' Sindiel said quietly.

'Enough,' said Morr. 'Assist us or leave at once.'

'Oh, I'll help you. Don't you worry. The world-singer can't go back and you can't stay here, so you all have to go forwards along the path you've made for yourselves...'

The motley one paused and stood on tiptoe for a moment, hand cupped to one ear in a pantomime of listening. The howling burst forth anew, and monstrously misshapen silhouettes could be glimpsed sliding through the translucent blocks all around them.

'...There will be a small price, of course,' the grey figure continued. 'Tiresome, but there are certain customs and traditions that have to be obeyed.'

'Name it!' cried Sindiel, 'whatever it is!'

'Three guesses.'

'The worldsinger?'

'No, no, I already told you I can't take her back. Guess again.'

'...Me?' Sindiel swallowed.

The motley one laughed musically in response. 'Oh you don't understand the joke at all, do you? Poor Sindiel. Last try.'

'The... spiritstones,' Sindiel said, sounding ashamed.

'Yes! I'll be taking the spiritstones you filched from Corallyon, Linthis and Belth, I think. Their souls deserve a better fate than to be taken to the dark city, I'll see that they get home.'

Kharbyr, Aez'ashya and Morr, with more or less reluctance respectively, gave over the spiritstones they had taken from the Rangers slain on Lileathanir. The small gems shone with a lambent amethyst glow as they were brought out, the trapped souls within them seeming to blaze like stars in the darkness. The grey-clad one tucked them away carefully and the gloom rushed in again.

'You have your payment,' Morr rumbled. 'Now do your part. Lead us to Commorragh with no more games.'

'Lead you? Oh no, I never lead anyone anywhere – quite the reverse in fact. I simply make you aware of the paths available,. Whether you go down them or not is up to you. We'll discuss this further at another time, but time is pressing so listen to this. *Lil'ashya nois shaa oum.*'

The words rang in the air like clear bells. Enraged, inhuman voices burst out all around the agents, giving tongue to their frustration at their prey slipping away. The landscape of mist and translucent shards dissolved around them and was replaced by a timeless sensation of falling. A merciless black void rushed in from all sides to engulf them, dragging them deeper into the undertow.

They found themselves crouching upon a bleak heath that sloped downwards into roiling clouds of rust-red smog. Tilted shapes towered out of the smog like skeletal titans, the remains of machines or buildings long since rotted to their bare framework. Wan, ruddy light filtered from above, the pervasive smog turning the sky into an upturned bowl of blood.

'Iron Thorn,' breathed Morr, making the name sound like a curse or a prayer.

CHAPTER 9
PACTS AND BARGAINS

'Author of evil, unknown till thy revolt! These acts of hateful strife – hateful to all save thee and thy foul adherents – disturb our most holy peace. How hast thou instilled thy malice into thousands? Those once upright and faithful are now proved false and all is despair.'

– The Broken King to Duke Vileth,
in Ursyllas's *Dispossessions*

THE RAIDING FORCES were returning from Lileathanir in triumph. The barbed, predatory ships raced one another exuberantly along the webway back to Commorragh. Their crews were drunk with bloodletting and cruelty and their holds were packed to bursting with slaves, raw materials, exotic lifeforms and other plunder for the ever-hungry markets of the eternal city.

Of course a raid returning to Commorragh was always a triumph for the leaders of an expedition, or at least it was depicted as such if it could be viewed as anything short of the most unmitigated disaster. A failed raid reflected badly on every participant from top to bottom and so there were no failed raids. Everything from exaggerations to outright lies were expected and frankly encouraged on the part of all involved from the lowliest returning warriors to the highest commanding archons.

In the final measurement Malixian had escaped with his crop of captured beasts and his life intact so he was more-or-less happy. Xelian would be equally pleased with the selection of dangerous carnosaurs and over-sized invertebrates procured from the reeking jungles of the maiden world for her arena bouts. Even the lesser archons would make a small profit in addition to enhancing their reputation by participating. The value of eldar slaves, even regressionists like Exodites, far outweighed that of any lesser species by a hundred to one. That would go some way to compensating for the relative paucity of the harvest from such a large undertaking.

Soon enough the crews coming off the sleek and deadly ships would tell outrageous stories of their vicious cunning and derring-do. As the vessels disgorged their cargoes of bewildered slaves onto Ashkeri Talon tales would be told of the bloody massacres and mass suicides that were the reason that so few had been taken alive. By the time the wretched Exodites were being hauled onto the auction blocks in the flesh markets lurid stories would be circulating about the annihilation of their maiden world home.

Yllithian on the other hand, pacing impatiently on the elegantly appointed bridge of the *Intemperate Angel*, was distinctly displeased by the outcome of the raid. His agents had failed to return or give any other indication of their survival so their mission had evidently failed. That was a minor disaster in its own right and annoying if not entirely unanticipated. It was the continued absence of Kraillach's chief executioner that was proving unexpectedly problematic.

Without Morr to act as de facto head of the Realm Eternal the whole kabal was in danger of collapsing in on itself in a furore of backstabbing and politicking. The kabal's ships and warriors accompanying the raid were already showing signs of internal strife that boded ill for their return to Commorragh. Kraillach was in danger of revivifying as an archon without a kabal.

Beyond such entirely practical considerations Yllithian also needed to know just what had happened at the World Shrine so that he could ensure nothing could be traced back to him. There could be no disguising the unusually bitter fighting during the latter stages of the raid, nor the seemingly unleashed fury of the planet itself. The spontaneous eruption of dozens of volcanoes that filled the atmosphere with choking ash was bound to be an event worthy of note even among the jaded citizenry of Commorragh. The rakes and sybarites would soon turn their attention to other gossip but for the present Malixian's raid was bound to become a hot topic.

The causes of such an event would become the

object of much speculation over the days that followed, some of it accurate, some of it wildly fanciful.
The absence of Morr would be noted by some, perhaps connected by others and then the pieces would
begin to fall into place. As such Yllithian had every
desire to get ahead of any rumours and have his story
straight before the tyrant's spies became too interested in precisely what had happened on Lileathanir
and why. The failed mission should be easy enough
to cover up as long as Yllithian could reassure himself
that there were no inconveniently surviving witnesses.

Among all the many subtle resources at his command Yllithian could think of only one that might
pierce the veil and give him the knowledge he sought.
He ordered the helmsman to bring his ship up to full
speed and promised a rich reward if they were the first
to dock at Commorragh.

WITHIN THE DARK pits below the White Flames' palace Syiin was busily hurrying to complete his own
preparations before Archon Yllithian returned to the
city. His workbench was strewn with tools and com-
ponents that made a dully gleaming landscape over
the stained metal surface. The object of his attentions
rose in the midst of it all, a miniature palace above a
shanty town of cogs and wires.

He had taken the runic tetrahedron so generously
donated by the coven of The Black Descent and placed
it within a framework of four tiny suspensor units.
These in turn were held in place by an open egg-like
contrivance of slender struts and tubes. Four different trigger sensors, motion, pressure, heat and aural,

were suspended from the egg. Syiin had configured the sensors to trip if the master haemonculus Bellathonis were detected within five metres, easily close enough to ensure his annihilation. Once the sensors were tripped the suspensors acted as blunt fingers to make the movements necessary to open the gate. That had been the hardest part to pull off by far and now, after much cursing and spitting along the way, Syiin was rather proud of the results.

The distinctly sinister looking device Syiin had built was going to be concealed inside an altogether more innocuous container. With the correct inducement the gourmand at the Red House had yielded a full description of the jar retrieved from there previously by one of Bellathonis's wracks. Now, outwardly at least, its twin stood before Syiin. In this case the hide-wrapped vessel also concealed a tiny mimic field built into its base that would defeat all but the most careful examination of its contents. The very esoteric nature of the threat itself would evade most tell-tales and detectors better than molecular explosives or binary poisons ever could, and the mimic field would render it completely undetectable.

In many ways hiding the dark gate was the easy part. Persuading Bellathonis to actually accept the gift would be the real trick. Syiin was counting on the confusion of Yllithian's return to be the right moment to strike. The archon would be flushed with success and fully engaged with his sycophants for a time after his arrival. Bellathonis, on the other hand, would be anxiously awaiting word of the capture of a pure heart and expecting a message or package from Yllithian.

Syiin licked his thin lips and smiled, picturing Bellathonis lifting up the jar triumphantly and unstoppering its lid moments before he was obliterated. Would the master haemonculus have long enough to realise how thoroughly he had been duped? Syiin hoped so. He had tried to imagine a way to be present at Bellathonis's death but decided it was simply too risky. Syiin's presence would make Bellathonis even more suspicious than usual, and the... event itself might be dangerously unpredictable. He was going to have to console himself with reports after the fact, and perhaps a little pilgrimage to the scoured circle left by the activation of the gate at some later date.

And yet... He was still concerned about the calibration of the triggering sensors. During his last meeting with Malixian and Bellathonis he'd had the presence of mind to surreptitiously read Bellathonis's vital signs and file them away for just such an eventuality. The problem was that haemonculi altered their bodies so frequently that such information had a distinctly limited shelf-life.

Syiin could broaden the parameters used by the sensors to account for a potential shift in morphology on Bellathonis's part, but that would increase the chances of accidental activation before the gate reached its intended target. As it stood Syiin had left the sensors tightly bound to Bellathonis's last recorded imprint, but he kept wondering uncomfortably about the wisdom of that decision.

Ideally he would have liked another reading to cross-reference against, but Bellathonis was nowhere to be found at present. The master haemonculus had vanished the moment Yllithian and Malixian left the city. He was not on the ships – Syiin's spies had been certain of that. No, Bellathonis was almost certainly hidden away in his secret laboratory in the catacombs, probably not far from Syiin's own domain. The thought enraged him and he snarled at one of his wracks, bringing the masked apprentice running over.

'What news of the raid?' Syiin demanded. 'How soon will the Lord Yllithian return?'

'The wager-slaves are giving the best odds for a return within the next six hours, master,' the wrack rasped after a moment. 'They say a signal announcing Malixian's triumph was received late yesterday. Crowds are gathering at Ashkeri Talon to welcome back the fleet.'

'To beg for scraps more like, and to do their utmost to separate our brave warriors from their new-found wealth before it can be brought into the city,' Syiin murmured cynically as he peered through a magnifying lens to make a final adjustment.

'Master?' the wrack asked in confusion.

'Nothing, wait there a moment,' Syiin grunted and turned his attention back to the device, tapping one of his tools meditatively. Wherever Bellathonis might be right now he would soon need to be on hand to welcome Malixian back to the Aviaries. Syiin could send the jar there and be fairly certain it would cross paths with the target, but would the triggers prove reliable? Without another reading it was impossible to be sure, but the attempt had to be made now when Bellathonis resurfaced – any later might be too late.

Syiin lifted the delicate egg-shaped mechanism

carefully by its uppermost struts. He moved it slowly over the mouth of the jar before lowering it inside. The framework expanded with a soft pneumatic hiss as it touched the bottom of the jar so that the device was snugly cradled within. He stoppered the jar, binding the lid in place with hide thongs. Finally he released a breath he didn't realise he'd been holding.

'Take six of your brethren and ensure this jar is delivered to the Aviaries of Malixian the Mad, intact and unopened, for the immediate attention of the master haemonculus Bellathonis,' Syiin said crisply.

The wrack gingerly lifted the jar with both hands. He was ignorant of the exact contents but he was fearful after seeing the care his master took with it. He started to leave the low-domed workroom but Syiin's voice stopped him.

'Wait,' the haemonculus said and stood from his bench, muttering. 'This won't do it, won't do it at all,' he said before raising his voice to the wrack. 'Are you aware of the thirteen foundations of vengeance? Could you name each of them to me?'

'Of course, master, though I've heard many more than thirteen maxims claimed as foundations.'

'Yes, yes, but are you aware of the one pertaining to individual as opposed to collective effort?'

The masked wrack appeared to ponder for a moment. 'If you want something attending to satisfactorily you must attend to it yourself?' came his eventual reply.

'Just so,' said Syiin. 'And as such I'm coming with you.'

* * *

BELLATHONIS HAD BEGUN surreptitiously moving some of his most vital pieces of equipment out of the Aviaries several weeks prior to the raid on Lileathanir. Deliveries were quietly redirected and devices disassembled to be placed into 'storage', ostensibly to make room for examining one of the giant pterasaurs Malixian planned to bring back from the maiden world. The normally cramped confines of the tower occupied by Bellathonis and his wracks were beginning to feel distinctly roomy.

Bellathonis had waited until Malixian and the bulk of the Ninth Raptrex were safely out of the way before moving the most sensitive items. His new torture-laboratories were buried within a honeycomb of hidden chambers and secret ways that touched on the White Flames' territory in High Commorragh. The main area comprised a wide, high chamber with rows of cells along one dripping wall and a cracked floor. Very safe, very secure – if lacking a little of the ambience of the old tower.

Bellathonis stood in the echoing space directing his wracks as they wheeled in examination tables and resurrection sarcophagi, lugged around jars filled with chemicals and less readily identifiable substances, connected cables to energy generators and strung lights. The master haemonculi ensured two sarcophagi were hoisted into place overlooking the examination table at the centre of the chamber. Archon Yllithian had indicated that Archon Kraillach would also need to be revivified when the Exodite catalyst was secured. This was in addition to resurrecting the mysterious and long-dead worthy that was the true subject of their bargain.

At any rate Yllithian appeared to think it was a mystery and thus far Bellathonis had chosen not to disabuse him of that notion. The master haemonculus took personal charge of the installation of a very special experiment in one of the smaller cells. Here three nerve-meshed subjects were hung together from chains to form a triptych of pain. A waist-high plinth installed before them accepted a special case Bellathonis carried there personally. The haemonculus locked the cylindrical case into place before releasing catches along its sides. Inside was the head of Angevere, quite Bellathonis's favourite experiment ever since he had procured it from Yllithian in exchange for his services.

The triple voice sighed in unison as Bellathonis connected the subject's speech centres to the crone to enable her to speak. Yllithian had told him that Angevere had spoken to him with her mind before he decapitated her. Bellathonis had little desire to have to speak to the creature mind-to-mind and so had devised this method to give her a voice. Pain receptors connected to the subjects also enabled the crone to be excruciated by proxy, a convenient arrangement that did not risk any lasting damage. All-in-all Bellathonis was extremely pleased with the experiment and considering its more general application.

'There we are, Angevere,' he fondly told the disembodied head, 'your new home.'

'*It is no different from the last,*' the subject's voices chorused petulantly. '*Promises were made – restitution and release.*'

'All in good time, my dear lady, all in good time.'

'Then what is it you wish of me? You only give me voice to torment me and question me, what is it you want this time?'

Bellathonis twisted a dial on the plinth that elicited a shout of agony from the dangling triptych of pain-proxies. The sound rang loudly in the narrow cell before it was instantly cut off as he twisted the dial back again.

'Firstly a little reminder to watch your manners, Angevere,' Bellathonis murmured as he worked. 'You are a guest and in no position to make demands of your host.' He fussed over the neural connections for several more minutes, fastidiously adjusting them until he was entirely satisfied.

'There. Now, tell me some more about this El'Uriaq character our mutual friend Yllithian is so keen to revivify.'

'What is there to tell? He was a great lord, he opposed Vect. He was destroyed.'

'Oh, you can do better than that,' Bellathonis said, sending the slightest trickle of energy through the pain amplifier.

'Sssaaahhhh! He was prince! A general! An intriguer! The pacts he made outlive him still, the oaths he took transcend life or death. Even now some in Commorragh still owe secret allegiance to the old emperor of Shaa-dom, and are bound to him forever by the most terrible vows!'

'Interesting, it certainly provides insight as to why the tyrant was so keen to be rid of him. Secret allies count for nothing while you're dead. Very well, then tell me more about this Dysjunction you claim to have predicted for Yllithian.'

'Dysjunction lay along the path from El'Uriaq's return, inescapable. When I beheld the sign of it I was suddenly afraid of the future the visionary sought. The visionary fears not to tear the universe asunder to make his ideal into a reality. I too would see Vect destroyed to avenge Shaa-dom but the price… the price…'

A hesitant rap at the cell door brought a frown of annoyance to Bellathonis's sharp features. He turned and plucked open the door to reveal one of his wrack servants almost literally crawling on his belly.

'Forgive me, Master!' The wrack wrung his hands contritely. 'But we have received word that the raiding force has returned. The Archon Yllithian has already disembarked and is on his way here!'

'Coming here?' Bellathonis said with some surprise. 'That is… uncharacteristically direct for one usually so circumspect. Hmm.'

He emerged from the cell and shut the door firmly behind him. Two possibilities suggested themselves to the master haemonculus. Either the mission had been a success and Yllithian was bringing the world-singer directly to him, or the plan had miscarried in some fashion and he wished to discuss alternatives.

Neither possibility seemed to adequately explain Yllithian taking the risk and inconvenience of a personal visit. Time was short. Malixian would not be much slower than Yllithian in disembarking, although transporting his prizes to the Aviaries should delay him for a while. Bellathonis hoped that he could deal with Yllithian quickly enough to return to the Aviaries before Malixian thought to wonder where his pet haemonculus had disappeared to. On consideration Bellathonis decided that it would be best to treat Yllithian's impending arrival as good news. He clapped his hands for attention, freezing the scurrying wracks in their tracks.

'Places everyone, we must be completely ready to begin the procedure when the noble archon arrives!'

The cavern-like chamber dissolved into a frenzy of activity.

ONCE ASDRUBAEL VECT had brought the great port-city of Commorragh to heel in his coup over the noble houses he turned his attention to conquering all the other sub-realms in the webway. Most fought and were crushed by the seemingly inexhaustible resources of the dark city. Some capitulated, thinking themselves able to buy their safety at the price of their freedom. Some realms were so wracked with their own internal dissension and disasters that they, at first, welcomed their invaders as saviours. Many sub-realms were found to be already dead, their inhabitants killed in the Fall or the privations that followed after it. Iron Thorn was one of the latter.

It appeared that the inhabitants of what came to be called Iron Thorn had been few and found themselves completely trapped in their sub-realm by the cataclysmic damage inflicted on the labyrinth dimension during the Fall. Some emergency or critical shortage of resources had forced them to take desperate measures to ensure their survival. In the end, either by accident or design, they had introduced a form of aggressively replicating nano-machinery into the environment of their sub-realm.

By the time the portals to Iron Thorn had been forced open by Vect's forces no one could tell how long the tiny machines had been at work or what their original purpose had really been. It was only apparent that some weird strain of accelerated machine evolution had occurred over the centuries in Iron Thorn. The practical outcome was that the nano-machines had gradually converted almost everything in the sub-realm to a skeletal framework of pure iron. The original inhabitants of Iron Thorn had survived after a fashion, although the curious machine half-life they exhibited bore little resemblance to that of their previous forms.

The tyrant's warriors had ruthlessly hunted down the ferric abominations and exterminated them wherever they could be found, but the altered beings had steadfastly refused to remain dead. Eventually Vect had nominally incorporated the sub-realm into Commorragh simply to save face and sent his frustrated archons elsewhere to conquer more rewarding lands. Iron Thorn had become another of the many strange sub-realms of Commorragh that were generally shunned by the citizens of the eternal city. Expeditions that entered such places were normally well-armed and of short duration.

Sindiel was horrified by the tale. 'Aren't we at risk, too?' he asked.

'Only if we remain here for a thousand years or so,' laughed Aez'ashya. 'This isn't the glass plague we're talking about.'

'The glass what?'

Sindiel was even more horrified by the tale of

Jalaxlar the sculptor and his vitrifying helix.

'Gates must exist connecting this sub-realm to the corespur,' Xyriadh said. 'For that matter, where's the gate we arrived from? There's nothing here.'

Morr ignored her and addressed Xagor instead. The worldsinger looked fragile in the wrack's arms. The ruddy light of Iron Thorn cast a pinkish pallor over her features and touched fire from the blonde hair that spilled over Xagor's shoulder in a river of gold.

'Is your prisoner intact, wrack?'

'Yes, yes. Without consciousness, but most healthy.'

'Why not waken her?' Kharbyr said with a leer. 'She should be enjoying the scenery with the rest of us.'

'No, no. The Master said to bring her to him unknowing of her fate,' Xagor said emphatically. Kharbyr mouthed a silent 'oh' and said nothing more on the matter.

'We will proceed to the gate,' Morr rumbled, swinging his blade up onto his shoulder.

'And which way would that be?' Sindiel called to Morr's retreating back as he tramped off into the red smog. The incubus did not respond and they hurried to catch up with him before he vanished from sight.

YLLITHIAN TOOK MORE than an hour to reach Bellathonis's hidden lab, having first to accept the plaudits of the common dross that flocked to Ashkeri Talon on hearing news of a returning raid. The word had spread with the wildfire speed of all gossip. There were cheering crowds of wretched, toothless slaves completely covering the docking talon before Yllithian's vessel even lowered its boarding ramps.

Standing proud and haughty at the prow of his personal barque Yllithian drifted slowly over the teeming masses. Inner turmoil clawed at him with the desire to depart directly but it was equally important for his face to be seen and for his personal legend to be enhanced just a little more. There goes the archon of the White Flames, they would say, see how powerful he's become.

Some of the wretches had seized several of their number and hung them up by the wrists to impress the archons with their fervour. As Yllithian passed metal-bladed whips were being used on them, beginning at the shins and working their way upwards. The surging crowd revelled in the crude display of pain and cruelty, shouting curses at the victims and laughing at their agonised screams. Blood and viscera flew, splattering from the barque's protective shields like rain.

It was a gratifying diversion certainly, but of little direct benefit to his current machinations. After a cursory parade, Yllithian's barque swept away towards his palace in the spires of High Commorragh at its highest speed.

He came to Bellathonis's new laboratory by hidden ways from the White Flames' palace, negotiating the labyrinth alone as he would trust none of his own retinue with the secret. The laboratory chamber was much changed from his last visitation. Harsh lights had been strung from the walls that seemed to emphasise rather than relieve the gloom. Two crystal-fronted sarcophagi dangled from the unseen ceiling by chains. The equipment and stores piled along the walls had a sinister aspect to them, some gleam of sharp edges and oiled metal that spoke of cutting and crushing. A table had been placed in the exact centre of the chamber, scrubbed and horrid in its clinical simplicity.

Bellathonis was waiting for him, the haemonculus's wrack servants lined up behind him like a class of nervous schoolchildren. He took one look at Yllithian and then dismissed the wracks so that they could continue their work. It was self-evident that the worldsinger was not present and the mission had been a failure. The master haemonculus bowed deeply.

'Archon Yllithian, I am honoured that you grace us with your presence. My apologies that we are not fully prepared to receive the catalyst at this time.'

Yllithian accepted the proffered bait graciously. 'Fear not, Bellathonis, I am not fully prepared to supply it at this time,' he said.

Bellathonis's brows rose marginally at the news. 'Oh? How regrettable. I presume that the mission was unsuccessful?'

'That is… undetermined as yet,' Yllithian glanced around at the masked wracks now hard at work. 'I would speak to you of this matter privately. Not to impugn the trustworthiness of your minions, but I trust no one.'

'Of course, my archon, very wise.' Bellathonis clapped his hands and the wracks fled from the chamber at once. Yllithian waited until they were alone before he spoke again.

'Something unusual certainly occurred on Lileath-anir, it's my belief that the World Shrine was breached by my agents.' He went on to tell Bellathonis briefly about the raid and its outcome. The haemonculus stroked his long chin and nodded in sympathy.

'Very disappointing. No agents and no worldsinger either. I see your dilemma but I confess myself at a loss as to how I can assist you in resolving it.'

'I do not require your assistance, Bellathonis, I require access to Angevere. Don't insult my intelligence by denying that you've perfected a way of interrogating her by now.'

Bellathonis made the briefest of internal calculations before replying. It would be unwise to let Yllithian know how much of his plan had already been revealed by Angevere. 'Of course, my archon, it was an intriguing diversion. I have had little opportunity to exercise the array but it is fully functional. If you would be so kind as to step this way...'

The crone and her three pain-proxies were unchanged from when Bellathonis had left them earlier. Yllithian took in the arrangement with a single glance as he stepped into the cell with the haemonculus.

'I'm afraid I still fail to understand,' said Bellathonis. 'A warp-dabbler casts runes or cards or bones to tell the future. This one has no hands.'

'I'm surprised at you, Bellathonis,' Yllithian admonished. 'Had you pursued your arcane studies sufficiently you would know those are only safeguards – psychic fuses, if you will. Angevere can peep beyond the veil all on her own with sufficient inducement.'

Bellathonis smiled grimly. 'Ordinarily the existence

of safeguards implies an increased risk is incurred by their absence.'

'A risk I'm prepared to take under the circumstances. I need to know what happened, whether any of the agents survived and, if so, where they are now. If you can offer me an alternate method of securing that information I'm quite prepared to consider it.'

Bellathonis remained silent. Like all Commorrites he had a deep repugnance spiced with a mixture of terrible fascination and atavistic fear when it came to the warp-touched. All eldar possessed an intuitive psychic ability; it built their first golden empire and almost destroyed them by creating She Who Thirsts. Most in Commorragh used drugs and intensive training to seal off the dangerous psychic conduits in their minds. Some broke Vect's laws by embracing their gifts and flirting with them briefly – typically to the great woe of anyone in the vicinity – before being consumed by She Who Thirsts, if Vect's castigators didn't find them first. Only a bare few survived long enough to gain any true insight. Yllithian chose to interpret Bellathonis's silence as acquiescence.

'As I thought, you see that this is the only way. Activate your device and proceed with the questioning at once.'

Bellathonis nodded and made the appropriate connections. The hanging bodies of the pain-proxies stirred as if they were ruffled by a spectral breeze.

'Yllithian, my slayer, returns to ask forgiveness? Bellathonis and I were just – Saasaaaaahhhhh!!!!'

Yllithian glared at Bellathonis darkly. 'Apologies,

my archon, momentary feedback on the regulator,' Bellathonis said contritely.

Yllithian turned his attention back to the crone. 'Tell me what occurred in the World Shrine on Lile-athanir during our recent raid,' he ordered.

'I cannot see beyond these walls, your own blade ensured that.'

Yllithian gestured to Bellathonis and triple-voiced shrieks ripped through the narrow cell. He gestured again and the nerve-tearing flow of pain was halted.

'Do not lie to me, Angevere, the knowledge is there. All you must do is reach out for it. Consider for a while the momentary dangers of this small thing when weighed against an eternity of pain.'

Bellathonis moved the regulator to its highest setting and waited with Yllithian while the resultant screams became hoarse.

CHAPTER 10
ESCAPING DEATH

MORR FORGED A straight path towards the highest of the skeletal shapes rearing up out of the red murk of Iron Thorn. His sabatons left deep imprints in the scrubby grass as though he were crunching through hoarfrost and tiny puffs of rust billowed up from each footfall. Xyriadh pushed ahead to scout, followed by Aez'ashya and Kharbyr. Eventually Morr seemed content to fall back to act as rearguard with Sindiel while Xagor continued to carry the worldsinger.

The smog became denser, filling their mouths and noses with a sharp metallic tang as they pushed deeper into it. The ground levelled out and they began to pass irregularly jutting shapes that might once have been trees and bushes, now rendered into corroded masses of thorn-like spars. Occasionally the ground trembled and they heard distant gurgling sounds somewhere beneath their feet as though they were walking on the belly of some giant. Rhythmic hammering drifted into their hearing and faded out again, only to return redoubled a few minutes later.

They slithered through the choking smog as quickly and quietly as they could but they soon spotted silent watchers paralleling their course. Luminous eyes glittered in the red mist and weirdly distorted shadows limped in their wake. The strange denizens of Iron Thorn were gathering, one by one at first and then by the dozen. The presence of life seemed to draw them forth, the hated biological excrescence within their realm pulling them in like white blood cells fighting an infection. Fear was keeping them at bay for the present but their unthinkable lust to destroy would soon overcome it. The remade half-life of Iron Thorn had long since learned to hate the biologicals that invaded their realm.

Kharbyr suspected that the fear that held the shuffling multitude in check was not inspired by their scurrying quarry but by mightier hunters that were abroad somewhere in the sub-realm. He couldn't shake the feeling that some vast, cool intellect perceived their progress, something that brought with it a twisted sense of wrongness that resonated through the whole sub-realm. The presence felt close, as if its chill breath were already on the nape of their necks. Its chosen instruments had found the spoor and were remorselessly closing in on their prey. It might be better to take his own life now, rather than wait to be hunted down and torn apart by iron fingers…

Aez'ashya reached over and slapped Kharbyr around the side of the head. 'Focus!' she hissed. 'We aren't caught yet.' He realised with a shock that the blade gripped in his hand had been creeping towards his throat, seemingly of its own volition. He gazed in confusion at his companions and wondered how many of them were being assailed by insidious thoughts that were not their own.

Ahead of them the vague distortion that marked Xyriadh's progress slithered to an abrupt halt.

'No way forwards,' Xyriadh's voice hissed anxiously in their ears.

'Explain,' rumbled Morr.

'Dozens of those things up ahead, maybe hundreds. They're blocking our path forwards.'

'What are they doing?' asked Sindiel.

'Standing there, swaying. I'd say they were singing, but there's no sound coming out.'

'They are emitting ultrasonics intended to disrupt our cognitive processes,' said Morr.

'Or they're supplicating the master of this place and begging to be given our souls,' suggested Aez'ashya. 'Either way I honestly don't think we're going to be friends.'

The sense of wrongness wafted more strongly around them, like a foetid breeze. The smog rippled and the harsh lines of the skeletal ruins wavered for a moment before solidifying into subtly altered shapes. The rhythmic hammering rose in intensity, now accompanied by an endless squealing as of great wheels turning. The hunters were coming.

'Defensive positions,' Morr ordered. 'Get out of the open.'

The towering incubus took the lead and battered his

way into a row of ferric shrubs that resembled spear-pointed railings more than vegetation. The strange entities in the mist seemed emboldened by cornering their prey and quickly pushed in closer to surround them. As they did so, the cursed dead of Iron Thorn became clearly visible for the first time.

They were hollow, mannequin-like forms that mocked life with their mismatched limbs and patch-work bodies. A hideous, sighing moan could be heard from the things as they pressed in closer around the makeshift fortress. Step by step the agents moved back into a defensive ring, confronting the creatures across bulwarks of rusting, twisted iron. With nowhere else to go they halted and readied themselves for the inev-itable attack.

'From peril, into peril they flee, carrying with them the pure heart. Into the lands of the lost they travel, hunted by many enemies. The Masquerade follows their every move but will not aid them, save with a clean end if they should fall.'

The temperature in the cell had dipped sharply as the head of Angevere began to speak through its pain-proxies. Glittering hoarfrost bloomed up the walls and a chill breeze had sprung seemingly from nowhere. Yllithian paced in the narrow confines of the cell, a sign of frustration he seldom permitted himself.

'This talk about lands of the lost tells us nothing!' he snapped. 'Where can they be found now? How can the pure heart be secured?'

The crone's voice changed, distorted into a coarse grumble. *'What is "now"? From one moment to the next is a skipping stone, our lives mere ripples intersecting.'* The voice changed to a high, nasal whine. *'They remake their future with every movement. The pure heart! Everything around it is distorted, a mirror. Hatred begets hatred!'*

Bellathonis looked at Yllithian questioningly. The haemonculus did not look frightened, but seemed intensely wary and curious. This sort of warp-babble was entirely outside his experience and Yllithian's own studies extended more to control and manipulation than interpretation… Yllithian stopped pacing and cursed himself for his own ignorance.

AT SOME UNHEARD signal the thornlings suddenly attacked. Four wedges of them pushed their way through the barriers in a flailing mass. Hinged blade-arms thrashed and peg-toothed jaws snapped as the horde rushed in. They were so closely packed that they resembled rust-coloured worms as they squeezed through the breaches in the iron hedge.

Morr's blade swept ruin through them with hurricane force, hurling about heads and limbs as if they were confetti. Aez'ashya's knives wove a deadly web, quickly piling up a drift of flopping, clattering bodies around her feet. Kharbyr lashed out wildly at the tide of iron limbs threatening to engulf them, Sindiel and Xyriadh fought desperately with knives and pistols, their rifles rendered useless at such close quarters. Xagor crouched in the centre protecting his prisoner as if his life depended on it, which in point of fact it did.

The thornlings were quick and strong but they made awkward fighters. More often than not their own numbers impeded them in the confined space.

Nonetheless if they felt pain or fatigue they did not show it, and their extremities had a disturbing tendency to continue attacking mindlessly even once they had been separated from their owners. Sindiel and Xyriadh soon began to busy themselves by grabbing severed clockwork limbs and tossing them outside the improvised barricade.

The rust-red tide suddenly ebbed away, stumbling back from the relentless blades of Morr and Aez'ashya. The survivors rallied amid the newly created junkheaps and began refitting lost limbs to shattered stumps, their cold and unblinking eyes lit with the promise of renewed violence. Morr watched them for a few seconds before hefting his blade and striding out to confront the half-made horde.

'Allow them no chance to recover,' he said simply.

Aez'ashya needed no second invitation and leapt forwards to add her knives again to the devastating arcs carved by Morr's klaive. The others followed more slowly, kicking away the limbless torsos and chattering skulls left in Morr and Aez'ashya's wake. The surviving thornlings limped away into the choking smog to escape the merciless assault, suddenly seeming more like living creatures for an instant as they fled. The ground shook and gurgled beneath their feet in impotent protest.

'Ha!' spat Aez'ashya. 'Not so–'

Something big and fast came hurtling out of the murk and leapt straight at Morr. Spike-studded wheels tore at him as he was borne backwards, knocking his great blade from his grasp. The thing was a chimerical offspring of predatory cat and cycle, its piston-like fore and hind limbs twisted to hold scythed wheels beneath a curving armoured back. Another machine roared in and tried to sideswipe Aez'ashya but the nimble wych was too quick to be caught by its blades, somersaulting over the machine at the last moment. Xyriadh ran out of the path of a third set of eye-lights, chased by chattering trails of solid slugs that stitched through the earth at her feet.

Morr was wrestling with the beast machine that had pinned him, holding its madly spinning fore-wheel away from his body. Bloodstone tusks on the incubus's helm suddenly spat a pulse of ruddy energy into the guts of the machine that struck sparks and flame from its innards. He twisted and threw the thing aside with a mighty heave, sending it crashing into the ground where it lay with wheels spinning feebly. Eye-lights stabbed through the murk as the rest of the hunting pack came roaring back around for another attack.

Aez'ashya immediately turned and sprinted away from the scant protection of her comrades. The beast machines swung aside to run down the fleeing figure, dirt spraying from their hind wheels as they accelerated after her. She dodged aside from their whirling spikes at the last instant, slapping one palm down on a machine as she vaulted over it. The machine was spinning around to chase her when the device she had attached to it detonated. Lightning burst from it, enveloping its entire body in crackling skeins of electricity. Fat blue sparks flew and the beast machine toppled over helplessly. Its companions slewed aside and vanished into the all-enveloping red smog with a despairing shriek.

'Haywire grenade,' Aez'ashya said with a wicked grin. 'These have to be some of the stupidest ideas for death machines I've ever seen. What use is something that can't stop without falling over?'

Morr bent and retrieved his klaive. His armour was dented and scored in a dozen places but he showed no signs of harm, save perhaps for moving a little more stiffly than normal.

'We must continue. This resistance is intended to keep us from the gate,' he said.

'VESLYIN THE ANCHORITE said that time has no meaning in the Sea of Souls. The warp can give glimpses of the past, the future and the present because within it they are all one. According to him when dealing with its denizens trying to attribute events to a timeframe in terms of past, present or future, is pointless – they must be addressed in terms of absolute actions.

'With that in mind tell me this, crone, where will my agents carrying the pure heart re-enter the city?'

'They will return in triumph at the feet of giants if they return at all. The guardians of the gate must be defeated first, and that outcome is unknowable.'

THE GATE TOWERED five stories high, gnarled metal pillars supported a thick lintel inset with wraithbone. It was open, the portal's mirrored surface clearly visible shimmering between the uprights. It was also guarded. A squad of Black Heart kabalite warriors lounged insouciantly in front of the gate with their Raider craft landed so that it restricted entry. They were heavily armed and despite their relaxed demeanour they looked ready to spring into action at the first sign of trouble.

'Vect's curs, what a coincidence,' Xyriadh said when she concluded her scouting report. 'Do you think they're here on our account?'

'Unlikely,' replied Morr. 'They guard the gate to prevent the denizens of Iron Thorn troubling the city.'

'Why even bother keeping it open at all?' Sindiel asked. 'There's nothing here!'

His naïveté prompted a laugh from the towering incubus, a short cough of levity that burst and then swiftly vanished like a bubble emerging from tar.

'You have much to learn of our ways, foundling,' Morr said. 'On this occasion I shall instruct you. The gate remains open because this sub-realm belongs to the tyrant. If it were closed he could no longer claim to dominate it as he does all the others. Some of the other sub-realms make this one seem a pleasure garden. Vect lays claim to them all. They are territory, and territory within the webway is finite.'

Sindiel blinked, slightly rocked by the incubus's intimidating declamation.

'Why not simply guard the other side then?' the renegade ventured. 'That would be safer than risking it out here, surely?'

'Truly you have much to learn,' Morr intoned and said no more.

'The risk is the whole point, Sindiel,' Aez'ashya whispered conspiratorially. 'If there were no risk they wouldn't stay on guard at all, they'd go and find something more exciting to do. They probably haven't even been ordered to guard the gate, they're just here because they feel it needs doing and they think that doing it might win them some favour.'

Sindiel's mind whirled at the thought of such ill discipline.

'Can't we just wait until they wander off then?' he asked.

'Could be an hour, could be a week. We don't have the time to wait,' Xyriadh said with an air of finality.

'We lack the strength for a direct assault. We must employ subterfuge,' Morr said. 'Sindiel, Xyriadh, move forward to hidden positions with sight lines to the Raider crew. Kharbyr and Aez'ashya will accompany me. Xagor will remain here with the prisoner.'

'What's the plan?' asked Xyriadh.

'We will approach them and negotiate,' Morr replied.

'And what happens when they've decided to kill us because we're so weak that we tried to negotiate?'

'We will already be close enough that their considerable advantage in ranged weaponry will be negated.'

The incubus hefted his klaive on to his shoulder, the single eye in his blank-faced helm glaring around at them in challenge. Sindiel and Xyriadh obediently took up their rifles and crept off towards the gate.

BELLATHONIS CROUCHED UNCOMFORTABLY on the open deck of a dart-like Venom grav craft as it hurtled through Low Commorragh carrying him back to his tower in the Aviaries. Fascinating as it had been to witness Yllithian at work, it had delayed Bellathonis's departure to an almost critical degree. In the end he'd had to leave Yllithian alone with some basic instructions on how to operate the array, make his apologies and leave.

It went against every instinct for a haemonculus to leave one of the uninitiated to conduct their own procedures, let alone using experimental equipment, but self-preservation had to come first. Yllithian's description of the raid made Bellathonis fear that Malixian might be returning in less than ideal humour. Under those circumstances attracting questions about Bellathonis's own whereabouts and activities could prove decidedly fatal.

Slipstream clawed at him as the Venom dipped between domes and needle-pointed antennae to intersect with the Beryl Gate on the Grand Canal. This close to them a trick of the wardings made it appear as if the Aviaries really existed in a pocket of reality just beyond their thick, oily membrane instead of an unguessable distance away in a different part of the webway. Bellathonis's hire-pilot descended slowly to the gate, finding it open and guarded by a handful of warriors eagerly awaiting Malixian's return.

Arriving at his tower Bellathonis found another craft already docked there, a Raider bearing the icon of the White Flames. Absurdly he thought for a moment that Yllithian had arrived ahead of him, but that was impossible. He entered his tower warily but was greeted by his two door-grotesques with the usual slobbering joy he would expect from the slab-muscled brutes. One of his wracks, Menetis, stood wringing his hands in the entry hall.

'Master! Guests arrived in your absence!' Menetis bleated. A nasty stab of concern shot through Bellathonis's mind.

'I hope you were not indiscreet enough to mention

I was not at home?' Bellathonis said gently.

'No! Master, no! They were told only that you were busy and could not be disturbed. They elected to wait until you became available.'

'Ah, I see. And just who might these guests be, hmm? An essential point that I note you've so far failed to communicate.'

Menetis looked horrified. 'The haemonculus Syiin and seven of his attending wracks are here, master!' he blurted. Bellathonis smiled disconcertingly at that news.

'Is he really? That's extremely interesting,' the master haemonculus purred. He pondered for a moment. 'Tell Syiin he may come and see me in my private quarters presently if he'll forbear bringing his attendants with him, we do have some private matters to discuss.'

SINDIEL COULD COUNT ten warriors through the scope of his needle rifle. They wore black armour burnished to a high gloss with functional-looking spikes and blades protruding from shoulders and elbows. They had caught some wretched denizen of the sub-realm and were amusing themselves by blasting parts off it then waiting for it to struggle back to a semblance of life before blasting it to pieces again.

The warriors tensed as they sighted Morr and his two companions moving forwards. Ten weapon muzzles simultaneously rose to aim at them as they approached. Morr held up an open hand to show he intended no violence and kept coming. This was the danger point. Morr had to lead his party blithely across the open ground and gamble that the warriors' curiosity would stay their hand. Sindiel's role was to target the Raider's gunner, Xyriadh was covering the steersman perched at the back of the ornate craft from another position a hundred metres away.

The gunner was a difficult shot because the target was half-hidden behind curving prow armour and pintle-mounted weapon. Sindiel carefully placed a targeting reticule on the gunner's face and then zoomed the scope view out so that he could see Morr and the others. A mental impulse was all it would take to fire the needle rifle and send its deadly shard of poison hurtling across the intervening space. He slowed his breathing and waited for the signal.

Morr tramped forwards, relentlessly closing the distance. One of the warriors lowered his rifle and raised one hand in an obvious 'stop' gesture while the incubus and his two companions were still a dozen metres away. Sindiel readied himself, his world focusing down to the pinpoint of the targeting reticule on his target. The progress of Morr and the others receded to barely float at the edge of his consciousness.

His concentration was shattered when a powerful grip unexpectedly fastened onto his ankle.

'Ah, Syiin, how good to see you.'

'Bellathonis. You appear in the very prime of health.'

The two haemonculi regarded each other for a moment across the riotous clutter of Bellathonis's private quarters. Tables, divans and bureaus peeked from beneath a thick layer of spilled vellum sheets, metal models, jars, vials, surgical tools and open tomes. Syiin's gaze was particularly searching as he looked at the taller master haemonculus. It was Bellathonis that first spoke again to break the silence.

'So to what do I owe the pleasure, Syiin? I regret that I've been unavailable of late but my Archon Malixian is a demanding one. At this very moment I should be making preparations for his triumphant return.'

'Yes. Your archon, Malixian,' Syiin mused. 'I wonder how he would respond to the knowledge that he's being cuckolded by another? One with ambitions that would bring terrible woes down upon the city.'

Bellathonis appeared genuinely taken aback by the statement. What had Syiin's determined digging turned up? He answered carefully.

'If such a theoretical situation were to occur I'm sure the consequences would be dire, an effect that I'm equally sure would be felt in various reciprocating quarters.'

'You think that Yllithian would avenge you?' Syiin said with the delighted incredulity normally reserved for the antics of particularly naïve children. 'I'm afraid you're sadly mistaken in that regard, he is a far from sentimental individual. I suspect he would be too concerned about the tyrant's castigators sniffing around.'

Silence descended again between the two. Bellathonis turned away and idly rummaged through some small objects scattered on a lacquered bureau. At the motion a row of carnivorous plants in a trough nearby began to writhe and snap hungrily. The tall haemonculus quietly admonished them for their greediness.

'Hmm. I think that you're just fishing again, Syiin,' Bellathonis said eventually, 'and that you have no intention of going to Malixian with what you have, which is nothing. If you had some evidence of these outrageous claims you would present it rather than try to blackmail me with vague innuendos.'

Syiin licked his lips. Bellathonis was right, he had nothing he could take to Malixian that would prove his claims. That didn't really matter, the accusation alone could make heads roll, but in the absence of damning proof Syiin was just as likely to feel the edge of a blade as Bellathonis.

Fortunately it didn't matter.

Syiin had all the readings he needed. Just by looking at his wasp-waisted frame Syiin could tell that Bellathonis had indeed altered himself, eliminating several organs and reconfiguring others. With the pulse echo, thermal imprint and voice patterns he now had it would be simplicity itself to set the triggers on the dark gate to precisely fit Bellathonis's profile. The jar with its concealed payload lay below with his wracks. He would configure the triggering devices to Bellathonis's bio-signs and leave one of his wracks behind to ensure delivery once the trap was properly set. Bellathonis was as good as dead.

'You know I can't escape the feeling that you don't really have Yllithian's best interests at heart, Syiin,' Bellathonis said mildly.

It was too much for Syiin, and his thin veil of civility dropped suddenly. 'He wants to spawn an abomination and you want to help him!' Syiin snarled.

'You don't think that perhaps your own jealousy

and ambition are clouding your judgement?'

'No! If you'd read the lore of The Black Descent as you should you'd know the risks yourself! My judgement is not the one in question here!'

'Oh, I really think it is,' said Bellathonis softly and held up a shining object in his hand.

The reflected light was impossibly bright. It seemed to expand before Syiin's eyes until it was as if he stood on a limitless white plain. White light blinded his eyes, shining through him from a hundred different directions at once, inside and out. Only then did he realise the source of it and begin to scream.

Bellathonis dropped the Shattershard in his hand and quickly ground it beneath his heel, the thick crystal readily breaking into pieces with a brittle crack. Syiin quite literally shattered at the same moment, his hunchbacked shape flying apart with a flash. The jagged chunks winked out of existence as whatever was left of Syiin was sent to a thousand different places at once by the collapsing fragments of the dimensional mirror. Bellathonis found it all very satisfactory and clapped his long-fingered hands in delight.

'There now, what did I tell you?' Bellathonis smiled to the empty chamber. 'Your judgement was impaired.'

'THAT'S CLOSE ENOUGH,' the warrior said. Kharbyr caught the slight catch in the way he said it that told him that the speaker wasn't the leader of the group. He wondered which one it was, smart enough to lead but not strong enough to do so openly.

'By what right do you bar our passage?' Morr rumbled.

'Nothing leaves Iron Thorn by order of the supreme overlord, Asdrubael Vect, may he forever reign eternal,' came the arrogant reply.

Morr took another step forwards and lowered his klaive to rest point first on the ground as though it wearied him to carry it further.

'I had heard no such ordinance before we came here,' the incubus stated flatly.

'I told you!' shrilled Aez'ashya, turning on him viciously. 'You wouldn't listen and now we're stuck here!' The lithe succubus contemptuously turned her back and stormed away, coincidentally bringing herself closer to the knot of warriors. Kharbyr scurried after her, solicitously trying to calm the fiery wych. She struck at him, forcing him to skip back in the direction of the warriors to avoid the blow. The kabalite warriors' levelled weapons were wavering and lowering a little as they enjoyed the unfolding drama.

The Raider's gunner suddenly cried out and clapped both hands to his face before toppling out of sight. The warriors were distracted for barely a heartbeat and their reaction was instantaneous – they opened fire in unison.

In the fraction of a second they had available Kharbyr and Aez'ashya had already closed the range to arm's length, hurling themselves into the warriors' midst to impede their fire. Poison-laced splinters ricocheted from Morr's armour as he strode forward and gutted a warrior who was struggling to bring a cumbersome dark lance to bear. The Raider's steersman was pitched over the side of his craft by another unseen shot just as two warriors ran to mount it. The warriors had to leap aside to avoid the Raider as it swung out of control and buried itself nose-first in the dirt.

Surprised and suddenly cornered by a rush of foes at close quarters the kabalite warriors leapt into the counter-attack without hesitation. They still outnumbered their enemies and they were battle-hardened, well-armed and better armoured. It was a dreadful miscalculation.

Morr's blade rose and fell with the mechanical precision of a metronome, carving straight through parrying splinter rifles and the armoured limbs that held them. Any warrior that jumped out of the path of the rampaging incubus found the blades of Aez'ashya and Kharbyr at their backs. One warrior that succeeded in gaining enough space to bring his own rifle to bear for a shot found the unseen snipers waiting to pick him off.

In a few seconds only a handful of the Black Heart warriors remained standing. They broke and fled for the open portal behind them. Kharbyr moved to pursue but staggered and clamped one hand over his blood-drenched thigh when he tried. Aez'ashya was able to bring down one warrior with a thrown knife but the remaining two vanished into the shimmering surface like divers entering a pool.

A combat blade had opened a wound in Kharbyr's leg that had gone unnoticed in the rush of combat. It proved to be as long as his hand and more than finger-deep. He struggled to apply a heal patch over it while Aez'ashya stood by coolly watching him, offering no help and waiting to see if he would collapse from blood loss. Morr moved around methodically dispatching the injured kabalites in silence.

First Xyriadh came up, then Xagor joined them carrying the prisoner, and eventually they were followed by a limping, pasty-faced Sindiel.

'You shot prematurely!' accused Xyriadh as soon as Sindiel was in sight. 'And then didn't shoot again at all. It's your fault two of them escaped!'

'It isn't my fault!' whined Sindiel. 'One of those… dead things must have followed us, it attacked me! I was fighting for my life!' His lightly armoured boot was indeed scratched and scored as if lifeless hands had clawed at it. Morr's single eye gazed at him for moment, judging… measuring.

'Unfortunate,' he said eventually. 'Get onto the Raider. I will steer us to the corespur.'

'I'll steer,' said Xyriadh. 'It might be best if the one doing the steering had some depth perception.'

The Raider was undamaged and slowly rose in response to Xyriadh's tentative movements of the tiller. The agents climbed aboard and Xyriadh smoothly brought the grav-craft around before sending it shooting through the gate.

The transition took only a second and they emerged thankfully into the familiar light of the *Ilmaea*. The very air around the Raider seemed cold and bright after the ruddy smog of Iron Thorn. An obsidian roadway stretched away below them supported on either hand by angular towers. Each tower was topped by a titanic statue, blank faced and highly stylised. Each statue's pose was subtly different but all of them held vast oval mirrors over the roadway.

'I know this place,' said Kharbyr weakly. 'It's the Eidolons' Pavane, we're on the tip of Ghulen spur.'

'I can't see the warriors that ran from us,' Sindiel reported as the Raider sped along the roadway. Their own images raced with them, caught and reflected in the giants' mirrors above. A mismatched and beaten group they looked too, stained and weary as they fled through the darkness aboard their stolen craft.

'Don't look at the reflections for too long,' Kharbyr admonished. 'That can be... bad.'

Xyriadh shouted a warning as a swirl of specks came into view, racing along the obsidian strip towards them. Hellions, at least a score of them, were arrowing towards the lone Raider. They split and drifted to either side of the craft to look over its occupants from beyond weapons range. Seemingly satisfied that there was sport to be had, the pack rejoined in the Raider's wake, curving around and rapidly accelerating to pursue it.

'How long to reach Nightsound Ghulen?' called Aez'ashya. The sloping tiers of that outer district could offer some shelter from the hellion's slashing attacks.

'Too long, they'll overhaul us before we're halfway there,' said Kharbyr resignedly.

'Sindiel, Xyriadh, take up your rifles,' said Morr. 'Kharbyr will steer.'

'And just what are you going to do?' Aez'ashya asked impertinently.

'I will bring the forward weapon to bear.'

'They aren't stupid enough to come in at us from that angle,' Kharbyr snorted. 'That's half the reason they're chasing us instead of going head on.'

'No matter,' Morr said. He took hold of the dark lance at the prow and, with a heave, tore it free from its mounting.

Sindiel and Xyriadh took down a hellion each before the others realised they were being fired on. Morr's dark lance shots were horribly inaccurate but they kept the rest of the pack more concerned with dodging and weaving than returning fire. However, once a few more of their compatriots were punched off their skyboards by Sindiel and Xyriadh's accurate rifle fire the survivors decided their best chances, in fact, lay in shooting back.

Splinters ricocheted wildly from the Raider's stern as the hellions opened fire, driving Sindiel and Xyriadh back into the scant cover available behind the stern. Morr resolutely stood his ground and reduced a hellion to a flaring cinder with a lucky bolt of entropic energy. One of the Raider's engines coughed and died immediately afterwards, causing the speeding grav-craft to lurch alarmingly.

'Can't take much more of this!' Kharbyr yelled.

'Set it down,' answered Morr.

'Madness!' shouted Xyriadh. 'They'll tear us apart on the ground!'

'We cannot risk a crash. Set it down. Now'

The Raider slid inelegantly down onto the obsidian road, trailing sparks and flames as its drives failed at the last moment and it kissed the smooth black stone. The hellion pack shot past, decelerating rapidly as they readied their hellglaives for the altogether more satisfactory work of chopping off heads and limbs. The agents abandoned the dubious cover of their wrecked grav-vehicle and made a rush for the nearest tower a hundred metres away. The dozen or so surviving hellions swirled around and came plummeting down to finish off their fleeing prey.

To Kharbyr, falling ever further behind as he tried to force his stiffened leg to function, the rush to the tower looked futile. He knew just how quickly a fighter on a skyboard could run down some fool on foot, he'd done it himself on many occasions.

He turned and flourished his long-barrelled pistol, preparing to sell himself as dearly as he could. He could see every detail of the hellions as they dived towards him; he could make out the wild faces yelling and screaming with pleasure, the pieced-together array of armour and stolen finery that marked the gang as being real steeple-scum, opportunistic scavengers of the kind he had run with in his formative years. He felt bitterness that he was fated to fall beneath the blades of such sky-pirates now.

Kharbyr was thus perfectly placed to witness streams of splinter cannon fire suddenly rip into the diving hellions from above. Riders were pulped like ripe fruit and skyboards detonated under the vicious barrage. The hellions broke off their attack and scattered like windblown leaves.

Three Raiders packed full of kabalite warriors dropped into view, sliding smoothly down to surround the fugitives. Kharbyr recognised the sigil on their prows with an almost palpable sense of relief. They were in the custody of the White Flames.

CHAPTER 11
THE COURT OF THE BROKEN KING

LARYIN AWOKE IN a strange, cold place. Returning consciousness brought hard on its heels the realisation of just where she was, and pure panic flooded in after that. She wanted to curl in on herself and vanish, flee, die, anything but remain where she was. She could do none of these things. She was restrained by hard circles that cut into her flesh, chaining her like an animal. A darkly melodious voice spoke from close by.

'Physical restraints are always best,' the voice said. 'We could simply disable motor control and trap you inside your own unresponsive body, but that is less effective. The primitive part of the brain, the animal part which I'm sure you're well-acquainted with, my dear, thrives on the physical sensation. Internalised horror has a disappointing passivity to it, although that too has its place, of course. Now open your eyes or I shall be forced to cut away the lids, and I do not wish to do that. If you open your eyes now I promise no harm will come to you.'

Laryin's eyes flew open of their own volition and she found herself staring into a face from nightmare. Dead white porcelain skin stretched tautly over a pointed nose and chin before flaring out to accommodate gaunt, lined cheeks and a high brow. The cheeks were dimpled to accommodate an impossibly shark-like smile. The eyes seemed completely black, visible only by a few vagrant glitters of reflected light that escaped their hungry depths.

'There now,' the nightmarish face said. 'I am Master Bellathonis and you are in my charge. We are going to make such miracles, you and I, that our names shall be remembered in future aeons. You shall become like your precious Isha at my hands, my dear, giving birth to new life.'

The face stared pointedly upwards for a moment and Laryin followed his gaze with trepidation. Above her hung what looked like two cabinets with glass fronts to them. One was empty, the other held a red-raw skeleton covered with scraps of flesh, like something left behind by scavengers. The dead held no intrinsic terrors for Laryin; death was part of the cycle of life. However when the dead thing moved and flopped its raw-meat hands against the crystal she shrieked like a terrified infant, earning a dark chuckle from Bellathonis.

'Well, strictly speaking we'll be giving rebirth to old life I suppose,' he admitted. 'But don't mind Archon Kraillach there. He's been very impatient for us to begin.'

Laryin's lips worked as she struggled to find her voice. The haemonculus turned his gaze back to her.

'You have a question, my dear?' he asked with disarming politeness, 'or a request? Ask and it shall be yours, saving for your freedom I'm afraid.'

'Why are you doing this?' she asked with child-like naïveté. Any but the blackest heart would have been crushed by her innocence. Bellathonis was possessed of the very blackest of hearts and even his reply was surprisingly kindly-sounding.

'A range of reasons to go with a range of individuals, my dear: some wish to restore lost glories, some wish to alter the status quo, some wish to bring harm to others. In my case I do it for the most personal of reasons – because I like it and because I can.'

YLLITHIAN LOOKED AROUND at the survivors from the Lileathanir mission with mixed emotions after hearing their report. He'd had them brought to a hidden annex close to Bellathonis's newly installed laboratory. Once the haemonculus's wracks had hurried off carrying the captive worldsinger, Yllithian had arrived to listen while the agents were having their injuries tended. What they told him gave him a great deal to ponder. He clinically studied the knot of emotions inside, surgically stripping them down to their essentials.

There was certainly relief, mostly relief that he no longer had to take account of the agents' whereabouts or concern himself about who might have captured them. There was pride too that his plan had succeeded and secured the catalyst the master haemonculus required. Despite the manifold obstacles the unlikely group had overcome them successfully, although in many cases it sounded more by luck than judgment. Unfortunately underpinning that feeling of relief was a growing sense of concern.

It was not so much concern about the destruction wrought on the maiden world that troubled him. Yllithian cared not one whit that the desecration of the World Shrine on Lileathanir had induced convulsions in the planet that probably set its carefully metered development back by thousands of years. Truth be told he took some pride in having a hand in that atrocity, albeit unrecognised. No, what was concerning him was the scale of forces that had been unleashed seemingly so readily. For the first time Yllithian was gaining some real sense of the power that Bellathonis was intent on tapping into for the purpose of rebirthing El'Uriaq. Again the crone's warnings of Dysjunction came back to haunt him. Hearing the stories from Lileathanir made it suddenly seem a lot more possible.

Yllithian sighed inwardly, keeping his face carefully neutral. One of the thirteen foundations of vengeance equated to 'once committed, do not fear the blade'. Yllithian himself had berated his allies on the need to wield the biggest weapons they could find without hesitation, yet now he found he hesitated. He sought after something to distract himself from the thought, a niggling piece of the puzzle that had been incongruous at the time.

'And what of this individual that helped you in the webway?' Yllithian asked. 'They witnessed you carrying off the worldsinger and yet they live. Why so? Who are they?'

'I don't know his name, my archon,' Sindiel replied promptly, lingering over the honorific as if tasting something for the first time. 'I don't even know if it's a he or a she, really; the Rangers knew it. When they talked about it, which wasn't often, they called it Motley, as if that said everything you needed to know about it.'

Yllithian fought with the urge to strike the renegade. The easy familiarity he spoke with and his professed ignorance were insults a kabalite would have suffered grievously for. Yllithian quelled his feelings carefully before responding. The whelp was fresh and it was not the proper time to begin his re-education.

'I shall make enquiries from sources that may prove more educational,' he said acidly. 'For the present it is my belief that we must proceed with the next phase of my plan immediately. Between this Motley character and the guards that escaped you in Iron Thorn we must assume that the tyrant has heard of your mission by now.

'Therefore we must act before Vect can start imagining what uses we might have for a captive worldsinger. He need only demand her as tribute and the whole scheme is ruined. In order to prevent the plan being further compromised it's my intention to use the group of you for this next phase. With the exception of Xyriadh you are not of my kabal and I cannot compel you to go on what will certainly be another dangerous mission, but know that your perseverance will be repaid a thousandfold should you succeed.'

Yllithian paused and looked around at the agents levelly before continuing. 'Also know that if you refuse to go you will earn my eternal displeasure.' Morr was the first to break the resulting pall of silence.

'When will Archon Kraillach be restored?' he said.

'Bellathonis tells me that he cannot begin the process until the second phase of the plan is completed.'

'And what does that entail?' Sindiel asked, earning himself a sharp look from Yllithian.

'The recovery of a relic,' Morr said, 'from a highly dangerous place. That is all you need to know.'

'Just so,' said Yllithian smoothly. 'Preparations have been made that will ensure your success. There is no cause for delay.'

'I will go,' Morr said immediately, to Yllithian's surprise.

'In your case you might better serve your archon by ensuring the Realm Eternal doesn't tear itself apart in your continued absence.'

'Unnecessary. I will issue orders to my brothers in Kraillach's service and they will keep the peace until I return with my archon restored.'

One by one the others assented to go: Xyriadh out of loyalty, Aez'ashya out of curiosity, Sindiel and the rest out of fear of Yllithian's displeasure.

'Very well then.' Yllithian gestured and his guards brought forward a slim black case. He opened it to reveal a row of silver amulets. Each comprised a simple chain holding a smooth gem in an ornate, clawed mounting. Soft inner lights swam in the depths of the gems and they exuded the unmistakable allure of captured souls.

'Spiritstones…' Sindiel whispered in dismay.

'Just so,' replied Yllithian, openly enjoying the renegade's discomfort before shutting the case with a snap. 'Attuned so that their contents will mask your presence and completely protect you from the… influences of the place where you must go. My guards will guide you to the appropriate portal as soon as you are fit to travel. Mind that you do not tarry here overlong.'

Yllithian swept out, leaving the case of amulets and a dozen kabalite trueborn to 'guide' the agents on the next part of their journey. He wondered briefly whether the half-finished amulets he was pressing into service would actually prove to be of any help whatsoever when put to the test. It was a gamble, only the latest in a succession of gambles he was being forced to make. He consoled himself that if the amulets only persuaded his agents to enter Shaa-dom by convincing them that they stood a chance of survival then they had served a substantial part of their purpose.

KRAILLACH STARED HUNGRILY down at the white form on the slab below him with his regrown eyes. His raw-meat hands grasped for her warmth but met only cold, unyielding crystal now fouled by his own pale blood. He sensed a thin etheric twist of life and energy emanating from her, squeezed out by her trepidation and discomfort.

Kraillach lapped thirstily at the psychic stream, aching for the full richness of life he could sense contained in the frail body below. In his weakened state it seemed like the promise of paradise lay there, a warm and sensuous ocean into which he ached to plunge and achieve rebirth. He beat his raw-meat fists uselessly against the crystal in frustration, croaking feeble imprecations. The black-clad haemonculus and his scurrying wrack servants paid him no heed.

'WHAT MADE ALL these scratches on the walls? They're everywhere.'

'Daemons. The archon of Talon Cyriix tried making a pact with daemons to help him overthrow the tyrant. The tables were turned when he got trapped in here with them.'

'That's… that's, gods, that's awful. Did everyone die?'

Aez'ashya snorted. 'Only the lucky ones.'

Sindiel absorbed that piece of information in silence. The worming passages they were following had seemed claustrophobic before and they felt doubly so now. He was starting to realise that the wisdom of Commorragh, such as it was, was entirely communicated through grisly tales of failed plots and successful ones, incautious leaders and vengeful families. Their lore was to be found in a dark tapestry of plots and counter-plots that had been weaving through the city for ten thousand years.

He had been doing his best to befriend Aez'ashya. Initially it had been out of sheer cupidity. No eldar female he'd ever met was as alive and passionate as she was and it kindled a feeling in him he'd never encountered before – the desire to possess something and deny it to all others. Aez'ashya knowingly welcomed his attentions, getting seemingly endless pleasure out of alternately encouraging him and mocking his virginal awkwardness. That had bothered Sindiel at first until he noticed that she acted in almost exactly the same way towards any male, including the hard-faced youth, Kharbyr, and the terrifying incubus, Morr. She assiduously ignored the ugly servant that hung around with Kharbyr as if he were beneath her attention, which was entirely possible given the way the servant grovelled to her all the time.

Aez'ashya was a mine of information on the realities of living in the dark city and seemed to actively enjoy educating Sindiel. However he was beginning to find all of her answers about Commorragh quite predictably coloured by an underlying ethos.

When he asked why they didn't use a portal or a flyer to reach Talon Cyriix she'd laughed at him. 'If we want everyone in the city to know where we're going there'd be easier ways to announce it. Yllithian's enemies would try to interfere with us just on principle. All craft leaving the White Flames' fortress are watched and all portals are guarded, so we walk. That's just the way it is.'

That's just the way it is. Even the rich and powerful had to live like hunted animals, because they truly were hunted by those with less power than themselves. The entire hierarchy of the dark city seethed constantly as those on top repressed those below, while those below rebelled in every fashion they could.

Aez'ashya's personality was as smooth and as impenetrable as a river-smoothed stone. She apparently lived entirely in the moment with no thoughts of the future beyond the immediate consequences of her actions, and that only in a limited sense. As best Sindiel could tell she was motivated by a kind of restlessness that would culminate in her sticking knives in people if she drummed her heels for too long. She was constantly looking for the next fix of adrenaline. Sindiel's attraction to her had begun to fade but he still found he liked her.

'So… this place where we're going now, it's supposed to be worse than here?'

'Much worse. They say that after Vect wrecked Shaadom the daemons never left it.'

THERE WAS A breathless moment of cold and then a rush of sultry heat. Yllithian's agents found themselves standing at the edge of a thoroughfare. Blackened flagstones lay beneath their feet and the twisted remnants of trees and statues clawed at the roiling skies. Warp-taint hung heavy in the air and reality itself had a sickly, greasy feel to it. The horizon was lit by unearthly fires and flakes of ash drifted in the air.

Kharbyr could barely make out the shell the protective amulet cast about him, it was a faint sheen that barely flickered on the edge of perception and failed to engender much confidence. He looked around at the others and found them all glancing around nervously with the exception of Morr. He seemed as imperturbable as ever regardless of the freakishness of his environment.

'The palace of El'Uriaq lies at the heart of the conflagration,' the incubus rumbled. 'We must move swiftly before our arrival is noticed.'

'Do we have anything even resembling a plan?' asked Sindiel with shaky levity.

'Get to the palace without being torn apart by daemons, after that we wing it,' Aez'ashya told him sweetly.

Their course was not hard to set; the invisible heat of the breach beat upon their faces even at a distance, and the eternal fires lit their way. The group made their way cautiously along ruined thoroughfares and boulevards trying to balance speed and stealth. The way became progressively more difficult as they moved forwards, and they increasingly had to backtrack from rubble-choked streets as they sought a clear path. The ravaged city appeared to be deserted but the sensation of being watched remained unshakeable.

Xyriadh was the first to spot one of the soulless. It was a wretchedly emaciated figure squatting on the curb ahead of them, arms locked around knees and rocking gently.

It raised its face at their approach, its luminous, hungry eyes searching hopelessly, slack jaw working mindlessly. It could sense a presence nearby but did not seem able to perceive them properly. It whined in frustration as it cast about seeking the souls it could feel nearby. They edged around the creature and moved onwards with many backward glances from Sindiel.

'That's what happens if your soul is taken by… Her… isn't it?' he whispered to Aez'ashya.

'If you're lucky,' she replied. 'That one must have had some shred of intelligence left to it. Most don't have so much self-possession.'

Sindiel shuddered. At the edge of his consciousness he could sense a dull, keening wail that seemed
caught forever on the verge of rising to a shriek. His
sense of vulnerability constantly left him weak at the
knees as he trudged onwards. He couldn't shake the
idea from his mind that the times of the Fall must
have been something like this, only infinitely worse.
The feelings of bravado that had driven him here had
evaporated and now he clung to his sinister companions desperately, terrified of being left behind.

Soon they encountered more soulless wretches
wandering aimlessly through the streets, clustering in
small groups here and there. The structures around
them were becoming more ruinous as they wormed
their way into the guts of the slaughtered city; increasing numbers of them were just empty shells staring
hollow-eyed across blasted lots. The flames on the
horizon were closer now, forming an eerie blue-green
aurora that covered half the sky.

Many of the soulless seemed to be pathetically re-
enacting parts of their lost lives, strolling with dead
friends, visiting destroyed bazaars. As the warp-taint
blew stronger reality flickered with fragments of memory: clean white streets, multi-coloured minarets,
children at play. The vision blew away like smoke just
as quickly as it came, scraps of it stuttering and recur-
ring again and again in a hundred variations.

Morr had led them with certainty thus far, but now
he stopped, seemingly confounded by the twisting
realities. The sky cracked and fragments of twisted
stone whirled past above them in striated bands.
Shadow-forms in the crackling atmosphere above

erected palaces and towers in mockery of the shattered street beneath, the dark stones flowing together and spinning apart to reform again in a thousand different shapes.

'Something's happening up ahead,' gasped Xyriadh.

'Handmaiden,' Morr warned.

The soulless were gathering, seeming to ooze from the shadows. They were clustering about a lambent figure at a crossroads, kneeling and fawning before it. The entity moved among them enveloped in a golden glow, astral fires chasing across its limbs and brow. It was a perfectly formed eldar female in shape and stature, but its shining eyes spoke of nothing mortal. Tiny sparks of light dripped from its extended fingers, sending the soulless into paroxysms of ecstasy. It gestured beatifically with a cruel half-smile on its lips as it scattered its bounty, exactly like a farmer feeding their livestock.

The agents froze in place, melding themselves into whatever cover they could find. The shining eyes swept languidly in their direction and away again. Long moments dragged past before the glowing figure moved away and disappeared from sight still trailed by a body of soulless supplicants.

'Handmaiden?' Sindiel whispered fearfully.

'A corrupted vessel,' Morr answered. 'There are said to be seven of them if the legends are to be believed. They minister to the outer precincts.'

'How do we fight them?'

'We do not unless we have to.'

'And if we have to?'

'We must destroy their bodies completely.'

'Is that why you made me bring this?' Sindiel hefted a stubby-looking blaster he carried that seemed to be entirely constructed of hooks and blades. Xyriadh had also exchanged her splinter rifle for a monomolecular shredder, a similarly dangerous looking weapon that projected clouds of monofilament mesh.

'Excessive questioning, in particular on the subject of the obvious, becomes tiresome. Be silent.'

The agents proceeded in silence, bypassing the crossroads where they had seen the Handmaiden and cutting through a rubble-choked alley. Reality shuddered again and for an instant they found themselves walking beneath balconies garlanded with flowers. Noble lords and ladies called languidly down to them with offers of entertainment and companionship. The bubble of unreality burst as quickly as it had come and they found themselves back beneath crumbled walls and a bruised-looking sky. They came to a great crack that spread across the street from building to building, almost three metres wide at its narrowest point and unguessably deep. Blue and purple vapours rose from the depths, twisting unnaturally together into half-formed faces or limbs that chased one another upwards until they were obliterated by the invisible pressures of the breach.

'It's blocked! We'll have to turn back and find another way!' said Sindiel with some relief. Something about the vapours was deeply disturbing to him, altogether too reminiscent of the hungry flames of a funeral pyre.

Morr merely glanced at him contemptuously before backing up a few paces and running forwards. He leapt across the yawning gulf and landed on the other side with an echoing crash, the vapours writhing in agitation about him as he stood. Aez'ashya was close behind, executing a flip halfway across as she made light work of the jump. Kharbyr and Xyriadh were less certain, in particular Kharbyr took an excessively long run-up before he made his leap. Xagor hurled himself at the jump resignedly, evidently expecting to plummet to his doom. The wrack jumped too soon and landed right at the crumbling edge of the precipice. His arms flailed hopelessly for a moment as he teetered backwards on the edge, his companions watching dispassionately to see if he fell. At the last possible moment Kharbyr seemed to relent and leaned forwards to grasp Xagor by the shoulder to pull him to safety.

Sindiel was left on the wrong side of the crack, wondering how long the others would wait for him. If his understanding of Aez'ashya was anything to go by it would not be long. Once again the terrors of being alone in this daemon-haunted place drove him forwards. His legs pumped maniacally as he sprinted forwards, determined not to repeat Xagor's mistake by jumping too soon. Instead he almost left it too late; as he pushed off from the near edge he felt the stones crumbling away beneath his feet, robbing him of the vital push he needed to cross the gap. The multi-coloured vapours issuing from the crack hissed and spluttered about him, tangling his limbs and miring his thoughts. There was a timeless moment as he realised he wasn't going to make it, and his mind filled with giggling, whispering, insinuating voices that were not his own.

The far edge of the crack rose up and smashed him in the midriff, knocking the wind out of him. His hands scrabbled desperately for grip among the broken stones as he slid backwards, his legs kicking into empty space devoid of any footholds.

'Help me!' he gasped to the others, the words contorting the vapours around him into mocking, screaming faces. No one moved. Sindiel slipped a few centimetres further as he tried to lever himself forwards with his elbows. Still no one moved to help him and Sindiel suddenly understood a new truth about the dark city. None of them, not even Aez'ashya, valued him enough to take the small risk involved in pulling him to safety. They would stand and watch him die, feeding on his desperation to the last moment rather than lift a finger to help him.

Sindiel cursed and kicked out to one side, catching his feet at last. Little by little he managed to scrabble over the edge in an undignified heap, experiencing a horrible sensation of vertigo at the last moment as he feared he was about to push himself back into the chasm by accident. He lay on his back panting, feeling the bright torch of hate truly kindle in his heart for the first time. He'd felt a spark of it before when he killed Linthis, a quick pulse as he excised all his anger at her in a single blow that saved his own life by taking hers. This was different: deeper, more affecting. He had sold his soul to join these people, given everything to be with them, little realising how twisted they truly were or how little value they placed on him. He nurtured his hate and allowed it into his heart, the heat of it anchoring him amidst the swirling madness.

After a moment he wordlessly picked himself up and rejoined the others, still feeling the pitiless intensity of their gaze upon him.

The agents had emerged onto the edge of an open space, perhaps once a wide promenade or a parade ground but now only a wilderness of cracked stone and windblown dust. Soulless wandered here and there among the ruins, picking listlessly at the bones of their lost world. In the distance to their right the twisted remnants of a mighty palace clawed out of the earth, its melted towers of quartz tilted over sagging walls of obsidian and alabaster. Strains of weird music drifted from the place, a convocation of shrieking laughter and sobbing misery. Above it loomed a horrible black cloud ripped by bursts of multi-coloured fire, writhing snakelike and revealing sudden flashes larger than lightning.

'It looks more inviting than I'd imagined,' whispered Aez'ashya. 'How are we going to find anything in that?'

'El'Uriaq was no fool, the roots of his palace burrow deep,' replied Xyriadh. 'I'll wager his bones are underground.'

Morr shook his head. 'We see only ruins now,' the incubus said. 'Closer to the breach things will be... different.'

Morr hefted his blade and moved forwards more cautiously than the others had seen him wont to do in the past. The towering incubus moved with surprising grace, gliding through the expanse of tumbled stone with barely a sound. The others followed, emulating his stealth with more or less success. They skirted open areas and worked their way carefully forwards. The first few soulless they encountered still seemed to be unaware of their presence, but as they came closer to the hydra-headed storm cloud marking the breach the wretches began sensing a disturbance. The emaciated figures started to lurch around randomly, heads twisting as if they were casting about for a scent.

'The amulets are failing!' hissed Kharbyr. 'We'll never make it!'

'Silence,' said Morr. 'Retreat is not an option.'

They could all feel the sinister thrill of She Who Thirsts brushing at their souls by now. The faint fish-scale shimmer that had surrounded them when they first entered Shaa-dom had intensified into a solid glow. The spiritstones they wore around their necks shone like red embers.

'No, no. Not failing,' muttered Xagor quietly. 'Straining, working hard.'

'Well, that's reassuring,' said Aez'ashya. 'Like Morr said, there's no use talking about going back, Yllithian will feed us to the daemons personally if we fail him now.' Her voice sounded brittle, apt to break into hysterics at any moment.

Ahead of them the palace was breaking up into fractal landscapes of possibilities. Towers reared and fell, walls crumbled and rebuilt themselves. Warring shards of possibility inverted the topography at will, doorways opened on empty air and stairs spiralled through impossible geometries.

Gazing into the maelstrom Sindiel felt a persistent part of his mind gibbering at him to flee, but the terror of having to do so alone still kept him trapped in lockstep with the others. His companions might not help him survive individually but they would defend themselves as a group, knowing that therein lay their only chance of survival. He felt a strange mixture of admiration and abhorrence for the Dark Kin in that moment, even though the torch of his hatred for them was undimmed. That they could be so seemingly undaunted by such a place almost defied his belief. It was as if they were all deaf and he was the only one that could hear the roaring, snorting monstrosity that was treading at their heels.

Each step they took brought the confused whirl ahead into sharper focus, slowly resolving into what was at once a parody of what had been the palace of El'Uriaq and an outraged denial of what had become of it. Its walls reared above them like a giant's castle, decked with kilometre-long banners proclaiming the ascendance of the emperor of Shaa-dom. Horrid seneschals mounted on strange beasts stood guard before a gate shaped like an open maw. The change in perspective reduced the agents to crawling insects inching below the titanic fortifications as they made for the gate. The seneschals regarded their slow approach with amused disdain.

Without doubt these were daemons of the old tales, sinister and beautiful in some lights but hideously twisted in others. The slender arms terminated in long crab-like claws and their knowing smiles revealed rows of sharpened fangs. Six of them sat before the gate upon sinuous bipedal beasts with curiously equine heads that tasted the air with obscenely long pink tongues. As the agents came closer the daemons chattered excitedly among themselves in a dark tongue that hurt the ears and seemed to brand the air with its eldritch tones. One more supremely hideous and beautiful than the others spurred her mount forwards and called out in a honeyed travesty of the ancient eldar tongue.

'Welcome, brothers and sisters!' the thing said. 'You've chosen to cast aside those tiresome bonds of mortality and join us at last. Your coming will be exalted until the stars burn out! A billion slaves will scream your praises for all eternity!'

The agents felt joy at the warmth and friendship in the thing's words and at the thrilling, secret promise that lay beneath every syllable. Morr's voice croaked unpleasantly by comparison, filled with doom and woe.

'Our business is with El'Uriaq and not for the likes of you. Stand aside and let us pass,' the incubus intoned.

The daemon licked its fangs lasciviously. 'I think not. One of you must remain with us for our mutual satisfaction, and know that once you enter the palace you will not be permitted to leave it under any circumstances.' The agents glanced around at one another wondering who might be chosen, and Kharbyr took an excited half-step forwards before Morr's grating voice halted him.

'I will not *bargain* with you, daemon,' the incubus said. His words were still hanging in the turgid air when his two-metre blade flicked out like a serpent's tongue. The daemon's headless mount began collapsing, almost unravelling as the energies holding it together flew apart. Morr neatly caught the daemon on his outstretched weapon as it fell forwards, and flung its thrashing, disintegrating shape into the path of its compatriots as they spurred in to attack.

The glamour of the daemon's words fell away as violence flared. Xyriadh's shredder immediately puffed out a cloud of harmless-looking gossamer strands that carved apart one charging mount and rider as if they had run headlong into a wall of rotating blades. Sindiel's blaster burped out a gob of emerald fire that ate straight through another daemon. Aez'ashya and Kharbyr leapt forwards to fight off the questing tongues of the mounts and the flashing claws of their riders.

An obscene tongue wrapped around Kharbyr's ankle, writhing up his leg like a constricting snake. The pain of his recent wound rekindled into an incandescent ecstasy that made him howl like an animal. Aez'ashya's knives lashed out and cut him free. The sellsword rolled on the ground moaning as the succubus stood over him with her blades carving a protective web.

Morr's blade crashed through another mount and rider in a single stroke, just as Aez'ashya's knives slashed across an equine face and sent a mount rearing backwards. A cloud of monofilament strands from Xyriadh's shredder engulfed a daemon rider before it could bring its mount back under control.

Kharbyr recovered sufficiently to redeem some shred of his ego by shooting the last daemon in the face. Psychically infused splinters from his pistol cratered its head as if it were made of soft clay, the daemon collapsing into a cloud of sickly sweet vapour. Morr dispatched the remaining riding beasts with economic sweeps of his great blade.

'Daemons,' Morr spat with contempt. 'Come, we must move on. They will soon reconstitute themselves and return with others.' He turned and vanished into the shadows that clustered within the maw-like gate.

'You never even considered accepting their bargain?' asked Sindiel as he hurried after the disappearing incubus.

'Daemons always lie,' Morr said with finality.

Beyond the gate lay a restless columned hall, at one moment the pillars standing proud and upright to support the high roof like mature trees, the next tumbled like the vanquished ranks of a defending army. Ghostly shapes moved through the hall, servants, guards, courtiers and patricians faded into view and vanished again, spirit shadows left behind when the blade of Vect plunged into the heart of the palace and annihilated them in a nuclear inferno. The agents' amulets blazed brighter than ever, painting the scene with a lurid ruddy hue. At the end of the shuddering hall double doors ran from the mosaiced floor to the high-groined roof. The mind's eye sometimes caught the unbreakable panels of the doors being hurled to the floor bent and twisted by unthinkable fury, chunks of frescoed ceiling raining down from above.

They stepped through the doors into a vast amphitheatre hung with a galaxy of golden lamps. Another glance saw a blast crater, glowing shrapnel caught in a timeless moment, spinning in place as it blossomed outwards in an imperfect sphere. At its centre a handsome eldar knight sat deep in thought upon the steps of a mountainous throne. From a different angle the throne was a kilometres-high mass of blackened wreckage and the pondering knight was a grinning crimson skull that peeked from the edge of it, preserved from the annihilating fires that had consumed its owner. A raging darkness split the air above the throne-wreck, the breach itself rippling and convulsing as it fed raw warp energy into the corrupted sub-realm.

To speak, even to think so close to the breach was almost impossible. Words took flight as half-formed living things, ideas became jerky flick-book montages of potential outcomes. Yet when three red-eyed, black armoured shapes rose to bar their path the intent of the guardians was clear.

You will not disturb our archon, the shadow-incubi seemed to say. *Long have we watched over him in this place, our souls forever bound to him. You shall not have him now or ever.*

The figures hefted great two-handed klaives that were cousins to that borne by Morr and strode forwards. At first they were insubstantial, but warp-stuff wove about them as they walked, lending substance to their tenebrous limbs. Morr roared an inarticulate challenge that formed a spectral dragon-head, hissing and spitting flames. He charged into the fray hammering at their blades as a smith hammers on an anvil. Sparks flew as their weapons clashed, carving out arcs of destruction that in this energised air could level mountains or cleave rivers.

A hissing blade swept down at Kharbyr and sent

him sprawling, his knife half-melted by a foolhardy attempt to parry. The others fell back firing their weapons desperately, unable to stand before the tsunami power of the shadow-guardians' rush. Green fire from Sindiel's blaster splashed harmlessly from the black carapace of one red-eyed fiend. Xyriadh's shredder proved equally ineffective, its deadly strands passing through the guardian's armour like smoke. Splinters from Xagor and Kharbyr rattled off the impervious figures to no avail.

Aez'ashya sprang forwards with a bright laugh of discovery. Darting beneath a scything blow she struck out with her knives. The gleaming blades sank into the guardian's armour and tore a ragged wound, its flapping lips drooling multi-hued warp-stuff. Spinning and dodging, the succubus continued to worry at her foe, a slice here and a thrust there, always one step ahead of the swinging blade. Thunder crashed as Morr duelled the other two guardians, the blows they exchanged sending shock waves booming through the amphitheatre.

Xagor leapt forward with desperate courage, rushing past Sindiel and Xyriadh and their useless weapons before jumping at the guardian attempting to swat Aez'ashya. The wrack grasped the thing's arm, his hands sizzling at the contact, and wrestled frantically. He might as well have been wrestling a pillar of iron for the impact he made. The red-eyed helm turned towards Xagor and he was flung aside with a contemptuous gesture.

The momentary distraction was all the opportunity Aez'ashya needed. She leapt and plunged both knives into the thing's neck with her whole weight behind them. Lightning flashed from the wounds, the invulnerable-seeming guardian lurching backwards and unravelling before the agents' eyes.

Xyriadh dropped her shredder and ran towards Morr to help him. However the same trick would not work twice on such superlative opponents. A spinning blade caught Xyriadh and opened her up from shoulder to hip before she could react. She might have survived even such a terrible blow to be rebirthed later, but the scything blade tore away her spiritstone amulet. Xyriadh only had the time for one piteous shriek before her soul was shorn from her body and sucked away into the raging breach. Sindiel, about to follow Xyriadh's rush, reeled away from her eviscerated corpse with a look of horror on his face.

More practically minded, Kharbyr, Aez'ashya and Xagor scrambled after the skull at the foot of the wreckage-throne. This proved to be a better distraction than Xyriadh's unfortunate demise. One of the shadow-incubi fighting Morr attempted to break away, plunging after the thieves before they could lay hands on his master. The creature either underestimated Morr's speed or overestimated its companion's ability to keep the towering incubus at bay. It did not get more than one pace away before Morr's blade separated the fiend's head from its shoulders.

The lone survivor wove a dazzling web of defence as it backed towards the throne, but Morr was in full fury now and not to be denied. He beat aside the shadow-incubus's blade and sent its owner back to hell with a disembowelling sweep of his mighty klaive. Xagor grasped the skull of El'Uriaq with his burned hands and wrenched it forth with a croak of triumph that disintegrated into a rain of crowned frogs. He found the skull to be smooth and heavy as if it had been re-cast in some strange, red metal.

Images filled Xagor's mind when he lifted it – parades and palaces, skulduggery and secret pacts, a thousand schemes and plans of the old emperor. With a tiny shriek that fluttered away as birds Xagor stuffed the skull into a casket he had brought for the purpose of containing any relics they might find.

As the lid clicked shut a tremble ran through the amphitheatre and the raging breach swelled with redoubled fury. The agents turned and ran.

A slow-spreading dawn dogged their heels, a hideous rising light of destruction that pursued them into the columned hall outside. The crowding ghosts perceived them now and they reacted with anger and alarm: spectral fists were raised against them, voiceless mouths opened calling for guards. The agents swept through the ethereal host scattering them like leaves. Bright light burned at their backs, heat and sound seeming to crawl behind it in slow motion, bursting apart the shifting columns and consuming the phantom court. They burst out of the maw-like gate as the fantasy palace of El'Uriaq collapsed in on itself, slumping into a mass of tumbled walls and shattered stone.

Morr paused after they passed the threshold, gazing back into the heart of the warp breach dancing triumphantly over the ruins.

'What happened?' asked Aez'ashya.

Morr was silent for a long moment before he replied. 'The bones of El'Uriaq anchored this shadow-play. His ruined palace, his dead courtiers and all the rest of it endured only by his will. With his absence they are lost.'

'Wait, what?' gasped Sindiel. 'He's dead! How can he have willed anything?'

'No, no. Mistaking dead flesh for dead mind,' whispered Xagor, holding the casket containing the skull at arm's length from himself.

Sindiel remained unconvinced. 'How can his soul have survived? You saw what happened to Xyriadh!'

'Well, maybe you can ask him when we get out of here,' Aez'ashya replied flippantly, 'which we had better do soon if we don't want to stay permanently.'

Morr straightened as if shaking off a deep reverie. 'Yes. We must leave now. Prepare yourselves, the return journey will not be so easy.'

Rushing winds were birthing in the wastes, rapidly growing from vagrant zephyrs to a yelling torrent that beat against their faces as they struggled into the teeth of the tempest. Periodically, soulless wretches blew past, flailing idiotically, their flickering life sparks sucked voraciously into the screaming void. Slowly they struggled towards the shelter of the surrounding ruins, pulling free step-by-step from the kraken-like embrace of the breach.

'Oh no!' Sindiel gasped, pointing frantically. Riders on sinuous bipedal mounts could be glimpsed in the distance behind them, while ahead of them an emergent glow was painting the shattered walls with reflected glory.

The Handmaid swept into view, her delicate feet walking on air and with banners of aetheric fire wreathing her limbs. A stillness surrounded her, her own personal eye in the hurricane force of the winds. There was no doubt she perceived them this time. Bright, inhuman eyes looked down on the agents with deliberation. Lambent power flowed from her, forming an incandescent rosette in the darkness. When she spoke her voice was chimes and bird calls, infinitely sweeter than the sickly, persuasive words of daemons.

'What noble suitors are these, that would brave the perils of Shaa-dom?'

'We came to rescue the bones of your old master, El'Uriaq, that he might live again and avenge himself at last. Let us pass and we would leave this place without delay,' said Morr carefully.

Complex emotions chased across the Handmaid's too-beautiful face at Morr's words. Rage and sadness were there in equal measure and it was a bold heart that did not quail before the sight of her passions aroused. The moment passed as quickly as it had come, and when she addressed them again it was with unreadable serenity.

'You are bold indeed to make such claims. Grant me but one simple boon, noble knight, and I will let you pass.'

The agents tensed for sudden violence, watching Morr carefully for their cue. To their surprise the incubus did not move.

'What is your desire?' he asked.

She smiled with hellfire burning in her eyes. 'Show him to me.'

Morr gestured Xagor forwards and with shaking knees the wrack complied. He lifted the casket he bore and opened it to reveal the polished red skull of El'Uriaq. The Handmaid crouched in genuflection, a tragic smile on her ethereal features.

'Long has it been, my lord, since we danced and sang for your pleasure. Do recall it? Endless nights in gardens wrapped in the scents of asphodel and nenuphar. How we loved you and your lady! You were our sun and moon! I'm saddened to see there's no pleasure left in you now.'

The too-bright eyes looked away before rising to examine them again, dangerous fires smouldering in their depths.

'Go. Take your prize,' the Handmaid said. 'I will spare you in honour of him. Revel in your lives while you still have them, my gift to you for bringing him back into the world. Remember, if you can, that he was once greater than you can know. Remember also that you chose this path for yourselves, wherever it might eventually lead.'

The Handmaid vanished like a blown-out candle, and as the shadows crowded in closer the sudden absence of her light seemed blinding.

CHAPTER 12

A RESURRECTION

El'Uriaq! El'Uriaq!
Shaa-dom was his realm.
How proud he stood! How low he fell!
El'Uriaq! El'Uriaq!
Felt Vect's blade and went to hell!

— *The March of the Vanquished*

A BREATHLESS AIR of anticipation hung about the shadowy chamber. The worldsinger Laryin lay captive on the examination table at its centre, unrestrained but seemingly pinned beneath the unwinking glare of a dozen harsh spotlights. A diadem of cold metal pressed at her brow, its silky leads trailing off to sinister-looking boxes of equipment to one side. The gaunt scarecrow figure of Bellathonis bent over them, his white, long-fingered hands like anxious birds flitting across the polished controls. Twin crystal-fronted sarcophagi overhung the scene like the faces of eldritch gods sitting in judgment.

'There,' the master haemonculus said to Laryin, 'we are almost ready to begin. You must forgive the lack of physical restraints – as I mentioned a sense of utter helplessness does sometimes have its part to play.' He delicately raised one of her slender wrists between thumb and forefinger before allowing it to drop limply back onto the slab. 'Have you ever heard of a weapon called a terrorfex, my dear? I suppose it would be surprising if you had, it's an extremely rare device even here in the eternal city. A terrorfex is made out of wraithbone, you see, and that's hard to find as it cannot be made in Commorragh. Wraithbone has to be... harvested from the divergent branches of the eldar, like the craftworlders and your own people. We have a lot of other uses for that resource I can assure you, and hence few terrorfexes are made these days. Sad to see such an elegant device fall out of use, but I digress.

'The way the terrorfex works is by psychically inducing visions so nightmarish that the victim is rendered helpless. The wraithbone is imbued with negative energy to act as a sort of catalyst. All it does really is to blow open the gates, so to speak, and allow your own worst fears to reign supreme. You're placed into a personal hell of your own making.' The haemonculus paused and turned to smile at her. 'Quite delicious really.'

He stepped across to look closely into Laryin's face. She had spent hours in his presence and not once had he done anything directly to harm her. If anything he had been unctuously charming through-out. She was unable to move but her very psyche still flinched instinctively from his hooded malice, trying to crawl away into some safe inner haven. Bellathonis chuckled.

'I have been working for some time,' he continued, 'on isolating the principles of the noble but sadly neglected terrorfex. I believe I can employ those principles in a more carefully metered form suitable for my own purposes. My initial tests have been most promising, and in your case I believe I have hit upon the perfect means to exercise full control.

'Physical pain has its limitations, you see. The body is most wonderfully equipped to inure itself to physical pain, and the mind is equipped to achieve a state of dull acceptance – some would maintain a transcendence – with a rapidity that is really most unhelpful. Mental anguish, on the other hand, is always fresh, immediate and utterly inescapable.'

'Is your creature liable to actually *do* something any-time soon, Nyos?' Xelian asked languidly.

Yllithian shifted uncomfortably beside Xelian where they stood in the shadows watching the haemonculus at work.

'Certain preparations have to be completed in the correct order and at their own pace,' Yllithian replied, stifling his own irritation at the haemonculus's lengthy discourses. 'Such great undertakings cannot be expedited on account of our own level of boredom or discomfort, more's the pity.'

Xelian remained petulant. 'El'Uriaq is unlikely to be impressed by resurrection into a dank hole like this one, you know. You could have at least supplied some refreshments or better entertainment than this.'

In truth Yllithian was beginning to regret choosing what was in effect a deep, dank sub-cellar to conduct these affairs. He'd had several surrounding chambers refurbished and used as stockpiles and armouries, but his fantasies about it being a secret base of operations did nothing to dispel the pervasive miasma of decay.

'What we begin here will be a slow process,' he explained with a patience he didn't feel. 'It could take months, years even, before El'Uriaq is able to fully emerge from his sarcophagus. I'll move him to suitably salubrious surroundings before that day comes. For the present privacy is more important than an impressive or especially comfortable locale, noble lady.'

'Oh really? And what measures have you taken to silence wagging tongues, Nyos? Aez'ashya can be trusted of course, but Morr is with the Realm Eternal and I see one of the haemonculus's scrofulous underlings here in this very room. Where's the other? And the renegade? Considering a loose word from any of these individuals could bring the tyrant down upon us in full fury, your requirements for privacy don't seem to have extended far enough to my mind.'

'The sell-sword, Kharbyr, is being watched and may have an unfortunate accident very soon, although Bellathonis has some unfathomable attachment to the scum so I have held back my hand thus far. The young renegade, Sindiel, is busy learning to appreciate the pleasures that indulgence can bestow and his loyalty is cheaply bought. All is under control, Xelian, do relax and try to enjoy the moment.'

Bellathonis glanced somewhat sharply at them both before stepping over sulkily to stand by his torture devices, waiting for permission to proceed. Seeing that the moment was upon them Yllithian raised his chin arrogantly and spoke.

'Begin.'

Bellathonis made the tiniest of adjustments to the engine and Laryin was instantly plunged into soul-searing horror. She relived her awakening in Bellathonis's torture laboratory for the first time breath for breath, feeling every pin-point prickle of sweat on her limbs. Her sense of helplessness and sick fear shone so bright and sharp in her mind that it made her gasp. The moment repeated, focused, stabilised and then went on and on and on.

'Perfect,' a distant voice said. It seemed a complete irrelevance amidst the crashing waves of terror.

In a flash the memory was gone. The metal diadem pressed coldly against her brow and she fancied she could almost feel it inside her skull, a twisted interloper riffling through her memories. Shame, disgust, humiliation writhed inside her and she could no longer tell if they were creations of her own mind.

'Now that we have a baseline we can proceed,' the voice went on, sounding pedantic but excited now, almost gleeful.

The World Shrine rose about her, the dank torture chamber rolling back like stage scenery to be replaced with walls of living rock and gently tinkling waterfalls. She relived the sensations of violation and horror as the Children of Khaine crept into the sanctum. Once again she was paralysed by her own fear, rooted to the spot as the killers moved in and forced to watch as they slew the guards that had given up their lives to protect her. Her fault, her shame, her punishment.

THE TWISTING ROPE of psychic energy passing before Kraillach's sarcophagus thickened into a river, aetheric ambrosia that laved his raw body and fed his parched soul. The breath of true life gusted through him, satiating him in a way he had not known in a thousand years. New skin, fresh and pink as a newborn's, was already spreading over his red-boned hands. He mewled with pleasure as he basked in the suffering of a pure heart.

Suddenly Kraillach felt that something was wrong. Very wrong. A… presence was growing close by, a faint trace of spirit that he had originally dismissed as irrelevant. He felt it become stronger, forming a hole like a chink in reality that widened inexorably. The flowing river of revivifying energy was being drawn into it like a whirlpool, torn away from Kraillach to feed the burgeoning entity. He whimpered helplessly as he was starved of the essence he so desperately wanted, but his attempts to attract the attention of the dimly perceived minions below were once again ignored. Worse still, he felt the presence coming to full sentience like the slow unfolding of a dreadful flower.

No.

Laryin's mind reformed around the syllable and clung to it as a rock in the midst of a raging flood. *No.* She grasped the tiny shred of self, struggling to free her psyche from the mire. *No.* The deaths and suffering were not her fault, the Children of Khaine had slain them, not her.

Bellathonis cursed softly as the dark energy pouring out of the girl wavered and dropped to a tenth of what it had been. He adjusted, searching through her consciousness to find new vulnerabilities. Something from her earliest childhood memories perhaps, where reason could less effectively raise blocks. Maiden worlds came with a fine pedigree of voracious, primitive arthropods that could be encountered by a young Exodite... A few seconds of fine-tuning and the full flow of Laryin's fear was released once more by a tide of bloodsucking ticks that were each larger than one of her young hands.

KRAILLACH RECOILED AS the psychic torrent was unleashed again. For a few precious moments the hideous presence opposite him had receded as the energy flow dropped away. Now it was back, more voracious than ever. The vortex reopened and the awful sentience behind it leapt to full life.

Newly-formed eyes pierced Kraillach from all directions at once, inside and outside and from angles that have no name. It perceived every part of him, every moment of his long life from birth to death was examined, mercilessly turning him inside out in a horrific spiritual vivisection. A conclusion was reached, septic energies narrowing their focus and erupting into Kraillach's quivering form, psychic pus from cancerous realms outside reality jetting into his hollow soul. Life-matrices were remade and altered accordingly, the daemonic loom of fate howling as it shuttled out his new destiny with feverish intensity. Caught inside his crystal-faced tomb, Kraillach writhed in eight dimensions as he was reborn from within.

With its seed planted, the multi-dimensional sentience set to completing reconstruction of its own form. Reaching into the energy flow it wrapped itself in the necessary trappings, transfiguring raw warp-stuff into cohesive matter. Bones reknitted, sheathed themselves with cartilage, tendons and ligaments whipped into place and muscle tissue flowed to cover new-formed limbs and torso like hardening wax. Within seconds skin was spreading over the manikin-like cadaver, ballooning to accommodate thickening muscles and a deepening chest. Fingers flexed with new life, balled into fists.

YLLITHIAN COULD FEEL the backwash of psychic energy from the worldsinger even with most of it being channelled to the sarcophagi above. Spectral fingers plucked at his mind, bringing an unbidden smile to his lips. Xelian gave a little moan of pleasure beside him as the flow increased, the ghostly fingers becoming a thrilling caress. Static electricity sparked from every piece of exposed metal and glowing witchfires crawled around the hanging sarcophagi. He felt some alarm, but the sensation transformed into a throb of pleasure.

Every moment, every detail was pleasurable – the wracks rushing around clownishly in their rubberised coats, the gleam of the lights, the white-faced haemonculus intent at his engine, the pallid pain-bride on her slab and the hungry not-quite-dead raging in their coffins above. It seemed pure theatre being played out for his benefit, comical manikins scurrying on a tiny stage for his pleasure.

The sense of alarm returned, surfacing from the wave of pleasure like a dark rock at low tide. Too fast. He locked onto the thought and clung to it. Too fast. He had believed the process would be long and tedious, only being begun today and achieving its end at some unforeseen point in the future. Feeling the power unleashed made him know he was wrong. Yllithian was no master Chaotician, his studies of the veil were limited to what was most useful to him. Even so he could *feel* the strain on reality building up in the chamber. The energy could not continue to flow at this rate, it had to be stopped before disaster struck.

He opened his mouth to call on Bellathonis to halt the procedure. Before the words could form, the crystal front of one of the sarcophagi burst in a shattering explosion and simultaneously every light in the room went out. Shouts of dismay went up from the wracks, quickly silenced by a snarl from Bellathonis.

'Lights, quickly!' Yllithian commanded. Some hand-lamp was kindled and the shadows fled from it grotesquely. In their dim illumination a new figure could be seen beside the slab in the centre of the chamber. Broad-shouldered and golden-haired, it was still slick from the sarcophagus's amniotic fluids and covered in superficial cuts from the broken crystal.

He was crouched beside the worldsinger and he was stroking her wide-eyed face. When he glanced up everyone in the chamber was frozen in place for a moment, feeling that he looked straight at them, reading them personally and learning more of them than they knew of themselves.

'She's been hurt,' he said in a rich, mellifluous voice. 'Help her.'

Fallen shards of crystal had pierced the worldsinger's pale flesh, and she lay now in a spreading pool of crimson. Wracks tumbled to obey, hurrying forwards with dressings and syringes in an unseemly rush. The newcomer rose and strode confidently to Yllithian and Xelian; completely ignoring, Yllithian noticed, the tumbled shards that cut his feet as he walked across them.

Yllithian scrabbled for some sense of control over the situation. This was not, in even the vaguest sense, going according to plan. Majesty radiated from the newcomer, a sense of confidence and nobility that inspired admiration and commanded instant obedience. Obedience, thought Yllithian sourly, born not out of fear but from a desire to please him and, perhaps by working long and diligently, earn his praise. Even now, clad only in smeared ichor and his own blood, the stranger dominated the room as if he wore a hidden crown. Yllithian found he hated him immediately.

'Welcome–' Yllithian began before the stranger cut him off.

'Please, before you speak allow me to give my thanks to you both for my safe return. Without your help I would still be trapped in Shaa-dom. How long has passed?'

'Three thousand years,' Xelian said with a knowing smile.

'Small wonder I feel so parched! And Vect still rules, I take it?'

'Why would you say that?' asked Yllithian, sounding sharper than he had intended. El'Uriaq threw his head back and laughed. It was the honest laughter of a joke shared between friends.

'Why else would you need me?' he said 'Only Vect's enemies would want me back, and that means Vect has to be alive. If Vect is alive he must still rule.'

'All too true,' Yllithian said bitterly. 'Then I'll be direct – will you join us and help to overthrow the tyrant? Will you dedicate yourself to it?'

To Yllithian's astonishment the tall eldar hugged him, the movement so quick and the grip so inescapable that he momentarily feared for his life.

El'Uriaq stared into his eyes intensely and said, 'I will reforge your armies into engines of destruction that will conquer each and every one of your foes, I will subvert your enemies and bring such a reckoning down among your friends that they will never again question their loyalty to you. I will help you to ascend to the very zenith of your power and together we will destroy the tyrant as I should have done so long ago. I would promise you this simply out of love for you after what you've done for me, but I'll swear to it on the lives of the very people that Vect murdered in my realm. *This* time I will strike first. This time Vect will feel *my* blade.'

El'Uriaq released him and Yllithian took a half-step back, dazed. Bellathonis was nearby, becoming increasingly agitated as he tried to get Yllithian's attention. It didn't look like he had good news. Yllithian seized on the opportunity to tear his attention away from the emotional whirlpool of El'Uriaq.

'What is it, Bellathonis?' Yllithian snapped, finding most of his irritation had now zeroed in on the master haemonculus as being its source. He could see that the wracks had lowered Kraillach's sarcophagus on its chains and were removing his fresh, pink body from its nest of tubes, filaments and sloshing amniotic fluids inside. The archon of the Realm Eternal looked like a newborn with his eyes squeezed tightly shut.

'I need to discuss some... anomalies that may have occurred with you, my archon,' Bellathonis said between bowing and scraping frantically. The master haemonculus must have been deeply upset about something to risk the archon's anger so thoughtlessly.

'Out with it, haemonculus,' Yllithian said coldly. 'We have a great deal of work ahead of us and I don't have the time to tarry here. What of Kraillach? Is he properly reborn?' He noticed that the master haemonculus was taking pains not to look directly at El'Uriaq.

'Yes, my archon, but that's just it: the issue, the anomaly. Altogether too rapid. Both were impossibly fast. By my calculations–'

'Enough!' roared El'Uriaq. Bellathonis was suddenly flung aside as if he had been swatted by an invisible fist. The lanky haemonculus's body crunched into the chamber wall five metres away with a bone-snapping impact before slithering down it to lie, unmoving, in a crumpled heap at the bottom. Psychic energy crackled through the chamber and El'Uriaq's eyes glowed with inner fires in the aftermath. All present froze in shock at witnessing such power used so flagrantly.

Yllithian gasped as one of Bellathonis's wracks, the one named Xagor, hurled himself at the reborn archon with a knife naked in his fist. His hand darted for his own weapon to cut down the deranged fool before he could harm El'Uriaq. He was too slow to affect the outcome. A single glance from El'Uriaq and the weapon in the wrack's hand flashed into a mass of molten metal. The wrack screamed and collapsed, his hand burned away to the wrist. The undercurrent of psychic energy in the chamber thickened until it seemed to drip from the air, dense and treacle-like.

'You're right,' El'Uriaq said with icy calm, 'we have a great deal of work ahead of us, my friends, far too much to be distracted by trivialities. I have waited long enough already. Let's be about it with no more delays.'

Yllithian found himself nodding with agreement, all thoughts of the haemonculus's fate temporarily forgotten under the spell of El'Uriaq's charisma. Yllithian felt elated again. Everything was coming together perfectly.

CHAPTER 13
THE REALM ETERNAL

THE DREAM HAD changed for Kraillach. He still saw Commorragh as he'd seen it before: a glittering crown of spires surrounded by a jewelled diadem of serenely orbiting sub-realms. Now his dream-self reached out for a passing gem as it swung close by, knowing that if he could only hide it in his palm he could draw it away from the dark city and cherish it all for his own. Often he hesitated at the last moment, confounded by the bright moving shapes, or was seized by a sudden and unaccountable fear, but each night his hand crept inexorably closer to his goal.

The result was always the same. Even as his fingers closed around the bauble it blackened and cracked, slipping away into the void. As it fell ripples of entropy spread, racing through the sub-realms with hurricane force, sending them clashing like beads on a wire. The mountainous spires of High Commorragh shivered and groaned, its jagged minarets and barbed steeples swaying like trees in a storm. Debris rained down: tiny, fluttering petals in his dream-sight but in reality gigantic avalanches of metal and ceramic destined to wipe out tens of thousands on their arrival in Low Commorragh. The sub-realms spun wildly, scattering outwards as fire and lightning wreathed the glittering crown.

KRAILLACH STIRRED PEEVISHLY in his nest of golden silks. The preceding night of exhausting and ultimately unsatisfying entertainments had taxed his newborn vigour. For a brief time he had almost felt like his old sybaritic self, but somehow the moment had never quite arrived. He had wanted to punish a few of his minions to excise his frustration and spur the rest to greater efforts, but he could muster little enthusiasm even for that diversion at present.

He had retired into his inner sanctum in the hopes that it would bring him some sense of serenity in the unfulfilled aftermath of his orgiastic pursuits as it had done so many times in the past. Today the walls of unbreakable stone and their linings of unbreachable metal were availing him nothing of the sort. His enemies were already inside, masked little conspirators of doubt and fear that were stalking around in the dark recesses of his mind.

He could not understand it. Everything should be perfect. The Realm Eternal had rebounded from its internal machinations and was growing more strongly than ever. Kraillach had always kept the kabal's recruiting policies as open as polite etiquette made possible, following the maxim that quantity has a quality all of its own. Lately he had been forced to consider becoming more selective just to cull the herd as the Realm Eternal's ranks swelled.

He found that he liked the idea and made a mental note to discuss it with Morr. Stringent controls would go some way to whipping the kabal into a more formidable military force over the long term. He briefly indulged himself in a fantasy of commanding powerful, disciplined forces rather than the armed rabble currently at his disposal. With sufficient force he could impose his commands on lesser kabals, seize more territory and make the Realm Eternal a name to be properly feared.

At least the bloating numbers had brought with them a shower of wealth that warmed even what passed for Kraillach's shrivelled black heart. Riches were flowing into his coffers from a variety of lucrative tithes and trades, erasing all of Kraillach's concerns about his future fortunes.

Yes, everything was perfect, everything for once seemed to be going his way. His new body was young and vital as it had not been in centuries, his appetites were if anything redoubled and yet... And yet it seemed, despite everything being so perfect, he could never quite quench his inner thirst. It was as if a hole had been made in his soul, or rather that the existing one had been widened from a keyhole to a gaping portal. He could never stop feeling hollow inside, almost as if every morsel fell straight through into an empty, unfillable void.

Something had been done to him during his rebirth, he felt sure of it. Trapped in his sarcophagus, metres away from the old emperor's resurrection, he had felt the monstrous, naked presence of the entity that settled on the frantically reknitting bones and sinews. He had perceived El'Uriaq's unthinkable hunger before it was clothed by flesh and hidden away from mortal eyes. The experience had marked Kraillach then and it still marked him now, as if El'Uriaq had pierced him with an icy lance that was still in the wound. He found himself trembling at the thought.

Again and again he found himself thinking about Dysjunction. He had lived through Dysjunctions before, witnessed the anarchy that ensued in their aftermath. They were dark and terrible times when feral necessity swept away the sophisticated face of Commorraghan politics and revealed the howling savage lurking just below the surface. There was another Dysjunction coming, he felt sure, just as Yllithian had said there would be. He already fancied he could almost feel the stresses developing and hear the distant creak of sub-realms straining at their connections to the core.

Kraillach glanced suspiciously around the chamber. Beyond his inner feelings of disquiet, something external *was* troubling him. Some element of the reassuring tableau of his inner sanctum was missing. Kraillach looked about with increasing alarm as he considered carefully what it might be.

The blood-daubed sigils covering the walls, floor and ceiling were fresh and unbroken. The censers hung about his bed silently dispensing their metered narcotics. The hermetic shields buzzed quietly at the edge of perception as they always did. The metre-thick iris valve of inscribed metal still sealed the only entrance to the sanctum and... Kraillach did a double-take.

The entrance was sealed but Morr was not in front of it.

Kraillach struggled to remember a time when he had awoken to find Morr absent, and failed. The towering incubus was such a fixture of the scene that now Kraillach was alerted to his absence he could virtually see a Morr-shaped hole where his chief executioner should be standing.

Kraillach rose quickly, gathering his robes about him as he walked hesitantly to the sealed portal. Morr would surely only have left under the most dire of circumstances and even then why did he not awaken his master to ask for permission before leaving his side? He called out, on all channels, but received no response.

Wracked by indecision, Kraillach retreated to the edge of his bath. A frightened part of his mind told him to arm himself and don the rainbow-hued armour standing nearby without delay. Another part of him quailed at the mockery he would glean by leaping out fully armed from his sanctuary if nothing truly threatened. The assassination attempt and the duel with Xelian had already hurt his reputation badly enough that he was sensitive to anything that might make matters worse. As the kabal grew it became more tempestuous, drama-filled and harder to control. Whatever his inner fears might be he had to present a composed, relaxed face full of confidence to the world. In Commorragh, living in fear of assassins was virtually guaranteed to bring them to the door.

He plucked a belt of linked metal plates from a table. He had grown wary of trusting to his doppelganger field to protect him after the fight with Xelian. He'd had this new protective device made by his artisans, a phasing shield that converted potentially deadly amounts of incoming energy into heat and light that was reflected outwards at the attacker. Kraillach cast the intricate belt back on the table petulantly. While it made for an excellent defence against high-energy weapon strikes, the shield was nowhere near as effective against the slow assassin's blade.

Swallowing his fear, Kraillach decided he was being ridiculous. Clearly something was amiss, the absence of Morr and any form of communication were quite alarming enough to warrant taking basic precautions like wearing armour. He started donning the rainbow-hued plates with fumbling hands, unaccustomed as he was to arming himself without assistance.

He had a nasty moment when the portal refused to open. The considerable irony to be had from simply trapping Kraillach inside his lair to starve to death had never really crossed his mind before. Sure enough he had victuals on hand to live for a while, but what if they ran out and he was still trapped? He steadied his nerves with a stiff drink and keyed the runic sequence again just to be sure. The iris slid open this time as it should, filling Kraillach with relief. At least something still worked. The shimmering surface of the portal was revealed and he waited a moment to see if enemies came plunging out of it. Seconds stretched by and nothing happened. Kraillach took another drink, snorted a large pinch of *agarin* and ventured out.

THE HALLS OF the palace were dim and quiet. The night before the halls had been filled with chattering crowds of brightly dressed revellers, but now Kraillach walked through echoing corridors devoid of any living thing. He had never seen his own palace so empty; the huge numbers of slaves, retainers, guards, sycophants, concubines and courtiers around him at all times had long since attained the status of ambulatory furniture in Kraillach's mind. He noticed their individual presence or absence no more than divans, hangings and ornaments. He now perceived just how much servile activity had surrounded every moment of his waking life, only becoming apparent by its complete absence.

At first he went by secret ways, going by the hidden stairways and concealed doors littered throughout his demesne. Kraillach had grown up in this palace and he knew them all, including the many additions of his own down the centuries. Each passage was decorated with the bones of the slaves that built it. Their skulls grinned down silently at him as he crept between spy holes, their lips forever sealed.

He stopped abruptly, nostrils flaring at a familiar scent. Turning aside from the narrow corridor he was following he moved to a hidden entrance to one of the many boudoirs scattered along its length. Deep shadows lurked within and limp hangings obscured his view through the spy hole until he gave up and pushed his way inside. The smell was stronger now and it overwhelmed the scents of sweat, musk and perfume he expected to find.

It was the coppery tang of freshly spilt blood that he had smelled. The floor was swimming with the stuff and the hangings were soaked with it. Kraillach was well aware of the extravagant-seeming quantities of blood to be found in an individual. He was in no doubt that several people had messily died here and yet there was no trace of bodies among the blood-soaked furnishings. He backed out of the intimate little charnel house into the colonnaded hallway outside, leaving a trail of crimson bootprints behind him.

Panic tried to lift his feet and propel him back to his inner sanctum but fear, mixed with morbid curiosity, held him back. The image of being trapped inside his sanctum kept resurfacing in his mind and would not leave it. He walked further down the hall to check an adjoining niche and found a similar scene of carnage. Again there were no bodies or even parts of bodies to be seen, but copious quantities of blood had sprayed everywhere with appalling vigour. Part of his mind couldn't stop wondering how all the bodies could be gone without leaving any trace of it in the hall.

He spun suddenly at a sound, the faintest breath of chittering laughter. Shadows, emptiness confronted him. He was alone.

HE FOUND ALL the bodies eventually, as he knew he would. They had been brought to the great hall and arranged around the throne of splendours. The vast space of the hall was covered in a pallid carpet of corpses, naked, white and drained of every drop of their blood. Most had been placed to make it appear as if they were sleeping or copulating, casually intertwined with their heads gently at rest on outstretched hands or cold shoulders. Others were placed as if they had been sitting up carousing together and momentarily drifted off into slumber. Others were caught in the act of murdering one another with slack hands around bruised throats or disembowelling daggers. Every single white corpse bore a red-lipped wound somewhere on their person, a yawning throat, a split back or an opened chest that spoke of their death blow.

Some sixth sense drew Kraillach's attention to the throne. It had been empty when he first approached, tumbling with kaleidoscopic images on every facet.

It was occupied now.

'Consequences,' the figure on the throne said distinctly. Kraillach's heart jumped into his mouth.

'Consequences,' the grey figure said again. 'There are always consequences for everything we do, for every step we take. It always saddens me immensely but here we are.'

Kraillach struggled to regain some hint of composure. He looked around fearfully, expecting an attack at any moment. The figure on the throne did not move and no hidden confederates sprang into view. After a few seconds Kraillach recovered sufficiently to ask: 'Who are you, why…?'

'Why, forgive me! I'm forgetting my manners!' The figure rose and moved towards him, dancing a few half-steps with an imaginary partner along the way. It was an eldar dressed in an archaic-looking doublet and hose made with so many variegated colours that from a distance the cloth appeared grey. A black and white domino mask hid the upper part of his face, and the mouth beneath the mask was twisted into a mournful, comically unhappy frown.

'You can call me Motley and it's my pleasure to make your acquaintance, Archon Kraillach.' The figure sketched out a mockery of a deep bow. 'But you're mistaken thinking that I did all this on my own. I admire the artistry immensely, of course, and I wish that I could claim all of the credit for it, but the truth is that all of *this*,' Motley gestured vaguely to encompass the evidence of massacre spread beneath their feet, 'was of your making. I may have wielded the blade in part but you were the one to press it into my hand, even though in truth I had considered myself only…' the figure poised and tilted its half-masked face in consideration, '…an interested observer.'

Motley began to dance slowly around the throne

in courtly fashion, bowing to his imaginary partner and rising on tiptoe to lift their imaginary arms
before spinning them lazily. Kraillach watched him
carefully.

'I know of your kind. By what right does the Masque
deign to interfere in my affairs?' Kraillach whined. 'Or
do you simply come to revel in my downfall?'

'Oh don't be so coy, archon, you know what's happening better than almost anyone – you must suspect
what's gestating inside you.' Motley shrugged. 'And if
things had continued the way they were I would have
arrived at your door at some point.'

Motley halted his pavane and pirouetted to face
Kraillach. 'As it stands that's become irrelevant as I
was invited in early to prevent a tragedy becoming
a catastrophe. Or was it a calamity becoming a cataclysm? I don't recall.

'If you want to find the real sculptor of this particular exhibit you'll need to look closer to home than my
good self, I think. He seemed a joyless fellow when
I first met him, but now I can see that he really has
a poet's soul beneath all that gruff. He's waiting for
you, I believe. Perhaps you should be running along
before his other friends come back?'

Motley gazed pointedly toward the far end of the
hall. Shadows were oozing out of the corners and
slithering along the walls towards them. Kraillach
fled.

AT FIRST KRAILLACH had tried to make his way to the
docking ports in the upper levels of the palace but
restless shadows dogged his heels at every turn.

They trailed him unerringly through the secret paths he took and lurked in wait for him at concealed portals they could not possibly have known about. He knew that he was being deliberately hemmed in and driven back towards his sanctum, but he couldn't muster the courage to turn and face the sinister, slinking shapes – not yet. The sick fear of being trapped was back again, edged with gibbering panic at being hunted through his own realm. He kept hoping to find some of his retainers alive, some embattled pocket of resistance somewhere in the palace that he could shelter in. His feet clattered along empty corridors, the lonely noise only serving to emphasise the complete absence of other sounds.

Suddenly the portal to his sanctum lay before him, two upright copper-coloured trees of fantastic craftsmanship that curved together to intertwine at the apex of an open oval formed between their trunks. Kraillach looked around desperately. He'd lost his way somehow, and force of habit had brought him unerringly back to the spot he had intended to avoid. The bright shimmer of the portal itself glowed between the shining trunks promising a false hope of safety. Desperate courage made Kraillach turn at bay before it, flourishing his blade at his shadowy pursuers.

'I'll not be driven into a trap like an animal! Come out and face me!' he shouted with more bravery than he truly felt. The corridor behind him was clotted with darkness, a gloomy stygian wall that denied the existence of anything but Kraillach, the portal and itself. The darkness rippled with silent movement and figures began to detach themselves from its embrace. Kraillach gripped his blade and wet his lips. They were mandrakes, umbral assassins from the depths of Aelindrach. Shadow-skinned and faceless, there seemed to be at least a dozen of them but there could have been a thousand lurking beyond the light and it would have been impossible to tell.

Sensing a presence at his shoulder he whirled suddenly, barely avoiding a sickle of etched bone that came slicing at his neck. He jumped back instinctively to avoid another half-seen movement at his side and found himself plunging through the portal.

With a flash he was inside his sanctum. The inscribed leaves of the iris door scissored shut behind him with a grim sound of finality. He blinked in the soft light, only now realising how truly dark it had been in the palace. He saw that he was not alone.

'Morr! Where have you been?' Kraillach babbled in relief, 'I am assailed! Assassins are at my very door!'

Morr's double-handed klaive came flashing down and tore Kraillach's blade from his hands.

'No!' Kraillach screamed, reeling back in horror. 'Not you! You're trustworthy! Loyal! All the years you served me…'

The towering incubus slowly circled his archon, blade at the ready for a killing stroke. When he spoke his voice was dispassionate, even disappointed.

'I am loyal, my archon. I served your father and his father before him. I am loyal to House Kraillach, and to the Realm Eternal as it has become. By my life or death I would have saved you if I could, but you are no longer Kraillach.'

'What do you mean I'm no longer Kraillach! I'm me! You're my chief executioner! Protect me, curse you!'

Morr hesitated and for a moment Kraillach dared to hope that his chief executioner, the most loyal and trusted of all his minions, would have a change of heart. 'I regret this has to be done, my archon, I regret all that has been done… I found out too late to prevent the outcome. If I had known my actions would bring this ending…'

Taking full advantage of the momentary distraction Kraillach whipped out his blast pistol and fired. The shot caught the incubus high in the chest, punching a ragged hole in his armour and spinning him about with the impact. Morr crashed into a table and fell on it, splintering the ornately carved wood into flinders. The giant two-metre klaive spun from his grasp and clattered across the chamber floor with its power field spitting angrily

'You've no idea what I've become!' Kraillach spat, his voice altering with each word. Worms of warp-spawned energy were writhing in his gut, transforming his flesh into a suitable vessel to accommodate a presence from beyond the veil. It was too soon, too soon by far. It had hoped to grow much stronger before emerging, but with its Kraillach-vessel under threat it had to come forth and protect its investment. The psychic seed planted during Kraillach's resurrection blossomed to began to bear horrid fruit. Pulsating energy flowed into his limbs and body, filling him with the fever-life of the possessed.

'All my new converts gone, you piece of dung!' roared the Daemon-Kraillach. 'You'll pay for that!' The air was buzzing with a demented choir of lost souls; obscenities were beginning to crawl forth unbidden from the dark recesses of consciousness. Quicker than thought the Daemon-Kraillach reached out with newly-formed claws to grasp at Morr. A shiver of anticipation ran through its multi-dimensional sensory lattice at the prospect of tearing the incubus limb from limb and consuming his soul.

'Thank you, my archon,' Morr whispered, 'for the gift of vindication.'

Too late the Daemon-Kraillach saw the belt of linked plates grasped in the incubus's first. The descending claws were met by a blaze of heat and a flash of light that violently threw them back. The warped entity staggered, struggling to control its new form in the blast of unexpected stimulus. Morr tossed away the smoking shield generator and painfully retrieved his fallen klaive, rising unsteadily to confront his daemonically-possessed master.

'Forgive me, my archon,' Morr intoned. The thing that Kraillach had become screamed with laughter as it swung its claws down in a killing arc.

The two-metre blade in Morr's hands swept up to sever the downrushing claws with a single, clean cut. The Daemon-Kraillach reeled back trumpeting in outrage, warp-spawned energy drooling from its wounds like white-hot liquid magma. Morr's horizontal return stroke severed the creature's horned head at the neck, the thrashing body falling at the edge of the sunken bath.

The bloated, altered corpse visibly deflated as the stolen warp energies fled from it in tongues of aetheric fire. Soon only the wizened, headless and handless corpse of Kraillach was left behind. His blood swirled into the waters of the bath forming submerged cloudscapes of pink and red, as it had done a thousand times before.

Polite applause echoed around the half-ruined chamber. A grey figure stood by the portal that a moment ago had been closed. Morr swayed and lowered his blade.

'Heroically executed, if I may say so!' exclaimed Motley. 'Bravo!'

The incubus inclined his head minutely, his contempt for the grey-clad interloper apparent in even that small gesture. Motley seemed hurt by this cold reception and became serious.

'Now finish it properly,' he said primly, 'and burn the body.'

IN THE CATACOMBS beneath High Commorragh a triple-threaded voice spoke in its dripping cell. *'The seed has been destroyed. The children of fury cleansed it from within before it could bear fruit. Its sire still remains, and his roots burrow deeper every day. The Realm Eternal crumbles but El'Uriaq's other schemes carry forward unchecked.'*

'Oh, but his time will come, Angevere, his time will come,' a crooked figure wheezed as it shuffled through the crone's cell. 'We must watch and wait as we prepare our plan. Our opportunity will arise and we must be ready for it when it does. The plan will work. It has to work.'

CHAPTER 14
DESIRES OF THE BLADE

XELIAN STALKED THROUGH the bowels of the practice chambers below her fortress followed by a cautious trail of sycophants and supplicants. In recent weeks the Blades of Desire had become favourites in the Commorrite arena circuit. Every wych cult, Reaver pack and hellion gang in the city had been clamouring for a chance to fight for Xelian's approval to enter her arena. Every day was marked with souls being quenched by the thousand for the vicarious pleasure of the kabals crammed onto her terraces. The roar of the crowd was an almost constant presence in the fortress now, echoing down from the arena above and giving the place an almost palpable pulse of excitement and energy.

The fortress was buzzing with purpose, minions leapt at her command, but Xelian felt curiously disassociated from it all. Beneath the sure hand of

El'Uriaq's guidance, her kabal was flourishing. She suddenly had connections all over the city, a hidden network that greased palms and removed obstacles seemingly at will. Despite the great tyrant's increasing suspicions everything had become so easy that it bothered her. She had started to feel unnecessary.

At times she had begun to feel as if her minions were merely humouring her, exchanging little knowing looks behind her back. The thought of it drove her into a vindictive frenzy, and had sent her lashing out at them so often that they now stayed well clear of their archon except at the most pressing need. Xelian's sense of isolation was increasing daily, in pace with the growing fear that hidden hands were slowly but surely wresting control of her own kabal away from her.

Seemingly overnight her favourite, Aez'ashya, had been catapulted to stardom and attracted her own following, and a cult was forming around her. The succubus still professed undying loyalty to Xelian of course, but all the warning signs were there. The day was coming when Aez'ashya would have to take her Hydra cult and leave the fortress to carve out her own territory.

Or not.

If Xelian were removed Aez'ashya could fight her way to the top of the Blades of Desire easily enough. She might even make a direct challenge, although it would be a bold move on her part to test her skills against her archon. Some, like Kraillach, might spend their fortunes on tricks and artifices in place of martial ability but Xelian kept her own counsel. Her fighting capabilities were honed to perfection through endless practice both public and private. She had always kept her grip on the Blades of Desire through the strength of her own arm and welcomed open challenges over slinking conspiracies anytime.

No, what troubled Xelian the most about the amorphous tentacles she could feel closing around her was that there was nothing to fasten on to and attack. At first she had begun to imagine that she was sensing Vect at work, subtly undermining her kabal from within. Lately she had come to believe otherwise. Something about the subtly dismissive manner of El'Uriaq in their last encounter had resonated with her, as if he had come to view her as an obstacle rather than an ally.

'You are such a wild beast, Xelian,' El'Uriaq had joked lightly in that oh-so warm and friendly way of his. 'I swear that the bloodletting is all that truly interests you. There's more to vengeance than simply throwing your enemy into the arena to become blade-fodder.' At the time it had seemed like a fine jest, but looking back now there was an undertone that the joke was on her. She found she was clenching her fists at the thought and briefly wished she had claws so that she could flex them.

Whether it was Vect or El'Uriaq, something was out there working against her. Something insidious, invisible and untouchable. The situation made her dangerously frustrated and spoiling for a fight. In an effort to work out some of her ire she had summoned her inner circle of wyches and succubi for a practice bout in a newly built chamber of her own design.

Some blade work might just give her the clarity she needed to dispel the clouds of paranoia and uncertainty that had begun to loom so large in her mind.

She descended a broad ramp to evade her fluttering suitors, disappearing into a series of low-ceilinged, cavern-like chambers filled with workshops and noisy activity to escape their platitudes. Here slaves were feverishly preparing grav vehicles of various types for the coming day's aerial bouts. Power units were being tuned, weapons loaded and bladevanes were being sharpened. The actinic glare of fusion torches lit the scene where the damage from previous skirmishes was being rapidly repaired. In another area piles of notched weapons and dented armour were being reconditioned for the use of fresh teams of doomed slaves.

Xelian had been secretly rather flattered by the notoriety she'd gained of late, even while she outwardly claimed it as her natural birthright. Some of the long-standing, infamous groupings of Commorragh had sent representatives to test the mettle of Xelian's patronage. From the Cult of Strife had come virtually legions of wyches eager to test the dire arts they learned among the Bone Middens on the outskirts of Aelindrach. The Crimson Ascension had dispatched a squadron of blood-red riders from their eternal battles among the upper spires of High Commorragh, and the hellions of the Savage Caress had followed them to carry their eternal enmity into a new realm.

Xelian left the workshops to see the fruits of their labour in action. From a windswept ledge on the inner edge of the arena she watched red-painted

Reavers duelling with fang-winged hellions over the fathoms-deep gulf. The angry swarm snarled back and forth in constant motion, the incredible agility of the hellions countered by the weight and acceleration of the jetbikes. The skills being displayed were nothing less than breathtaking, the expert riders flipping and whirling their machines through the air with reckless agility. These were legendary contenders from gangs that had torn themselves apart and been reborn, phoenix-like, from the ashes a thousand times over. When the time came for war their loyalty would be invaluable.

She allowed her gaze to wander upwards to take in the jagged bulk of Vect's ziggurat where it hung, dark and ominously silent, above her fortress. It had arrived unheralded within hours of the first news of Kraillach's assassination. Xelian had been summoned to stand before the titanic projected face of the tyrant and be questioned like some errant slave, an experience that still made Xelian grind her teeth with fury.

'I'm sure you've heard about the passing of our mutual friend Archon Kraillach, Xelian,' Vect had boomed down at her. 'Given that you had a recent and well-publicised disagreement with him it seems pertinent to discover your thoughts on the affair.'

'I had no part in it, supreme overlord,' Xelian had replied, truthfully for once. 'I heard that Kraillach fell to enemies within his own kabal, therefore he was weak and couldn't keep his own retinue under control.'

Dark eyes wider than windows regarded Xelian with ageless wisdom and bottomless malice. 'Weak?

Perhaps he was,' the tyrant's voice rumbled, 'but old Kraillach was also terribly, terribly cautious. Losing one of his pedigree is a rarity, he wasn't like you youngsters that rely on luck and a quick blade to stay on top. I must say I'm even slightly moved at his loss.' The cliff-like visage broke into a terrible smile at that thought. 'But only slightly,' the tyrant amended.

'Why concern yourself at all, great tyrant?' Xelian had shouted back, refusing to be daunted by Vect's tricks. 'Your laws have been kept. Kraillach failed to protect himself and his position so he paid the price. I had no hand in it but I applaud those that did the deed and I would give them a place in my own kabal without hesitation. They would find neither softness nor weakness in the Blades of Desire.'

'A fine speech, Xelian, I am warmed by your appreciation of the correctness of my laws and their manifest benefits. I think I shall keep a presence here for a time where I can fully appreciate that loyalty and strength through closer examination. Excitement does seem to attend your works here, I trust that you won't disappoint.'

With that the face of tyrant had winked out and had not returned. The ziggurat had remained hanging like a brooding sentinel over the games and blood-letting ever since, always silently observing. It galled her a little that the tyrant's scrutiny was probably at the root of some of her current notoriety but she had determined to brazen it out. Xelian's schemes were not going to be easy to uncover, and she had taken the ominous presence of the ziggurat as a sign of how little Vect knew, rather than how much.

Xelian returned inside and wove her way deeper into the bowels of the practice levels. She called her newest training area the crown of thorns. It was dominated by an interwoven ring made up of forty-metre-long spines tapering to razor-sharp points. Fighting inside or atop the ring took extraordinary nerves and footwork, with any slip in the mass of sharp points and honed edges liable to cost an inept fighter dearly. It was an energising experience in its own right that could be further heightened with gravity inversions and pressure waves. Xelian had hopes to perfect a larger version of it for use in the arena one day, although it was too deadly to be practical for most slave species. Still, their hopeless attempts to keep their footing on the sharp spines might well have some comedy value, particularly in combination with a pursuit by suitably agile predators of some sort, ur-ghuls or loxatl perhaps…

She surveyed the dozen assembled wyches with a critical eye. They were exclusively female fighters in half-armour or less, although none had quite gone the whole way to being entirely skyclad. All of them were possessed of the subtle grace only an eldar female trained rigorously from birth could aspire to, they could run on spear points or dance on a blade's edge – a matter that was about to be put to the test. These were her chosen, her hekatrix, the keenest blades at her command. Aez'ashya would have been among them once, the apple of Xelian's eye before Yllithian's scheming had ruined her.

The crown of thorns floated before them, a hundred metres across and filling the practice space virtually wall-to-wall as it slowly contra-rotated in a mesmerising lattice of sharp edges and needle-points. The pulse of it seemed to fill the air, relentless and implacable as the beat of a giant's heart. They mounted light grav platforms to elevate themselves to its upper surface before stepping off onto a shifting toroidal landscape of dully-gleaming blades. She gazed around at her hekatrix and raised her voice above the low whisper of the thorn-blades cutting through the air.

'To first *blood*.' Xelian found she savoured the word so unexpectedly that it made her hesitate for a moment before she recovered her poise.

'Begin.'

The wyches whirled into action, sprinting across the surface of the crown in a blur of flashing limbs. The unspoken rules of engagement were that everyone fought for themselves, but that meant temporary alliances of weaker fighters as they attempted to overwhelm the strongest. Xelian quickly had three of her wyches pressing at her defences. She ran along the blade she stood upon with quick, sure strides and sprang to another sliding past five metres away, daring her assailants to emulate her feat.

The first wych to try to follow her met her knives and slid into the maze of edged metal below, ending her short, painful journey impaled on an upward-tilting point. The other two thought better of making the jump and ran back to find a surer way around.

Xelian had problems of her own. She was caught blind-side by another opponent, a wych named Lorys recently risen from the Cult of Strife. Lorys's determined attack drove Xelian step-by-step to the very tip of the thorn she stood upon. There she turned at bay, her knives weaving a bright web that struck sparks from Lorys's thrusts.

The crown lurched slightly beneath Xelian's feet as its rotation began to speed up. Just as it did so one of Lorys's whistling blows slipped under her guard and creased her ribs, slicing though skin and muscle with surgical precision. The kiss of cold steel thrilled through Xelian's nerves and finally dispelled her fugue of doubts and concerns. She was totally in the moment at last, the dance of blades becoming her entire world. Lorys relaxed fractionally at the sight of blood, thinking her archon would stand down as the rules of the bout dictated.

'More!' Xelian shouted, whirling her knives furiously onto the attack.

Xelian's ferocious counter-assault caught Lorys off guard, driving her back down the gleaming thorn. She was soon bleeding freely from a score of nicks to her arms and legs as she fought desperately to keep her archon in check. The bloodshed seemed to drive Xelian into even more of a frenzy, raining her attacks down with no thought to her own defence. Lorys was soon reeling beneath the rain of blows, barely able stave off an inevitable deathblow.

The two wyches Xelian had evaded earlier suddenly rejoined the fray, leaping from blade to blade to attack Xelian's flanks. She turned on them with a scream of pure hatred, the glittering fangs of her knives carving into them with predatory swiftness.

'You are such a wild beast, Xelian.'

Xelian tore open a face and sent one of her chosen

companions screaming into the soughing blades. A stroke like white lightning came from her flank and sheared through her upper arm, the red lips of the wound parting obscenely as the bicep flopped loose. She laughed in wild ecstasy and pivoted to impale her other attacker on twin fangs, driving them deep into her body before ripping upwards with horrible strength. Bloody viscera slithered down her arms and painted them a fetching crimson.

'I swear that the bloodletting is all that truly interests you.'

A knife was sunk into her back, a penetrating shard of bright pain probing up under ribs and lungs for the heart. She allowed the weight of the eviscerated corpse on her own knives to carry her forwards, half-turning to smash Lorys's face with her elbow. They were falling, falling into the moving skein of bright edges.

A distant part of her mind was screaming that this was relevant somehow and that falling demanded action, but the all-consuming bloodlust that had been unleashed in her soul blotted it out completely. She twisted and caught Lorys on her fangs to drag her close for a final, deadly embrace as the churning blades rushed up to meet them. Blood sprayed over her, embracing her in a crimson flood of joy. The last blood Xelian saw being shed was her own.

CHAPTER 15
A CONFESSION

*'I raised a pillar above Cyllidh's city gate and I
flayed all of the dracons who had revolted, and I
hung the pillar with their skins. Some I sealed at
the base of the pillar, some I impaled upon the pillar
on barbs, and others I bound round about the pillar
with chains of burning ice… And I cut the limbs of
the officers, of the noble officers who had rebelled…
Many captives I burned with fire and many others I
took as living slaves into my own house. From some
I took their fingers and toes, from others noses and
tongues, of many I put out the eyes so that all might
know the hand of Vect.'*

– Asdrubael Vect

YLLITHIAN HURRIED ALONG through the secret ways
beneath his palace, his mind racing furiously. He had
been summoned by El'Uriaq, called like a slave to

attend on his master. The thought provoked the taste of bile in his mouth but behind it lay the omnipresent taint of fear. Xelian and Kraillach both lay dead at the hands of their own retainers. It was no coincidence that both of his old, most trusted allies had suddenly succumbed to plots after centuries of leading their kabals. Fear of assassination had grown to encompass every moment of Yllithian's waking life. Even his dreams were haunted by stealthy murderers that wore the faces of his most trusted servants.

By all accounts El'Uriaq seemed to thrive on danger. In the months since his resurrection he had survived no less than fourteen attempts on his life without so much as a scratch. His assailants were able to claim no such happy condition. El'Uriaq wielded raw psychic power with an effortless ease that was as terrifying to witness for those around him as it was brutally effective at crushing any threat to his person. Many of his most fervent followers had taken to hailing him as a demi-god. Just how the old emperor of Shaa-dom could wield such powers while avoiding any repercussions from beyond the veil was a matter of great interest to Yllithian, but it was immaterial at present. The simple truth was that El'Uriaq was in control and seemingly unassailable. Whatever hand had struck down Kraillach and Xelian seemed unable to harm El'Uriaq and, for some reason, had passed Yllithian by.

At first Yllithian had believed that Vect had become aware of their plot, that despite all possible precautions the tyrant had divined that El'Uriaq had returned. Then he began to fear that Vect was trying to turn El'Uriaq against him by deliberately targeting the others while leaving Yllithian himself conspicuously unchallenged. Lately Yllithian had come to the conclusion that El'Uriaq himself had to be behind the assassinations. His spies in the city had heard not a whisper, nor a breath of rumour that could betray El'Uriaq's return in the months since his resurrection, nor any indication that Vect was aware of it.

So it was that when El'Uriaq called for his presence, Yllithian, great and noble archon of the White Flames, came running. Yllithian had always prided himself upon, among other things, his clear insight. He could see the way that his allies had been swept away when they exhausted their usefulness and he was determined not to follow them into oblivion. For now he must play the devoted follower until he could find El'Uriaq's weakness. Yllithian consoled himself that he already had reason to believe the old emperor of Shaa-dom was not quite as resourceful as recent events might indicate.

Yllithian stopped short, pulled out of his ruminations to wonder at the sight before him. He'd heard that at El'Uriaq's instruction slaves had been labouring to break open new areas of the catacombs beneath. Yllithian had given little thought to the reports when he heard them, imagining only that El'Uriaq sought to open up a little more living space for himself while he plotted Vect's demise. It seemed the work being undertaken was more extensive than he had imagined.

Where there had previously been only a narrow corridor, rock-cut galleries now rose out of sight on either side. In each gallery gangs of slaves were toiling beneath the lash to widen the excavations further. It was still a hole, of course, in comparison to the sweeping grandeur of High Commorragh, but it was hard to deny that El'Uriaq's works radiated a crude strength and purpose not to be found in the glittering spires above.

Yllithian walked on more slowly, cultivating an air of bored disinterest as he observed the work in progress. The slaves were all fresh, their limbs hale and straight, their skins little marked by the sores and scars they soon accumulated. Yllithian wondered what had happened to all the previous gangs of slaves swallowed up by El'Uriaq's lair. He moved deeper, pondering the latest nugget of information he had uncovered about Kraillach's death.

There was no doubt that Morr had been the one behind the fall of the Realm Eternal. Scandalously the incubus, a faithful servant since before anyone seemed able to remember, had turned on his master and his whole kabal. Yllithian's spies had reported to him that the slaughter had been merciless. Kraillach's kabal was a broken reed now, its scattered survivors staying but one step ahead of avaricious rivals intent on carving up their remaining assets. Kraillach himself had met True Death, his body utterly destroyed.

Morr had subsequently vanished without trace. In Yllithian's secret consultations with Angevere she had said that Morr had returned to the hidden shrine of Arhra, Father of Scorpions. It was a reference to the legendary place where all incubi were said to learn their killing arts. Yllithian set little store in the existence of such a mythical location and took her meaning to be a metaphorical one – Morr had sought shelter among the ranks of his fellow incubi. Yllithian would have given a great deal to know just why the incubi had chosen to overlook Morr's blatant betrayal of their professed tenets of obedience and loyalty to their archons. Sadly that particular piece of information was also hidden from him, and if the crone knew more about it she refused to say.

Nonetheless logic dictated that if Morr had acted at the behest of El'Uriaq, why had he not come forth to claim his reward? It was an altogether more likely scenario that Morr had slaughtered his archon for transgressing one of the incubi's obscure ascetic beliefs. His flight to the incubi implied that some matter of honour was at stake. The Realm Eternal had been meekly falling in line with El'Uriaq's machinations but now it was lost to him. That spoke to Yllithian of some other hidden hand at work. He could only hope that it was not the hand of Asdrubael Vect.

Beyond the galleries the passage narrowed to the more familiar catacombs again, but even here new cross-passages had been made. Everywhere he could hear the buzz of low voices and the sound of hurried footsteps. Three times Yllithian was stopped by arrogant trueborn warriors and forced to explain his business there. When he named himself and his business they were deferential enough but the incidents chafed at Yllithian's already raw temper even further. He carefully kept his emotions in check; Xelian's recent fall from grace was still sharp in his mind.

Opinions varied as to whether the Blades of Desire had survived as a kabal because of or despite the tyrant's scrutiny at an especially vulnerable time. A new archon had been raised with a minimal amount of bloodletting after Xelian's death. Dark rumours persisted of Xelian being seized by a fit of madness immediately before her demise but the extreme damage her body had sustained precluded any practical attempt at investigation. Her resurrection was proving unfeasibly prolonged for a variety of ill-explained reasons. It had reached a point where Yllithian was beginning to suspect Xelian's haemonculi had been bribed to prevent, or at least delay, her return.

Yllithian was regretting the loss of the services of Bellathonis, himself incarcerated in one of his own sarcophagi since he had displeased El'Uriaq. Apparently the master haemonculus had sustained dreadful injuries during the resurrection, his own splintered bones piercing his organs in many places. Weeks of regrowth, Bellathonis's wracks had told him, would be required and they refused to rouse their master ahead of time. Yllithian had sensed deception from the wracks, a fearful taint that they were hiding something. No doubt they too were in El'Uriaq's employ.

Bellathonis would have been able to get to the bottom of things, or at the very least get Xelian back in the running. To Yllithian's practised eye the changeover at the Blades of Desire had been altogether too smooth, a sure sign that someone had worked hard behind the scenes to make it so. He had little doubt that the new archon of the Blades of Desire owed her allegiance to El'Uriaq body and soul. Xelian had so effectively eliminated rivals from her own bloodline that the remnants of her house were now helpless pawns and figureheads. It would be long – if ever – before House Xelian rose to any form of prominence in Commorragh again. In the old alliance of the noble houses that left only Yllithian and his White Flames free to act.

As free as fear would allow.

YLLITHIAN PASSED BENEATH what had been a low opening that was now an arch three stories high. Beyond it the way opened into an amphitheatre with a tall throne on a stepped dais at its centre. Yllithian followed a wide ramp down to the floor of the amphitheatre, noting how crude and unfinished everything looked; the ramp was rough and uneven, the angles of the stepped terraces mismatched. Slaves were scattered everywhere chipping miserably at the rock while being alternately harassed, goaded or abused by scores of guards with nothing better to do with their time. Messengers dashed in and out vying for attention with extravagantly costumed victuallers that were intent on displaying their wares: spice wines and stem meads that had been distilled from whole settlements, the cured flesh and pickled organs of extinct species, or the last living examples of endangered ones. Jewels and the richest finery lay in heaps like a mythical dragon's horde.

At the centre of this great constellation of activity was El'Uriaq himself. His personal gravity was such that it made every occurrence in the wide amphitheatre orbit around him. The guards abused the slaves for *his* pleasure, the piles of treasure were *his* tribute, the messengers clamoured for *his* ear, the hustlers showed their goods to win *his* favour. Yllithian approached the dais feeling lonely and vulnerable, a dark-clad non-entity in the multitude. As the proud archon of the White Flames he had already had to accept that his only protection against El'Uriaq was his continued usefulness. If that ever failed him neither guards nor walls would keep him safe, as Kraillach and Xelian had discovered to their cost. Even so it was still a test for his nerve to appear before the old emperor of Shaa-dom shorn of any such artifices and depend solely on El'Uriaq's good favour not to be killed on a whim.

El'Uriaq wore an open-fronted robe of pale silver over a suit of shining bronze-coloured body armour. His head bore a crown adorned with eight stars of shifting hues and his hand bore a sceptre carved from a single ruby. So had high archons appeared in the days before the rise of Vect, a wordless claim to nobility of a lost age – a time that Shaa-dom in point of fact was never a part of. Such panoply left little doubt as to El'Uriaq's ambitions to rule Commorragh in the tyrant's stead. Despite the crowd El'Uriaq sensed Yllithian's arrival immediately, turning to him with a delighted expression as if at the return of an old friend that had been long absent.

'Nyos! My thanks for accepting my invitation, I'm so glad you could come!' El'Uriaq called, his rich voice full of warmth and welcome.

'It was my honour, El'Uriaq, to be invited to your hidden kingdom,' Yllithian said as he looked about him pointedly. 'Your security is not a concern any more, I assume?'

'Fear not, everyone here can be trusted to take their own life before revealing my secrets to our enemies.'

'Reassuring. I would include myself in that pool of happy martyrs, of course.'

'Your devotion to our common cause is beyond question, Nyos, I know that,' El'Uriaq replied with heartfelt conviction. What did he know that Yllithian didn't? The thought was chilling.

'Which is why I have invited you here to come and share your thoughts about the unfortunate demise of Kraillach.'

Yllithian's mind went through an instantaneous flip. El'Uriaq was asking *him* for theories on Kraillach's murder? Perhaps the plan was to entrap him with a false accusation of complicity?

'I understand that Kraillach's own chief executioner, an incubus named Morr, was behind the heinous crime in question. He has evaded justice ever since as best I know.'

El'Uriaq was watching him carefully, weighing the truth or falsehood behind every word.

'Yes, that much is common gossip, so I hear,' said El'Uriaq lightly. 'The burning question is *why* the executioner slew his master. Why do you think he did it, Nyos? What was the motive?'

'I had assumed he was in the employ of our enemies,' Yllithian lied, noting that El'Uriaq didn't seem to require any theories about Xelian's passing. He decided to risk a probe in that direction. 'Perhaps this was an attempt to weaken our alliance, given the recent… disruption within the Blades of Desire. Our enemies sought to remove the Realm Eternal as a viable power block too.'

El'Uriaq did not rise to the bait, still seeming to weigh Yllithian's answer. No doubt El'Uriaq already knew more than Yllithian did about Kraillach's death and was feeling him out. No theories were really needed, merely an insight into how much Yllithian knew or guessed at. The true question now was whether an excess of knowledge or ignorance would be the fatal factor on Yllithian's part.

Yllithian decided he would rather be damned for knowing too much than too little, adding: 'Of course for an incubus, especially one of Morr's standing, such a betrayal is virtually unprecedented. And if one such as he betrayed us to our enemies how can we still be at liberty to be having this conversation? Vect's castigators would already be at our door.'

'Quite,' El'Uriaq nodded.

'So if not at the behest of Vect, then who?'

'Just so, Nyos, there are other forces at work here. The tyrant is still ignorant of my return, I'm sure of that, but I confess that Kraillach's passing is troubling to me.'

'With the perpetrator apparently vanished I'm afraid that I find it difficult to suggest a productive course of action.'

'Wheels are in motion, Nyos. My foes will find me harder to be rid of this time around.' El'Uriaq smiled lightly as he said the words but Yllithian caught a dangerous light glowing in his eyes.

'But let us lay aside such grim talk. There is another

matter I wished to speak with you about, a lighter one than the tragic demise of Kraillach. The time has come for a gathering of forces, for the conspirators to take binding oaths together and dedicate themselves fully to the cause.' El'Uriaq's gaze was far away, as though he saw another time and place in his mind's eye.

'Three days hence I will call together our chief supporters for a celebratory banquet, a show of strength so that they may take heart at their numbers and also a warning when they witness the fate of the traitors I've discovered among them. You will attend I hope, Yllithian. I owe you so much that it simply wouldn't be the same without you.'

El'Uriaq's solicitous invitation seemed so coy that Yllithian wondered if he were being mocked. 'Of course, it'll be my great pleasure to attend,' he replied mechanically as he wondered if he was being invited to his own public execution.

'Wonderful, it really was too kind of you to come and visit in person. You must forgive the disarray, there's still so much to do.'

Yllithian recognised that he was being politely invited to leave. He bowed. 'My thanks for finding the time to speak with me, El'Uriaq. It was an illuminating experience, as ever.' El'Uriaq nodded and smiled, and Yllithian backed away until the old emperor was swallowed up again by his constellation of followers. He swallowed dryly, but the taste of bile wouldn't leave the back of his throat.

Yllithian hurried up the ramp and out into the tunnels before his sense of impotent rage overwhelmed his discipline. Having to virtually abase himself before the creature he had helped to create vexed him sorely. He was so wrapped in his own thoughts that he barely gave heed to the crooked figure that followed him from the amphitheatre. He wound his way past the tirelessly working slave gangs to places where the sound of their tools and snap of whips receded into the distance. The walls of passages gradually narrowed to little more than shoulder-width and the turnings became fewer. The sepulchral quiet of the deep catacombs reasserted itself as his feet carried him automatically along memorised paths towards his palace above.

Only there, when he was upon paths seldom trod by guards and slaves, did he become aware that he was no longer alone. He turned at once and laid a hand on the hilt of his blade as he called a challenge.

'Who are you that dares to dog the steps of an archon? Come out and show yourself!'

A crooked figure limped painfully out of the shadows and into the light of a solitary gem overhead. It was a gaunt, black scarecrow-like figure that was bent unnaturally in back and limb.

'It is I, Bellathonis, my archon, and I would have words with you.'

'Bellathonis?' Yllithian exclaimed in disbelief. 'But your wracks told me that you were in the process of rebirth!'

'Forgive the deception, my archon,' the master haemonculus wheezed as he came closer. 'I have forgone more permanent restitution of bodily function for the present. There simply seemed too much to do and being thought of as... unavailable has allowed me freedoms I might otherwise have not enjoyed.'

Yllithian looked at the haemonculus more carefully. A host of slender rods had been drilled through his flesh into his bones. These were being held immobile by external clamps to brace his shattered limbs. A small pharmacopoeia made up of canisters and bags hung about his neck with lines running from it to feed needles pushed beneath his grey, waxy-looking skin. Pale blood oozed from the wounds and the haemonculus's eyes were fever-bright.

'I applaud your dedication,' Yllithian said, somewhat repelled at the thought. 'And what have you been doing with all the copious free time afforded to you by not being dead?'

'Trying to understand what happened when we brought back El'Uriaq,' Bellathonis said as he limped forwards. 'Trying to understand what happened to Archon Kraillach and Archon Xelian.' The twisted haemonculus leaned in closer and his voice dropped to a harsh whisper. 'Trying to understand what we called up, Yllithian, and how we can dispose of it.'

Yllithian drew back involuntarily at the implication. 'Are you mad?' he hissed angrily. 'It is death to speak such words and yet you speak them here, in his very domain?'

The haemonculus smiled at him apologetically. 'Better here than your own throne room, archon, you know yourself that the taint has spread that far. Why else would you come alone? You know that your warriors would follow El'Uriaq's commands rather than your own. You know that his very presence sways hearts and commands minds to do his bidding.'

Yllithian looked around the shadowed, empty passageway, self-consciously reassuring himself that they were alone. His hand flexed on the hilt of his sword with the momentary urge to draw it and slash the haemonculus's smiling face into red ruin. Yllithian mastered the urge and unwrapped his fingers with a conscious effort. Bellathonis was right, there was no denying it. The sense of helplessness he was feeling stemmed from the simple fact he could trust no one to obey him.

'Very well, I'm listening. But choose your words with care, crooked one, I'm not about to betray our beloved El'Uriaq no matter what your inducements.'

Bellathonis nodded slowly, recognising the old formulas of denial in his words.

'You've gone to speak with Angevere many times, but she is obstinate, is she not? I can assure you that a more certain hand at the controls has her singing like a bird. Add to that some investigations of my own and... well, here we are.'

Bellathonis sighed, his steel-pinned limbs winking in the dim light as he moved. 'You see, even with the worldsinger's power the regeneration couldn't be instantaneous – for that to happen it needed even more energy coming in from outside.

'When we recalled El'Uriaq something else found the crack in reality and came back with him, a great revenant from beyond the veil. It wears El'Uriaq like a mask, hidden for now but guiding his every action.'

'For now?' Yllithian asked warily, his face stony and unreadable.

'Yes, until it gains a strong enough foothold in our

reality that it can emerge fully and open a permanent breach,' Bellathonis said, cocking his head bird-like at Yllithian as if he expected him to already know the answer.

'In many ways it's a perfect symbiosis,' Bellathonis continued. 'El'Uriaq's residual personality and self-belief create an ideal framework for the entity to attach itself to. As his ambitions grow it grows with him, continually feeding him more power from the outside. It's a familiar pattern among the slave races. We set little value by their lore but in this area their experiences are in some ways more extensive than our own.'

The silence that fell between the archon and haemonculus was broken only by the drip of moisture and the sigh of a foetid breeze blowing through the tunnels. Yllithian was carefully weighing what secrets he could learn against the price of discovery. His curiosity gradually edged ahead of his caution. He could always present everything he was told to El'Uriaq and denounce Bellathonis later, although if the haemonculus was correct Yllithian held out little hope that would save his life.

'This is why Morr turned against his master? You're saying that Kraillach was… tainted by his association by El'Uriaq?' he eventually asked.

'Yes,' the haemonculus wheezed regretfully. 'In some fashion the entity that entered El'Uriaq also infected Kraillach during the resurrection. Through Kraillach's influences the Realm Eternal was being brought firmly under El'Uriaq's control – that is until their chief executioner saw the peril for what it was and took action. The Realm Eternal was always in danger of collapsing into a pleasure cult. Kraillach was preparing to take them the whole way.'

'So now the incubi shield him,' interrupted Yllithian, 'oathbreaker and traitor that he is. Few archons will trust that silent brotherhood again if word of this gets out.' Vague schemes for blackmail flourished in Yllithian's mind unbidden. To gain a hold over the incubi would be a fine prize indeed...

'Not when the whole of this sad tale is known, my archon,' Bellathonis replied, dashing cold water on the half-formed plans. 'As I understand it the incubi pledge themselves to serve their living lord and not some daemonically-corrupted imposter.'

'And what of Xelian?' Yllithian prompted. 'I can only assume that your grand conspiracy theory incorporates her death too.'

'Denial of the obvious is indeed the last refuge of the desperate mind, my archon, as I have seen on my examination tables many times.' Bellathonis smiled ingratiatingly. 'I was unsurprised that she, too, fell into El'Uriaq's web. In many ways the more surprising thing is that you have survived thus far, unharmed and untainted as best as I can discover. He finds you useful, Yllithian, more useful than your noble allies.

'Much like Kraillach, Xelian carried the seeds of her own destruction inside her, albeit in less spectacular fashion. It's my belief that the thing posing as El'Uriaq found Xelian too proud and intractable to be a useful tool. In order to remove her it tended those seeds of weakness until they blossomed and brought about her own death. The thirst for blood was ever at the fore of Xelian's mind. El'Uriaq's subtle prompt-ings cultivated that thirst until it consumed her.'

'What are you saying that you believe we've unleashed?'

'An old doom, my archon, one that has been unleashed and contained many times before in our city. Fear not, we are more cunning than our foes know. Our enemy still believes that his purpose is hidden, and although he wonders about Kraillach's destruction his fears are formless as yet.'

'You would be telling me none of this unless you needed my help. What is it you expect me to do?'

'A trifle only, I would not ask you to act directly against him. If El'Uriaq's personality is strengthened the entity will find it increasingly difficult to control his actions. It so happens that we have an artefact of El'Uriaq's past life in our hands, one that might focus his mind on the present juncture in a highly success-ful fashion–'

'The head of the crone,' Yllithian said flatly.

'Just so. Angevere knew El'Uriaq of old. I have no doubt that contact with her will trigger all kinds of memories. If you were to present the head to him as a gift and a keepsake at this gathering he's planning, El'Uriaq will not be able to refuse it.'

'Because naturally you wouldn't have infested it with something deadly, or simply turned it into a bomb. Crude, Bellathonis. I can't believe that you're serious. I'll not be your delivery slave.'

'Of course you will be able to fully examine the head before taking it, and I assure you that no assas-sination device will be carried within it or upon it in any fashion. I honestly imagine the gift will win great favour from both El'Uriaq and his hidden master.'

'How so?' Yllithian asked warily. He found that he was taking the haemonculus's proposition seriously despite his reflexive scepticism. He didn't doubt that Bellathonis had some ulterior motive behind the idea, but if he could discomfit El'Uriaq without openly dirtying his hands too much the idea appealed to him.

'Of El'Uriaq's seven handmaids, only Angevere escaped the daemons in the fall of Shaa-dom. Restoring her to him, even in such an attenuated form, will stimulate El'Uriaq's residual personality magnificently. The possessing entity will also be delighted to finally have her within its grasp and may not appreciate the danger of letting its disguise slip in its moment of triumph. I don't doubt for a moment that the entity is one of those that participated in the sack of Shaadom when the breach was made there.'

'But you're saying this gift won't harm El'Uriaq *directly* in any way.'

'It will not directly harm him, no, my archon.'

'Very well, then I accept your proposal. I trust I need not emphasise the consequences attached to lying to me or attempting to make me your dupe, Bellathonis. I do not accept your wild allegations about El'Uriaq, Xelian or Kraillach. More likely we're seeing the tyrant's hand at work. You see, you listen to the crone entirely too much, perhaps she's the true source of diabolical influences you perceive in every mishap. You forget she has already been proven wrong on one key point.'

Bellathonis was genuinely perplexed. Yllithian's dart was well-placed. Perhaps he had been entirely too reliant on Angevere for her interpretation of events...

'To – ah – to which key point do you refer, my archon?' Bellathonis asked humbly.

'Why the Dysjunction, of course! She firmly predicted one would occur if we resurrected El'Uriaq and yet here we stand with no ill-effects felt beyond incessant rumours and the baseless predictions of the warp-dabblers. I'll be doing you a great service by taking the crone's head back and gifting it to El'Uriaq: I'll be saving you from her insidious lies. Follow me no further, haemonculus, or I'll give you additional reasons to enter a resurrection crypt.'

Yllithian turned and stalked away without another word. Bellathonis watched him vanish down the ill-lit passage towards his own fortress, no doubt to huddle there in mortal fear of his own retainers. Behind him the shadows shifted restlessly, a sibilant whisper forming in the air.

'Of course he suspects something,' Bellathonis grumbled to the darkness. 'He always suspects everyone and everything all of the time – that's his nature. But he'll do it when the time comes, he's desperate to take back some control in any way he can.'

The broken figure of the haemonculus shuffled away, with dark shapes flitting at his heels.

'Now we must put our trust in the worldsinger,' he wheezed to the slinking shadows. 'Everything hinges on her.'

More urgent whispers hissed from the darkness.

'Dysjunction? Don't doubt it's still coming in spite of Yllithian's claims,' Bellathonis snorted. 'It is inevitable now.'

CHAPTER 16
THE PATH OF THE RENEGADE

SINDIEL CREPT FEARFULLY along the ill-lit corridors of El'Uriaq's hidden domain. He was richly dressed in shimmering Eol-fur and sun-spider silk, with precious metal and rainbow gems adorning his hands and throat. He was armed with a sinuously beautiful splinter pistol and the *Dai Saoith*, a long, straight blade that apparently had an ancient pedigree much finer than his own. The weapons were mostly for show, to be expected on a highborn of Commorragh. The mostly deadly device he carried was currently concealed at his wrist beneath the voluminous lace at his cuffs. He was hoping that he would not have call to use *that* weapon, but he'd also found that he felt desperate enough to bring it with him – just in case.

It was all so unfair. Despite being bedecked like some barbaric princeling Sindiel's external wealth did nothing to protect him from the internal sense of destitution he felt. His star had risen swiftly under the direct patronage of Yllithian and the indirect favours of El'Uriaq. He had already gained control of a squadron of sleek Corsairs berthed at Ashkeri Talon and a palatial manse to dwell in nearby. He had warriors at his command that knelt before him and called him dracon, he had the choice of slaves taken from a million worlds to do with as he would. Now he could explore every fantasy and indulge every hidden vice in a society that did not judge nor even care how its members behaved. The archon's rewards had been everything promised and for Sindiel, a relative newcomer to the concepts of ownership and property, quite dizzying.

Nonetheless he had felt himself slowly coming to an uncomfortable revelation about the Dark Kin. It was the kind of thought that once it had formed simply wouldn't go away. In their own way the eldar of Commorragh were just as stunted and narrowed as the eldar of the craftworlds or, for that matter, the Exodites. They were also denying a part of themselves in their bid for immortality, trying to turn a blind eye to their psychic nature in the hopes of cheating She Who Thirsts. He was secretly starting to wonder if the daemon-goddess had allowed some of the eldar race to escape simply to enjoy their self-imposed suffering as they eternally twisted and turned trying to evade Her claws.

He crept along with his heart in his mouth, unable to quite decide whether he should try to stroll brazenly or not. This part of the catacombs beneath the White Flames' fortress, roughly delineated as it was, had been taken over by El'Uriaq and his minions as their makeshift palace. He'd been told the foundation plates of the great port-city were riddled with secret ways, hideouts, mines and countermines constructed by competing kabals down the long centuries. The old emperor of Shaa-dom had declared himself happy enough with these troglodytic quarters and now seldom issued forth. Slaves disappeared into El'Uriaq's den with voracious regularity, but apparently in Commorragh this in itself was not worthy of any great excitement or interest.

Sindiel could not shake the sense that a lurking horror had manifested itself down here, and that it was growing stronger by the day. Although he often felt naïve and ignorant among the darkly brilliant citizens of the eternal city he was sure of one thing – that their psychic senses were dulled to the point of blindness. They saw the warp in terms of forces to be manipulated and refused to see that it was also manipulating them in return.

The sound of approaching footsteps interrupted his troubling thoughts. He turned and fled into a darkened cross-passage before pressing himself into the shadows behind a mouldering buttress. The measured tread of two pairs of armoured feet steadily approached the cross-passage and halted briefly before moving on. Sindiel crept cautiously back to the main path in time to see the backs of two kabalite warriors disappearing in the direction he had just come from.

He moved the opposite way, reflecting bitterly on how, once again, providence had demonstrated its habit of pitching him into situations he was ill prepared for. He had come to El'Uriaq's lair with no clear objective in mind; only some vague notion of seeing how it *felt*, as if that would confirm or dispel his fears, with an underlying idea that he would improvise heroically from there. Now he had wandered inside an area that was being actively patrolled with no adequate explanation for what he was doing here. Destiny had left him with no choice but to sneak in further, if only to look for another way out.

It always happened like this. Sindiel had never thought of himself as a renegade, indeed he felt he had laboured long and hard to try and find purpose in his life. He had come to believe that his being birthed on a craftworld was a matter of mischance and concluded that he had never really been intended for such a hard, narrow life until some hiccup in destiny had cast him into it. He had rebelled often and joyously against the strictures of the seers and moralising dogma of his companions, conceiving it as his adoptive destiny to mix things up a little.

The few pranks he had played and the lessons he had attempted to teach to his moribund fellow travellers on the craftworld had done little to endear him to them or vice versa. Slowly but surely he had been expelled into the chilly outer darkness of social seclusion, there to watch others undertake their meaningless journeys along different paths; gardener, sculptor, entertainer, philosopher, artisan, warrior, on and on. It appeared to him that their aim was a lifetime of well-rounded mediocrity and he despised them for it.

He had briefly flirted with the warrior path but found it to be the most tiresomely restrictive and ritualised of them all. Everything on the warrior path seemed focused on how to stop being a warrior, how to deny that part of the psyche that lusted for violence. When he was offered the opportunity to leave his beautiful prison and escape into the wider universe he'd jumped at the chance – even now he remembered the weary shrug the seer had given when Sindiel asked him what would happen if he chose *not* to go.

For the most part the great and wonderful universe had proved to be nothing but mud and squalor warring with ignorance and stubbornness. His supposedly disaffected Ranger companions proved to be merely tourists with a taste for the outdoors and a fondness for meddling in the affairs of others. None of them had the slightest intention of questioning their way of life or attempting to forge their own path. They were simply bored and disaffected so they took the prescribed craftworld path of life that was labelled 'for the bored and the disaffected'. Sindiel had wanted more out of life than that.

Well, he'd certainly found it now, and damned his immortal soul into the bargain. Listening to seers prattle about the perils of the warp and the spirit-self was one thing, entering the daemon-haunted ruins of Shaa-dom had been quite another. He found he now believed in the existence of his immortal soul as he had never done before.

He could also blame Motley for that. Ever since Iron Thorn the grey one's words kept coming back to haunt him. Sindiel had almost died of fright when his ankle was grabbed as he lay waiting near the gate, then grown furious when he saw the grinning half-masked face bending over him.

'*Don't think that this is The End*,' the masked one had said. '*You have more choices, more chances ahead of you than you can ever know. Your path will always be your own to make no matter what they tell you. Remember that it's never too late to try and reclaim your soul.*'

The nagging idea that he could still do… *something* to recover himself had stayed with him ever since. He'd thought himself committed to the dark path, that he'd finally spat in the face of the universe once and for all and sworn himself to win power by any means. Now he had it he found that the power he'd sought was meaningless. He could feel the first tendrils of the empty hunger of the Commorrites kindling inside him and he did not like it one bit. He was starting to understand the unremitting fury of the dark city and its need to consume everything that it touched. If they stopped for even a moment the yawning void that was constantly at their heels would engulf them all. Now that an eternal life of parasitism and exploitation was laid out before him he found the idea repellent.

So, Sindiel the fool had come wandering into the monster's lair without a plan, as if a single idiotic act could redeem the murder of companions and the betrayal of secrets he had sworn to keep for all eternity. It struck him that perhaps he was being moti-vated by some self-destructive urge to court death in an effort to assuage his guilt. He found the idea oddly cheering and pushed on with a lighter step.

By now his feet had carried him to a bell-shaped chamber with three other passages leading out of it. Down the left passage he could hear distant sounds like shrieks or skirling music or some mixture of both. From directly ahead blew warm, moist air that was heavy with the sickly-sweet scents of roasting meat. Neither sounds, smells nor lights emanated from the right-hand path, and after a moment's hesitation Sindiel turned and went in that direction.

The passage twisted and sloped downwards, the rough-hewn walls occasionally lit by a dully-gleaming light gem. The walls sweated moisture that dribbled down into a small rivulet that was slowly eroding a channel in the centre of the passage. Sindiel avoided the sluggish liquid with distaste, trying not to think about what manner of effluvia might have seeped its way down here over the millennia.

He already felt he could confirm his worst fears. There was definitely a pervasive sense of wrongness in the catacombs, and it was more than just paranoia that was making Sindiel fear some hideous monstrosity lurked in every shadow. He stopped in his tracks, trying to make out the blurred form he could just see up ahead. The corridor appeared to open out and there was... *something* just visible where the light grew dimmer. It looked uncomfortably like an uneven, vaguely conical boulder made of flesh.

Sindiel turned to retreat but a sound made him stop short. Thin and distant, it plucked at his consciousness, sounding as much in his mind as in his ears. His first flush of terror drained away as he listened.

It was a song being sung without words. There was nothing insidious or threatening about it as he had first feared, it was no net for the mind or soul except in the subtlest sense. It was a song filled with sadness and longing, with a faint but lingering undercurrent of hope.

Sindiel's mind staggered. Surely only one soul in Commorragh could give voice to its suffering so poignantly as this. A pure heart. He had convinced himself that she had been killed and her soul devoured in some hideous orgy by Yllithian and his cohorts long ago, never quite knowing if he should hope that the worldsinger was really dead or not. He had not heard the worldsinger's voice since Linthis had first introduced them at the World Shrine on Lileathanir. Happier times, of course, before he had decided to sell her into slavery for his own gain.

It had all seemed like a game at first, with Sindiel destined to be the winner. He couldn't believe his luck when he'd found the message sphere, apparently dropped in haste during the aftermath of a sharp skirmish with the Dark Kin. Lately he found he wondered about that seemingly chance discovery, knowing the depths of Commorrite cunning as he did now. Without really knowing why he'd concealed the smooth sphere of chalcedony from his companions and began to study it without their knowledge. After much secret experimentation he'd found the sphere allowed him to communicate with an earnest-seeming prince from the dark city, a semi-legendary place of wickedness and depravity that had always exerted a deadly fascination on Sindiel.

Archon Yllithian had made Commorragh seem romantically dangerous and alluring. He made no attempt to conceal the fierce competition and the high stakes, nor the boldness and determination needed to thrive there. It had all been music to Sindiel's jaded ears – freedom at last! An opportunity to live life to the full! Sindiel bitterly realised now that Yllithian had been artfully manipulating him, stringing him along with hints of the forbidden pleasures that came with mastery over others as he decried the dull, monastic strictures of the craftworlds.

Sindiel wondered how many other disaffected eldar had been drawn in by the siren call of Commorragh in similar ways down the centuries. Many, it seemed. Commorragh seethed with teeming multitudes more numerous than a thousand craftworlds, a million. From Sindiel's perspective it seemed as if his entire race was gathered in this one city, the craftworlds and Exodites merely country cousins that were indulged despite their introverted ways. The proud remnants of eldar power and majesty resided firmly in Commorragh, dark though it might be.

When Yllithian had asked for something it was always a trifle, merely warnings of where the rangers travelled to avoid accidentally clashing with his warriors or news on where the resource-starved city could find certain ores and minerals it required. In exchange Yllithian took Sindiel into his confidence and explained his hopes of reuniting the disparate branches of the eldar; a process that must be begun by confronting the cruel and terrible tyrant that ruled Commorragh, Asdrubael Vect, and making him mend his wicked ways.

One day Yllithian had told him that the dark city needed a sacrifice to usher in the new age, a sacrifice that they could not make themselves. Commorragh needed a martyr to break its chains and only he, Sindiel, had the strength and clarity to help his enslaved brethren in their hour of need. From there Sindiel had done most of the work by convincing himself that one life being sacrificed to save billions was a small price to pay. At the time it had seemed an absurdly simple conclusion to reach, so clear. Only later did Sindiel, fool that he was, begin to understand the dark schemes he'd become ensnared in.

He'd thought they had killed the worldsinger in some daemon's bargain to bring back El'Uriaq. But the worldsinger was alive, at least in some sense of the word. Sindiel wondered with sick horror whether she had been transformed into the lump of flesh ahead of him. That was apparently exactly the kind of twisted thing the haemonculi did with their spare time.

It took a long time for Sindiel to screw up enough courage to move forwards and investigate. He could think of a hundred reasons to retreat and only one to go on, but that one beat the rest hands down. He simply had to know. Eventually he drew his pistol for a little moral support and crept down the passage. He reached a point where he could see that the passage became a causeway across a darkly glistening pool. In the distance a single, broad pillar wider than a tower reared up to support a ceiling lost in the shadows above.

The fleshy boulder he had seen sat halfway between Sindiel and the pillar. He realised with a rush of relief that it seemed as if the singing was coming from beyond, from the tower-like pillar in the distance. Watching the disturbing object before him more closely Sindiel became convinced that it was a creature of some kind, a guardian sculpted by the haemonculi from living flesh. He could make out scarred skin stretched over bunched shoulders and thick haunches. The thing was squatting in the centre of the causeway, head tucked down and out of sight beneath slab-like arms. A miniature forest sprouted from its thick spine, rows of syringes and bio-pumps that were burbling quietly as they circulated whatever acidic ichor had been used to replace its blood. Sindiel felt absurdly relieved that he couldn't see the thing's face.

Sindiel edged out on to the causeway, his courage growing slightly when the thing didn't react to the movement. He walked closer slowly, placing each foot carefully to produce not a whisper of sound. The guardian-creature shifted slightly and Sindiel froze. The worldsinger's lament continued to weave through the still air, telling of a place where all life came together within the world spirit, where all anguish was eased and all enmities forgotten. Several deep breaths huffed from beneath the creature's arms before the thing settled down again into what Sindiel hoped was a deeper slumber.

There was barely enough room on either edge of the causeway to squeeze past the creature without touching it but Sindiel wasn't prepared to try wading into the pool instead. Something about the dark, still expanse seemed more dangerous to him than the guardian squatting before him on the causeway. The enigmatic tower and the plaintive sounds of the worldsinger's song drew him onwards.

He moved with painstaking precision, mastering his fear to walk softly past the thing. He reached the half-way point safely and drew a little courage from that, horribly aware of the animal warmth and closeness of the guardian. He had just stepped onto the causeway beyond the creature when the singing stopped. Sindiel froze again, willing himself to become invisible.

The mountain of flesh beside him erupted with a roar, its tree-trunk arms flailing at the causeway with hammer-like blows. A face masked in black iron glared out at Sindiel from beneath hulking shoulders, its red, soulless eyes aflame with hatred of all living things. Sindiel shrieked and leapt backwards, his heels skidding at the brink of the sinister pool.

With a motion almost too quick to see the thing grabbed for him with spade-like hands. Sindiel tried to hurl himself to one side but couldn't make his limbs move fast enough to evade the rampaging crea-ture. It seized him and pulled him close to its scarred chest in a bone-crushing embrace. Iron-fanged jaws scraped through his rich clothing to reveal the fine mesh armour he wore beneath. A few seconds more and the clashing fangs would bite through into his flesh.

Sindiel's pistol had flown from his hand in the instant he was grabbed. Now in desperation he tried to punch forwards with his pinned arm. The feeble impact of his knuckles barely scuffed the iron-hard flesh that they struck, but the device still bound to his wrist was infinitely more effective. Invisible strands of gossamer wire shot out of the concealed weapon, slipping through his sleeve, through the creature's scarred hide and into its flesh as easily as if they were all made of water. The guardian roared again and dropped Sindiel, bruised and bleeding, onto the causeway so that it could clutch at the tiny wound he'd succeeded in making in its side. Syringes in its spine hissed as they began automatically injecting coagulants to seal the minor breach and stimulants to provoke the grotesque guardian into a berserker frenzy.

But the wound was deceptive. Sindiel's hidden weapon was Motley's parting gift to him in Iron Thorn: an ancient type seldom seen in the later ages of the eldar, called a harlequin's kiss. In the brief instant that the kiss touched the guardian's flesh, metres-long monomolecular filaments were sent looping throughout its body. As tough as it was the altered creature could not survive having its insides reduced to the consistency of soup by the unfurling wires. The hulking guardian sagged and then toppled from the causeway with a final, despairing groan, disappearing into the dark pool with barely a ripple.

Sindiel lay where he had fallen, gasping for breath. He waited helplessly for a rush of running feet and hands roughly seizing him, but no one came. Slowly his heart stopped hammering and he began to recover his wits. He cautiously moved his limbs one by one to find if any of them were broken. Wrenched and painful as they all were everything seemed to be fully functional, although his ribs were aflame with agony at every breath he took. After some minutes he rolled over and cautiously levered himself upright. He stood gazing along the remaining strip of causeway to the tower, wondering if the unseen worldsinger had deliberately tried to bring about his death. He tottered forwards, unsure whether he now sought absolution or vengeance.

A rough stair had been hacked out of the dull stone of the pillar. The stair rose in a precipitous spiral from its base and quickly disappeared from sight. Sindiel wearily began to climb upwards almost on hands and knees, his torn clothes flapping about him.

After a seemingly endless climb the stair opened onto a low landing that had been made by widening a great horizontal crack in the pillar. Many lamps were hung within, illuminating the grotto-like crack with a wash of soft white light. Of the few furnishings to be found there the only one of note was a richly carved bed of dark wood, or more accurately its occupant. The worldsinger Laryin sat in the bed watching Sindiel struggle up the last few steps into view. She was bound at the neck by a metal collar with a chain attached that was in turn stapled to the wall. Otherwise she appeared unharmed, though her eyes seemed like limpid pools of misery. All thoughts of vengeance fled from him at the sight.

'It's you,' she said.

'That's right, me. The one that got you into this. I–' Sindiel fell silent, unable to meet her eyes. He had rehearsed many scenarios in his mind but found them all in tatters now that he had reached the moment of truth.

'I–I'm sorry,' was all he could think to say.

To his surprise she laughed, not with bitterness or mockery but with a pure sound of joy that seemed like a breath of spring in that dark place. Sindiel blinked at her in surprise and that made her laugh again. He wondered if she had been driven insane by her experiences.

'After all you've done you're still an innocent,' she said at last. 'That gives me hope. You're wondering if I've gone mad – no I haven't. They can hurt me but they can't touch me.'

'Then we can escape! I'll take you away from here!' Sindiel said, his mind whirling with schemes to escape the catacombs and reach a webway portal unseen. But then what?

Laryin was shaking her head sadly, soft golden hair brushing the dark metal collar at her throat. 'There's no escape for me now. I'm committed to this path. I've become Morai-Heg and given birth to a monster. Without me to nurture him who knows what he might become?'

'Nurture? How can you say such things?' Sindiel choked. 'Motley said there were always more choices, more chances to take...'

'And I choose to stay. What El'Uriaq takes from me would otherwise come from a hundred thousand of my brothers and sisters. I've accepted that burden in their stead. The thing that is El'Uriaq owns me now. We are bound together as tyrant and pain-bride.'

Sindiel's face was ashen, all the hopes that had blossomed in him a moment before withered utterly. The worldsinger looked at him sympathetically with eyes that seemed too old for her youthful-looking face.

'Don't be sad, Sindiel,' she said earnestly. 'I brought him to life and I hope to see him returned to death, for is that not the cycle of life? Birth and death? Your part in this is over, you should save yourself if you still can.'

'You're going to try and kill him?' Sindiel asked in wonder.

'I wouldn't know how. His is the power of domination and destruction while mine is in the nurture of growing things. But life will find a way to end in death as it always will, and when it does I will be there to mourn its passing and sing of the hope of a happier rebirth.'

'I was given this as a gift,' Sindiel said as he came to a decision, 'but I think that it was really meant to be given to you.' He unstrapped the harlequin's kiss from his wrist and laid it on the edge of the bed. 'Press the narrowest part of it against the target and the weapon will do the rest.'

Laryin looked at the elongated black diamond shape but did not touch it. 'Is that what you used to kill the guardian?' she asked eventually.

'Yes. Did you use the guardian to try to kill me?'

'No, it was just in such torment that I sang to soothe it. When I sensed someone coming near with purpose in their heart I stopped and hoped they would put it out of its misery.' The worldsinger smiled sweetly up at Sindiel. 'And you did. I'm sorry if it hurt you.'

'Should I put you out of your misery too?' he asked her quietly.

'No! My ending now won't solve what has been begun. I will follow the path to the end, bitter though it might be.'

Sindiel looked away for a long time in silence, only finding the bravery to meet her eyes when his own were blurred with tears. 'How is it that you can forgive me after what I've done?'

Laryin was silent for a long while before answering.

'You know I can't forgive you, Sindiel, you're the only one that can do that.'

But Sindiel, with the last of his courage spent, had already fled.

CHAPTER 17

A TRIUMPHAL BANQUET
(THE HANDMAID'S PROMISE)

*'Don't speak ill of father Shaimesh, he is a friend
and ally to all in need. The old and the weak he
lends his strength to equally, and lovers too call
upon him at need. Where would the widow and the
orphan find their bite if not in his fangs? He is the
gate keeper and the path maker, and he holds the
key to many paths to oblivion, full as many as his
forked tongues…'*

The fool Mecuto to the Broken King,
in Ursyllas's *Dispossessions*

To DESCEND INTO El'Uriaq's realm was to enter a
land of faerie. For weeks slaves had been feverishly
gnawing floatstone and cracking bedrock to enact
a transformation of the darkling catacombs that
almost beggared belief. Where there had been narrow paths and blind ways there were now wide halls

and passages opening to richly appointed chambers furnished with delicate chairs and tables of ivory. Lofty ceilings were supported by tapering pillars that reached up into the darkness, sloping runoffs had been cut into low steps, bottomless pits had been bridged. A hundred thousand lamps were suspended in the air lighting the way, their brilliance pushing back the reluctant shadows behind translucent hangings of many soft hues. In their golden glow El'Uriaq's excavations seemed rich and welcoming, a place of wonder and miracles.

The slaves that had laboured so diligently to effect the metamorphosis of foetid dungeon to noble palace were still present, after a fashion. Their hides hung from the walls in stunning profusion, their bones had been cunningly wrought into new forms to serve their master in death as they had in life. Of their flesh, their blood and their souls there was no sign, but an aura of death and suffering clung to the golden halls of El'Uriaq's hidden kingdom.

For months now the subtle tendrils of El'Uriaq's influence had glided outwards into the eternal city. His faceless agents had been moving among esoteric cults and obscure kabals reminding them of their forgotten duties. Guarded approaches had been made to the power-hungry and leaders had been bribed or replaced by the hundred. A thousand delicate movements were orchestrated to shift power or allegiance away from Asdrubael Vect. The great tyrant still knew nothing of El'Uriaq's return, but he had certainly sensed the movement of another predator in Commorragh's political jungle. Recently inter-kabal fighting had intensified as

Vect sought to reassert control. Vect struck blindly but often, and some of his blows fell true upon the slaves and property of El'Uriaq's followers. Fear gripped the city, and El'Uriaq's cohorts most of all. Just as the noose started to tighten the old emperor of Shaa-dom sent the coded call for his chosen to come to him.

El'Uriaq's secret followers trickled in from every corner of Commorragh both high and low. Petty archons came striding in the midst of their silent bodyguards, armoured sybarites rubbed shoulders with light-stepping succubi, mechanists walked beside beastmasters, gang lords exchanged taunts with flesh traders. All wore masks to conceal their identities, although some chose to flaunt themselves openly by wearing the barest mockeries of silk or crystal. The poet-philosopher Aclyriid duelled the philosopher-poet Pso'kobor with barbed words and mockeries, while the vivisectionist Zeelatar pointed out distinctive hides hanging from the walls and held forth on the virtues of the different slave races under varying states of duress.

'Sunlight! A lack of sunlight for greenskins, oh yes! All that vaunted toughness becomes as soft and malleable as boiled tubers!'

Many that came wondered at their numbers, the strength that they were a part of never made manifest to them before now. Each had thought themselves privy to secrets held by few others and now they found themselves in a company hundreds strong. A glittering river of warriors, assassins, leaders and spymasters flowed ever deeper into the golden halls, gathering rivulets and tributaries to itself as it drew nigh to the great amphitheatre below.

There waited El'Uriaq in his court, decked in the radiant finery of an earlier age. His robe of shifting midnight hues was slit at the chest and wrist to reveal glimpses of the bright armour he wore beneath as if he were clad in storm clouds that flashed with lightning. The crown of eight stars was upon his head and the ruby sceptre was in his hand and he looked lordly indeed, kingly even although the eldar had foresworn having kings long before. On the steps of the dais was a veiled female clad all in dazzling white, with a chain running from a collar at her throat to the foot of the throne as though she were an intractable pet or dangerous beast. Whispers flew through the throng at the sight of the veiled woman. Surely this was El'Uriaq's pain-bride, the pure heart rumoured to grant true immortality to whomsoever could master her.

Ranked tables about El'Uriaq's throne groaned beneath the weight of assembled provender. Plunder from a million worlds had been gathered for his guests: star-metal casks winked alongside spun crystal bottles, heaped trenchers of squamous ocean world delicacies wobbled beside platters of rare meats taken from every part of the Great Wheel, euphoric tinctures and narcotic powders were there in plenty.

'Welcome, my friends!' El'Uriaq called to the masked multitude as they spilled in. 'Kindly find the places appointed to you! Hurry now! I am anxious to begin the evening's entertainments!'

Entertainments were also there in plenty: musicians and dancers waited at the margins, along with savage looking slave-gladiators, orators and mimes, restrained slaves to torment in situ and loose ones to dominate at leisure. As the guests filed among the tables they found individual settings with plaques inscribed with messages thus:

'*The Aphor of the eleventh district*'

'*The right hand of Xarlon*'

'*The master of the stone road*'

Each held a clue that would be understood only by the conspirator and El'Uriaq himself, a reference to a coded missive from their past communications, in some cases now made dreadfully clear. Some took their seats with relief, flattered by the personal attention and evocation of past success, others sat filled with foreboding as they recognised their messages as inferring some oversight or failure on their part.

'*The broken promise of the sprawls*'

'*The Fortress Unvanquishable, save for Sacnoth*'

'*He who loved well, if not wisely, Cymbelline*'

Some were reluctant to take their places at first, but as more and more of their compatriots were seated they found themselves alone. Beneath El'Uriaq's searing gaze they hurried to comply until all of the assembled host sat at their tables at last. Archon Yllithian, clad in subtly differing lustres of black and wearing a crow mask, had found his setting to read:

'*Beloved Primogenitor and primus*'

Which he took to be a moderately encouraging sign, unless El'Uriaq believed that like the titans of old he should consume his parent. He placed the cylindrical container he was carrying beside a spindly bone chair and took a seat before glancing around disinterestedly at his table partners. He recognised several petty archons among them but the bulk seemed to be lowborn scum of one sort or another. Nyos wondered if El'Uriaq was deliberately insulting him by placing him in such company. At his side a rough-handed warrior wearing a mask with bulging jewelled insect eyes looked around with interest.

'What've you got there, brother? Something to share and share alike?' he said, gesturing at the container jocularly.

'Nothing for the likes of you,' Yllithian replied with contempt. His neighbour seemed to be under the mistaken impression that he was at some kind of social event to make friends. Yllithian was labouring under no such delusions. El'Uriaq bringing together so many of his followers could only mean one thing – that he was ready to act. The conspirators' banquet was an old institution in Commorrite lore, a final step to cement the plotters' commitment and weed out any naysayers. Not all of those that had entered the amphitheatre were going to leave it alive; instead they would become examples of the price of disloyalty in order to bind the rest together.

As the last guests were seated a fanfare of horns and trumpets blew to silence their chatter. El'Uriaq stood up proud and splendid upon the steps of his throne and spoke to the throng. By some artifice of the amphitheatre or his own powers his words were carried clearly to every ear as if he stood close at hand. They were low and thrilling, replete with all the power and confidence of his magnetic personality.

'Do you feel it, my friends? Do you feel history being made? This is a moment that will be cherished in our fine city for generations to come. They will look back upon this night with reverence, the night when the first blows were struck against the shackles of tyranny encompassing their lives.

'The tyrant told you that I, El'Uriaq, had fallen beneath his blade. He lied. He told you that no rival could match his guile and purpose. He lied again. He told you the city would flourish beneath his rule. He lied once more. Who here still believes in the lies of Asdrubael Vect?'

A chorus of denouncements and vitriolic curses at the perfidy of the tyrant echoed around the amphi-theatre from the assembled guests. Many of the lowborn drew weapons and clashed them together ferociously, eager to show their hatred and contempt for Vect. El'Uriaq smiled radiantly as he allowed the clamour to die away.

'So! Now I bid you feast and take your ease, for we have hard fighting ahead of us if our city is to be freed from bondage. I will speak with each of you to hear your concerns and further share my plans; for now relax and enjoy the hospitality of my court. To the future! To the doom of Vect!'

Another, perhaps more heartfelt, cheer erupted, drums thundered and pipes skirled in the tumult. Dancers stepped lightly among the tables to perform as the music calmed to a more languorous refrain. Yllithian turned his attention to a plate of jellied pin-stars harvested from sunless seas, pushing the luminous echinoderms around with a silver-tined fork. The accoutrements of each table were rich and finely crafted; the plates, bottles, chalices, goblets, bowls, the multitudinous and highly specialised knives, forks and spoons – all were made with fantastic artistry and skill, but all were mismatched with one another. No artisan of Commorragh had made these things to unify form and purpose as only eldar hands might do, rather they were articles of plunder taken from a million worlds. El'Uriaq's feasting tables had all the riotous barbarity of a pirate's lair.

The thought depressed Yllithian. Were there not artisans enough in the dark city to make goods of their own aesthetic? He already knew the sad truth. The kabals prized plunder more highly – what could be taken had become worth more than what could be made with their own hands. The chaotic diversity hid a message for the keen observer – El'Uriaq had reach. Even from hiding he could pluck treasures from anywhere in the galaxy at his whim and scatter them before his followers. Yllithian had no doubt that it was a display that impressed the lowborn members of the assembly, but it left him feeling cold.

Hoots and cheers drew his attention to where two gangly slave-gladiators were hacking bloody chunks out of one another in an impromptu bout between two tables. Beak-faced and quill-haired, the avian-looking creatures wielded hook-tipped staves with creditable gusto, hissing and screeching as they gave and received wounds. One eventually pinned the other down and tore out its still-pulsing heart before consuming it, to the great amusement of the immediate onlookers.

Sudden awareness of a presence at his elbow made him glance around sharply. An obese castrato in a furred animal mask stood beside him.

'Lord El'Uriaq bidth that you may attend on him now,' the castrato lisped, holding out his fat white hands to gesture towards the throne. Yllithian saw that a triumvirate of warriors in bull masks were stepping down from the dais after speaking with El'Uriaq. His time had come. He picked up the container beside his chair and pushed his way between the revellers towards the throne.

FROM BENEATH GAUZY veils of white Laryin watched the Dark Kin at their sport, forcing herself to take it in. Her whole body ached and she wanted nothing more than to crouch down and block everything out but she stood stiff and silent as the nightmare washed over her. She liked to think that it was pride that kept her so upright and unbending, that she simply could not give in to the urge to grovel before them. Fear of punishment was most likely the true motivator. She'd been ordered to stand and so stand she must. She'd also been shown that her body was capable of betraying her will in the most craven fashion and she'd found she hated that part of herself more than the pain. Against her wrist a hard, elongated diamond shape was digging into her flesh, surprisingly warm, almost pleasant to the touch.

A smallish Dark Kin wearing black with a crow mask was approaching the throne. Laryin's attention was caught by the container he carried, a cylinder of burnished metal with a handle at the top. El'Uriaq actually rose and descended the steps to greet this one of his followers; he was obviously a valued minion. Laryin wondered what was in the tithe he'd brought.

Something about it fascinated her, a forgotten sense of insight that tickled at the back of her skull.

'Ah, my primus!' El'Uriaq roared in delight, sweeping up his smaller follower with a hug that evidently terrified him. The crow-mask recovered quickly after El'Uriaq released him, bowing low and making his offering.

'What's this?' smiled El'Uriaq with his eyes glittering more sharply than his eight-starred crown. 'A gift for me?'

'Indeed, a memento of past times,' Crow-mask replied with an impish grin, 'the contents being perfectly harmless of course, as I'm sure you're quite aware.'

Laryin could see that the grin was just as much a mask as the beak and feathers worn above it. Hard, calculating eyes behind the mask flicked at her for an instant before returning to El'Uriaq.

'Naturally,' El'Uriaq said soothingly. 'Allow me to reframe my question – whose head do you bring to me?'

Crow-mask opened the container with a flourish, hinging open a curved lid to reveal another thing out of nightmare. The metal casing held a cylinder of crystal filled with colourless fluid. What was in the liquid was almost hidden by long, dark hair that floated slowly around it, but it was undeniably a severed head. Laryin took an involuntarily half-step back, the chain at her throat clinking gently as she did so. El'Uriaq turned and hissed at her playfully, freezing her with terror.

'Don't be like that, Laryin, you have more in common

with Angevere than you might think.' He turned back to crow-mask, smiling broadly. 'Quite wonderful. May I?' El'Uriaq took the container and lifted it to stare at the contents more closely. Crow-mask was watching El'Uriaq's face intently as he did so, so intently that curiosity overwhelmed Laryin's usual fear and she looked too.

She was surprised by what she saw on the monster's too-handsome features. Warmth and tenderness were written there, fond memories and sad recollections. She had never seen him look so... mortal before, even vulnerable. In that instant she also saw the thing that looked out through El'Uriaq's eyes. She saw it only for a moment, a flash of the terrible all-consuming fire that dwelt within his soul, an entity that gazed out at the world with obscene triumph and unspeakable malice. Laryin swayed and almost stumbled at the sight, the amphitheatre seeming to pitch beneath her feet. Crow-mask and the monster were speaking in low tones but she barely heard them over the pulse of blood in her ears.

The diamond shape against Laryin's wrist ached warmly. Despite her brave words to the renegade she wasn't sure that she had the strength to endure the river of fate flowing over her. The weapon he'd left gnawed at her mind constantly. One blow and it could be ended. She had made no conscious decision to bring the weapon with her or to use it but a part of her mind still clung to it like a talisman. It represented having some kind of choice for her now. The only choice she could still make.

* * *

YLLITHIAN SAW THE beast unmasked in El'Uriaq too, only for an instant but that was all it took. The flash of it seared his mind and it took all of his considerable will not to draw back immediately. Fortunately El'Uriaq seemed too enraptured by his gift to sense anything amiss – just as the damned haemonculus had predicted. Yllithian felt as if ice water were flooding into his veins, his knees suddenly seemed treacherously weak. The thing was talking to him, and a part of his mind was screaming at him to respond.

'–she speak?' asked the thing that looked like El'Uriaq.

'Indeed she does,' Yllithian replied, his well-worn instincts for dissimulation mastering his fear and rushing to the fore to save him. 'The – ah – haemonculi fitted a vocal synthesiser to the casket. She had a nasty habit of using mind speech she had to be cured of before she'd use it.'

The El'Uriaq-thing laughed heartily. 'Well now,' it said to the head, 'all your running and cleverness brought you to this, Angevere? I never imagined I would become better looking than you.'

Angevere's synthesised voice sighed like the wind through winter-stripped branches. *My life is fulfilled knowing that you are complete once more, my immortal lord,* she said.

'Indeed it is, we'll have a great deal to talk about, you and I, when time permits. For the present speak me a prediction, since now you have become a crone and I'll hear your sweet voice no more.'

In the amphitheatre El'Uriaq's guests were

beginning to slake their lusts in ever more outrageous fashion. Pipes skirled hauntingly over the clamour of cries and screams. As Angevere spoke her thin, insidious whisper seemed to mute the sounds of revelry.

'The Dysjunction approaches, the city will be riven asunder. Blood shall wash the spires and beasts shall stalk the streets. As they suffer beneath the lash of destiny the citizens will cry out for salvation but they will have no succour. Three shall rise but only one will endure.'

El'Uriaq smiled again, the picture of indulgence. 'Very nice,' he said. 'Everything I would hope for from a doomsayer.' He glanced about and then looked at Laryin with a knowing smirk. 'Come here, darling, I have a special job for you.'

Laryin walked forwards unwillingly. The diamond shape on her wrist burned like a brand. She took another step, almost within arm's reach of the daemon meat-puppet and the monstrous thing it held out to her. Now that the time had come she found that her choice was already made. She tensed her arm to lash out, probably the last action she would ever take. Her mind's eye expanded with the skein of possible outcomes. El'Uriaq slain, standing over his body splashed with crimson... El'Uriaq alive, seizing her wrist and twisting it back... Laryin dead, white dress blotched pink with leaking lifeblood... The drums pulsed louder in her ears, matching the rhythm of her heart.

+Don't.+

Mind speech. Laryin hesitated. It was the first time she had heard it used in the dark city; even the renegade had not dared to use it when he was alone with her. El'Uriaq looked at her sharply, his eyes seeming to pierce the veils and bore straight into her quivering soul... searching... probing. Crow-mask cleared his throat suddenly.

'Perhaps we should move on to more pressing matters, honoured host? I did not intend to distract you from your other entertainments this evening, forgive me if gift-giving was inappropriate.'

El'Uriaq's attention shifted to the eldar dressed in black and the moment was broken, his good humour returning flawlessly. 'Not at all, my friend, you've made me very happy,' he said. Laryin hurriedly reached out and took the horrid casket from him before backing away. Any excuse to move out of his immediate presence was welcome. El'Uriaq was deep in conversation with crow-mask and ignored her.

+Very good,+ the voice came into her mind again, stronger now but still only the barest whisper. +Remain calm. He needs fear to read you clearly.+

+Who are you? Where are you?+ Laryin thought back softly, whispering inside the monster's lair.

+The answer is in your hands, don't pretend you hadn't already guessed.+

Laryin had guessed. She nerved herself to lift the casket up and look at the face in its drifting nest of hair. El'Uriaq had called her Angevere. The crow-masked one was turning to leave and Laryin felt an illogical stab of loss at his going. He had helped her, probably saved her.

+Shed no tears for Yllithian, he's the one that brought you here in the first place. You and me, together, have made this abomination but he's the one that made it all possible.+

'Do try the haemovore cutlets at your table, they'll go well with those pin-stars you were trying,' El'Uriaq said to the departing Yllithian. When he was gone El'Uriaq glanced over at Laryin again, and raised his voice to speak to her over the tumult in the background.

'Have Angevere tell you of her services to me in Shaa-dom. You will soon be emulating them,' he said before turning away with a laugh. He went back to sit on his throne as a long-limbed, spidery-looking individual in a silvered skull-mask came forward and made obeisance.

+It wears the shape of my lord well, doesn't it? For now at least. Oh, but he's close to his dark apotheosis. It could be tonight or it could be in a hundred years but he's close.+

+Then why did you stop me?+ Laryin thought. +I might have ended it.+

The crone's laughter rustled through her mind, dry and dead. +I thought you had become Morai-Heg? Weren't you destined to succour your frightful off-spring? Child! No assassin's tool will end this, not even one supplied by a broken heart.+

+What then! My life was forfeit, I accepted that. But when I saw it I knew... I knew that it had to be ended.+

+Very good. You understand. There is a way if you are strong enough and clever enough. Shall I tell you what it is?+

Laryin looked around, struggling to keep calm as the crone had told her to do. Knives were out in the amphitheatre, their savage caress eliciting piercing shrieks that merged with the infernal piping and pulsing drums. Writhing knots of figures swayed through coloured smoke, dancing and fighting and copulating in equal measure. All the worst legends of her people about the decadence before the Fall and the cruelty of the Dark Kin were being played out before her eyes.

+Just tell me how I can end this.+

The low, dry whisper of Angevere's speech in her mind told her what she must do.

YLLITHIAN MOVED AS artfully as he could towards the exit. The shape of the amphitheatre meant that El'Uriaq could see any part of it from his throne at the centre. If he were watching he might realise that Yllithian was trying to leave. Nyos slipped around groups, politely refused invitations, exchanged pleasantries and ignored challenges as he worked his way to the ramp leading out of the amphitheatre. He was finally stopped by a troupe of dancing Lhamaeans and their wide circle of onlookers barring his path. The sharp musk of their poisoned perfumes filled the air as their tattooed limbs flashed in a fantastic, gyrating display that held their slack-jawed audience enthralled. Beyond them Yllithian could see the ramp was filled with masked guards anyway. There was no way out there.

He looked around casually, apparently busy fastidiously stripping the spicy flesh from a haemovore cutlet. El'Uriaq's gastronomic advice at least seemed excellent; the blood-soaked meat nicely offset the jellied echinoderms he'd dined on earlier. El'Uriaq himself still sat upon his throne receiving supplicants in the midst of the feast, an island of light in the dark revelry surrounding him. To one side of him the veiled worldsinger stood like a pale flame, gripping the casket with the crone's head. Yllithian experienced a moment of vertigo as he looked at her, the same sensation he'd had during the resurrection. He could almost *feel* reality straining. Eldritch voices seemed to be whispering and cackling at the edge of his consciousness. Something very bad was about to happen and he needed to get out before it was too late.

The serving slaves and courtesans had not entered down the ramp as the guests had. There had to be other exits to the amphitheatre. Yllithian watched carefully and spotted three slaves bearing away a huge salver piled with gnawed bones. They slipped behind skin curtains to one side and did not return until a short time later with a new salver bearing a steaming heap of broiled limbs. Yllithian calmly started making his way over to the spot the slaves had emerged from.

He could smell the heady scents of the kitchens when crashing drums and braying trumpets stopped him short of his goal. El'Uriaq was rising from his throne as the din in the amphitheatre was momentarily silenced by the savage fanfare. All eyes were drawn to him. The old emperor of Shaa-dom – or rather the thing that wore his flesh, as Yllithian now knew – gazed around triumphantly. His voice boomed through the amphitheatre with no artifice of personalisation for his listeners this time. This was the voice of a prophet addressing his believers.

'My friends, the time has come to strip fear from your heart and cast aside veils of anonymity. We are bonded together in the single, unshakeable purpose of overthrowing the tyrant. Therefore those gathered here have nothing to fear from one another and so I bid you now to remove your masks.'

An involuntary gasp rippled through the throng at the implication. Each of them would hold the lives of the others in their hands. Even one traitor in their midst could doom the whole conspiracy. Some threw off their masks joyfully, crying out their loyalty to El'Uriaq. Yllithian, like many others, was more reluctant but the implication was clear – anyone unwilling to remove their mask would stand revealed as just such a potential traitor. No doubt El'Uriaq was paying close heed to just who was quick and who was slow to obey him. It was a masterful stroke in its own way, self-preservation would enforce loyalty. Yllithian quickly removed his crow-mask before El'Uriaq thought to look in his direction.

'There. Excellent. Very good,' El'Uriaq said soothingly as his guests divested themselves of their masks and gazed around at their co-conspirators. 'There really is nothing to fear. To show you that I'd like to introduce the great friend and ally that has made all of this possible – Archon Yllithian of the White Flames.' The monster was looking straight at him as he said it.

Yllithian felt blood rushing to his cheeks. Suddenly exposed, literally standing in the stablights as he was, he forced a smile onto his face. 'Come down here, Nyos!' called El'Uriaq. 'Come stand at my side!'

Some uncertain cheers with a polite smattering of applause followed Yllithian as he forced his unwilling feet to carry him back into the monster's lair. El'Uriaq greeted him warmly once more and embraced him. Every ounce of Yllithian's considerable self-control was necessary to keep himself from flinching. El'Uriaq whispered enigmatically: 'I do hope you tried the cutlets, Nyos,' before he continued to address his guests.

'Yllithian here is a student of antiquities, a great raconteur in matters of the past – which I'm sure is why he took an interest in me.' Dutiful laughter fluttered in response. 'As such Yllithian here recalls many of the old traditions that have slipped away in modern times. For example I'll wager that Yllithian remembers the Feast of Shaimesh, an archaic practice long forgotten by some.'

Yllithian's mind raced. The black arts of Shaimesh pertained to poisons and toxins of all kinds. The greatest practitioners of the art were the Lhamaeans, courtesan-poisoners who could bring a lover to the edge of ecstasy with their virulent brews – or snuff out their life like a candle. But the Feast of Shaimesh? A poison banquet… Fear clutched at Yllithian's belly as El'Uriaq spoke again.

'Shaimesh, father of poisons, taught us that everything can be a poison in the correct dosage and that the little kiss of death we find there is what adds spice to life. The students of Shaimesh would gather for a feast and test their skills against one another, poisoning each dish a little differently.'

A deathly hush had fallen over the amphitheatre, his fearful audience hanging on every word. The low, rhythmic pulse of the drums continued, never speeding or slowing.

'The poisons would be too subtle to detect, too

mild and innocuous in effect to even classify as dangerous – on their own, that is. The combinations were the key, you see. Some compounds would cancel each other out… while others would combine and magnify their effects a thousand times.'

A groan and a crash sounded out in the stillness of the amphitheatre. El'Uriaq continued unperturbed. 'It is possible to predict the effects of resulting necrolixirs with astounding accuracy, even down to the second of demise. I have looked into your hearts this night. Those of you with faith and obedience have nothing to fear, but those that would betray us, those that would crawl on their bellies before the tyrant and sell their comrades to lick a few crumbs from his hands…'

El'Uriaq's voice had been rising, growing stronger with each word. Now he stood from his throne and roared, 'Now is the time you pay for your crimes!'

Pandemonium erupted throughout the amphitheatre. Not one in ten of the guests fell prey to the dreadful vitriolic compounds they had drunk or ingested, but those that had been targeted died in the most spectacular and painful ways. The Dark Kin's horrid talents had devised countless deadly effects down the ages.

The philosopher-poet Pso'kobor, replete after unknowingly dining on pantopherol and tocotheric, simultaneously ruptured every blood vessel in his body with explosive force. He exsanguinated himself in a fine, red mist.

The xeno-trader Mayylaenidian Vir twisted horribly as his bones were broken by his own spasming muscles. He howled wildly as his spine curved so far backwards his head emerged from between his knees before a final sickening crack made him silent. Even afterwards the muscles of the corpse continued to writhe and twist with a life of their own.

The myrmidon Kolaxian burst into flames, spontaneously combusting like a tallow candle beneath a blowtorch. Flaming drips of fat showered as the luckless warrior staggered between tables and was fended off by his compatriots.

The overseer Azurnal fell to a creeping vari-form of the glass plague, having had his own phagic inoculations against the deadly viral helix selectively neutralised by the delicious mirepoix he had tasted earlier. Sheets of black crystal shot through with lambent green slithered languorously down his legs and arms as he screamed for help that would not come.

The archon Slithiyyius collapsed in the midst of his bodyguards, fallen prey to a foe their blades could not stop. Skin sloughed off him in untidy lumps as he rapidly turned into a pile of corroding bones and necrotising flesh.

There were a dozen more equally horrifying deaths ranged around the amphitheatre, all of the guests seeing the price of disloyalty firsthand. Shrieks and laughter rang out in equal measure. El'Uriaq's surviving faithful gratefully warmed themselves at the dying soul sparks all about them, an unexpectedly rich and generous feast. On the dais at the centre of it all Yllithian felt as if reality were stretching still thinner, a balloon ready to burst.

'A fine jest, my host,' he dared to whisper. 'What

other surprises might be in store, I wonder?'

El'Uriaq grinned wolfishly, his eyes flashing dangerously with excitement. 'I haven't decided yet,' he confided in Yllithian. 'There may be a really big surprise still to come.'

The entity was there again, staring out at him through El'Uriaq's eyes. It knew. It knew Yllithian had seen it and it didn't care. It would continue to use him anyway, right until his usefulness was all wrung out, and only then would it end him. What alternative did he have but to play along – apart from making the fatal mistake of seeking help from Asdrubael Vect? Yllithian was trapped, he was bound to the monster he'd created and they both knew it.

'M… my lord?' a small, frightened voice said from close at hand.

El'Uriaq looked around at the speaker in some surprise. It was the worldsinger, her veils thrown back to show her pale face and vivid bruises. She cradled Angevere's head in its casket as if it were a babe in arms.

'My lord, may I speak?' Laryin asked sweetly. Intrigued, El'Uriaq nodded brusquely.

'I have a gift for you too, sire, if you'll accept it. I have little to give you but it is something unique in the dark city, and perhaps of passing interest even to one as knowledgeable as yourself.'

'A riddle? Quite charming. Very well, I accept and surrender; tell me of this mysterious gift that only you can bestow upon me.'

'A song, my lord, such as we sing in the World Shrine on Lileathanir at the birth of new life to welcome it into the world of growing things. I will sing in honour of your return, if you will permit me to.'

El'Uriaq's face was sour. 'If I want to hear wailing slaves I can make my own music quite successfully.'

Angevere's dry, rustling voice came from between Laryin's arms. *'Not a slave giving voice in terror, my archon, a pure heart rendering up her joy at your victories. Such sweetness as you have not heard since the fall of Shaa-dom when my sisters were all taken.'*

When El'Uriaq didn't respond the crone persisted. *'Will you not permit her to sing? If not for yourself then perhaps for the sake of the last of your poor, lost handmaids, Angevere?'*

Laryin's knees were shaking. Angevere had told her not to be afraid, that fear is the mind-killer. Easy for her to say, being a thing of nightmare herself. El'Uriaq seemed to loom over her, an impossibly tall silhouette in the harsh lights behind him. She tried to focus on the one Angevere had called Yllithian instead. Without his crow mask the Dark Kin was bland and unassuming except for his eyes. They were as black and merciless as gun barrels, and they were trained on her.

'Please,' Laryin said piteously to El'Uriaq. 'In my… realm it is traditional for the bride to bring a dowry to her betrothed. My father is dead and I have only this small thing I can give, but give it I must.'

El'Uriaq turned to Yllithian and raised his brows quizzically. 'What say you, Nyos?' he said to his companion. 'Should we permit this barbaric nuptial display in my hall?'

Yllithian coughed politely before answering. 'I don't

believe that it will impugn the dignity of your palace or office, no,' he replied levelly. El'Uriaq laughed uproariously at that and clapped him on the back, making the small archon stagger.

'Traces of a spine, Nyos!' El'Uriaq smiled. 'We'll make a true leader out of you yet! I was beginning to worry that too much time spent conspiring had softened your bones.'

'They remain yours to crush at will, apparently,' Yllithian said ruefully while rubbing his shoulder. 'I, at least, would like to hear our captive bird sing. Just as the girl said it would be a unique experience even here in Commorragh, the city of a thousand and one delights. It might go some way to repaying the considerable difficulties in procuring her – above and beyond the resurrection of your inestimable self and the sadly departed Kraillach, of course.'

'Of course,' El'Uriaq nodded. Turning to Laryin he said, 'Very well, as an indulgence to my friend here I will listen for a while. Ensure it's sweet to my ears or I'll soon have you singing a different tune.'

Laryin nodded nervously and knelt quickly to put down the casket she held before rising again, seeming to grow in confidence as she did so. She drew in breath once, twice, thrice and began her song alone and unaccompanied, somehow weaving it gently into the background clamour of the amphitheatre. It began with a thin, tremulous refrain that twisted to and fro, always questing, seeking like the first shoots of new growth.

Her song was a thing of beauty woven of sound and psychic energy in equal parts, tickling empathically like mind speech, affecting the body on an almost cellular level as it responded to the forgotten sounds of creation. The background noise seemed to fall away as Laryin's voice grew stronger, breaking to the surface with the joy of new awakening.

Yllithian basked in the glow of her power. It felt very much like it had at the resurrection but now the energy Bellathonis had wrung from her with his torture engines was being freely given. There was the slightest tingling sensation on his skin, as though every fine hair were straining to stand on end. Alarm registered in his satiated mind and then was swept away by a wave of pleasure as Laryin struck a high note, as clear and perfect as pure crystal.

El'Uriaq seemed enraptured, a horrible thing to behold as his face was written with all the lust, possessiveness and violence this bright, quivering spark of soul-life aroused in him. The worldsinger sang on, but she was not looking at the monster leering over her. She gazed full at Yllithian and something in her clear eyes held both a warning and a plea.

Yllithian suddenly understood and stumbled away, almost falling on the steps of the dais. The world song rolled around him, rich and potent. Laryin sang of flourishing life, bursting forth upon the canvas of creation, shaping it and changing it with endless potential. The tingling on Yllithian's skin had increased to a prickling. He staggered past unmasked guests and naked slaves, all seemingly frozen and silently gazing up at the dais. He desperately forced his stiffening limbs to carry him toward the servant's entrance he'd spied earlier.

The song swept over him, powerful and dirge-like now as it sang of death. It seemed too powerful, too sonorous to be coming from the little white witch on the dais, as though she had evoked an otherworldly choir of roaring spirits. His skin was burning, and he looked down in horror at his hands. A film of black-green crystal was creeping across his skin, starting at his fingertips and already grown back as far as the second knuckle. Yllithian gave a little shriek and found that his face and lips were frighteningly immobile. He lurched through the skin curtains ahead of him, battering them frantically aside with rigid hands.

Behind him Laryin sang of sadness and loss, of life returning to the dark place beneath the world. Her voice cracked, and she trailed off, unable to continue. Silence fell across the amphitheatre. The silence of death.

Her audience sat or stood or lay unmoving all around, frozen in the vitrifying grip of the glass plague. What had been a place of horrors now seemed like a work of stunning artistry, the faceless dark crystal rendering its victims into a form of transcendent unity. Deathly silence hung over the whole tableau.

'Are they really...?'

'Dead. Yes, their souls are flown.'

Laryin looked at El'Uriaq on his throne, caught leaning forwards, eyes wide, mouth set in an avaricious leer. He seemed to be gazing back at her, and she shuddered.

'Horrible, I didn't think I could do it. How could you know?'

'The viral helix is highly mutable, a living thing seeking

to spread and flourish, to overcome the barriers to its growth. The protection they had against the glass plague was a physical thing, tiny machines that destroyed the virus before it could grow. It was only a hope that you could help it grow fast enough to overwhelm the machines, but it was the best hope we could find.'

Laryin wasn't so sure that it had worked. The silence that had descended over the frozen scene didn't feel like ending, it was more like watchful imminence. The amphitheatre swam before her eyes as bonecrushing weariness swept over her.

'Laryin!' came a cry from the back of the shadowed amphitheatre. Shapes were moving there on the entry ramp. A detachment of armoured warriors spread out cautiously with weapons at the ready. Rushing from their midst came Sindiel, with a pistol in hand and his fine armour hacked and slashed in a dozen places.

To Laryin's surprise the grim-looking warriors didn't shoot Sindiel down in his tracks, instead they moved to protect his back. Sindiel ran to the foot of the dais and stopped, gazing up at the worldsinger uncertainly.

'It's you,' she prompted.

'I… it's me, I came to rescue you,' Sindiel stammered gallantly. 'It seems I'm a little late.'

Laryin glanced at the ominous crystal-glass statue of El'Uriaq. 'I'm not so sure about that,' she said shakily, 'your timing couldn't be better.' She rattled the chain at her throat helplessly and said, 'Could you…?'

Sindiel mounted the steps and gently took her wrist, guiding the harlequin's kiss to the adamantine links. A whisper of motion too quick to see and the chains fell away. Laryin leaned on Sindiel, suddenly exhausted and finding herself barely able to stand.

'How did you get those others to come?' Laryin managed to ask as Sindiel half-carried her down the dais steps.

The renegade glanced back at the knot of warriors reforming at the ramp. 'They're from my ships. I told them we were going to kidnap a great prize from fat and wealthy archons.'

'But *why* did you come back?' Laryin's vision was dimming, Sindiel's face was becoming a blur, but it seemed desperately important to hear him out.

'Because of what you said. I decided to forgive myself and act in the way I truly wanted to.'

'You would have been crushed.'

Sindiel was silent for a long time before he said eventually, 'I know... but I had to try.'

IN THE SILENT amphitheatre El'Uriaq sat frozen among his departed minions. The slightest discoloration could be seen spreading across his form, the subtlest marbling that spoke of changes occurring within. Its enemies had trapped it but they had not destroyed it. They had underestimated how tenaciously the entity could cling to even the slightest fragment of physicality, adjusting its own extradimensional lattice to fit inside the smallest space. Its bridgehead into the dark city had been reduced but not removed. With time it would alter this vessel until it could seek out a new host.

Even trapped as it was, the entity possessing El'Uriaq still had the senses to tell that it was not alone. A figure had entered the amphitheatre and was limping its way slowly to the throne.

'*I thought you'd never come,*' whispered Angevere from beside the throne.

'I had to wait for the foundling and his merry band to get out of the way,' Bellathonis wheezed reproachfully. 'They took the pure heart with them?'

'*Yes, it was all very moving.*'

'Let's hope our heroic idiot has the wherewithal to get her out of the city before more damage is done.'

'*It doesn't matter. Finish this so that we can be gone.*'

'Tsk, tsk, Angevere. This is a historic moment whether we like it or not. It should be treated with sufficient gravitas.'

'*There's no reason to relish it. The cost will be high.*'

'Vengeance is vengeance, my dear, doesn't the tyrant teach us that we must strike down those that wrong us no matter the cost? Isn't that a moment to be relished? And gloried in?' Bellathonis chuckled dryly. 'Besides which, there's no other way. To finish this a price must be paid. Now hush or I won't take you with me when I leave.'

Bellathonis dragged his crooked legs up the steps to the figure on the throne. He held a hide-wrapped jar in his hands.

'I too have a gift for you, noble El'Uriaq,' he said to the dark crystal form. 'A little something a colleague had thought to bestow upon me.' He placed the jar reverentially at El'Uriaq's feet, picked up the casket containing the head of Angevere and backed away.

The somewhat dimmed sentience of the entity still invested in the form of El'Uriaq registered the close presence of the dark gate with a sensation akin to fear. It represented a dimensional trap to it, a black hole in miniature that led to an oubliette crammed with starved remnants of its own ilk. It could feel them, beating hungrily at the thin membrane encompassed inside the runic tetrahedron. It grew very still and waited.

'My colleague placed a number of discreet triggers on the device he constructed,' Bellathonis called out as he shuffled away between the ranked tables. 'It was to be specifically attuned for my bio-signature, you see? But I destroyed him when he tried to get the readings he needed to calibrate the device. Rather ironic, no? I confess that I simplified his rather magnificently useless attempt by substituting a single trigger of quite mundane sort…'

Bellathonis reached the exit ramp and paused to look back at the frozen tableau for one last time.

'A timer.'

At the top of the dais reality cracked open for a fraction of a second as the dark gate activated. Purple-black light welled forth with retina-searing intensity and a clap of thunder rolled around the amphitheatre. For one dreadful moment it seemed as if El'Uriaq was enthroned in leaping purple flames. Then the sight was obscured by frantically looping darkness, half-seen ectoplasmic tendrils that writhed with eye-blurring swiftness. Writhing, looping, contracting. A flash and another peal of thunder and that too was gone, the very rock trembling with the sudden impact. The glass tableau in the amphitheatre shattered into a glittering cloud of shards as the shockwave hit it, the reverberating echoes booming from the walls like titanic laughter.

Bellathonis clutched at the wall for support. The trembling did not lessen, rather it intensified. Flakes of stone rained down, soon pursued by larger chunks. A chandelier of woven ribs crashed to the ground, smashing several victims of the glass plague into tinkling ruin. The haemonculus staggered away into the catacombs but he knew it was already too late to escape, nowhere in the city would be safe.

Even now ripples of entropy from the event were racing ahead of him to crash against the complex system of psychic wards holding together Commorragh and its sub-realms. Across the city formerly inactive portals would be flaring into life, while other vital arteries were being cut. The very foundations of the eternal city were shaking.

The Dysjunction had begun.

ABOUT THE AUTHOR

Andy Chambers is a veteran writer for
the Warhammer 40,000 universe with
more than twenty years experience
creating worlds dominated by giant
robots, spaceships and dangerous aliens.
He worked at Games Workshop as lead
designer of the Warhammer 40,000
miniatures game for three editions before
moving to the PC gaming market to work
on the hit real time strategy game *Starcraft2*
by Blizzard Entertainment. Andy has
written several short stories and two novels
for Black Library, *Survival Instinc*t and *Path
of the Renegade*. Andy has recently returned
to the UK and is living in Nottingham.

FOLLOW THE PATH OF THE ELDAR

UK ISBN: 978-1-84416-874-3
US ISBN: 978-1-84416-875-0

UK ISBN: 978-1-84970-080-1
US ISBN: 978-1-84970-081-8

UK ISBN: 978-1-84970-197-6
US ISBN: 978-1-84970-198-3

COMING SEPTEMBER 2012

Collect the entire series at www.blacklibrary.com